Freda Lightfoot was born and brought up in the mill towns of
Lancashire. She has been a teacher, bookseller and smallholder
but began her writing career by publishing over forty short
stories and articles and five historical romances. She has a flat in
the Lake District and a house in a small mountain village in
Spain. To find out more informaton, visit Freda's website at
www.fredalightfoot.co.uk

Praise for Freda Lightfoot:

'Charming and exciting . . . A lovely story by an author with
extraordinary feeling in her writing.' *Bangor Chronicle*

'Freda Lightfoot's talent for creating believable characters
makes this a page-turning read.' *Newcastle Evening Chronicle*

'The kind of character-driven saga that delights the Catherine
Cookson and Josephine Cox audience.'
Peterborough Evening Telegraph

Also by Freda Lightfoot

FREDA LIGHTFOOT

The Girl from Poor House Lane

CORONET BOOKS
Hodder & Stoughton

ACKNOWLEDGEMENTS

Poor House Lane and the Kirkland Workhouse in Kendal did exist but are both now long gone. The descriptions of the town are as accurate as I can make them but Tyson Lodge and Tyson's Shoe Factory are entirely fictitious. I am grateful to Spencer Crookenden for the information on the shoe industry from his book *K Shoes – The First 150 Years*. However, they were known as an excellent employer in the town and this is not their story.

1905

I

'Make no mistake, Kate O'Connor, this is the best chance you're going to get so don't mess it up. There's many a lass who'd give their eye-teeth to work for Mr Tyson, hard taskmaster though he might be, and who can blame him when you see some of the ne'er-do-wells he has to rely on for labour? Just watch that lip of yours and you'll happen be all right. And think on – Kirkland Poor House is closing before the week is out, so you'll have to cope on yer own from now on.'

With red hair which loudly proclaimed her Irish background, and apple cheeks made rosy by the sweet country air of the Westmorland fells, eighteen-year-old Kate O'Connor could easily have been taken for any simple, fresh young country girl. But looking closer, an interested stranger might note a bone-thin body, one that had not seen a good solid meal in a long while; a pair of scrawny ankles in over-large boots jutting out from beneath the loose-fitting gown made for some other, more voluptuous and better class of woman altogether. They might note that what little was visible of her skin was encrusted with ingrained dirt, the hair which fell about her slender shoulders matted and uncombed for all a portion of it was carefully knotted on top of her neatly shaped head.

'Oh, I can cope all right,' Kate responded tartly. 'I'm not afraid of hard work. Don't you fret none about that. Ye wouldn't find me accepting any of yer po-faced charity, not if I didn't have me babby to think of.'

Though she had only visited her homeland a couple of times as a child, there was a lilt to her voice, a musical intonation of sound, that she'd perhaps inherited from her father, or else been born in her. And if she appeared alarmingly fragile, the fire within gave off a radiance to warm the soul. Her grey eyes were alive with pride and passion and an anger as fierce, and as stormy, as the Lakeland skies. And something else: a softer inner core she was doing her utmost to hide, a sadness which still held the bleakness of grief. Whoever had made her hate the world with such a vehemence would not be let off lightly. That much was all too plain in the obstinate set of the small square chin, the way the eyebrows winged defiantly upwards and the nostrils flared with courage, revealing a rare beauty made all the more poignant by the outward image of a wayward young girl. For that steady gaze, the proud, proprietorial manner with which she held her child, the very truculence of her stance, proved that however low she had fallen, however downtrodden, the fight had only just begun.

The woman wagged an admonitory finger then jabbed it against Kate's thin shoulder, nearly knocking her over. 'Mark my words, girl, pride comes before a fall. You were glad enough of our so-called charity once over, not least when your poor husband was called to his maker. Think yerself lucky you were fed and sheltered here, in Poor House Lane. Next time it'll be the big Union Workhouse on Kendal Green, then you'll be sorry. They'll not treat you so kindly up there, and you'll have to work even harder, making Harden cloth from flax and hemp, laundrywork happen, or emptying chamber pots. See if you like that any better.' And with this parting threat, the woman nodded her head with gleeful satisfaction and slammed shut the door.

Kate stood for a second in silent contemplation of that battered, filthy door she knew so well, scratched and pounded upon by a million hungry hands over the years, all of them paupers, like herself, who had come pleading to be let in, to be fed and watered by the unfeeling guardians within. They would queue for hours in the soft Westmorland rain for a bowl of watery soup or lukewarm porridge then hurry back with it to feed their children in the hovel they'd been assigned in Poor House Lane; others would stand where they were in the rotting filth of a stinking yard, eating it quickly before anyone stole it from them. They might be given free coal in severe weather, a warm shawl, or a pair of boots that some poor soul no longer needed since scarlet fever or 'the visitation of God' had perhaps carried them off. And they were daily encouraged by the overseer to adopt the habits of 'prudence and virtue', no doubt on the grounds that it was their own fault that they were starving.

Perhaps, if Kate had been more fortunate in her family, she might not have needed to come knocking on that door at all. Things could have been so different. Her father had first come to Westmorland as a young man in 1870 as one of the navvies working on the new sewerage system, installing it over a period of five years so that for a time he'd enjoyed relative stability and prosperity, sufficient to take a wife and start a family, producing a son first whom they named Dermot, after his own father. But Kate's mother died giving birth to her just a few years later and the two youngsters had to be cared for by various well-meaning neighbours while her father moved on to other building work: the new Market Hall, Sandes Avenue and Victoria Bridge. He'd passed quietly away in the 'flu epidemic back in '92 when Kate had been barely five or six and Dermot had just started an apprenticeship with a shoemaker. Losing her beloved father had been so terrible, all such a blur, she couldn't quite remember the details but while Dermot managed to board with his master, for Kate it was one short step to Poor House Lane and the guardians.

The only bright spot in a grim youth was when she'd met and fallen in love with Callum, married at just sixteen and gone to live with him behind his tiny cobbler's shop. And then the River Kent had flooded, as it so frequently did – not quite so badly as when in 1898 the worst floods in living memory nearly washed away the new bridge Daddy had helped build, but badly enough to deprive Kate of a beloved husband, as if the gods resented even this little bit of happiness she'd found.

In Kate's eyes he'd died a hero's death trying to save her from the floods which had swamped their humble dwelling. Having helped her cling safely to a tree, her lovely Callum had lost his hold and been swept away by the swirling waters.

But what was the use in complaining? This was where she lived now, in one room of a cottage opposite where the pigs were kept.

Poor House Lane was typical of many of Kendal's yards, which were a distinctive feature of the town. These might be known by a number or a name, but all led off from the single main street that ran north to south, parallel with the river, in this case close by the church in Kirkland through a narrow entrance that led to a row of ten or eleven cottages which might house thirty or more families at any one time. The walls were built of limestone, blackened by age and grime, and high enough to block out most of the sunlight that might creep over the slated roofs. Within the narrow confines of the yard with its shared privies and central open sewer running over the rough cobbles, there was a degree of security to be found by the seething mass of folk, all victims of poverty like herself, who needed to draw strength from each other.

A short flight of stone steps led to the upper floor of each of the cottages and it was to one of these that Kate now went, holding her child close to her breast and ducking her head beneath the low lintel. Here, in number five, she'd been allotted a plank bed with a pillow and blanket, a straw pallet she scoured every day for bugs, and the facility to warm milk for her baby. As she entered, she saw that Millie, with whom she shared this room and had become friendly, was still asleep; no doubt having been kept awake half the night by her own brood which she'd produced at yearly intervals, regular as clockwork, since she was fifteen. All of them were constantly ailing from something or other.

Kate poured a small quantity of the milk she'd been given into a pan and set it on the hob to warm by the meagre fire, then sat on the corner of her bed, cuddling her child and humming softly as she laid him on his back on her lap to change his wet napkin. Freed from the encumbrance of the damp flannel, young Callum kicked his legs exuberantly, big grey-blue eyes fixed on hers, his beaming smile lighting up the gloomy room.

'Tha didn't get owt then, only the milk?'

Kate glanced up. Millie's old mother-in-law, Ma Parkin, sat rocking herself in a corner, cradling the youngest infant in her arms while doing her level best to keep the others out of mischief by having them unpick a moth-eaten old woollen jumper they'd no doubt picked up off the rubbish tip. The rest of the Parkin tribe were either at Kirkland School, if they'd felt inclined to go that morning, or out with their father Clem if they'd managed to avoid the truant officer. Clem had only one arm, having lost his other to gangrene following an accident at work, and could do little more than clean middens, or search for scraps to sell or use in their hand-to-mouth existence. Generally speaking he was a patient, kindly man who adored his wife, though if he did get any money in his pocket, he was fond of stopping off at the Cock and Dolphin and spending a good part of it on booze

'That's right, Ma, just the milk. And it's all for you, me grand boy, is it not?' Kate crooned, tweaking her baby's dimpled cheek and kissing him. 'And how many teeth can I see? One, two, three, four . . . ah, 'tis too many to count now. Aren't ye the clever one?'

The old woman heaved a sigh, cursing softly under her breath. 'What are we supposed to eat to keep body and soul together then, bloody muck off t'cobbles?'

Kate said nothing, but the small crust of bread she had carefully secreted in her pocket seemed to press heavily against her thigh. She was fond of Ma Parkin yet she couldn't give it to the old woman without depriving her own child. She meant to soak the crust in the last of the milk for Callum's supper, so that at least he didn't go to bed hungry. She washed and dried his bottom with great care because whatever pains she took it was always a little red and sore, there being nowhere to dry his napkins properly. She neatly pinned on a clean one, then poured the warmed milk into the curved bottle and fixed on the rubber teat which he at once grabbed and began to suckle greedily. At fifteen months, he was really getting too big for this to satisfy him and Kate would have liked to give him something more solid, but the bit of bread was all she had. She'd given no thought to her own supper yet, relying on providence, Millie or Clem to provide it. She had a couple of pennies tucked into the pocket of her shift but that would have to last until she was paid, which could be a few days, even a week or more, before she produced anything worthwhile.

'It'll all be better soon,' she told her child, rubbing her nose against his and making the baby chortle with glee. 'Mammy's going to make us a fortune, so she is, sewing shoes like yer clever uncle. Except that unlike yer Uncle Dermot, and most round here, I'll save every penny, so I will, then we can get out of this God-forsaken place and start to go up in the world. Won't that be grand?'

Ma Parkin gave a snort of disbelief.

'I will so,' Kate insisted, just as if she had spoken.

A loud sniff this time, 'I wish I'd a penny for every time I've heard that.'

'Ah, but I'm the lucky one, Ma. It might not look like it to some, but this is a red letter day for me.'

The old woman gazed back at her, blank and uncomprehending.

Kate simply smiled and returned to talking to her child, who was much more responsive, 'I will so,' she repeated in a whisper against the baby's soft cheek. 'I'm not having my fine little man being brought up in this hell-hole, so help me.'

At her brother Dermot's suggestion, she'd gone knocking on Tyson's door just a few days ago, spoken to the foreman and got herself some outwork, stitching the soles on to women's shoes. She couldn't believe her own good fortune. Kate saw this as the first step on her road to freedom; an escape from the Poor Law Guardians who'd largely brought her up after her father died. As a child she'd worked in the mornings on the carding and knitting, learning the basics of the three Rs in the afternoon – if she could stay awake long enough to take anything in, that is. After she left school at twelve she'd been found a bit of domestic work here and there but most people didn't care to have a pauper child about the place, so it was never easy to make ends meet. And only months after Callum had been drowned, she'd been forced to move back to Poor

House Lane, worse off than ever. Heavily pregnant, she'd been grateful for their care, rough and ready though it might be, if only for the sake of the son she'd given birth to within these damp, rat-infested walls. At least the guardians had provided her with a midwife, seen that her child was born alive and well, and put food in her belly at a time in her short life when she hadn't cared whether she lived or died, heartbroken as she was over losing her lovely husband.

Each morning and evening since that day, she'd joined the queue for food at the door of the Poor House which gave the lane its name, done her allotted chores, then spent the rest of the day helping Millie to clean the overcrowded room, do the washing and care for her numerous children.

Desperate as Kate was, and grateful for a roof over her head, she'd somehow never become inured to the squalor of their living quarters: running with damp and vermin and stinking of stale urine, vomit and the sweet-sour odour of decay, with Millie making scant effort to keep it clean. The state of it still turned Kate's stomach. You could pick the bugs one by one off the crumbling walls, though they as quickly returned; see the cockroaches scurry across the floor; hear the mice and the rats squabbling and squealing.

'We can't put up with this! The pigs live better,' she'd cried, when she'd first clapped eyes on her new quarters. But no one cared about Poor House Lane now that the big new workhouse up on the hill was in operation.

Millie had simply shrugged her shoulders in helpless defeat, all the fight in her having long since seeped away, destroyed by lack of sustenance and too many demands upon her which she'd no hope of fulfilling. Kate had briskly complained to the overseer, whose only response had been the loan of a brush and a bucket of whitewash with the curt instruction to clean it up herself if she wasn't satisfied. This was accompanied by a lengthy lecture on how she should consider herself fortunate that the Misses Tyson were generous enough to provide such implements for the betterment of the poor.

'The Misses Tyson, whoever they might be, should be ashamed of theirselves for having such places in their fancy town,' Kate had responded tartly.

Clem, when he heard, had ranted and raved at her. Filled with fear for his family, for once he'd thoroughly lost his temper. 'Were you trying to get us evicted, was that the way of it?' he roared, his face so scarlet with rage she feared he might burst a blood vessel. 'Where the hell would we go then, will thoo tell me that? In t'gutter? And have you the fare home to Ireland?'

That was the moment when Kate finally realised how very serious her situation was, that she too was trapped with no hope of escape, her future in ruins. She'd no one to rely upon but herself. Worse than that, she had a small baby entirely dependent upon her for survival. She'd long ago learned that she couldn't expect help from her brother who never had a penny to his name, wasting it all on beer and the turn of a card, far too much the rabble-rouser to be anything like dependable. It was a wonder he hadn't ended up on Correction Hill, the fights he got himself into. Being deprived of a father seemed to have affected him badly. Dermot was filled with bitterness, carrying a grudge against society as big as a rock on his skinny young shoulders.

But for Kate a lesson had been learned and from then on she struggled to be as accepting and uncomplaining as everyone else in the yard, although she found it far from easy. She strove to keep herself clean, going frequently to draw water from the Anchorite well on Kirkbarrow, the hill that backed on to Poor House Lane. The walk gave her a chance to smell the sweet green grass and breathe fresh, clean air into her lungs. She'd take her time walking back through Vicar's Fields and think herself in the country. Then, with her face and hands scrubbed till they were red-raw with the effort, she'd spend hours trailing around the streets of Kendal in the vain hope of persuading someone to offer her work. Mostly, they took one look at her tell-tale institutional clothes and scrawny appearance, and shut the door in her face.

Some days, though, especially when the rain sheeted down and even the comforting sight of Kendal Castle was blotted out by cloud and mist, she'd lose the will to do that much, and would simply get through the day using as little energy as possible so as not to worsen the constant and gnawing pangs of hunger.

Oh, but today was different. She at last had a proper job so wasn't she the lucky one? And even if it was ill-paid and Mr Tyson didn't enjoy the reputation of being the most amenable or caring of employers, it represented a whole new beginning for her, a chance to give her son a better future.

Kate's first morning was to be a training session with the foreman. A small, rotund man with a bristly moustache and a manner to match, he had hard, self-seeking eyes, one of them with a slight cast in it, which left Kate unsure as to whether he was looking at her or addressing someone else entirely.

The sight of this strange man filled her with trepidation and for some reason she felt reluctant to enter the shabby little workroom with the big counter where he handed out leather, sometimes ready-cut into soles, sometimes still in the bend, which was an oddly shaped piece looking as if it came straight from the cow. Kate hovered uncertainly at the door.

'Well, are you coming in or not? Don't waste my time if you're not up to the job. You lasses are too flighty to my mind. Reckoning you want work, and then not turning up fer it.'

The thought of anyone having the energy to be flighty in Poor House Lane struck Kate as so funny that she almost laughed out loud. But managing to keep her gaze downcast, she meekly responded, 'Sure, I'm a fine worker, so I am.'

'Women never were any use. On the work front, that is.' And he smirked, giving a dirty little laugh as if he'd said something amusing.

'Well, I'm different. So long as I know what's expected of me.'

He rubbed the snot from his nose with the back of one hand. 'Don't stand about then. Get in here and I'll show thee what's what.'

He made her sit on a stool, pressing himself hard against her back, trapping her within the circle of his arms as he began to demonstrate the job to her, in a sketchy, hasty sort of way. He smelled strongly of leather, which was not unpleasant, and something else she couldn't put a name to, which was. As he adjusted her hands, showing her how to hold the shoe, he let his own hand slide over her breast, giving it a quick squeeze before circling her waist and finally dipping into her crotch, fondling her with a boldness that shocked her to the core.

Kate leaped to her feet, knocking away his hand and dropping the shoe and leather sole in her haste to escape his probing fingers.

'What the hell's wrong with yer, girl? Can't a chap be friendly? You'll have to learn better if yer to work fer me, lass. Show proper gratitude.'

'And why the hell should I?' She was breathing hard, her cheeks rosy with outraged fury. But the foreman simply smiled at her, revealing yellowed, tobacco-stained teeth.

'Because you don't want that bairn of yours to starve. I'd say that was as good a reason as any. But it's no skin off my nose. If you want the job, pick up them uppers and soles and go and get on with it. But you'd do well to mind yer manners better next time, 'cause I don't take kindly to uppity girls. There are rules, and if you want work, you have to keep 'em. Understood?' His greedy little eyes were narrowed, challenging her to object.

For a moment, she very nearly did. Kate almost told him to stick his job and walked out in bold-faced defiance. But beggars couldn't be choosers. Kirkland Poor House had shut its doors for the last time, and, as had been clearly explained to her, if she wasn't to end up in a worse situation, sleeping in regimented dormitories in the big Union Workhouse on Kendal Green, year after year till she was old and grey, she had no choice but to make a go of this precious opportunity she'd been given. She'd just have to learn how to handle this toad, that was all.

Her son needed feeding, and there was no one else going to see to him but Kate. This was her big chance. Now it was up to her.

2

The work started well enough. Each week, Kate collected the shoe uppers and leather soles, and set about her task according to the instructions she'd been given. The leather was of the finest quality, soft and supple, and Kate loved the feel of it. Vegetable-tanned, with oil and grease and wax rubbed in to give it strength and flexibility and make it water-resistant, this process was known as 'currying' and could take months as Tyson's prided themselves on tailoring the finest leathers, calf and kid, to a customer's specific requirements. They produced a comprehensive range of men's and women's shoes and boots as well as bridles, harness and military accoutrements. The uppers were stitched together in a room at the factory but outworkers were still used to attach the soles by riveting or stitching. This was to be Kate's job.

Dermot too did outwork, usually men's boots: Hessian, Shooting, Peel Riding boots or Napoleon, and fine workmanship was required. He collected the basic materials from the workshop in exactly the same way, and returned days later with the completed boots ready for polishing and finishing. So as Kate started on her new job, for once in his life her brother came up trumps and carefully demonstrated what she must do. She was grateful for his help since Ned Swainson, the despicable foreman with the self-satisfied leer and wandering eye, offered no further assistance.

Even before Kate had experienced Swainson's over-familiar

attentions at first hand, she'd been warned of his low opinion of women; of most people, in fact, other than himself. Evidently he believed that Tyson's could not operate without him. It was said that he was so determined to buy himself a life of ease and comfort that he was filled with bitter envy of all those more fortunately placed. He was equally contemptuous of those below him, no doubt because they reminded him from whence he'd come, using them for his own ends, greedily making a profit from any little sideline he could devise.

'Don't enquire too closely into them,' Kate was warned by other women in the yard such as Sally Sibson, Joan Enderby and Nell Benson.

'Do as thoo's told and don't argue. You get off more lightly that way.'

Kate's first attempt was a mess but she soon began to improve, though had it not been for what she'd learned by watching her late husband work the leather, and from Dermot, she would have been in a complete fog. When she took in the batch of finished shoes, Kate could see at once that Swainson was surprised.

He muttered and harrumphed, turning the shoes over and over with hands deeply ingrained with the dyes used on the leather, evidently seeking some way to find fault with her work. 'Quite the little clever-clogs, eh?' Almost as if he were disappointed that she'd done so well as it disproved his theory that women weren't up to the job.

Aware of Dermot standing quietly beside her with his own load, and anxious not to upset the foreman since she needed regular work from him, Kate hastened to set the record straight with what she believed to be a proper show of modesty. 'Not really. Me brother here showed me how to do it, as it was me first time.'

'Tha could have come and asked me, girl, if there were

summat tha didn't understand. We wouldn't want a nice li'l lass like you fretting, now would we?' Swainson accompanied this offer with a smirk that chilled her, so that when he slipped a hand consolingly about her slender waist, letting his fingers creep up and squeeze the fullness of one breast beneath her arm, Kate managed 'accidentally' to step on his toes with the heel of her boot. It gave her immense satisfaction to see him struggle to disguise the flicker of pain that came into his eyes; but the flare of anger was all too evident.

He stepped back, scowling at her, smoothed down his moustache with two brown-stained fingers and then glowered at Dermot even more fiercely. 'Happen I should pay him then, and not you, if he med 'em up.'

'Oh, no, he only demonstrated. *I* stitched them.' It had been harder on her hands than Kate had expected: waxing the thread, holding the two parts of the shoe together with a special tool called a clam, and pushing the hog-hair bristle which served as a needle through the tiny holes she'd pricked with the awl in the stiff leather. She certainly wanted to make sure that she got her just rewards for her labours. 'It's all my own work, isn't it, Dermot?'

Before her brother had the chance to reply, the foreman brusquely interrupted. 'Happen he's got too much time on his hands if he can afford to give demonstrations, and he's not doing his own work reet.'

'Ye'll find no fault with them,' Dermot said, setting three pairs of boots on the bench before him. 'My work is as fine as ye'll get in London Town, so it is.'

Swainson harrumphed again as he snatched up the boots and turned them over to examine the soles, picking at the stitches, pressing here and there with the heel of his thumb, then resolutely shook his head. 'This in't the leather you were given to use.'

'Indeed it is!'

'Nay, I don't reckon so. This is inferior stuff. See how thin it is? No doubt you've sold the decent leather I gave you for extra beer money.'

'That's a lie, and I'll ask you to take it back afore I knock yer block off.'

Swainson flinched slightly, as if he half expected fists to fly there and then, while Kate frantically tried to calm down her brother. Wasn't she familiar with his quick Irish temper – forgetting that it was her own that had landed them in this pretty pickle. 'If you've been up to more mischief, Dermot, I'll skin you alive, so I will.'

'Indeed I haven't!'

'Oh, aye, thoo has.' Seeing he was in no real danger from either one of them, the foreman quickly recovered from his show of nerves, determined to reassert his authority as he pounded the counter top with one fist. 'Seems to me, tha's got too big for yer boots, Dermot O'Connor. Tha's been laiking about stitching tha sister's shoes and then rushing to finish yer own batch in an inferior fashion. I don't believe this li'l lass capable of doing this class of work herself, not fost time, and you happen fancied some extra money to feed yer drinking habit. If you think you can cheat Mr Tyson and get away with it, thoo's mistaken. Neither of you will get a penny out of me today.' And he tossed both the boots and the shoes Kate had stitched under the bench, as if the very sight of them offended him and he'd no wish to clap eyes on them again.

Dermot looked as if he might leap over the big wooden counter and throttle the foreman with his own bare hands. Kate, equally incensed, got in first by yelling at the top of her voice, 'Ye can't do that!'

Swainson's moustache twitched and his eyebrows shot up into his thatch of dark, greasy hair, 'I can do owt I want to.

I'm the foreman, in case you haven't noticed. What I say goes.'

'But it's not fair. Dermot only showed me how to get started. I put every stitch in meself. By hand. Look!' And holding out her hands, Kate showed him the welts and segs and coarse patches scarring the rough skin. He was unimpressed.

'Show me a woman round here with soft hands and I'll show you a whore. It proves nothing. The pair of you is nowt but offcomers. We don't want no Irish rubbish here. More trouble than you're worth. Be off with you.'

Dermot took a step closer, his voice dangerously low. 'Why don't you stop hiding behind that high counter and come round this side and say that to me face? Go on, show me what a fine, strong man ye are. I dare you.'

Uncertainty flared in the other man's mean little eyes as the right one focused furiously upon Dermot and the other roamed wildly, as if seeking escape. But aware of his power, Ned Swainson soon recovered his composure, 'I could give you the push for that alone, tha knows. However, thoo's caught me in a mellow mood today, so get on with your next batch and we'll say no more about it. Just see that you do better next time. But tha'll get not a penny out of me for this lot.'

A wave of sickness came over Kate. 'No money? Next batch? But how will we eat till then? I've a babby to feed. Dermot has rent to pay. He's only just finished off his apprenticeship, with nothing behind him, and he has to find a place to live. You can't stop the pay for both of us! We'll starve, so we will. Besides, we didn't try to cheat anyone. We've done a grand job and deserve to be properly paid for it.'

'Are you questioning my judgement, young woman?'

A stain of red spread over her cheekbones and the fighting spirit returned to Kate's stormy eyes. Fists firmly planted into her slender waist, she faced him head on. 'I certainly am. I'm questioning your right not to pay what's due to us.'

It was Dermot now who was urging Kate to be quiet. 'Will ye shut yer face or ye'll get us both the sack?'

Swainson gave a harsh bark of laughter. 'Tha niver spoke a truer word, lad. Take it or leave it, it's all the same to me. Do the next batch, or you can sling yer hook and never show yer faces in t'shop again. Suit theesen.' And giving a shrug, he removed the bend of leather he'd just placed on the counter top and put it away again.

Seeing her brother's shoulders slump and her own dreams slip away did nothing to calm Kate, rather the opposite as fresh anger kindled deep inside her, hot and fierce. The soft Irish lilt had never seemed more pronounced and more at odds with her temper than it was at this moment. 'Indeed it looks to me like you're the one doing the cheating round here, not us at all.'

'For God's sake, Kate, shut yer noise. He'll hang, draw and quarter us, so he will.'

'Not before we get our money, he won't. We'll have that off the bastard first, to be sure. You can string me up when I've fed me babby and not a minute sooner, Ned Swainson. So, what's it to be?'

'*Mr* Swainson to you, girl, and you'd do well to hearken to your brother's advice, if'n you wish to keep your job.'

'Indeed? And where's *Mr* Tyson? What would he have to say about all of this? I'm wondering. Now wouldn't I like a word with the grand man himself, and to hear his opinion on the way we're being treated.'

'Hear what the grand man himself has got to say about what, may I ask?' And Kate turned to find herself face to face with her employer. Behind her, Dermot began to mutter quietly, 'Oh, Hail Mary, Mother of God . . .'

Eliot Tyson viewed the scene before him with the jaundiced eyes of one who had seen it all enacted too many times before.

The underfed waif, the rapscallion brother, both no doubt ready to swindle and cheat while being anxious to save their own skins, obstinately maintaining they had right on their side. He was all too aware that his reputation among the outworkers was not good, yet despite common opinion believed himself to be a fair and just employer, if perhaps somewhat neglectful. He provided much-needed employment in the town in a business which was expanding rapidly, paid above the going rate, and contributed generously towards a recreation room for his workers, and an annual outing for them every July.

He didn't greatly care for Swainson, who was admittedly a bit of a bully, but the task of keeping outworkers in line couldn't be an easy one. Many of them were only too eager to get one over on him, at the least opportunity. The most favoured method was substituting cheaper quality leather for the soles while selling off the better stuff to dealers. Another way was farming out work to women at a cheaper rate while pretending to do it himself, so that a man could take on more than he could personally cope with, which easily boosted his own income.

Eliot glanced at the girl and saw, to his surprise, that she was a beauty, from what he could see of her beneath the grime. She'd obviously made some effort to clean it off for which he gave due credit even if the attempt didn't meet the standards he was personally accustomed to. Her eyes were the softest grey he'd ever seen, admittedly with not much evidence of compassion in them at this precise moment; and the lashes long and curling. But her hair was filthy and matted, more like a rook's nest save for its fiery colour. He considered it with a detached fascination, trying to put a name to the particular shade: auburn; ginger; titian . . . no, none of those. But how could he even begin to guess? It would take several buckets of hot water and a large cake of soap to discover the answer.

Startled out of his reverie, he realised that she was speaking to him directly and Swainson was jumping about like a cat with his tail on fire as a consequence.

'You'll address your questions to me, miss, not bother Mr Tyson with your prattling.'

'I'll speak to whosoever I wish, and since you've just given both me and me brother the push for doing an honest week's work, we owe you nothing, I'm thinking.'

Eliot hid a smile for the girl's forthright manner was refreshing and having a decidedly unsettling effect upon his surly foreman, which was most amusing. 'If he sacked you, I'm sure he must have had good reason. Perhaps you'd best listen to him, and go quietly.'

The young man beside her, Eliot noticed, was growing agitated, plucking at her sleeve and begging her to hush. His own thatch of hair was not quite so red and cut exceptionally short, but the pair were undoubtedly related.

Eliot resigned himself to a long, convoluted wail of self-pity from all parties concerned. It didn't happen. Instead, she marched right up to him, hands on hips. Sticking her chin in the air, with steam practically billowing from her ears, she began to rail at him.

'Not while I've breath left in me body! I never did anything quietly in me life, and I don't intend to start now. Just fer the record, it's this man you should be watching, not me. He's the one doing the cheating which you'll discover to your cost one day, mark my words. But you can stick yer rotten job. I don't work for them what twist me and steal the bread out of me babby's mouth.'

Startled and perplexed by her daring, Eliot narrowed his eyes in a questioning manner as he swung around to his foreman, demanding clarification. 'Well, Swainson, is what she says true?'

'Not a word of it, sir, as well you know.'

'Hmm, as I would expect. Then can you perhaps explain to me, briefly, and in words of one syllable, what this fracas is all about?'

'No, he cannot,' cut in Kate before Swainson had chance to draw breath. 'Because he hasn't a leg to stand on, isn't that the truth? Me brother here showed me how to do the work since that eejit didn't have the time nor the patience to show me right, and for some reason this is not allowed and so we've both got the push.'

'The work is rushed and inferior,' Swainson blustered, finally finding his voice.

' 'Tis not! It's just that your foreman here doesn't believe a woman to be capable of such quality work.'

'And the boy hasn't used the right leather.'

'I have so.' This from Dermot, who suddenly took it into his head to speak up and defend himself.

But a tell-tale flush was creeping up his neck and along his jawline, a sure sign of guilt in Eliot's opinion, one he had seen too many times before. He came to a swift decision, more out of admiration for the girl's cheek than anger, and because he was in a hurry.

They were expecting the Whinerays for supper this evening and he was anxious to get back home to soothe his wife's jitters. Her nerves always played up when everything needed to be absolutely correct and she found herself required to give precise instructions on menu and flowers and goodness knows what else. Of late, her depression had been such that she couldn't even control her own servants, particularly the dreaded Mrs Petty. Amelia had grown far too indulgent of her cook's failings, a woman easily diverted from the task in hand by her facility for fanciful superstition and gossip.

'Give the young man his cards but keep the girl on. He

seems to be the one at fault.' And she has a baby to feed, added a small voice at the back of his head. But Eliot didn't say this out loud, in case he failed to disguise the envy in his tone. It always seemed so utterly unfair that those who had least to offer could breed so easily, while he, who had everything – a fine house, a thriving business, a beautiful, adoring wife – couldn't get himself a son for love nor money. A child of either gender would, in fact, have been most welcome. But, apparently, it was not to be.

Having issued his judgement, Eliot Tyson turned on his heel and walked smartly away. The last thing he wanted was for any of his own workers to feel sorry for him.

The supper party was not a success. It had begun badly when he'd found his tailcoat had not been brushed and his white tie was crumpled and dingy so that he would have to use the black one instead. Really, this household had gone to pot ever since Beckworth had retired. He should somehow find the funds for a new valet despite dear Amelia's insisting she enjoyed laying out a clean shirt and handkerchief for him. She'd had young Dennis polish his shoes and press his trousers, but the boy had put out his velvet smoking jacket by mistake so the tailcoat was still hanging, unbrushed, in the wardrobe.

Eliot had always been most fastidious about his appearance and now quietly completed these essential tasks himself rather than upset his wife by pointing out the inadequacies of her preparations. He'd painstakingly shaved the whiskers from his chin with a cut-throat razor, slapped cologne on the long, narrow cheeks and jutting jaw, then brushed his hair, striving to flatten the dark curls into some sort of order. His own brown eyes stared broodingly back at himself from the mirror, already expressing doubt as to the wisdom of hosting this occasion.

Did he really wish to become involved in local politics? Was this a wise move on his part? Almost as if he wished to fill the gap in his life, as if he needed to keep every hour of his day fully occupied. Yet could he afford to take his eye off a business which seemed to be flagging of late?

Tyson's Shoe Manufactory had been his father's pride and joy, and his undoubted obsession. Eliot was all too aware that he would never be able to match up. Hadn't his father told him so a dozen times? George Tyson had started the company from scratch, cycling the length and breadth of the country as a young man in order to win orders, devoting his life to building up the company but his success had brought little happiness in its wake, resulting in him rarely showing his face in the gracious home he provided for his family. His wife had grown bitter and disillusioned and, not surprisingly, had ultimately refused him her bed, so that he'd turned to other women for consolation and had taken a string of mistresses.

With the business an endless bone of contention between his parents, Eliot had watched in helpless misery as the pair barely spoke a civil word to each other, living entirely separate lives within the claustrophobic four walls of their home.

George Tyson had jealously guarded his creation, declaring that he wished his sons to climb above trade and any necessity of earning a living for themselves. They were assured that there would be no need for them ever to work, that there would be sufficient money for them to live a life of ease, as gentlemen. Charles, the younger son and apple of his father's eye, accepted this unquestioningly, preening himself on his own good fortune. Eliot was different. He wanted to be a part of the company, to be active in its growth. But when he asked if he could learn the business from the shop floor upwards, his father had simply laughed, telling him he knew nothing about shoes, and never would. That he should stick to his books and his gardening.

But then nothing Eliot ever did, or suggested, was considered good enough so far as his father was concerned. He dubbed him a 'mother's boy' in that sarcastic, derogatory way of his, all because Eliot took his mother's side in the inevitable and frequent arguments between them.

Feeling rejected and unwanted, he had buried his disappointment by spending much of his youth studying art and history at university, and in travelling, at least until his father's stroke. That had been so dreadful, so incapacitating, that George had been forced to allow Eliot to take over, albeit with furious resentment, viewing his son as an interloper and resisting him every inch of the way.

This cold and empty childhood was perhaps the reason why a desire for a child so consumed him now. Eliot still longed for the family life he'd been deprived of as a boy, to be the kind of father his own never was. But even that was denied him.

Tonight dinner had been late, no doubt due to some other distraction in the kitchen, and yet the lamb was woefully underdone, too bloody for his taste. Young Fanny, the bows of her starched apron sticking out like cow's ears, had spilled soup on Gilbert Whineray's pristine white cuff. The wine hadn't been allowed to breathe for nearly long enough and darling Amelia was taut with tension, as highly strung as a young thoroughbred. Which was what she was, in a way. Far too well bred for her own good. Ah, but what she lacked in organisational skills she more than made up for by her beauty.

She had looked utterly delightful in a coffee and cream lace gown, a pink rose tucked into its trim waistband. Her skin was clear and rose-flushed, lips generously curved into a gracious, rather wistful smile, and her eyes as bright as a summer sky.

With her blonde hair puffed out entrancingly about the pale oval of her lovely face, his wife sat at the head of his table with all eyes upon her: a perfect vision of loveliness, a picture of serenity. Only he was privy to the true turmoil within. But then Amelia looked wonderful whatever she was wearing, even in the thick woollen stockings and tweed skirts she adopted to 'help him' with the gardening, which never managed to become mud spattered, however inclement the day. And when she was asleep, neatly curled up like a child with one hand cupped beneath her cheek, she was never anything but entrancing.

Oh, how he adored her. She was the sweetest, most delightful woman he'd ever met, and despite everything, he had never, not for a moment, regretted marrying her. She was his very reason for existence. Without her, he would be nothing.

But yet he longed for a child.

When all their guests were gone, Eliot came out of his dressing room to find Amelia already sitting up in bed, cheeks flushed, blue eyes bright as they always were after such an evening. 'It went well, don't you think?' she asked excitedly, 'I thought Mrs Petty surpassed herself with the pear tart, didn't you? A quite unusual dessert. I'm sure Olive Whineray was thoroughly impressed.'

Dear Olive, he noticed, had left half of it untouched, the pastry being slightly soggy. He leaned over and kissed Amelia's soft, pink cheek. 'It was wonderful darling, as ever. A superb evening, and I'm sure it will bear fruit. Whineray is keen to have me on the Council.'

'And will you agree to it?' She sounded anxious, knowing his doubts.

Eliot suppressed a sigh, 'I dare say I might in the end. It can do no harm to be seen about more, I suppose. But what about you? You must feel quite worn out with all the preparations and organisation you've had to do.'

Her cheeks, if anything, flushed even pinker. 'Not in the least. I feel perfectly marvellous.'

And so he climbed into bed, turned off the light and made love to his wife. But sadly, as he knew only too well, their passion for each other would bear no fruit at all.

3

'I'm done for. This is it, the end. If I'd known that helping you get started in the job would lose me mine, I'd never have offered. Years of apprenticeship, a trade at me fingertips, and now I'm all washed up, finished before I hardly get started!' Dermot stood in the midst of the muddle and squalor of the single room Kate called home, Millie and Clem anxiously looking on, Ma Parkin oblivious as she sat and hummed some ditty, surrounded by a gaggle of children. His hands hung at his sides, shoulders slumped, dejection written all over him. 'What am I supposed to do now? I don't even have a home to go to, not now me apprenticeship is over, and I've no money coming in to pay rent.'

'You could stop here with us,' Millie offered, generous to a fault, as always, even though she had nothing much to give.

Dermot gave her a weak smile and said nothing. He'd no wish to give offence but the idea of bunking down with Millie, Clem and their noisome brood didn't bear thinking of.

'What about yer master?' Clem put in, clearly thinking that a man fortunate enough to have two arms and a trade as well as youth on his side, didn't have too much to complain about.

'Old Gabriel barely has enough work to keep himself going, he's certainly none to give me, I've already asked him. I was depending on Tyson's.'

'Couldn't you get work someplace else?'

'And who would that be with, would ye mind telling me?

What other employer of size do we have hereabouts? None that won't be influenced by the fact Tyson laid me off. No, I'm done for. There's no other word for it.'

'Aw, don't keep going on about it, Dermot. I know what I've done to you and I'm right sorry for it, so I am.' Kate could hardly bear to look at the bleak misery in her brother's face, see the tightness of his jaw and the way his mouth trembled very slightly despite his best efforts to prevent it, just as it had done when he was a boy. 'I never meant for this to happen. It was just that it was all so unfair – I couldn't bear for Swainson to cheat us. He wouldn't accept that a woman can do as good a job as a man.'

'You and your blethering pride!'

' 'Tis not *my* pride at fault, but his. To blame you for helping me wasn't right, not right at all. The miserable scoundrel! I'd wring his scrawny neck with me own two bare hands if ever I got the chance.'

'Ach, don't start again. I'm the one who has to suffer, not you. You're fine and dandy, so you are. It's me what's got the push.' Dermot pounded a fist into his chest, made to storm off but then, realising there was nowhere for him to go, stayed where he was, flapping his arms about in frustration. 'What am I going to do, Katy?'

He hadn't called her by this pet name in years, not since they were children together. Kate felt a lump come into her throat and couldn't help but wonder what Daddy would have said to see how her show of temper had landed their Dermot in this mess. She could almost hear his soft voice just as if he were standing right beside her, the lilt in it as he put the long 'A' in her name. 'Houly Mauther, what've ye landed us in now, Katherine child?' Kate couldn't help but smile at the memory, for all she could feel the prick of tears at the back of her eyes. She came to a sudden decision.

'I'll put it right, I'll go and see himself. Apologise for being so forward, so filled with pride and impudence. I'll speak to the priest too, get him to put in a word for me. I'll tell himself it was all my fault and it's me should be given the old heave-ho, not you.'

Millie said, 'Don't talk daft, Kate. How will you feed the bairn if you've no work, nor money coming in?'

'Aye, she's right. At least I'm still single.' Dermot had been hoping to change that lonely status and ask Dolly to wed him, once he'd got a bit put by. They'd been walking out for years and had both been very patient, but the waiting was driving him mad. He was desperate to bed her, but she wouldn't let him go beyond a chaste kiss and a bit of fondling till she had a ring on her finger. Now he was further away than ever from that hoped-for happy state.

Kate was saying, 'I'll go up to the Union Workhouse, then, so I will.'

'You'd rather be a skivvy in the kitchens or scrub laundry up there, would you, than work for Mr Tyson?' Millie asked in disbelief. 'And what about your dreams for Callum? Look at us, is that what you want for him too?' She became distracted as one of her babies started to howl. Picking it up, she lifted her blouse and watched in pained resignation as it clamped its greedy mouth tight on to a scraggy breast. It sucked for no more than ten seconds before it began to howl again. 'See what I mean? No food left anywhere.'

Kate shivered. 'Well, they'll feed us up there, at least. We'll manage, don't you fret.'

She'd meant to sound jaunty and decisive, but the words emerged as a hollow-sounding squeak because she could barely get them out for the lump of fear and bitter disappointment that was clogging her throat. Why was it that everything turned sour for her? What had she ever done to deserve such ill luck? Kate didn't care on her own account. Hadn't she endured the rough and ready ministrations of the Board of Guardians for years? But what Millie said was true. She did want something better for Callum.

Besides, they'd take him away from her, she knew they would. They'd put him to work along with the other children by the time he was five or six, crushing bones for fertiliser, or breaking stones. That's if they hadn't already given him away to some better-off family in need of a fine healthy son. For as sure as the Virgin Mary is on the side of all sinners, he wouldn't stay healthy for long, not in that great, huge monstrosity of a place where hundreds of men, women and children were slowly reduced to human wrecks. It was said that the bed frames were already rusty as the mattresses were rarely dried properly, let alone aired. Kate knew well enough that this was the overseer's way of discouraging malingerers, as if anyone would willingly choose to be incarcerated in such a hell-hole.

'I'll go and see himself, so I will. Put this mess right. Mebbe he'll change his mind and keep us both on, if I ask him nicely.'

'You think Tyson will listen to you? Don't make me laugh, Katy. He'll not even see you.'

'He will, so. I'll make him see me. He won't be able to resist.' She gave a little smile, for hadn't she seen a flare of interest in his eyes? She might be poor and uneducated but she knew when a man liked the look of her right enough.

Dermot rubbed his hands through the wild thatch of ginger hair that topped his round head and gave a grunt of impatience. 'There ye go again, so damned sure of yourself, so filled with yer own self-importance. He's a happily married man, Kate, and even if he weren't, he'd never be interested in the likes of you, a girl from Poor House Lane.'

'He will so, you'll see. I'll put it right, so I will.'

★

Kate had hoped to leave Callum with Millie while she put her case to Eliot Tyson, or even with old Ma Parkin, but when it came to it she changed her mind. The youngest Parkin child had woken fractious and burning up with a fever this morning and Kate had left the cottage as soon as she possibly could, anxious to get away, frantic that whatever was ailing Millie's children this time, Callum wouldn't come down with it too. Fortunately, he never seemed to catch their coughs and colds, or their frequent bouts of diarrhoea, and had so far proved himself to be a happy, healthy child. Even so, Kate never stopped fretting about him, not in that place, it was a breeding ground for disease and fever of one sort or another. Rarely a week passed without a child in the yard contracting measles or chicken pox, whooping cough or mumps, and too many of them didn't have the strength or the will to survive. Lice and scabies were all too common, and sometimes there were more serious complaints such as diphtheria or scarlet fever that could carry off an entire family of children in the blink of an eye.

So here she was, dashing across Nether Bridge with her baby tucked under her shawl, the rain sleeting down in typical Lakeland fashion, soaking her to the skin, and Kate still hadn't decided what, exactly, she would say when she got to the factory.

'I'm a blethering idiot, so I am, Mr Tyson, and I'd like you to sack me instead of me brother because he's desperate to wed.' Would that do? No, that wouldn't wash at all. He'd take her for the fool she claimed to be, laugh fit to bust and probably sack the both of them. Oh, this was a pretty kettle of fish and no mistake.

She paused to wait for a waggonette to go by, stepping quickly back as it sprayed yet more mud and water on to her skirts. 'Shall I say that your clever Uncle Dermot is the one with the skills, or is that going too far?' She pulled the shawl closer around Callum so he didn't catch cold as she addressed the question to him. The baby beamed up at her, a happy, toothy grin, and kicked his legs against her hips, making her laugh. 'Or shall I simply say that he's the man, and deserves a job more than me?'

Ach, how could she even think to say such a thing? Didn't she have a little man in her arms who deserved the best that life could offer? Besides, it went against the grain to set herself lower than the male of the species. Even for the sake of her own brother. Come to think of it, particularly for her own brother. Had she lost her senses completely even to be thinking of saving Dermot's position?

'Doesn't he lose most of the money he earns on the dogs, the cards or the booze anyway?'

With her head down against the tearing wind and rain, she made a dash for it across Aynam Road, splashing through puddles and getting further soaked for her troubles.

Yet she couldn't let him starve, now could she? Not her own brother. What would Daddy have said? Kate let out a bubbling laugh. 'He'd have said, "That son of mine is the greatest lump of useless pudding I ever had the misfortune to . . ."'

She got no further with the thought.

Kate didn't even see the carriage coming full tilt from the direction of Thorney Hills where the nobs lived. Wasn't aware of its presence as she rehearsed her thoughts aloud, entranced by her sweet memories, the rain drumming on the pavement and the wind howling in her ears – or not until she smelled the horses, heard the jingle of a bit and a warning snort of alarm from wide, flaring nostrils. The next instant she seemed to be tangled in a mesh of harness, desperately trying to fend off two terrified animals and prevent them from ploughing down herself and her precious child under their prancing feet, even as she felt Callum slip from her grasp.

When she came to, the world was spinning slowly round and small explosions of light were going off inside her head. Kate came to with a start and tried to sit up. 'Callum! *Callum!*'

'Ah, good, we have life.' Hands pressed her gently down again; a round, cheery face swam into view. It bore whiskers and sideburns, steel-framed spectacles, and there was the strong smell of burning feathers under her nose. The stink was appalling.

'Where is he? Where's me son?' She seemed to be on some sort of couch, evidently inside a doctor's surgery, and there was no sign of Callum anywhere. The doctor had turned away, was walking to the door as if not wishing to answer her question, and Kate's heart plummeted. She felt certain that the bile she could taste in her throat would erupt at any moment, all over the doctor's clean floor. 'Mary, Mother of God, will ye tell me where he is before I go demented? Is he all right?'

The doctor hurried back to her at a brisk pace, quietly hushing her, his expression stern. 'By some miracle the baby is well. Must have bounced like a rubber ball for there's barely a bruise on him. You have a fine healthy son, my dear, so stop fretting and stay calm while I fetch him for you.'

Kate sank back on to the leather couch with a sigh of relief and let the tears slide down her cheeks. What would she have done if she'd lost Callum? It really didn't bear thinking about.

By the time she heard the door open again she was sitting up, had made some attempt to smooth her muddy skirts, push the tangle of hair from her eyes and was patiently waiting, arms wrapped about her thin chest for she felt chilled to the bone, despite the thin blanket the doctor had draped about her shoulders. Still dazed and in shock, she looked up eagerly, arms reaching out for her child.

It wasn't the doctor bringing Callum but quite another figure altogether who emerged from the shadows, bearing down upon her like the angel of doom. His voice rang with anger. 'What the hell do you think you were doing, running around the town with a babe in your arms in this weather?'

Kate took a quivering breath. She recognised him instantly. Oh, why did things always go wrong for her? Wouldn't Dermot kill her, to be sure? She cleared her throat, reminding herself to take care to address him correctly, 'I was coming to see you, as a matter of fact, Mr Tyson, sir.' It was amazing that her voice sounded so calm, when inside she was a turmoil of emotion. *Where was Callum? Was the doctor lying?*

'If you mean to plead for that wastrel brother of yours, you can save your breath. Swainson is certain he cheated with the leather, and in any case I'm reliably informed that he generally spent three days working and two drinking. He can be replaced by a dozen better men any day of the week. As for you, young lady, you should be ashamed of yourself, taking a child out in such a rainstorm. Don't you realise he could have caught a chill, got pneumonia even.'

'Oh, so he'd be better off catching scarletina in the stews of Poor House Lane, would he?' Kate retorted, cocking up her chin in exactly the sort of truculent manner she'd vowed not to use with him again, and taking enormous satisfaction from the stunned expression that came over his face.

'Scarletina? Are you saying there's an epidemic about?'

'I'm saying he's no worse off in the rain than staying in the pit we call home.' Had the man lost his wits completely? But then, wasn't she supposed to be trying to butter him up, to wheedle him into a more benevolent mood so that she could indeed put Dermot's case? She softened her stance, attempted an alluring smile. 'Look, the fact is that me brother had done nothing wrong, nought but help me get started with the stitching.'

'That's not what I heard.'

'He showed me what Swainson should have done himself, if only he'd had the patience. And there was nothing at all wrong with the boots Dermot made neither. Your precious foreman was just determined to be nasty and have his own way, so help me.'

The look Eliot gave her was scathing. 'What are you saying? That he wanted to have his wicked way with you, is that what you're accusing him of now? What else? Murder and mayhem too perhaps.'

Kate flushed with annoyance, hating the way he kept side-tracking her from the point she was trying to make. She wondered whether she dare accuse Swainson of having wandering hands, but decided that was too risky, even for her. Besides, she couldn't prove a thing. But recklessly, not wanting to be beaten, she decided to try a different tack. 'If ye think Tyson's is still producing the quality work it allus used to when your father was alive, ask your precious foreman to prove it.'

'I beg your pardon?'

'Go on, why don't you? Me brother says there's no comparison between the old and new.'

'We're not discussing Tyson business here.'

'I am.'

'We are discussing how you risked your own child's life in order to save that useless brother of yours.'

'I did not risk my child's life!'

'Running around, not looking where you were going . . . Do you realise that child could have been killed?' He kept his voice low although it crackled with wrath. It showed not a trace of the harsh overtones of a Westmorland accent or the slightest hint of a flat vowel. Eliot Tyson's voice was clear and well-modulated, as one would expect from one of the gentry.

'That was not the way of it at all. If you hadn't been tearing down the road so fast in that fancy carriage of yours, ye might have seen us. Do you always drive so recklessly?'

'A gentleman doesn't drive his own carriage.'

'Aw, now why didn't I think of that? Doesn't that make all the difference in the world? Well then, you should employ someone who isn't half-blind or plain daft. A woman with a babby can't be that difficult to spot, surely to God, even in the rain.'

'You were reckless in the extreme, so don't try to turn the blame on to me or my driver. Not for this unfortunate accident, nor for that other little matter.'

'Little matter?' Kate was incensed. ' 'Tis our livelihood we're talking about here. You robbed us of it, turned me brother off without a penny.'

'Accept what fate and your brother's own folly has brought you, Kate O'Connor. I never back down from my decisions. Never! As I understand it, he got what he deserved. You both did.' Eliot Tyson's anger and obduracy suddenly seemed awesome, leaving Kate stunned into silence for a whole ten seconds before she found her voice again.

'Then you understand wrong.' Despite her defiance, a tiny shiver ran down her spine at his vow that he never backed down from a decision, rather like a premonition, just as if a goose had walked over her grave.

He stepped closer in a manner she took to be threatening, except that in that moment she became aware, for the first time, how very handsome he was. He had a chiselled, sensitive mouth and a high forehead from which sprang dark, wavy hair that just touched the collar of his greatcoat. The nose was perhaps more hawk-like than aquiline but no one could deny the fine bone structure, even if the lines of his face did look as if they'd been dragged down by some disappointment or other. His eyes were a deep chestnut colour though worry and strain seemed to have created a fog of abstraction in them, the sentiment echoed in the slump of his shoulders.

Until that moment Kate had never imagined it possible to be both rich and unhappy, it somehow seemed a contradiction in terms but she knew hurt when she saw it, only too well, and this new insight surprised her. She longed to reach up her hands and stroke away those cold, harsh lines, to ask him what had put them there. But then the doctor came in, carrying Callum in his arms, and the moment passed.

Kate leaped from the couch and ran to gather her child to her breast. Callum stretched out his arms to her, giving her his cheeky, toothy grin, and her heart melted with love for him. Cradling him close she began to sob quietly, breathing in the dearly familiar, baby smell of him, admittedly much fresher and sweeter than of late as someone had evidently bathed and changed him, dressing him in clean clothes she didn't even recognise. He looked quite the little dandy, but he was still her babby, her lovely Callum, whole and well.

'Leave us,' Eliot Tyson instructed the doctor with a brusque nod, and the man discreetly withdrew. 'Sit down, I'm not done yet. There are things which need to be said, matters requiring attention.'

Kate pouted her resentment, 'I thought it was all settled. You said you never changed your mind.'

'I'm not talking about that dratted brother of yours, but this child here and your inadequate care of him.'

'Inadequate? How dare you? I . . .'

'Don't interrupt, girl, when I'm speaking.' He was ranging

about the room in a restless, agitated manner, as taut as a coiled spring. Wisely, Kate sank back on to the couch and held her tongue.

'I assume there's no husband,' he snapped, glancing across at her with open contempt, and Kate bridled.

'There was once but he was drownded, God rest his soul. Saved me life, as a matter of fact, but lost his own.'

'I'm sorry.'

Eliot Tyson didn't sound in the least bit sorry, or even convinced by her tale, but Kate let it pass. He was striding about the room again, rubbing a hand against his chin, apparently deep in contemplation of something or other, and she began to feel alarmed and very slightly troubled. Why didn't he just let her take Callum and go? He'd made it perfectly clear that he'd no intention of relenting over his decision not to give Dermot any more work. This whole trip had been a complete waste of time. She'd put herself and her child through all this agony for nothing and nearly got them both run over in the process.

Eliot was speaking again, in slow, measured tones, almost as if the facts of life had only just become clear to him. 'You can't pretend your situation is ideal. Living in Poor House Lane as you do, trying to get by on an outworker's wages, running around town in rags and with your child in a pitiful condition . . .'

Kate gasped, cut to the quick by the insult. 'Pitiful condition? Isn't he the finest boy you could ever hope to see? Sturdy and strong and full of good spirits.'

'Indeed he is. Surprisingly healthy, in fact.' There was a moment's silence while Eliot paused to consider the baby seated on her lap which, as the silence dragged on and lengthened, became ever more strained and awkward, making Kate fidget and feel increasingly uncomfortable. Finally, he seemed to stir himself and recollect what he'd been saying. 'That's exactly my point. He deserves better.'

'Well, isn't that what I'm trying to do for him? Which is why it's so important I get regular work with decent pay.' She made a sound of disgust deep in her throat. 'Only it seems you have to be on the right side of your foreman to get it.'

'You can't blame Swainson. He's only doing his job. He has to guard against scoundrels who are only too anxious to cheat me.'

'You think everyone is dishonest, just because they're poor? Let me tell ye, there's plenty in the same situation as me, and once you're down there's no way back up that flaming ladder to a decent life, or so it seems, but that doesn't make us all cheats and liars. Honest to a fault, that's me, so help me God, though not a living soul cares.'

She noticed that he very nearly smiled at this, but then thought better of it. 'I dare say there are indeed plenty in as bad a situation, but that doesn't make it right – for you.'

'Why should you care about me?'

'I don't, not in the least. It's the child I'm thinking of.'

'Then think about all the other children and their poor mothers.'

He ignored this. 'Wouldn't you like a decent life for him? Something better than Poor House Lane?'

Kate felt suddenly overwhelmed with frustration at his stupidity. He was so naïve, so blinkered, he couldn't seem to recognise the day-to-day reality she had to live with – a dire situation not helped by a nasty foreman with wandering hands. Didn't she do her level best for her child, poor as she was?

Kate got to her feet, filled with a sudden impatience to leave this clean sanctuary, this man whose wits had clearly been addled by soft living. Annoyance flared once more into hot temper.

'Of course I'd like something better for him. Haven't I said as much? Dermot would like to start a family too, if he could afford one.' She made for the door, ready to flounce off home in high dudgeon, to put her child to bed and hope and pray she could find something for his breakfast on the morrow. *And* try to think of some way to soften the disappointment for her poor brother. In any case, where was the point in going round and round in bloody circles, repeating the obvious? Her hands were actually reaching for the handle when Eliot's next words brought her to a skidding halt.

'I have come to the decision that it would be by far the best thing for me to adopt him.'

'*What?*'

'That is, for my wife and I to adopt the child. We can give him a much better home than you could ever hope to. He would be properly fed and cared for, schooled and educated, turned into a fine gentleman to live a life beyond your wildest dreams. What do you say to that?'

'I'd say you've run stark, staring mad.'

'It's a generous offer. Take it or leave it. You'll not get a better.'

4

Amelia gazed at her husband in astonishment. Had she not been properly brought up, she might very well have allowed her mouth to drop open in shock.

'I'm sorry, Eliot, but I think you're going to have to explain this all over again. You plan to what?'

He'd wisely left the girl kicking her heels in the hall while he brought his wife around to the idea. Despite Amelia's having suffered a disastrous end to three pregnancies, the last more than two years ago with no sign of another since, he knew that she still hadn't given up hope. Her longing for a child was such that whenever he'd tried to reassure her that it really didn't matter, that he loved her anyway, it always upset her. It seemed too cruel simply to tell his beloved wife that Doctor Mitchell had confidentially informed him it was highly unlikely she would ever bear another. Aware of Eliot's desire for a family, she longed to provide one. In the end, they'd stopped discussing the matter as it was far too painful a subject for them both, and generally reduced Amelia to tears. Even the shattered remnants of the dreams that she clung to had seemed better than no hope at all. Until now.

'The boy is healthy and strong, and in need of a good home,' Eliot told her.

'You speak as if he were a stray dog or cat.'

'Then I am sorry if I have given that impression. He will, I am sure, grow into a fine young man. He does have a mother who loves him but she is penniless, without the means to care for him properly. My plan is that we should adopt him as our own.'

Amelia looked at him askance. 'And she is agreeable to this? Is she asking for money? What kind of mother is she?'

'A desperate one. And no, she has asked for nothing for herself. The suggestion – the idea – was mine. She isn't, as yet, too comfortable with it but is prepared to consider it, for the child's sake, and is willing to meet you.'

'But handing over her own child? That seems so heartless. Can't you simply give her some work?'

'She has work, but neither home nor family beyond a rapscallion of a brother. She lives in Poor House Lane but wants something better for the boy, and who can blame her? I wouldn't let a dog of mine live there. Will you speak to her at least? Will you agree to see the boy? He needs our help. Can you imagine, Amelia, how it must feel to be starving?'

She could not, unfortunately, imagine anything of the sort. Not out of any sense of unkindness or lack of caring on her part. She held a strong sense of *noblesse oblige,* loved to give to those less blessed than herself, indeed felt it her bounden duty to do so. She would take them the preserves made by Mrs Petty in the kitchen; the flowers or fruit which grew in abundance in their garden, thanks to Eliot's green fingers and to Askew's back-breaking efforts. But it never crossed her mind to worry over the differences between her own good fortune and station in life, and those of the blighted poor. 'The rich man in his castle, the poor man at his gate' were to Amelia facts of life over which she had no control. God had ordered their estates, as the words of the old poem clearly stated, and therefore they could not be altered.

She certainly believed that she treated her servants with benevolence and generosity. They were well-fed, had access to regular hot baths, fresh air, and ample time off. Some mistresses, she knew, were so unkind to their maids that it was more than likely she could be accused by them of pampering her servants. Social change, with its connotations of politics, economics and other weighty matters, was something best left to men, in her opinion. It was a part of their rhetoric and therefore quite beyond her. In Amelia's world a woman should concern herself solely with the moral tone, with social etiquette. She must train her daughters to be ladies and her sons to take over the business, assuming she was fortunate enough to have children. Which Amelia, sadly, was not.

'I – I'm not sure, Eliot. I'm not certain that I can do that. I mean – take on another woman's child? Indeed, it is asking a great deal of me when we may yet have our own.' She turned her lovely, pale face up to his, eager for his assurance that this was probably true, but instead read bleak disbelief in his eyes. A small sob escaped her and she got up from her chair and fled to the window, pressing her lace handkerchief against her mouth to stifle her tears.

Following her, he quickly gathered her into his arms and held her close against his chest, stroking her slender shoulders till the weeping eased. 'I don't mean to be unkind, my darling. I would never ask this of you if I thought there was some other way, but you know – we both know, in our hearts – that there is little chance of that now. And if you did have a child of your own, all well and good, then we would have two children. What is so wrong with that? And you will love him on sight, as I did. I know you will. Shall I bring him to you?'

'He is called Callum. Say hello, Callum, to the nice lady. He's only just starting to talk but he's bright as a button, ma'am.'

Kate was aware that she was talking too much but this woman in the dark grey dress, a dull muddy shade that did nothing for her complexion and made Kate think of old ladies and funerals, was sitting bolt upright, saying nothing at all. Kate had placed Callum on the rug before Mrs Tyson then stepped back quickly, mindful of her boots, but the woman had scarcely given him more than a passing glance.

Kate sent a silent appeal to Eliot Tyson, standing behind his wife's chair. He seemed anxious and uncomfortable, and rested a hand gently on her shoulder. 'Speak to the child, Amelia. Perhaps he would like one of your sweets.'

Obedient to his direction, she took a peppermint drop from the bag on the small round table beside her and held it out to the child with a trembling hand, rather as if he were a rabid dog and she half expected him to snap off her fingers. Callum had never in his life tasted such a thing but curiosity and the sweet, peppermint scent of it intrigued him. He reached up and grasped it with one small fist and, as is the way with babies, put it straight to his mouth. Suddenly his eyes opened wide in delight and he began to suck upon it noisily. In seconds it was gone and he was reaching out a sticky hand for more. 'Again,' he said. Amelia burst out laughing and gave him one.

'What a greedy boy you are,' she said, reaching for another, her blue eyes suddenly shining. 'Say "please".'

'Peas.'

Amelia clapped her hands with delight, half turning to look up at Eliot. 'Did you hear that?'

'I did.'

Kate moved a step closer. 'Not too many, ma'am. He'll get bellyache.'

'Oh, of course. I wasn't thinking.'

Satisfied that some progress at least had been made, Eliot muttered something about having one or two matters to attend to. 'I'll leave you to get acquainted.' And when Amelia put out a hand to him in alarm, he grasped it, kissed her fingers and assured her that he wouldn't be more than ten or fifteen minutes at most.

When he was gone, closing the door softly behind him, Kate felt quite at a loss to know what to do or say next. Standing there in her rags and tatty boots on an expensive Persian rug made her feel like something the cat had dragged in. She glanced anxiously down at her footwear, at the shameful trail of dried mud behind her, and thought that perhaps she should have taken them off, after all.

The house had astounded her. It was built of limestone, as was usual with these square, Lakeland mansions, with tall, wide windows looking out over the river, its roof a complicated arrangement of gables, even sporting a tower in one corner with a battlemented top. The coachman, Dennis, had driven them into a big paved yard surrounded by a bewildering number of outbuildings and what she took to be stables, larders and dairies. Kate couldn't imagine how two people could need so much space, and why they didn't frequently lose each other within it. She guessed there must be a number of servants living here too. She'd already met Fanny, the maid who had opened the front door to them. She'd peered at Kate with frowning curiosity as she'd sat waiting on the carved wooden bench in the hall, Callum on her knee. Clearly Fanny wasn't accustomed to seeing ragamuffins in dirty boots spoiling her mistress's polished floor, and had stared pointedly at them.

'Are you here for a job? Because by rights you should come in t'back way and see Mrs Petty, the housekeeper,' she'd asked Kate, in her blunt way, implying that she was getting above herself by sitting there, even though the master himself had instructed her to do so.

Kate had shaken her head. 'No, I've not come for a job.'

'I didn't think you could have, because there isn't one going.

Not that I know of.' A short silence and then, 'So why have you come, if I might ask?'

Kate had smiled. 'I'm not too sure. Perhaps he's not the only one to have gone funny in the head.'

And since this made no sense at all, Fanny had redirected her attention to the offending footwear. 'Were you planning on going into t'parlour in them things?'

'I wouldn't know.'

'Are your socks any cleaner?'

Kate had managed a little giggle at this. 'What socks? And before you ask, me feet are filthy too, so they are.' And Fanny had put her nose in the air then and stalked off.

Now it was too late to take off the boots, the damage was done, and she would really have to risk stepping on the rug again before Callum sicked up all the peppermints Mrs Tyson was stuffing into him. 'I think mebbe he's had enough, ma'am.' And, very daringly, Kate did indeed step further on to the beautiful cream rug to reach for her child.

'May I hold him? Just for a moment. He's such a cherub, isn't he? Just look at those enchanting blue-grey eyes.'

Warming to her kind words, Kate picked up Callum and placed her son on the other woman's lap. She was used to others holding him, to Ma Parkin minding him, and Millie once or twice putting him to her own breast when she'd been overflowing with milk and Kate had dried up. Yet this felt different. Seated on this woman's clean, sweet-scented lap, he seemed slightly removed from her, distanced by the strangeness of the situation. Kate saw how poor and grubby her baby really was, even in the borrowed clothes. His eyes were indeed bright, and his hair undoubtedly marked him as her own, but his skin had that dingy quality of all underfed babies, and he was much too thin. Dribbles of peppermint ran from the corners of his laughing mouth and when he suddenly reached up and playfully tweaked Amelia's nose between his finger and thumb, making her giggle with delight, Kate saw the woman's earlier resistance melt away. She saw love spring into her eyes, and felt, in that moment, a deep sinking of her own heart.

'Oh, he's wonderful. What a little dear!'

Uncaring now of the rug, Kate marched across the huge expanse of it and made to reclaim him. Callum wriggled his legs with excitement as his mother approached and reached up his arms to her. Kate would have taken him but Amelia held him fast on her lap, preventing her from removing him, stayed her with a gentle touch of her hand.

'Eliot says you are willing to allow us to adopt him. Is that correct?'

'It's a mad idea. The daftest I ever heard.'

A small frown puckered Amelia's smooth brow. 'I can see that it would be hard for you to part with him. When he first put the notion to me, I asked Eliot what kind of mother would give up her child, but I can see you have no wish to do so, not deep down. You love him too much to give him up, is that not so?'

Kate dropped her hands to her sides, not knowing what to do with them since the urge to snatch up Callum and run from this house was almost overwhelming. 'I want a better future for him, 'tis true. I'd got no further than that,' she said, speaking so quietly that Amelia had to lean forward slightly to hear the half whispered words.

Amelia again smiled into the grubby face of the child. 'And doesn't he deserve it? He's a delight. And healthy?'

'He's never ailed a thing, by a miracle, praise be.'

'All the more credit to you as his mother that you have kept him so fit and well, particularly considering the circumstances you must have had to endure.'

'Life is never easy for the likes of us, ma'am.'

'I'm quite sure that it is not.'

'And after me husband was drownded, I'd no choice but to manage on me own.' She wanted to make her son's status quite clear, yet the bitterness in Kate's tone spoke volumes, implying the additional, unspoken thought: What would you know of dire poverty?

But Amelia seemed unaware of this. 'You have done a grand job, Kate.'

Neither woman spoke for some moments after this exchange as they both watched the child. He was playing with Amelia's beads now, jiggling and sucking on them, making her laugh all the more. And then suddenly she gasped. 'I've had a marvellous idea! There's no reason at all why you should give him up, not entirely.'

'Begging your pardon, ma'am?'

'We shall adopt him, as Eliot suggests. We'll bring him up as our very own son to be a fine gentleman, and won't we be proud to do so,' she said, rubbing her nose against his in just the manner Kate herself was fond of doing – a gesture which brought an ache to her heart. But then, smiling up at Kate, Amelia added, 'And you shall stay and care for him too. You shall be his nursemaid, his nanny. How would that suit? Isn't that the perfect solution?'

Kate stared at her, unspeaking. Was she truly being asked to give up being the mother of her own child to be his nursemaid instead? This seemed to bring a whole new twist to the Judgement of Solomon. But what was the alternative? To take him back to Poor House Lane, or up to the Union Workhouse where they'd separate him from her anyway? Kate shuddered at the thought. He could very likely take sick and die in Poor House Lane. And she had to admit this was an unbelievable offer, a marvellous opportunity for him. Had she the right to deprive Callum of it because of her own over-sensitivity? Kate knew she had not. She loved him too much for that.

'Your background, or lack of it, will not be a problem. Maids are treated well here, so long as they are willing, good-tempered and honest.'

'I'm sure they are, ma'am.'

'Are you a regular church-goer, Kate? Ah, perhaps you're a Catholic. Because we would expect you to attend family prayers. Would that be a problem for you?'

Kate stared at her, her mind in a whirl. This woman was asking her to give up her son, and yet was fussing about family prayers! 'I'm sure it would not, ma'am, so long as I had time off to go to mass.' Kate, who had never been much of a church-goer in her entire life, managed to give the expected answer. Her gaze, and her thoughts, were fixed on Callum. The way his bright little eyes roved about the room, seeking mischief, his hands reaching out again for the bag of peppermints on the nearby table.

'Perhaps you'd like time to consider the offer?' Amelia kindly suggested.

Kate swallowed, cleared her throat as if about to speak but still no sound came. Her eyes were still fixed upon her child, drinking in the sight of him as if she were dying of thirst and he alone could quench it. Yet what she'd seen of Eliot Tyson's wife had impressed her. Amelia Tyson may be a woman of her class, sheltered and pampered, very moral and proper, no doubt with strict rules on etiquette and fussy about how he must hold his knife, how he must say his pleases and thank yous and learn to share and take his turn – but was that a bad thing? If Callum were to make his way in the world, he'd be much better equipped if he knew all about such niceties. And Amelia would give him book learning and figuring, and no doubt put him up on one of them fine horses they kept in the stables. Wouldn't it be cruelly selfish, a crying shame in fact, to deprive him of such a grand chance in life?

And this fine lady was even offering her the chance to stay with him.

Kate found her voice. 'I don't need no more time. 'Tis very thoughtful of you to consider my feelings, and I'd be pleased to accept.' Not for a moment had she considered the effect of this decision upon her own life. Kate's one thought was for the well-being of her son, and she was of course eager to grasp at any opportunity to stay close by him.

When Eliot Tyson returned, some twenty minutes later than he'd promised, all the details had been finalised. Kate was to occupy the nursery landing, close by Callum's side at night, and be entirely responsible for his day-to-day care except for the hours each afternoon and evening that he would spend with Amelia. This regime would continue at least until he was old enough to have a governess. It seemed, to Kate, like a miracle. They would both have clean clothes provided, regular meals and a warm bed to sleep in. One each, in fact. It might have seemed like paradise, save for the fact that from this day forward he would be deemed to be the son of the house, the child of Amelia and Eliot. Callum Tyson, not Callum O'Connor. That would be hard to come to terms with, but she'd do it, for his sake.

When these arrangements were explained to Eliot, he looked momentarily taken aback. 'Then you'll be staying too?' Kate detected a note of surprise, a hint of irritation in his tone. Eyes as brown and hard as polished pebbles were glaring at her, as if he believed the suggestion had come from her. He clearly hadn't bargained on having the child's mother around, a thorn in his side, which gave Kate a surge of satisfaction as if she'd scored a small victory over him.

'I will so.'

'Better for the child, I thought, darling,' said Amelia sweetly. At which comment he seemed to pull himself together and smiled affectionately down upon his wife. 'If that is what you wish, my dear. Whyever not? Sounds a very practical, sensible arrangement.'

Millie was surprisingly cool when she heard the news. Kate had returned to Poor House Lane, of course, to collect her few personal possessions: the cap her father had worn when he'd first crossed the sea from Ireland, the bible he'd given her when she was a small child, and a tiny pair of clogs Dermot had made for Callum to wear when he started to walk. She gathered other things into her bundle too, scrappy items of clothing mainly, knowing they'd be thrown away, probably burned, once she arrived back at the house on Thorny Hills, but her strong sense of independence making her cling on to them.

Besides wanting her precious belongings, Kate naturally felt the need to explain all that had taken place that morning, to tell her friends of her good fortune. Surprisingly, their reaction was not at all what she'd expected or hoped for. She'd wanted them to be pleased for her, to wish her well. Instead, all Millie could say, over and over again, was: 'You've given away your child? You've given Callum to Eliot Tyson? How could you do such a thing?'

'For Callum's sake, because it will be better for him.' But no matter how forcibly Kate put her case, Millie wouldn't even try to understand, which left her feeling sick at heart. Was it all a terrible mistake? Had she made the wrong decision? Yet just looking at Millie's whimpering brood with their runny noses, scabs and sores all over their emaciated bodies, never mind the child who even as they talked lay in a feverish state watched over by an anxious Ma Parkin, she knew that no matter what it cost her personally to give up Callum, she was providing her son with the best possible chance he could have. And she would be there with him, every step of the way. Where was the harm in that?

Clem said, 'How can you trust that man after what he's done to Dermot?'

In a sudden flash of intuition, Kate realised that Dermot might see her action as a kind of betrayal, as if she'd abandoned him. It came to her then that she'd been so taken up with her own concerns, worrying over whether to agree to this outrageous plan of Tyson's, whether she could bear to relinquish her son to another woman, that when she'd made her decision, she hadn't given Dermot a thought. Her brother's plight had gone clean out of her head. She must make it clear she hadn't forgotten him, that she'd do something for him too. 'It was Ned Swainson who gave Dermot the push, not Tyson himself.'

'Aye, but from what you told us, Tyson got you your job back but left poor Dermot high and dry. I doubt your brother will see what's happened to you as quite the good news you're making it out to be. Good for Callum, happen, and for you too in a way, but it don't do much for Dermot, poor lad, now do it?'

'Tell him I'll sort it, so I will.'

Clem looked doubtful, 'I'll try, but whether he'll believe me or not is another matter. You said that before, Kate, isn't that why you went to see Tyson in the first place?'

'I did try but got nowhere. But I'll see it's put right, to be sure. Make him believe that, Clem, please?'

'I'll do me best lass.' Though he still looked doubtful.

She went to say goodbye to Ma Parkin where she sat hunched in a chair, smoothing the child's fevered brow with a cold compress, and kissed the old lady on her sunken cheek. 'I'll come and see you, Ma, to be sure I will.'

The old woman turned from the sick child to look into

Kate's eyes, imparting a knowledge of his condition in the glance exchanged between them that Kate would rather not have shared. The wrinkled old hands clasped hers hard, and the faded eyes were fierce. 'Nay, don't. Once you leave this yard, lass, don't ever come back. Tha's doing reet by that child o'thine, hard as it might seem. Don't ever think otherwise. And you'd do him no service to come back here and risk catching summat. Tha's med up thee mind. Stick by it. Don't come back.'

'Oh, Ma, what will I do without you?' And she hugged the old woman tight, the closest contact there'd ever been between the two of them in all the long months they'd shared the misery of this single room. During that time Kate had been unaware how deep their affection ran. She'd thought the old woman senile, but her shrewd advice now gave the lie to that. Amelia had already denied Kate's request to bring Callum back with her, so that he too could say his goodbyes to Millie and the other children on the same grounds.

'Best he stay here with me, Kate, where he's safe,' had been her uncompromising decision. Quite rightly, as it had turned out.

Kate shook Clem's only hand then hugged him too, both of them aware of Millie standing close by, wringing her hands in silent anguish, pretending to be inured to the likely loss of another child, for all she never would be. 'Take care of Millie and the childer.' He solemnly nodded, looking sad-eyed as the two young women faced each other for what each knew must be the last time.

'Ma's right. You'll not venture round these parts again. I wouldn't, if I were you.'

'We might see each other about, round town. Kendal's not so big.'

'Aye, 'course we will. And we can have a bit of a crack.' But they both knew that if they did chance upon each other, in the market place, for instance, there would be little possibility of Kate being allowed to acknowledge her friend, let alone have time for gossip, not if she were accompanying her mistress on some errand, or wheeling Callum out in his perambulator as the nursemaids of the nobs did. If she was on her own, mind, that would be a different matter.

'You'll always be my best friend, Millie. I'll never forget you.' And Kate's eyes suddenly filled with tears. 'Look at me. Best bit of fortune I've ever had in me life, and I'm crying buckets, so I am.'

Millie was crying too. 'Oh, but we'll miss you, love.' They hugged each other tight, made all kinds of unlikely promises, and then Kate picked up her bundle and set out on her new life.

5

Fanny, the stuck-up maid who'd thought so little of her mucky boots, was allotted the task of showing Kate around, and supplying her with the facilities to make herself presentable before introducing her to the rest of the staff. She brought out an old tin bath, placing it in one of the outhouses because she said she'd no intention of carrying pans of hot water up three flights of stairs, thank you very much. Together the two girls filled it and then, lip curled in distaste, Fanny waited for Kate's clothes as she took them off one by one before carrying them away to put on the garden bonfire.

When she returned, Kate was still standing shivering, not quite able to pluck up the courage to put even a toe in the water. Amelia had elected to mind Callum for a while to allow Kate time to settle in, the baby having already been bathed and changed and checked over by the doctor. But although Kate had seen how splendid he looked, she was less keen to try out the experience for herself.

'Well, get on with it then. Hasta niver seen a bath before?'

''Course I have. We got one every month or so at the Poor House, though it was generally cold.' And the water shared with a dozen others, she might well have added. Kate had generally avoided them, not trusting what those who went in before her might be carrying.

'Aye, and this will be too if tha dun't look sharp about it.'

And then, looking more closely at Kate, 'By heck, tha's thin as a drink of water.'

'So would you be if you'd lived on porridge and Poor House soup.'

Fanny said nothing to this, but set about helping her to scrub herself clean, wash her hair and comb it free of any head-lice, Kate watching in amazement as the soap did its work. As Fanny scrubbed at the filth and the muck, little pink patches of flesh began to emerge among the bubbles and Kate was entranced. Although she'd done her best to keep clean by scrubbing her face and hands regularly with cold water, the rest of her body and hair had largely been left to its own devices, it being far too cold and damp to remove any item of clothing in Poor House Lane, even if there'd been such a thing as privacy. She'd never realised how very soft and silky was her skin, how gloriously soft and slippy her hair.

'Well, isn't this the grandest way to spend an afternoon?' she said, unable to contain her excitement, 'I won't know meself when yer done.'

Fanny tightened her lips, staying oddly silent as she poured jugs of clean, warm water over Kate's head, splashed and scrubbed at her back and shoulders. There was none of the jocularity or good-tearted teasing one might expect from a couple of young girls set free from their labours to enjoy a little bath-time fun. She didn't even seem curious about the new-comer, not asking a single question but remaining tight-lipped throughout.

'There you are then. Tha'll smell a bit sweeter and be nicer to be near, at least.' Almost as if she were relieved that the task had come to an end.

Perhaps, Kate thought, she preferred cleaning out fire grates to scrubbing filthy paupers. 'Thank you so much.'

'I reckon tha's left half of Poor House Lane behind you in

that bath water. We could happen grow a crop of spuds in that muck.'

Kate simply laughed, not caring a jot if Fanny did make rude remarks about the amount of filth which caked the surface of the water; she couldn't ever remember feeling so wonderful in all her life. The water had been piping hot, the soap rich with frothy bubbles. Her hair felt marvellous, so clean it squeaked after being thoroughly washed and scoured with sulphur soap, and rubbed dry with a rough towel.

Fanny handed her a set of clean clothes. Fresh flannel underwear, a clean shift, then a simple, pale grey cotton frock with a belt that buckled about her waist, darker grey woollen stockings and shiny black boots that were exactly her size. Kate couldn't remember ever having boots that fitted before. Fanny attached a stiff white collar about her neck, fastening it with a stud at the front. Last, but by no means least, there was a crisp white apron which almost completely covered the dress.

And as Fanny helped her to do up buttons, tie laces and apron strings, Kate risked a few enquiries of her own. 'Are there many servants? I'm thinking they'd be needed in a grand big house like this.'

'Not that many, not enough in my opinion, and we're a motley crew. There's Askew the gardener, he's getting on a bit and should retire only he loves his garden too much. Dennis the coachman – he's my intended, so keep yer hands off him.' Fanny's round cheeks went slightly pink at this. 'Then there's old Jinny who comes in daily to do the laundry, and Mrs Petty – she's the cook and housekeeper all rolled into one, and a right roly-poly she is too. There's Ida, the skivvy, who helps with the veg and the washing-up, and such like. We've no butler here and Beckworth, the master's valet, recently retired and is not to be replaced, apparently. Again, to save a bit of brass, I reckon. And there's me. I'm the only maid so I 'as to run up and down all them stairs, clean all the rooms, answer the door, take in tea . . . the whole bloomin' lot. Run off me feet, I am, most of the time.'

'And now there's me.'

Fanny cast her a sideways glance as she carefully parted Kate's hair down the middle and, looping it loosely back over each ear, set about tying it firmly and tidily into a bun on the top of her head before pinning on a cap. The latter was, apparently, looked upon almost as a badge of office. It was sternly plain and stiff with starch, without any of the frills that distinguished Fanny's own cap. 'Aye, well, we'll see how long thoo lasts. Most new maids don't stop long. Too much like hard work, or they find it lonely and prefer to work in the finishing room at the factory where they can gossip with their friends. They're usually gone afore t'month is out.'

'I won't leave. I'm different.'

'Oh, aye, sez 'oo?'

'I shall stay because of Callum, my baby. Mrs Tyson is . . .' Kate started to explain but Fanny cut in.

'Aye, I saw yer bairn when you arrived.' And giving a loud sniff of disapproval, she continued: 'Lucky you had that accident with Mr T's carriage. Soft as butter the mistress is over bairns, since she's none of her own, more's the pity. A year or two back thoo wouldn't have got yer foot through t'door. So what wages will thoo be getting?'

Surprised by her obvious hostility, Kate quietly responded, 'I – I don't know. I haven't been told yet.'

Fanny had begun to ladle water from the bath, now she paused in her labours to look at her askance. 'Nay, that should be t'first question thoo asks. I get eighteen pound a year. It should be twenty, by rights, being the only housemaid. But you should get less, since you're new.'

Kate quickly picked up another can and began to help. 'Why

is the work so hard? There's only Mr and Mrs Tyson to see to, is there not?'

'Aye, usually, though we get visits from the two aunts, Miss Vera and Miss Cissie, from time to time. Right pair they are. Create more work than a houseful of nippers would, had the mistress been fortunate enough to hang on to 'em, that is. Clever of you to win her round with the bairn, appealing to her soft side, 'cause she's been telling me for years we don't need another housemaid.'

'It's not like that at all!'

Fanny gave a half shrug and setting aside the ladling can, gave Kate's apron strings a final tweak and said, 'There you are then. All done and dusted.'

Kate twirled about in her new crisp uniform. Beaming with delight, eyes gleaming with such excitement and happiness that even the tight-lipped Fanny was moved to say, 'By heck, tha looks grand. A new woman.'

'I feel like one too.' Kate had never felt so fresh, so clean, so bright and shining in all of her life. It was a miracle. 'Do I get to keep all of this?'

'There's another set, for when this one's in t'wash, and work aprons, of course. Brats, we call 'em. None of it's new. These uniforms have been in the family for years. Tha wouldn't believe how penny-pinching they are in this household. Still, better than having to pay for it, like in most places, so mind you look after it. Thoo's expected to keep it neat and tidy, wear yer flippin cap at all times, and don't lose owt or tha'll be fined a shilling. The mistress has been a bit below par and neglectful of her duties of late, but slatternly maids give a house a bad name and if she don't sort you out, Mrs P certainly will.'

Not these dire words of warning, nor even the undercurrent of Fanny's disapproval and hostility could dent Kate's high spirits. She felt wonderful, so clean! Reborn.

Fanny herself was smartly attired in a well-starched print, covered by an equally capacious work apron in a matching plain blue, a frilled white cap perched precariously atop a mass of dark curls. She was a plump girl with boot button dark eyes, and had she chosen to smile a little more, might well have been pretty. 'Happen tha's noo ready to meet thee doom in the shape of our Mrs Petty. Don't be put off, her bark's worse than her bite. Generally speaking.'

Kate would have liked to ask what she meant by this, but no opportunity was given her. They had to finish emptying the bath, wipe the floor clean, put the towels to dry, and all at record speed as Fanny had to change into her black uniform dress and white frilly apron before serving afternoon tea. Mrs Tyson was most particular about meal times being punctual.

'Look sharp.' And then she was off, clattering across the yard in her button boots, and Kate had no option but to run after her and save any further questions for later.

Mrs Petty was the fattest woman Kate had ever seen in her life. But then, there hadn't been sufficient food in Poor House Lane for obesity to be much of a problem, so everyone seemed plump and well-fed to her. Mrs Petty, in her turn, took one look at Kate, then set her hands on her ample hips and shook her head in despair, her several chins shaking with mirth.

'By beck, what have we here? Is it a sparrow or a stick insect? Tha's that thin, lass, one puff of wind would blow thee away. I'll have to tek care not to cough too loud. Come from the paupers' cottages in Poor House Lane, I'm told? Well, no fault o' thine, I suppose. Don't thoo fret, we'll soon fatten thee up. Put some meat on them bones.'

Kate politely thanked her. Already her mouth was watering at the wonderfully appetising smells emanating from the huge cooking range that stood in the chimney inglenook in the big kitchen. Oh, and hadn't she fallen on her feet here right enough?

'Course, you're lucky to have got tekken on. Workhouse children normally only get a position with small-time shop-keepers, shoemakers and the like. Most folk don't care for the scraggy appearance of a pauper child, wondering where they come from and what their background were. You're fortunate, girl, that our mistress is a sweet, generous-hearted lady who dun't trouble her head over such things. Play thee cards right and you'll be set for life here. You could work yer way up to my job, if you've a mind to it. Once I retire to the Fylde Coast with me sister Annie, that is. I've told that to our Fanny here. Not that she listens, too starry-eyed over our lovely Dennis to bother. You strike me as a very different kettle of fish altogether. Good head on them shoulders, I'd say. Nobody's fool, eh?'

'I try not to be. I can stick up fer myself, for sure.'

'Aye, tha does right. Many of them poor nippers, like our Ida here, were badly treated, beaten and ill-fed by folk what thought they could treat a workhouse brat like muck. Tha'll get none of that here.'

'I'm glad to hear it.'

Mrs Petty nodded briskly, as if she'd said her piece, then turning to Ida shouted. 'Nay, have you not mashed them spuds yet? Gerron wi' it, girl. I'm fair clemmed.'

The master and mistress had already dined, having been joined by Mr Tyson's brother Charles and his wife Lucy. Kate had bathed Callum, dressed him in a warm nightshirt she found in a chest in the nursery, and given him his supper: delicious hot cocoa which she'd warmed over a spirit lamp, and an arrowroot biscuit. It had been wonderful to see the little boy drink every drop, smacking his lips with pleasure over the good food. Kate had been about to put him to bed in the big ancient crib which stood in the night nursery when Amelia had come bustling in to collect him: 'So that I can show him off to my dear sister-in-law.' Kate didn't dare point out that it was already past his bedtime and meekly, if rather reluctantly, handed him over, agreeing that it would allow her the opportunity to eat with the other servants in the kitchen, on this her first night.

A long deal table ran the length of the kitchen around which they were now gathering, taking their seats preparatory to eating supper. Kate could hardly wait, for, apart from sharing a few sips of Callum's cocoa, she'd eaten nothing all day and her stomach ached with hunger.

Mrs Petty took her place at the head of the table, grace was quietly recited in unison, and then the food was placed before her: thick slices of roast lamb, a mound of mashed potatoes, heaps of peas and carrots, all drenched in a delicious rich gravy. Kate just sat looking at it in wonder, not daring even to lift her fork in case she should puncture this dream and it would all vanish in a puff of steam.

'Eat up. Nobody's trying to poison thee, tha knows.'

Kate cleared her throat. 'Is this all for me?'

A bark of laughter. 'Well, I dun't know what you do in Poor House Lane, but we can afford to have a plate of us own here, tha knows. We don't all share t'same one.'

Everyone was tucking in with great appetite and gusto, and, glancing surreptitiously around the table, Kate saw that they were casting equally curious glances in her direction. The old codger at the end with the white whiskers must be the gardener, Askew. She recognised the handsome young man with the dark brown curls as Dennis the coachman. Fanny was seated close beside him, constantly nudging his elbow and whispering in his ear. Next to her sat a snotty-nosed girl Kate understood to be Ida, the skivvy. The girl smiled kindly across at her, revealing a mouth full of blackened and broken teeth, and Kate smiled back, sensing a kindred spirit. Perhaps she too had lived in Poor House Lane, or up at the Union Workhouse.

The ache in her stomach had turned to a dull pain now, and still she didn't pick up her knife or fork. Just looking at all this food was doing funny things to her insides. Suddenly Kate knew that she couldn't eat a morsel. It was all far too exciting and terrifying. She'd bring the whole lot up again, she was sure of it. She was worrying far too much about Callum and this shocking decision she'd made. Where was he? Was he behaving himself? Was he wondering where she'd gone? Was he crying for his mam? Did he imagine that she'd abandoned him completely? 'Perhaps I should go and find Callum.' She half rose from her seat but Mrs Petty waved her down again.

'The missus is taking good care of the li'l lad. He's your brat, I take it, so you should be grateful for her care. She dun't usually tek on girls lumbered with a bairn, with or without a father. Mind, we could do wi' a bit more help round here, so we won't complain. Hard to come by, these days, is a good housemaid, and our Fanny is fair whacked.'

Kate's first reaction to this was a fierce desire to defend her son, to insist he wasn't a 'brat' and that he'd had a father once, one she'd been legally wed to, but, mindful of her place and that she was a newcomer, she swallowed her pride and said nothing. Instead, just to set the record straight, she haltingly explained that she wasn't going to be a housemaid. 'It's Callum she really wants, not me. Mr and Mrs Tyson mean to adopt him, but I'm to be employed as his nursemaid.'

The silence which fell upon the assembled company at this was deafening. Knives and forks were stilled as each pair of eyes turned to stare at her, bringing a stain of colour to her cheeks with embarrassment of being the focus of so much attention. Had she said the wrong thing? Let the cat out of the bag? Not that Callum could rightly be called a cat, or kept quiet. She'd been seen arriving with him, after all, and he was all too evidently her son, a pauper's child, thin and scraggy, copper-haired and pale. And Mrs Tyson could hardly keep it a secret, what she planned to do. So why were they all looking at her with this strange condemnation on their faces?

'I thought you all knew,' she mumbled, wishing Mrs Petty's clean flagged floor would open up and allow her to fall right through it. 'I – I assumed word would have got around. Or that Mr Tyson would have mentioned it.'

Mrs Petty was the first to speak. Laying down her knife and fork and rubbing a rough hand over her plump cheeks, she said, 'By heck, I've heard of some wheezes to land a job, but this one just about takes the biscuit.'

'And what would ye be meaning by that, may I ask?' Kate burst out, feeling bewildered. The tension in the room was such now that her skin felt ice cold, despite the heat in the kitchen. What was happening? What had gone wrong?

'Nay, to give away your own son in order to get a job and escape Poor House Lane . . . that's a bit rich that is. I've niver heard of such a thing in all my days.'

'It's not like that at all! I didn't give Callum away. It's for his own good, not mine.'

'Oh, aye? And do I look fourpence to the shilling to believe such a tale?'

' 'Tis so. It was Mr Tyson's idea, not mine, and Mrs Tyson just loved him on sight. Everybody loves Callum. Isn't he a grand little chap?' Kate demanded, gazing around at them all. Then her eyes filled with a gush of tears. How could she even begin to explain what it felt like to give him up so that he could have a decent future, survive even? Nobody noticed her distress as they'd all turned their faces away from her, picked up their knives and forks again and steadfastly concentrated on their food. Only little Ida gave her a half-hearted smile.

'I were abandoned by me mam an' all.'

'I'm not abandoning him. *I'm not!* I'm staying right here.'

For the length of the entire meal no one spoke another word to her. Kate did her best to ignore them, and to eat the wonderful food set before her, but somehow she couldn't chew the tender lamb and the potatoes tasted like dry flour, clogging her mouth. In the end, she gave up the effort and left it largely untouched. Even the hot apple pie and custard which followed was too much for her, and she was relieved when the endless meal was finally over.

'Can I help with the washing-up?' she offered, but Mrs Petty gave a loud sniff and turned away. 'Ida can manage. That's what she gets paid for. It's her job, and she at least come by it honest.'

The rest of the servants settled down for the evening, happily chatting to each other and relaxing after a hard day's work. Mrs Petty was showing Ida how to knit, Askew contentedly snoring, and Fanny and Dennis doing a bit of canoodling on the settle under the window. They all continued to ignore Kate. Whatever their liberal views of employing pauper girls in general, those who gave away their sons were obviously beyond the pale.

Kate crept quietly back upstairs. She wasn't sure if this was allowed, having seen the lengthy list of rules stuck up on Mrs Petty's larder door which included such items as:

No maid to go into the still room, china closet or larder without permission.

The linen cupboard will at all times be kept locked and freshly folded linen cannot be returned until it has been properly checked.

Requests for soap, oil or candles must be made direct to the housekeeper's room by 7.30 a.m.

There were various others of a similar ilk, concluding with a lengthy instruction on how waste was an abomination, with precise details on how various items such as rabbit skins, old tea leaves, dripping and the like, must be dealt with.

But, since no one had brought Callum down to her, Kate felt she'd no choice but to go looking for him. Perhaps the Tysons were waiting for her to collect him and put him to bed, the ways of the upper classes being a bit of a mystery to her. She was ready to go to bed herself, come to think of it. What a day it had been. She was quite worn out. Things might look better after a good night's sleep, but if they didn't, she would leave first thing in the morning, taking Callum with her, to be sure. This whole idea had been crazy from the start. She must have lost her senses to agree to it. They'd just have to take their chances with all the rest at the Union Workhouse, but at least they'd be together.

The small parlour was empty so Kate decided to head for the upstairs drawing room, but as she passed the dining room she became aware of loud voices coming from within. Perhaps they were all still in there. She tapped on the door, hopping from foot to foot with impatience as she waited for permission to enter. Pressing her ear to a door panel, she tried to hear what was being said: a man's voice, loud and booming, and very angry.

'You're damned well being taken advantage of! Surely to God, Eliot, you don't seriously intend to go through with this madcap scheme?'

This must be the brother, Charles. Perhaps, after all, the two ladies had retired to the drawing room for coffee, since Eliot Tyson and his brother were apparently in the midst of one almighty row. And it wasn't difficult to guess the subject of their argument.

'For God's sake, you'd risk putting a workhouse brat in line to take over the factory, just because your own wife is barren? You must have taken leave of your senses.'

A furious mumble, which she couldn't quite make out beyond a few firm opening words. 'How dare you accuse my wife . . .'

'Well, however you like to dress it up, don't think you'll get away with this. Father's will made no provision for such an eventuality, and I'll see you live to regret it if you insist on going through with this idiotic scheme. I'll not see my inheritance lost to some tart's bastard!'

At which point the door was flung open and, losing her balance, Kate fell into the room.

6

'I'm sorry you had to hear all of that, Kate. Most unfortunate. My brother is not an easy man to understand. He has a different set of moral values from my own. Money is his driving force, I'm afraid, with not a charitable bone in his body. Other people are of no account to him whatsoever, so long as he has what he wants – power and wealth. We try to operate by different standards in this household, I hope his words won't make you have second thoughts about our agreement? My wife has already taken little Callum to her heart. It would break now, were you to remove him.'

Eliot was standing with his back to the fire, gazing down upon the top of his new maid's head. Pity for the girl had caused him to offer her a restorative glass of port, which she'd very properly refused. Nevertheless, he'd seated her on an upright chair where she remained as still as a statue, hands clasped, head bowed in abject misery, which he did not wonder at. To be caught eavesdropping at her employer's door on her very first night was not a good beginning. Charlie, praise be, had stormed off after a few choice words on the subject of servants getting above their station, calling for Lucy, and his carriage, in one single breath.

Eliot had dealt with him calmly, as was ever the best way, telling his brother to get off his high horse, reminding him of how their own origins had been humble enough, their father possessing nothing but faith in his own abilities when he'd set about starting the business all those years before.

Nonetheless, Eliot was beginning to have doubts: to wonder at his own impulsive folly, and think that perhaps Charlie might have a point about the wisdom of taking this waif into his home and adopting an unknown child. It was a somewhat reckless act on his part, with possibly more repercussions than he had at first anticipated. And, for all he knew, the infant could be carrying all manner of unknown ailments, and have a temperament quite unsuited to the life before him. Yet simply to see the joy on his wife's face told Eliot that he'd done the right thing.

So long as he could deal with the consequences of having the child's mother live on the premises too, which was something he had not anticipated. Kate O'Connor was undoubtedly attractive; a rare beauty with that indefinable quality of sexual allure that any man would find hard to resist. Not that this cut any ice with him. Eliot felt himself impervious to feminine charms, however tempting, as he would never betray the wife he adored. If he defended the girl it was out of common humanity, because she seemed so fragile, and because, deep down, he admired her spirit. She'd displayed amazing strength and resilience in the face of adversity, for all she was at times far too quick to stoke herself up into a temper.

No, young Kate O'Connor was like a wire about to snap, and he really didn't have the patience to deal with any histrionics from her. Conflict over to whom the child truly belonged was the last thing he needed. The boy must be entirely theirs. Eliot made a mental note to get the adoption papers drawn up by his solicitor with all speed, and duly signed.

He was beginning to wonder if she would ever speak again when the girl suddenly got to her feet and stood before him, her face parchment-pale but with its chin set characteristically high.

'I'd just like to point out that I never asked you to take my child. Nor would I *ever* give him away in order to put food in me own mouth. I'd die sooner than lose him.' She was still smarting from the treatment meted out to her by the other servants, it seemed excessively cruel for them to jump to the wrong conclusion, and a worse insult for Mr Tyson's brother to brand her a tart without ever having met her.

Eliot nodded, 'I understand.'

'I hope you do. Your servants have a different opinion. I want you, and them, to understand that I'm doing this for Callum – for *his* future, not mine. Nor is my son a bastard, and I'll not have him so addressed. I'd be obliged if you'd make that clear to your esteemed brother, among others.'

Again he quietly agreed, inwardly smiling at her use of the ironic description. 'Esteemed' was not a word he himself would use to describe Charles. But then, sensing she had more to say, he urged her to relax and to be seated again. Kate ignored his instruction, treating it as a request, not an order. The set of her shoulders remained stiff, grey eyes meeting his with a barefaced stubbornness which he knew Charlie, for one, would call insolence.

'I'm wondering what you mean to do with me brother? *If* you recall, Dermot was unjustly given the sack by your foreman whose own practices are highly doubtful. I'm thinking that mebbe it would be a charitable act for you to reinstate Dermot.'

He had to hand it to her, she had guts, and the most outrageous cheek. There was more courage in her little finger than most people could summon up in a lifetime. Whether that was a good thing or a bad rather depended on how she chose to use it. Given the wrong slant, her audacity could turn into obstinate pigheadedness. So far, she was employing it for the good of her nearest and dearest, fighting for her son and brother, which he supposed must be commendable.

But however much he might privately admire her robust spirit, he'd be damned if he'd be bullied by a slip of a girl, a mere pauper from Poor House Lane. He wondered what would happen if she ever needed something for herself. What tenacity would she display then? She might have tantalising charm as well as captivating beauty, but these attributes were quite at odds with her tempestuous nature. And her brother was another matter altogether.

No, Eliot decided that he'd done what he could, and that was an end to the matter.

'You were badly used by Swainson, I agree, but I've already spoken to him on the subject. Your brother was blatantly cheating me. My foreman assures me that the leather he used on those boots was not of the same quality as that which was issued to him. He'd clearly sold it at profit to himself, and no doubt gambled the money away. Swainson says this is not the first time.'

'If that's true, and I'm not saying it is, I'll speak to Dermot about it. He'll have learned his lesson, to be sure. He'll not do it again.'

'I can't take the risk. I'm sorry, but if I let him off everyone will see me as soft and attempt to take advantage likewise. Then the standards for which Tyson's are famous will be seen to fail, and I can't risk that. We have our reputation to think of. Besides, I feel our arrangement is a fair one. Your son will be well cared for, and you yourself have been given a position in my household to allow you to continue to be close to him. That seems more than adequate to me.'

'But what am I to tell Dermot? I cannot allow me own brother to starve.'

'He should have thought of the consequences of his actions before he attempted to cheat me. Now, I think we are both tired. It has been a long day and perhaps you are not thinking too clearly. Go to bed.' And as he turned from her, intimating that the subject was closed, Kate had no choice but to comply.

But it was a long time before Eliot felt able to retire. He smoked a second cigar and chided himself for all kinds of a fool for embarking on this dangerous venture, before finally he went to his wife's bed.

Despite the troubles in the kitchen, and her failure to secure any reversal of the foreman's decision about Dermot, Kate passed a blissfully contented night sleeping beside her child in a deeply comfortable bed. She'd gone straight from the difficult interview with Eliot Tyson to collect Callum from the drawing room where he was again being fed sweets by Mrs Tyson. Probably in an attempt to keep him quiet, Kate suspected, because the poor little mite was worn out, his eyes big and wide and dark from lack of sleep.

'I know it must be well past his bedtime but we couldn't resist playing with him, could we, Lucy? He's so full of beans, quite the life and soul of the party. Though of course he must have a proper routine in future, as my dear sister-in-law has quite rightly pointed out.'

Kate barely glanced at the visitor, who was standing ready dressed in her outdoor attire of coat and hat and muff, evidently waiting for the carriage to be brought to the door. At first sight, despite her obvious dark-haired beauty, she appeared sour-faced, with lips as tightly pursed as a wrinkled prune. There was no sign of her bad-tempered husband, for which Kate was vastly relieved. She gathered Callum in her arms, inwardly cursing herself for leaving him so long and for making such a fool of herself by listening at the dining-room door, then scurried to the nursery, thankful to make her escape and be alone with her child at last.

Ignoring the ancient crib which stood four-square in the centre of the floor, Kate took the child into bed with her. The sweet, baby scent of him seemed like a miracle, as if the pair of them had indeed been reborn. Clad in a nightgown of softest lawn, she felt like a princess lying between the crisp clean sheets with her son snuffling contentedly beside her. No matter what difficulties might lie ahead, this must be right for Callum. Wouldn't he thrive in such a place? She refused to be bullied, not by prating servants nor by ill-mannered brothers. She'd stick it out, for the sake of a glorious future here for her lovely boy.

Until now she'd only been planning on Callum getting regular meals, a safe place to lay his head, and an education. Now Kate saw that there was much more involved, enough to make Charles Tyson furiously jealous. And in a way, she didn't blame him. A fine house and a business employing hundreds of people would be worth fighting for, would they not? To think of her son gaining such an inheritance was astonishing to say the least, more than Kate could take in right now. Oh, but wouldn't he make a fine gentleman one day? Strong and healthy and handsome. As she slid into sleep, a small part of her was still trying to decide how she could persuade her mistress to stop giving Callum sweets before the woman ruined all those brand new teeth of his.

When next Eliot Tyson confronted his foreman, the man's attitude could only be described as truculent. Swainson obviously bore a grudge over the fact that his authority had been undermined by his employer speaking up for the girl and not allowing her to be sacked. Not that Eliot allowed this to trouble him in the slightest. He was anxious to know what had happened to the brother; if he really was the troublemaker Swainson had made him out to be. They went through their usual morning routine of checking on the status of the work being brought in, new orders needing to be filled, and then Eliot asked, 'Did you stick with your decision not to use Dermot Flannegan again?'

'Dermot Flannegan?' Swainson could remember the name of each and every outworker he'd ever employed, particularly those who made him the most profit. His prevarication was simply to buy himself time to marshal his thoughts.

'Kate O'Connor's brother.'

'Oh, him. Aye, I stuck by it all right. Nowt but a rabble-rouser that one. Born troublemakers, these Irish immigrants. Girl an' all, if you want my opinion.'

Eliot didn't, but kept his own counsel on that one. 'She won't be a trouble to you any more, she's been given employment elsewhere.'

Swainson's bristly eyebrows shot upwards, his wandering eye seeming to cavort with fury. 'And where would that be?' If it was one of the independent shoemakers, he'd make the man sorry for taking on someone the foreman of Tysons had chosen to dispose of. Swainson didn't care to have his authority challenged, not by the firm's competitors, nor even his own boss. He'd had every intention of defying Tyson's orders and ridding himself of the lass. A troublemaker if ever there was one, with her fire-brand temper and hair to match. Now he'd been denied even *that* satisfaction.

Not for the first time, Eliot felt a prickle of discomfort in front of this man who'd worked tirelessly for his father for as long as he could remember, and was never slow to point out failings in others. Despite being accustomed to battling against a constant sense of inadequacy after taking over the business, at great cost to himself, Eliot was keenly aware that it wasn't really his place to interfere in the foreman's duties, certainly not to the extent of publicly undermining the man's authority in the way he had.

There were times when he wondered why he persisted with this crazy ambition not only to equal his father's success but to surpass it, for all he had no family to follow him in the business. And for some reason he couldn't quite work out why, despite all his efforts, Tyson's was no longer as successful a company as it had once been. Proof, perhaps, that his father had been right. Eliot understood nothing about shoes and never would.

So there was the nub of it: little though he cared for Swainson, the man was a long serving employee whom Eliot's father had trusted implicitly to act in the best interests of the firm. He was conscientious and diligent and kept the outworkers up to scratch, which was no mean task. So who was he to find fault with such a man?

'As a matter of fact, Mrs Tyson has taken a shine to the girl and provided her with a position.'

'In your own household? Is that wise?' Ned Swainson's astonishment was not feigned and Eliot felt a surge of annoyance. It certainly wasn't the foreman's place to question *his* judgement.

'It may suit her better.'

'Oh, aye, I'm sure it will. Nice easy billet, and better for the bairn.'

His tone was caustic and Eliot found it a struggle not to leap to the girl's defence yet again. He didn't usually concern himself with selecting domestic staff, but this was an extremely sensitive situation. He concentrated on checking a column of figures, asking a few questions about them along the way. Even so, he couldn't resist confirming the rightness of his decision. 'Amelia certainly seems well pleased with her. Gets her out of our hair at least, eh?' And he gave a little laugh, as if this were all women's business and out of his hands entirely.

Swainson couldn't quite believe the evidence of his own ears. He was aware that Eliot Tyson's reputation as an unfeeling employer was due more to a sense of inadequacy than genuine harshness; an insecurity he hid behind a façade of aloofness typical of his class. And he was soft as putty where his wife and family were concerned, fool that he was. But this display of sympathy was excessive even by his standards. Swainson felt a raw fury kindle within that his authority had been flouted, that the girl had apparently been rewarded for defying him. Not that he gave any sign of this but if there was some particular reason why that fool Tyson was protecting her, he'd dearly love to know what it was. She was a good looking little filly, no denying that. Happen Tyson fancied her, although that would be a shaker, him and his good wife still apparently acting like cooing lovebirds. Still, you could never tell with toffs. Ned Swainson decided to err on the side of caution, for the moment at least. 'It's not for me to comment upon Mrs Tyson's choices, sir, but I'd keep an eye on that li'l lass, if I were you. Full of fire and brimstone, that little madam.'

'I'm sure she is but Amelia is skilled at managing her maids. Probably do the girl good to have a touch more discipline. But what of the brother? Has he found work elsewhere?'

By heck, Swainson thought, he's persistent. Happen he's bursting out of his trousers with need for the girl, eager to coax her into his bed. Well, Swainson, knew how that felt. He'd fancied the lass himself and been annoyed to be so rebuffed, so he wasn't going to be the one to help another enjoy what he couldn't. Besides which, the leather he'd given the lad had been of poor quality from the start, but he'd no intention of allowing his boss to discover that fact. Didn't he, Ned Swainson, the man who had held this company together for so long, deserve every penny he made out of these little sidelines? He took the view that if Tyson was so green he didn't pay proper attention to what his staff were up to, more fool him. 'Nay, I wouldn't know owt about him but I'm sure it's not the first time the lad's tried to cheat you.'

'Indeed, I'm sure it isn't. But I wouldn't be best pleased if I learned that we had – shall we say – jumped to the wrong conclusion.'

'Oh, and in what way might that come about exactly – sir?'

'I simply want to be sure we aren't making a mistake in accusing him.'

'Nay, I wouldn't waste your time worrying over that scoundrel. He can easily be replaced with any number of better men. Dermot Flannegan will survive.'

Eliot detected a certain insolence in the man's tone but didn't remark upon it. Nevertheless, he held his ground, 'I would be unhappy if, following his discharge from my employ, word got about that the lad was considered untrustworthy and unemployable, yet proved to be innocent after all. We do need to be sure of our facts.'

'Are you doubting my judgement?'

'I'm saying, don't take me for a fool, Swainson, or it will be your head on the block.'

Swainson experienced a prickle of unease between his shoulder blades. There were times, he had discovered to his cost, when this apparently well-meaning and ignorant employer of his could suddenly turn into a shrewd and sharp operator. Eliot had spent hours on the shop floor since his father died, doing what he called 'learning the trade', which had largely left Swainson to run the factory as he thought fit. Now he seemed to be taking much more notice, which was a mite worrying, and all because of some jumped-up little tart and her disreputable brother. Swainson manufactured a look of pure innocence and mock outrage.

'Don't you fret. You can rely on me, sir, as you well know. And how is your garden looking at the moment? Lovely time of year, spring, isn't it?'

Again Eliot hesitated, not entirely trusting the man's fawning manner, but finally decided he was probably worrying unduly. Nevertheless, he did not reply to his foreman's question, not being in the mood for idle chatter or wishing it to appear as if he could be easily diverted by trivial matters. He turned to leave the workshop, satisfied that he'd done all he could for the moment; made his feelings on the matter plain. Eliot felt relieved that this particular problem seemed to have resolved itself. The lad had no doubt found work elsewhere, and, as Swainson said, wasn't worth the candle anyway.

Then for some reason he was never afterwards fully to understand, he paused to make one final point. 'Should Dermot Flannegan reappear, send him to me, will you? It might only inflame him, and cause further problems, if you try to deal with the lad yourself. As I say, Amelia has taken quite a shine to the girl and her child. As a matter of fact, we're thinking of adopting him. Amelia sees it as her Christian duty, an act of mercy, to save the little one at least.'

There it was, out in the open, and why not? Where was the shame in it? Although Eliot was still careful to give no indication of their despair over ever being able to produce a child of their own. 'I'd like them both left in peace, the girl and her brother, and would be grateful for your co-operation on this. Right, I'll leave you to it then. See that the Dixon order is ready by the end of the week, will you, please? I'll deliver it myself.'

Ned Swainson was left standing with his mouth hanging open with astonishment. Adopted? Bloody hell, that was a twist he'd not seen coming.

The girl must have got her feet under the table good and proper, the clever little madam, and happen got between the master's sheets long since. She'd certainly ideas above her station. For all Swainson knew, the child could be Eliot Tyson's bastard. No wonder a humble foreman were nowhere near good enough for her! He might be a bit long in the tooth, a bit individual-looking as you might say, but many a woman had been glad of his attentions. Indeed, still were. While that canny little whore had sold her body, and her son too by the sound of it. No wonder Tyson was looking so pleased with himself. Who wouldn't be, with that luscious little filly warming his bed? Not that Tyson had a reputation for womanising but this so-called happy marriage might all be a sham, a lie. Who could tell? The nobs had different standards, different ways of going about things. If that were so, then it was Mrs Tyson Ned felt sorry for, not only having her husband's by-blow foisted upon her, poor woman, but having to employ his mistress as well.

'And what will Master Charles think of this new development?' Swainson muttered to himself. As younger brother and junior partner always having to play second fiddle, Charlie Boy was unlikely to be pleased that an obstacle had been placed in the way of his inheritance. It had probably quite suited him that his sister-in-law had failed to produce an heir, but this would change everything.

Swainson realised that it might be worth a few discreet enquiries to discover exactly what Charles Tyson's reaction was to this unexpected turn of events. It wouldn't pay to go barging in, mind. He'd need to play it canny but, who knows, the man might be glad of a bit of help one day, and doing favours in high places wouldn't do Ned himself any harm either. But first he must make sure that the Flannegan lad didn't trouble any of them, ever again.

'Time he learned that I'm not a man to cross. I can teach him a lesson, at least. One he's long been in need of.'

Having made this satisfactory decision, Swainson wasted no time in putting it into effect. He strolled out into the factory yard and called over a couple of his trusties. It only took a matter of minutes to outline what he needed doing, and how he would make it worth their while. The pair went on their way with grins on their faces. Dermot Flannegan would never know what had hit him. As for the rest of this puzzling affair, Ned Swainson would just have to keep his ear to the ground.

The night they came for him, Dermot was entirely unprepared. He'd been feeling much better of late, quite pleased with himself in fact, having got a bit of work from his old master plus some repair work on the side. Cobbling bits of leather was a waste of his skills as a shoemaker but at least there was money coming in and Dermot was beginning to think that maybe he could set up on his own account. There were surely plenty of people who'd be glad to buy handmade shoes, and be prepared to pay the price for quality work. He didn't have to depend on someone like Tyson to provide him with outwork. Of course, he needed a bit of capital to buy the materials, the leather and nails, a last, and such like. He already possessed his own set of tools in which he took great pride. And he'd need to afford to pay the rent on a place. He didn't need much, a room in some yard would do nicely. Perhaps then he and Dolly could get wed after all. He was chewing all this over in his head as he sat on the doorstep outside Clem's place when they came for him, two great bruisers. One glance told him that they spelled trouble, and that it was meant for him.

'Dermot Flannegan?'

'Who wants to know?'

Everything was a blur after that. There was the sound of Clem shouting, of Millie frantically screaming and God knows how many kids crying, but he barely managed more than the odd surprised grunt as they laid into him. His last memory was of them dragging him between them over the cobbles. Ahead, just across the road, was the dark glint of the river.

7

Charles Tyson was not a happy man. At a stroke, every-thing had changed. All his carefully nurtured hopes and dreams had crumbled to dust because of one pauper child who was to be elevated above his station. *Adopted into the family, for Christ's sake!* It really didn't bear thinking about.

Younger than his brother by little above a year, despite his cosseted upbringing, or perhaps because of it, at twenty-five Charles felt cheated, believing that life owed him much, much more. As boys, he and Eliot had got along tolerably well, largely because they'd had separate groups of friends, and mixed very little. But once his elder brother had been left full control of the company Charles had felt shut out, given scarcely any say at all in the way things were run. He'd once accused Eliot of only allowing him on the board as some sort of sop. More to the point, his salary and profits received from the business did not, in Charles's opinion, properly reflect his status as a member of the Tyson family. To add insult to injury, Aunt Vera and Aunt Cissle received nearly as much as he did, simply by virtue of being shareholders, and did no work at all. It really was too bad. But when he'd voiced these grievances aloud, Eliot had simply laughed them off with some droll remark about him always being a greedy little boy, and nothing ever being good enough to please him.

But why should Eliot be the one to take over the company, *and* the family town house, *and* run everything, without so much as a by-your-leave? No wonder the business wasn't doing well. Admittedly, Father had left Charles the house at the foot of Lake Windermere but Eliot still held the lion's share. He complained frequently about Charles's spending and yet had recently set up a scholarship for poor grammar school boys to go to university, having some outlandish notion that education should be available to all. In Charles's view, educating the masses could well prove to be the touch paper which set society alight and brought it tumbling down around their ears. Eliot was thinking of endowing some land for almshouses now. The man was a liability, with his philosophy that wealth was a responsibility which should be shared. How could he even consider handing it over to strangers, and undeserving ones at that, while denying his own brother the increase in salary he deserved? Why should everything always be done Eliot's way? The whole caboodle handed to him on a plate?

His 'good works' were of course the reason Whineray had invited Eliot to stand for the town council, which again was infuriating. Absolute nonsense, in Charles's opinion. Such concerns should not be the province of a gentleman at all. It was surely women's business to tend the poor and ineffectual. What else did his brother's useless wife have to do with her time?

And why was *he* never considered for elevation in the community? Why did no one think to give *him* the opportunity to shine? Charles certainly knew how to lead and take control much better than Eliot did. And he would make really rather a dashing Mayor.

He preened himself before his dressing mirror and thought himself a fine chap. Admittedly he cut a slightly more substantial figure than in his salad days, but if he did not possess his brother's more classical good looks, there was surely power in his square, robust features. His hair was darker and more smoothly shaped into the head, and, unlike his brother who was clean-shaven, he sported a neatly clipped, fashionable moustache, kept so by an excellent barber so that the whiskers did not quite conceal the noble line of his jaw or the fullness of his mouth. He made a point of wearing suits of the finest cloth, made up in the latest style by a wonderful little Italian tailor he'd found in Manchester.

Yet it always seemed to be Eliot who got the better bargain. Eliot who had won the place at university. Eliot who was considered the more gifted of the two brothers, both in intellect and in his precious painting, or 'daubs' as Father had termed them even as Mama had gushed about her favourite son's prodigious gift. Eliot had also displayed an unnatural talent for gardening, seemingly fascinated by growing stupid flowers, even able to remember all their blasted Latin names. Furthermore, when he had travelled as a young graduate from Cambridge, he'd come back able to speak fluent Italian while Charles had been accused by his darling mama of 'wasting his opportunities', since he'd spent months enjoying the Bohemian life with like-minded individuals on a Greek island, not going anywhere near Renaissance Florence. Charles was pleased to say that he wouldn't recognise a Botticelli if he fell over one.

Fortunately, their father had largely taken his side, calling his elder son a useless fop and a mother's pet, which had made the division of spoils after his death all the harder to bear.

There'd been the most fearful rows of course when their father had taken to his bed following his stroke: Pops yelling like a banshee, Mother sobbing, and Eliot storming about as grim-faced as one of his favourite Shakespearean heroes. But after Pops's death, it seemed to be taken for granted that Eliot, the elder brother, would take over the company as well as the family home on Thorny Hills. Charles himself had been left the family country home, a decaying mansion at the foot of Lake Windermere in dire need of complete refurbishment, certainly in Lucy's view. Of course, he'd also been left a substantial sum of money, quite a sizeable amount in fact, but nowhere near as much as he'd been promised. No hope of living the life of a gentleman, not with a growing family to consider. But then everyone appreciated how expensive it was to maintain a family, save for his brother who of course didn't have one.

Charles had felt compelled to join the firm and, refusing to sell the Windermere mansion, had bought a fine town house on Stramongate, with the aid of a substantial mortgage, where the family could reside during the week. Then there was the question of decent schools for the children, and a seemingly endless array of new gowns and furbelows for his beloved wife.

More recently there was the hoped-for purchase of a steam yacht. Charles already possessed a carriage and the governess cart which Lucy used, but the roads were so dreadful, one couldn't live on the lake without the facilities of a private yacht. He intended to have it all rigged out in polished mahogany, naturally, with monogrammed cushions and china crockery, together with the customary Windermere kettle which would boil tea for them over the steam boiler. Lucy had a fancy for weekend picnics on the lake, delightful social gatherings with friends – and why shouldn't she? – while he could enjoy his favourite country pursuits of sailing, riding, shooting and fishing. But all of this cost money and Eliot absolutely refused to increase Charles's salary, saying he should sell the Windermere mansion if he couldn't afford to keep it, which was grossly unfair.

Charles scowled as he adjusted the pearl studs of his dress shirt. He could hear Lucy scolding her maid, telling her that if she didn't buck up her ideas, she'd be out without a character come Monday morning.

It was alarming how much servants cost these days, and did one get value for money? Not according to Lucy. And if Charles sometimes worried about his mounting commitments, he did not allow his wife to guess it. Lucy believed in always buying the very best. She'd once picked up a Constable at auction which had practically bankrupted him; worse, doubt had then been thrown upon its provenance, which had left her in a sulk for days. Nevertheless, he enjoyed the kudos of being able to acquire decent stuff: the kind of bric-à-brac which gave an indication of their status in society – garden statues, Chinese pots, gilt vases and marble busts being among his favourites. Their town house was adorned with fine rugs and furniture kept immaculate by the substantial and overpaid staff they employed.

But didn't he deserve to live in a decent style, commensurate with his position in the community? He was, after all, an Edwardian capitalist, if not quite as rich as he would have liked.

Lucy stormed into the bedroom and stamped her foot in temper. 'That girl will have to go! She's broken one of my best vases. She's weeping about her mother needing the money she brings in, but I've told her she should have thought about that before she dropped it.'

Charles wasn't interested in the plight of her maid. He looked at his beloved wife and helpmeet, and his heart sank just a little. 'Is that a new gown, beloved?' he mildly enquired, because Lucy was just as likely to fire up at him too.

'Is that some sort of criticism? You surely don't expect me to wear my old one? The Cowpers are practically aristocracy. Her father was knighted, don't you know?'

Charles sighed. 'Yes, I do know, my love. But I am still at a loss to understand why that should require you to buy a new gown every time we have dinner with them.'

'Don't be peevish!' Lucy marched over to her long mirror and began to tweak the frills of her gown and fiddle with her coiffure. 'The girl never did manage to do my hair right, in any case. I shall get a French maid next time. More skills in their smallest finger than a Westmorland girl. And so much more stylish.'

'I'm not sure we can afford a French maid, my love.'

'Oh, do stop complaining about money. I hear nothing else from you these days. You're getting to be quite a bore on the subject, Charles, every bit as mean as your brother. I suppose you'll be saying next that I can't have new curtains for the dining room?'

'No, no, I wouldn't dream of interfering with your plans, beloved, I only wonder if they have to be Chinese silk? And I thought the peacock blue gown you bought last week looked superb on you, and it has only been seen by a very few people.'

'How parsimonious you are of a sudden. It's so upsetting. Don't you like me to look well? And I feel so fat and weary in this particular pregnancy.'

And then to his utter dismay she burst into noisy tears so that it took fifteen long minutes before he could calm her again, largely with the promise to take her to Italy once her confinement was safely over. Not that he minded too much. He liked Italy and was really rather in need of a rest himself. Eliot might place unnecessary restrictions upon his influence in the company, but he certainly didn't hold back on the work he piled on to Charles.

Besides, Lucy was a fine, handsome woman with her ebony hair and violet eyes, a startling beauty in her day – still was, he supposed, despite the plumpness due to her delicate condition, and a certain discontented set about the mouth. She deserved a treat now and then, to cheer her up. This pregnancy had distressed her more than the other two. She claimed it was too soon, and blamed him for that, though he needed only to tip his hat on the bed and she was off. Secretly, it gave him enormous pleasure that she was again *enceinte*, proving himself to be virile and his wife fertile. Quite unlike poor Amelia, who still showed no sign of producing. Why didn't anyone appreciate what a credit his darling Lucy was to this family by keeping the blood line going?

He had rather hoped that this would be to his advantage, that the aunts would see that he deserved decent prospects – in the fullness of time, of course. But they had bluntly informed him that they had not the slightest intention of leaving him a single penny in their respective wills; insisting that as a man with youth and vigour on his side, he was perfectly capable of making his own fortune. Aunt Vera had declared she would leave all her money to the Church, and Cissie would no doubt bestow hers upon some animal charity or other. But surely, he thought, family was far more important than any religious establishment or stupid dogs' home?

Moreover, Lucy had never enjoyed the same advantages or opportunities in life that his brother and Amelia, for instance, so took for granted. Her parents had been simple country folk, nothing but an ordinary farmer, land rich but cash poor, most of which would pass to her elder brothers, leaving little for her sisters or Lucy herself. But then, didn't they both suffer from being the youngest in the family, with little hope of a decent inheritance from any direction?

Completely in tune with his mood, as ever, Lucy broke into his thoughts. 'Has Eliot agreed to give you a more prominent role in the company now that I'm expecting again and our commitments will increase? Perhaps even permit you to take it over completely and be given the lion's share of the profits, since you are the one with a son to follow on, and possibly a second on the way?'

He did agree that this made perfect sense. Unfortunately, Eliot viewed the matter quite differently, and Charles felt a moment's irritation that his wife had raised this matter while it remained unsettled, had in fact turned it into a bone of contention between them. 'He's said nothing on that score at all.' In fact Eliot had laughed out loud when Charles had put the suggestion, baldly stating that feeding his family was Charles's own responsibility and not that of the company. There was also a great deal more said about not believing everything their father had told them, of cutting his coat according to his cloth, and other such nonsense which he preferred not to reflect upon. 'In any case, from what we learned last night, it would seem that he means to get himself a son after all, one way or another.'

There was a quick intake of breath from Lucy. 'You mean, the adoption of that pauper child? Surely you don't seriously believe that will take place, do you? I assumed it was some stupid fancy of Amelia's and would quickly die the death. Eliot's bound to put paid to such nonsense.'

Charles looked grim, 'I very much fear that he means to go ahead with it, and with all speed. He is as much besotted by the boy as his pathetic wife.'

Lucy put a hand to her throat and her cry of dismay made her voice rise in pitch to a frightening level. 'Then how will we manage? Didn't you tell him about the planned refurbishments to the Windermere house, for the sake of the children?'

They'd both convinced themselves that the planned addition of a nursery wing, plus a new conservatory, not to mention the steam yacht, would be for the children's benefit and not their own pleasure at all. That they needed to keep this exceedingly expensive property on the lake for the health of their growing family. Nevertheless, inwardly Charles squirmed. He'd made a point of not mentioning these plans to Eliot, knowing what his reaction would be. The mortgage on the Stramongate house was already straining his bank account to the limits; a further loan for the improvements could sink it entirely. 'Time enough for such details later, beloved, when the work begins.'

'But if he does adopt this child, where will that leave our own precious darlings? Without any inheritance at all, that's where.' And once more the tears spurted. 'We'll be the paupers then. Oh, what are we to do? We are ruined, ruined!'

'Not at all, my sweet. No, no, indeed not! Do not fret yourself.'

'Oh, my, I fear I am about to faint. Please, Charles, bring my sal volatile. Hurry!'

At his wits' end, Charles hurried to carry out her order, as he always did, endeavouring to keep her calm, reminding her of the child she carried, warning that she'd make her face all red and blotchy and ruin her hair, and when all of that failed, of their dinner date with the Cowpers, which rapidly brought her back under control.

'There's my girl. Chin up, we'll find a solution to this conundrum, make no mistake about it. I'll not see our little treasures pushed out into the cold, as I was. Oh, dear me, no. Now, beloved, go and freshen your pretty face with a little cold water and we'll be on our way. You know how you always like to be punctual, and you do look charming, quite delicious . . . the new gown was worth every penny of whatever it might have cost. I am a most fortunate man, most fortunate indeed.' And pulling her into his arms, he kissed her heartily while fondling her breast. That was another thing he enjoyed about Lucy: her full breasts, ripe as plums. But then, pregnancy always suited her.

Blushing bright pink, she playfully slapped his hand away. 'Shameful man.' But he could see that she was pleased by the attention. Perhaps he'd be able to talk her out of those Chinese silk curtains after all, on the grounds that they were about to restore their other house and must save every penny for that. If not, then he'd just have to bring his dratted brother to heel, one way or another.

Kate was up with the lark every single morning, marvelling at the clear view of the distant mountains she could see through the bars of the nursery windows, their peaks dusted with a frosting of snow against a clear blue sky. Closer to hand she could look down upon the river; sluggish this morning as it slid quietly along past wide, grassy banks, most unlike the raging torrent which had swept away her lovely husband. Beyond the church, which she could just see if she strained her head to one side, lay Poor House Lane and the yards where she had spent her youth. In crossing the river, she seemed to have crossed a Rubicon in her own life just as the bible stated. She'd made a decision and Kate realised there would be no going back, even if she wanted to.

She meant to write to Dermot, tell him that she'd tried at least to help him and that she wished him well. Sure and it was vital that they kept in touch.

The door opened and Fanny entered, a pail of hot water dangling from one arm and a tray of breakfast in her hands. Kate could see boiled eggs, tea and toast, and her mouth began to water. Would she ever recover from this perpetual feeling of hunger? she wondered. Fanny set down both in tight-lipped silence, as always not responding when Kate thanked her. She hadn't spoken to her since that very first meal in the kitchen, nearly a week ago now. None of the servants had. It had been a depressingly silent time. On this occasion, it was only when

Kate offered to fetch her meals herself in future that the girl was finally driven to speak.

'Thoo's not allowed to leave the bairn unattended, instructions from the mistress, otherwise I wouldn't be waiting on you, thoo can be sure of that. Oh, and the mistress says when baby is dressed, would you please go down to the small parlour? She would like to talk to you about proper arrangements for his routine.'

'Of course. And thank you again for bringing up breakfast for us, Fanny. If you've not the time, we'd be happy to eat in the kitchen instead.'

She looked shocked. 'Nursemaids stay in the nursery, with the bairn, for everything, including meals. That's how it's done.'

It had already been made clear to Kate that she was not expected to appear below stairs, a state of affairs which made her thoroughly depressed and quite at a loss. It was going to be very lonely indeed if she was never allowed below stairs with the other servants, and they didn't speak to her if she should happen to go down. Clearly, there were all kinds of pitfalls ahead, all manner of rules and regulations she needed to learn and understand. Even so, she persisted in her attempts to be friendly, thankful that Fanny had at last responded, and so eagerly addressed her departing figure.

'Perhaps you and I could come to some arrangement then, whereby I could help you with some of your chores in return?'

But Fanny simply gave a loud snort and stalked out of the room, head high, closing the door with a sharp click behind her. Kate felt certain that had it not been for the close proximity of her mistress taking breakfast in her own room nearby, the maid would very likely have slammed it.

'Ah, Kate. I hope you are happily settled in? I've left you in peace till you felt quite at home but now I think it time we sort out essential arrangements. Sit our little cherub down on the rug, there's a good girl, while we chat. We've a great deal to discuss.' Amelia did not invite Kate to sit.

Every morning during this last week the mistress had visited the nursery, cooing and gurgling over Callum for so long that getting him up and dressed had frequently been delayed by a half-hour or more. At first Kate had been at a loss to know what to dress him in as his old clothes weren't even fit for the rag-bag, but an inspection of the mahogany chest of drawers in the nursery revealed many items of baby wear, mainly undergarments and old-fashioned dresses, of the finest materials and beautifully clean. Some of them she considered to be rather girlish and at times she struggled to find something that was just right for him. This morning she'd chosen a dress with pleats and a sailor collar, and a matching set of pants to go underneath, so today he looked a fine little chap, sitting happily on the rug playing with a wooden engine Kate had found in a toy cupboard, his cheeks all pink and surely plumper already.

Amelia said, 'While you've been settling in, I have not been idle but busily taking advice. Now I've made a list which I'd like you to peruse with care, at your leisure. Oh dear, you can read, I trust? I quite forgot to ask.'

'To be sure, ma'am, Daddy taught me fine how to read. And Dermot can read too, so he can.'

'Excellent, and most commendable of your father. Well then, I shall run quickly through the bare essentials and if you see any problems, you have only to say.' Hardly pausing to draw breath, Amelia proceeded to read from the paper. 'The nurseries must be painted and redecorated according to the dictates of *Dr Barker's Advice to Mothers*, a copy of which I have here, loaned to me by my dear sister-in-law who has two children of her own and a third on the way. It must be quite plain and unadorned, with a table and a couple of chairs. A rocking chair, a shallow bath on a stand for baby, and a place to store his clothes, most of which we already have. There is also a toy cupboard, and the crib which has been in the family for generations and will serve him well, of course. But he is to have no pillow, as that would make him round-shouldered, and the mattress must be changed to one of straw, which is healthier, I am told.'

'Very good, ma'am.' Kate couldn't help wondering how it was that so many babies and children who slept on a straw mattress in Poor House Lane and had never seen a pillow in their lives, grew up round-shouldered, bow-legged and very far from healthy.

'He will take breakfast at eight with porridge and an egg. Luncheon at one, upon which I have given full instructions to Mrs Petty. Generally chicken or fish, perhaps boiled mutton on occasion, and plenty of fresh vegetables, rice pudding and fruit jellies. Tea with jam and bread and cake at four, then milk or cocoa and biscuits before going to bed. He must also take a little fruit each day.'

'And not too many sweets, ma'am?'

Amelia gave her a sharp look. 'Indeed not. His diet must be healthy. And he needs lots of exercise and fresh air.'

And so the list and its accompanying instructions went on and on till Kate felt dizzy with trying to remember it all. How on earth would she cope?

8

Kate might have been taught the rudiments of domestic labour by the Poor Law Guardians, but the finer, more delicate work was quite beyond her and she discovered she had much to learn. She must remember to keep Callum's play clothes separate from his walking-out clothes, for the sake of hygiene, and Kate herself was personally responsible for laundering and ironing all his garments. For all he was now a sturdy toddler who loved to play and get grubby, as all children did, he must be presentable at all times, and since his clothes were generally pale in colour, showing every speck of dirt, much frilled and beribboned, this was no mean feat.

There were a multitude of rules to be learned which Amelia would explain to her with endless care and tact: such as that she must always keep her hands still when being addressed by her betters, and not fidget. She must look at a person directly when being spoken to. Should she be required to walk out with Amelia or her master, on some errand or other, she must always walk a few paces behind.

And, most startling of all, she must address her own son as Master Callum. Kate found this dreadfully difficult, as well as oddly distancing and unfeeling, so only obeyed this rule when Amelia was present.

There were, of course, difficulties and differences of opinion. Kate thought the bath on the stand too small for Callum and would have preferred to use the bathroom, where taps jetted streams of hot water. This, however, was not allowed. It was the only bathroom in the house, servants having to make do with the old hip baths, and kept for the exclusive use of the master and mistress. Besides Amelia considered it far too dangerous a place for a child of such tender years. What if he were to slip and drown in that great bath?

Kate maintained that he was often overdressed, with so many layers of clothing that at times it restricted his movement and he would become frustrated in his play. But Amelia would not hear of a single layer being removed, not until May was out at the very least.

Putting all the new information and instructions she'd been given into effect seemed fraught with pitfalls. The contents of the nursery medicine cupboard alone were difficult enough to understand, with strange names such as Gregory Mixture and Godfrey's Cordial, Daffy's Elixir for Colic and something called Dr James's Powder which claimed to be for ailing infants and looked highly suspect. Kate felt certain the box must have been in that cupboard for fifty years or more. Nothing would induce her to give Callum even one grain of it, though she did administer the prescribed regular doses of castor oil every morning, and as the days slid past, thanked her lucky stars for his robust health.

There was one occasion when Amelia was quite certain that he was starting with a cold and instructed Kate to give him hot blackcurrant tea at bedtime. He was only teething, but enjoyed the juice and perhaps it did help him to sleep a little better.

The routine continued assiduously with twice-daily walks, morning and afternoon. There were set times for play and he must be rested on the nursery sofa to strengthen his back, and bathed in salt water to get his strength up. After his afternoon nap he was changed and allowed downstairs to see Amelia in the parlour where he was taught to colour in pictures or stick scraps in a book while she read extracts from Sir Walter Scott to help form an appreciative mind. Eliot would come in later and play more boisterous games with him, declaring himself to be looking forward with pleasure to tutoring the boy in backgammon and draughts. Kate thought that her son might turn into a little adult before ever he reached his second birthday.

And each and every bedtime, Amelia would come to kiss him goodnight. Kate found this the hardest part of the day. She would stand some distance away with her hands firmly clasped behind her back, so as not to be tempted to interfere, watching as Amelia dandled Callum on her knee, kissing and cuddling him, before settling him in the great crib with many soft words and yet more kisses.

It was a week or two later that, quite by chance, or so Charles assumed, he discovered Ned Swainson still in the office one evening long after his shift should have ended.

'No home to go to, Swainson?'

The foreman had lingered on after work on numerous occasions recently, and was delighted that at last his patience had been rewarded, 'I was hoping to have a private word with you, as a matter of fact.'

'Problems?'

'You could say so.'

'Then perhaps you should discuss them with my brother. He's the one with power round here, as you well know.' Charles's tone was bitter and he did not pause as he made for the door. He, for one, didn't care to spend any extra hours, minutes even, in this place since he didn't consider that he received proper remuneration for his work. It shamed him to have to admit to needing to earn money at all. He was anxious to get home, pour himself a large brandy and relax. Besides, the foreman was an odd cove with that permanent leer and his wandering eye.

'It was about your brother that I wished to speak to you,' Swainson announced to Charles's departing figure. 'And this new addition to his family.'

Charles paused, his hand sliding from the brass doorknob as he swung back into the room. 'How do you know about that?'

'Mr Tyson himself told me that he was going to adopt the child. Pardon my presumption, but I thought it were a rum do, like, and it crossed my mind that such an eventuality might put your good self into a tricky position. And I wondered – I wondered what you intended to do about it?'

Charles considered the man with fresh interest, eyes narrowed in a speculative gaze. What was he getting at? What point was the fellow trying to make? 'What's it to you?'

'Nowt, save fer the fact that lass, the mother of the brat, and her ruffian brother did their level best to besmirch my name, and I don't care for that, not one little bit. They nearly got me the sack with the accusations they were making. If Tyson's isn't run quite as it used to be, the fault isn't mine. I've had to learn to look after me own interests, and so should you. I were thinking like, if'n you were needing someone on your side . . . someone who could keep his ear to the ground and didn't mind getting his hands dirty, so to speak . . . we might be able to do each other a good turn. That's if it should prove necessary like, for you to stand up for your rights, or even if you should fancy feathering yer own nest a bit more, if'n you catch my drift?'

There followed a short, thoughtful silence and then Charles said in low urgent tones, 'Is there somewhere we could enjoy a drink without interruption? I'd like to hear more.'

*

There was no doubt that Amelia doted upon her adopted son and spoiled him dreadfully. She devoted hours to playing hilarious games with him: Tiddlywinks, Old Maid and Snap. The little boy would shout out so loud, whether or not he had successfully matched two cards, that Amelia would hold her sides from laughing so much.

And if having two mothers sometimes caused confusion for the child, there were other occasions when he took advantage of the situation. Kate would recognise when he was 'playing-up' and firmly attempt to control his temper. Amelia, however, did not have the heart to chastise him or listen to his tantrums and would dash to pick him up for a cuddle, despite Kate's protests.

'That does him no good at all, ma'am. He has to learn that he doesn't get his own way in everything.'

'Oh, but he was so distressed. Look at his scarlet face.'

'That's temper, not distress. He must learn manners if he is to be a proper little gentleman.'

'Oh, he will, he will, but he is so small yet, and still much too thin. Come along now, Callum, Mama will find you a nice peppermint if you promise to be a very good boy in future.' And off she would go, leading a triumphant Callum by the hand, and Kate would sigh with exasperation.

One evening towards the end of the first month the boy was not being quite so co-operative as usual, resisting all attempts to make him lie down and be still. He kept sticking his legs in the air to push off the blankets, and waving his arms about. Then of a sudden he rolled over and pulled himself to his feet by the rim of the crib, beginning to shake it vigorously, making it rock. Amelia grew quite frantic, certain he was about to turn it over, but paying her no heed he suddenly spotted Kate doing some mending in the rocking chair in the far corner of the room, and cried out to her.

'Mammy!' When she didn't come to him immediately, he cried out again. '*Mammy, Mammy. Want Mammy!*' And as Amelia hushed and shushed him, he refused to be comforted and began to cry.

'Kate, you'd better see to him tonight. He's perhaps teething and feeling fretful.' And so, on this occasion, she was allowed to put her own son to bed.

Afterwards, when he was happily settled and drifting into sleep, Amelia turned to Kate, a smile on her face which looked somehow stiff and awkward, and very slightly embarrassed. Kate was soon to discover why.

'I know it can't be easy for you, my dear, but I think it's time we settled one little matter between us. I believe it would be best in future if Callum were to learn to call you Nurse. I am his mama now, after all. Could you please see that you teach him to do this? Better to start as we mean to go on, don't you think, and that we do things correctly in order to avoid confusion later. You do understand that I'm not trying to shut you out? It is Callum I am thinking of, and his future.'

'Y-yes, ma'am. Of course.' Kate was startled. She knew she should have expected this but somehow it came as a shock, like a bolt from the blue.

'It wouldn't do, would it, were you to meet up with other nurses out on your walks, if he were to call you by the wrong name?'

'I – I understand.'

'Good, good. I believe we will suit very well.' And having settled this most sensitive matter, Amelia swept out of the nursery, leaving Kate to sink into a chair and quietly sob into her apron.

As spring changed to summer, Amelia began to take Callum out on railway trips to Grange-over-Sands or Arnside, with foot-warmers and waterproofs in case the day turned inclement; once as far as Morecambe where, armed with bucket and spade, shrimping net and sailing boat, he was indeed as happy as a sandboy. At home he was allowed to run about the house and garden in plimsolls and with bare legs, teasing Amelia to chase him and giggling ecstatically when she succeeded in catching him.

Sometimes the entire family would visit Charles and Lucy's mansion on Lake Windermere, where they would take a picnic on a steamer trip and find a quiet cove to enjoy it.

'We really should have our own private yacht,' Lucy would frequently be heard to declare. 'Then we would no longer be obliged to endure the proximity of all these other people, the riff-raff.'

'Oh, but that's part of the fun,' Amelia would maintain.

They would boil tea on a spirit stove, enjoy jam and bread and an assortment of delicious cakes which Mrs Petty would make up for them. Kate had never known so many treats, or such contentment. Every day brought new pleasures and was a wonderful journey of discovery for her. And if sometimes she thought herself overworked, being left to mind Lucy's two offspring on these occasions in addition to Callum, a mischievous duo to say the least, she shouldered the chore with goodwill and gratitude, for wasn't she the lucky one?

The weeks and months flew by and Kate grew used to the nursery routine, discovering in it a security she'd never known before. She took increasing pride in the newly painted nursery, keeping it immaculately clean and tidy, and came to love living in this fine house, revelling in her new status. And if what Mrs Petty said was true, that other girls were starting to look down upon domestic service and wish for more freedom, Kate thought them wrong. To her it felt like paradise.

Dermot was the only blot on her horizon. She worried about her brother a great deal, had written him several letters but received not a single reply to any of them. Once she asked Amelia if she might call upon her friends, Millie and Clem, in order to make proper enquiries about him. But her mistress wouldn't hear of it.

'Who knows what diseases might be lurking in those yards? I'm surprised you even ask, Kate.'

And because Amelia was so kind and showed the patience of a saint in every other way, Kate felt obliged to let the subject drop. She would simply have to trust in Dermot's ability to survive on his wits, as he'd certainly done thus far.

Mrs Petty's attitude remained obdurate and, faced with the stone wall of her resistance, Kate wisely decided not to make a fuss as she felt sure this would only make matters worse. If the woman chose to think the worst of her, then there was little Kate could do to change her mind. Following the house-keeper's example, the other servants held fast to their unwillingness to speak to Kate and the atmosphere, whenever she ventured into the kitchen, remained cold and strained. She resolved to deal with the problem by tackling each of them one by one.

She first approached Ida, who was only too eager to make friends and tell her own sad tale of being ill-treated: a far worse story, Kate felt, than her own as the girl had been frequently locked in a cupboard for hours at a time and kept on starvation rations. She was saved one day when the local vicar called and heard her crying. The woman of the house was prosecuted but, following her dreadful experience, Ida had been too scared to venture out of the workhouse again until Mrs Tyson person-ally called while carrying out her charitable duties and took pity on her.

The gardener, old Askew, Kate found to be no trouble at all.

He hadn't so much sent her to Coventry, he assured her, as not realised what was going on. She needed only to show a little interest in his tomatoes and he instantly was her friend.

Fanny was more tricky, blowing hot and cold. Some days she was willing to exchange a few chill words, generally comprising the relaying of instructions from Mrs Petty or the mistress; at other times her mouth would be pursed so tight it looked as if she'd swallowed a lemon. Kate just kept smiling and agreeing with her, hoping for the best. And she kept her distance from Dennis who was only too ready to smile and wink at her at every opportunity. He'd once caught her on the back stairs, told her what a pretty little bird she was, and asked, how about a kiss? Kate had made a joke of it, managed to wriggle from his grasp and fled.

He was a pert, cocksure sort of fellow who knew everything there was to learn about the workings of the internal combustion engine and was evidently hoping to persuade his employer to abandon the carriage and buy a motor. He also appreciated the value of polished brass and shining paintwork and was frequently heard to declare that if he didn't get proper treatment and promotion with the Tysons, he would move on somewhere more forward-looking and amenable, and of course take Fanny with him.

According to his adoring fiancée, he would easily pass muster as a gentleman's gentleman, since he knew how to be discreet.

'Not that our Mr Tyson would ever stray, any more than my lovely Dennis would, so don't you cast an eye in that direction either, madam.'

'Huh, as if I would,' Kate replied tartly, but the comment made her consider her employer in a different light, and if he passed her on the stairs, or was reading at his desk when she took Callum into the drawing room before dinner, she would cast covert glances in his direction and wonder what kind of man he was, what sort of husband he made. Was he loving and kind, or firm and dictatorial? Kate knew very little about marriage, not having any memory of her mother's and father's life together, and her own marriage had been too short-lived to teach her anything save that men had their own view of the world, their own way of looking at things, which wasn't necessarily the same as a woman's. This meant that they were not always easy to understand, or bend to your own will.

But she remembered also, from those few blissful short weeks, that a man and woman could have a deal of fun together. And so Kate would look at Eliot and wonder what kind of bed-mate he might make.

Eliot Tyson had certainly turned out to be very different from her expectations. Far from being the unyielding tyrant she'd been led to expect, with his quiet brown eyes and winning, slightly diffident smile, he'd proved to be a pleasant, easy-going sort of employer who was prepared to discuss matters with his servants as if he truly valued their opinion. Kate had personally witnessed him thanking Dennis for keeping the harness and other trappings so clean and neat. He would ask the gardener if he would mind feeding the pigeons, or politely request a sandwich from Mrs Petty should he feel hungry after an hour or two of work pruning his trees or if he'd come home late from the factory.

He was liberal in his views, a definite individual, and not in any way a man to ignore.

If he had a fault it was that his approach to life, and to business, was perhaps a touch too casual. In Kate's humble opinion he seemed to spend less time at the factory than he properly should, spending hour upon hour with his beloved wife and Callum, much of it in the garden. She thought all of this rather strange for how could he possibly manage to keep a proper eye on things when he was so often absent from the factory? No wonder the likes of Ned Swainson got a bit above themselves and took advantage, with a largely absentee boss.

When once she'd dared tentatively to ask if he was perhaps neglecting his business rather too much, he'd laughed and asked if she wasn't pleased he was proving to be such a diligent father to her son? 'Haven't I wanted this all my life, Kate? Where's the harm in spending a little time with my son? And here, in the garden, is where I find the peace and solace I need, a time which welds us together as a family. Doesn't that have a value equal to making money?'

Kate could not deny it, yet experienced great pangs of jealousy watching the three together. Eliot was planning a new design for the garden, and worked happily side by side with old Askew, reshaping it to a scheme he had drawn up with meticulous care, describing it all to Callum as if the little boy could possibly understand.

'It is not in any way to be a grand design, you see,' he would explain to the child, who would gaze up at him with wide-eyed adoration, 'but a series of small intimate outdoor rooms, linked together to form a composite whole. Won't that be nice?'

'Me like pretty flowers,' Callum said, nodding vigorously, clearly enchanted with the garden.

In the weeks following, Kate too grew to love walking there, admiring the fruits of her employer's labours. There was always something new to see: perhaps an unexpected artefact at the turn of a path, the minutiae of a mosaic patio laid by his own hands, or a showy exotic plant to delight the eye. He was a collector, a creator, and, like all good gardeners, a patient optimist, content to plant trees he would never see mature in his own lifetime.

Master Eliot, as old Askew insisted on calling his employer, certaintly displayed a fine eye for detail.

And a winning way with her child.

On one particular morning in early-autumn Kate discovered him planting a dozen young saplings, or 'whips' as he called them.

'Haven't you enough trees already?' she laughed, looking about her at the gracious line of beeches along the drive, and the woodland copse of ash and rowan that stood behind the house, shielding Tyson Lodge from the terrace of fine houses beyond and the High School from which each afternoon burst a chattering mass of giggling girls.

'One can never have enough trees. We must plant for the next generation,' he explained.

'For Callum, you mean?'

He gave her a wry smile. 'For Callum, and for his children, and for all future generations to come.'

'Then will you tell me why you don't take the same care over the business as you do over your blessed trees?'

Eliot paused in his digging to glance up at her in surprise, a frown puckering his brow, perhaps affronted by her cheek. 'Dammit, I do! I always have taken proper care of the company. I run the factory with great care and attention to detail.'

'Not recently, you don't. Not since you got Callum, which seems odd to me. Doesn't he, let alone these future generations you talk about, deserve to have some money coming in? Then he can carry on living in this grand house and enjoying this wonderful garden you've made?'

Kate thought for a moment that the master was going to be angry, though she'd never yet seen him lose his temper. Nor did he on this occasion. Instead his frozen expression was finally warmed by a lazy smile. 'My word, you have a way with words, Kate O'Connor; a happy knack for cutting to the heart of a matter. But it is a justified criticism. I should spend more time at the factory, I don't deny it. I've been enjoying my new son.' He glanced fondly down at the boy, digging beside him in the rich earth with a small trowel.

'Well then, what are ye going to do about it? Or this little chap could suffer and then I'd have given him up for nothing. Why don't ye get back to work?' She seemed to be growing more daring by the minute. Surely to God he'd bite her head off for such barefaced cheek?

Frowning, Eliot leaned on his spade to give the matter closer attention, just as if nursemaids questioned his judgement every day of the week. 'I suppose because I'm not a greedy man and would much rather spend my time here in the garden, or with my wife, than in the office. Amelia is so much improved now that she has Callum, and you to help her. Am I not the most fortunate of souls, with all that a man could wish for? With sufficient funds for our needs, I am content.'

'But will you continue to be so if the money runs out? Will there be sufficient funds, as you call them, if you carry on in this fashion? Sure and I'm no expert but if you neglect the business too much, and leave it in the hands of that nasty Ned Swainson, then may the Good Lord save you!'

He shook his head sadly. 'Oh Kate, I'm well aware of your dislike of my poor foreman. Spare me further complaints about him, I beg you, on such a golden autumn day.'

She was not to be distracted. 'Why not let Mr Charles run the company for a while then?'

At this, Eliot Tyson put his head back and laughed, a harsh, brittle sound with little humour in it. 'Because he'd have us bankrupt in a matter of months! Fortunately I've an accounts clerk to keep an eye on the financial side of things. Charles has his place in the company, as junior partner in charge of over-seas orders. Plus, of course, whether you approve of him or not, I do have a most able foreman to deal with everyday matters.'

'Saints preserve us, I wouldn't trust the little toad as far as I could throw him! Begging your pardon, sir, but the man's nought but horse shite, so help me God.'

Eliot let out a great shout of laughter, a genuine, heartfelt sound which went on for so long that Kate found her own lips twitching into a smile. 'Begging yer pardon over me language, sir.'

'I wouldn't ever let Mrs Tyson hear you use such words, Kate. She'd faint clean away.' He took out a clean, linen hand-kerchief and wiped tears of mirth from his eyes, blew his nose, then tucked the handkerchief away again, a smile still playing about his mouth. Kate found her gaze fixed upon that mouth, upon the wide, upward curve of the lips, wondering what they might feel like pressed against her own. Cool? Firm? Or warm and soft and persuasively seductive? She pushed the thought away and concentrated on what he was saying to her.

'While I don't share your harsh opinion of Swainson, in other respects, Kate O'Connor, your criticism is justified. I should, *and will*, strive to be more assiduous in my duties in future. You are quite right that I have a son to think of now, and Callum's future should be made safe. I promise I will be more diligent in that respect. I shall even go in tomorrow and check that everything is in order. There, does that suit?'

And they both smiled into each other's eyes, aware of the incongruity of the exchange and yet both well satisfied with it

Nevertheless, Kate couldn't help wondering if, despite these fine words, Eliot would keep his promise. Why would someone who'd never needed to think too much about money in their life, find rent or worry about where the next meal was coming from, trouble himself over much how of it arrived in their pocket?

The next morning he was off to the office by six. Admittedly he was home again by lunchtime, after which he took himself off to the summer house where he set up his easel and spent the rest of the afternoon teaching Callum how to paint his beloved trees. The child was soon plastered with the stuff, and daubed in green and gold and yellow from top to toe by the time they were done for the afternoon. Drat the man, he was too relaxed and easy-going for his own good, allowing the joys of fatherhood to cloud his judgement over the business. A flaw in him, to be sure, but, in Kate's opinion, understandable, and his only one. In every other respect he seemed to her quite perfect. So perfect, she was having trouble getting him out of her mind.

She'd go to mass on Sunday, so she would, without fail.

9

Lucy looked on with increasing alarm and despondency. Despite Charles's promises that he had the matter in hand, nothing seemed to have changed. The workhouse brat had indeed been adopted and accepted into the family, papers duly signed, and now her own expertise as a mother was frequently called upon to supply advice to Amelia. Admittedly the woman followed every word of it to the letter, using that stupid book of Dr Barker's Lucy had given her, as some sort of bible.

What Lucy really longed to say was 'put the dratted infant back where he belongs', but she dare not. Amelia could be remarkably stubborn, as could Eliot, and relations between the two branches of the family had never been easy since Eliot simply didn't appreciate his brother as he should, nor provide proper recompense for the hours Charles put in at the factory. Lucy had hardly seen her husband lately. It really was too bad.

For her nothing was certain, nor quite as it should be. She still felt bloated and tired after her latest pregnancy which had resulted in another boy whom they'd named George after his grandfather, needing to make a point. She'd wanted to do this with their first-born but Charles had been so furious with his father for not leaving him a proper share in the business he wouldn't hear of it. He'd regretted it ever since, of course, particularly as Eliot refused to share with him the task of running the company properly, claiming that he had no real

head for business. Arrogant nonsense! Eliot never had appreciated Charles's virtues, his ambition or his drive, not to mention
his clever way of looking at things, Lucy thought admiringly,
if with no small degree of prejudice.

Now it looked as if their precious children were to be
deprived of their proper heritage as well. It really was too
much. She mustn't let that happen. Nor would it. Not if she
had any say in the matter.

One day in late-autumn, with the first crispness of winter in
the air and Callum having celebrated his second birthday,
Amelia declared her intention of taking him shopping. 'He is
no longer a baby. Now that he is grown so big, our little man
should have some new winter clothes, don't you think? You
must come too, Kate, to help me choose, and to wheel his
pram.'

They walked him out the very next morning in the big, black
perambulator which, to Kate's mind, resembled nothing so
much as an invalid carriage in every respect save for its size.
As always, she felt hugely conspicuous as they strolled in
leisurely fashion across the new Victoria Bridge which her own
father had helped to build, opened only a few short years ago
to celebrate the Golden Jubilee. Then along Stramongate and
up into town, Amelia stopping frequently to chat to ladies she
met along the way as she so liked to do.

When they had first come into town with the baby, she had
been delighted to show off the new addition to her household.
Several ladies had expressed surprise, saying they hadn't even
known a 'happy event' was due. No one remarked on the unlikely size of this new baby, but it was surely observed. Amelia
did not enlighten them as to the truth of the situation, merely
smiled and looked suitably proud. Today they agreed what a
fine boy he'd grown into, and if privately they understood

more of the situation than had been officially revealed, they were certainly not letting on. Kate, naturally, said not a word.

On this particular morning they called at Blacow Brothers on the corner of Finkle Street and Branthwaite Brow to collect a new hat which Eliot had ordered, and then proceeded on to Musgrove's where, comfortably seated on a chair, Amelia proceeded to buy outfits for Callum, an event which seemed to take most of the morning, putting to the lie Fanny's insistence that the family was parsimonious to a fault.

The ubiquitous 'Jack Tar' suit was the first item selected. It was something all gently reared little boys possessed, and made them look like sailors. A kilt was chosen next, in which Kate thought her son looked a 'right little doat', to use an Irish expression she'd learned off her daddy. Then a cream woollen coat with a broad blue silk collar, and shorts that reached almost to his ankles to allow room for growth. These suited him better. They even had a matching waistcoat so that he could be a 'proper little man'. Kate thought he looked fine, though how she would manage to keep it clean was another matter altogether.

Several other items followed, including nightgowns, smocks, shorts, shoes and socks, so that Kate marvelled one small child could need so much in the way of clothing.

'Oh, Kate, what do you think of this?' Amelia had him rigged out in a Tyrolean-style short jacket with a round Tyrolean hat with ribbons, which she declared was 'quite perfect for sporting occasions'. Kate kept her opinions to herself.

Last, but by no means least, came a blue velveteen suit with girlishly pointed-toed shoes for parties.

'Is this what Doctor Barker, the author of your book, recommends you should buy?' Kate dared to ask.

'Indeed no, I'm sure it is not, Kate dear, but I simply can't resist it. Doesn't he look heavenly?'

She almost burst out laughing on the spot, saying he looked like a miniature Little Lord Fauntleroy. All he needed was a white lace collar since he already owned the flowing locks, albeit in bright copper. But she managed to restrain herself just in time. 'Doesn't he just!'

Callum was, in fact, beginning to grizzle and complain from all the tryings-on and fussing he'd been subjected to for the entire morning, and once having ordered the shop assistant to deliver the items, a service carried out by a porter on a bicycle who would pedal about town with the boxes perched on the handlebars, Amelia instructed Kate to wheel him home as she intended to meet up with Mrs Dawson for lunch at the Rainbow Hotel.

'You may walk him back the long way, down Highgate, through Kirkland and across Nether Bridge then back along by the river, so that he has had plenty of fresh air. But please do not make any detours into any of the yards along the way – the air is so unsanitary in those dreadful places. No visiting old acquaintances, Kate. Remember our agreement.'

'Very good, ma'am.' She gave a wry smile, and could only marvel that her robust son had survived that unsanitary air for as long as he had, living in 'those dreadful places'. Even so, she was equally unwilling to jeopardise his health and didn't in the least mind giving her word. Much as she longed to see her old friends again and discover what had happened to Dermot, she wouldn't take the risk. She'd kept to her word to stay away.

But then on her way back through Kirkland, close to the Parish Church, she ran into Millie

Her friend was so surprised to see her that for a moment she was too startled to move an inch. All her children were gathered about her, clinging to her skirts or to each other like a brood of raggedy-eared puppies holding on to each other's tails, the youngest cradled in the arms of the eldest girl since Millie herself was laden down with kindling she'd collected on the river bank. She dropped it all to the ground and the next instant the pair were hugging and laughing, thrilled to be reunited.

'By heck, you look a right toff all dolled up in that rig! Well, I never! And what about young Callum in his knitted pram suit? Doesn't he look the cat's whiskers?'

'Oh, Millie, you've no idea how pleased I am to see you. You must tell me everything. How is Clem? And Ma? And little Ruby?' referring to the little girl who'd been sick when Kate had left Poor House Lane. Millie simply shook her head, saying nothing, putting up a hand to prevent her from asking more. Kate swallowed, squeezed Millie's hand. 'And our Dermot? I wrote him so many letters but he never replied to any of them. I did what I could, you know, but got absolutely nowhere. Will you tell me how he is managing before I burst?'

'Hush, hush! One question at a time. To tell the truth, we're all fine. Well, much the same as ever, if I'm honest. Clem has still had no luck with finding work, but he scratches a living and we muddle through as best we can. Ma misses you, and speaks of you often. But the news about Dermot is not so good. Oh, Kate, how can I tell you . . . Someone came looking for him one dark, wet night, beat him up and took him away. God knows where to, we've not seen hide nor hair of him since.'

Kate was devastated and asked a dozen more questions, wanting to know who was responsible, but Millie could tell her nothing more. 'Sorry, Kate love, two men came for him is all I saw. I don't who they were, or where they took him.'

'Ach, don't ye worry, I reckon I can guess.'

'I thought mebbe they were some of his gambling cronies, they were so nasty. They frog-marched him away between them, holding fast to his arms like he were some sort of drunk.

The poor lad didn't stand a chance, and we could do nowt neither. Our Clem were reet cut up about it. Waited up half the night fer him, then gathered together some of his mates and they all went out searching for the poor bugger, but, like I say, they found not a sign.'

Kate felt sick, not wanting to think too closely about what fate might have befallen her brother. But, as always, this was swiftly replaced by anger. Oh, she knew who to blame right enough! The rotten, nasty, no-good piece of work! And wouldn't she give him a piece of her mind, so she would. The temper was rising in her, as it so often did, and before she knew it she was saying, 'Here, take care of Callum for me for ten minutes while I go and have a word with that Ned Swainson. The nasty, rotten, no-good piece of shite! He's not getting away with this . . .'

'Swainson! Nay, lass, don't be daft,' Millie protested. 'That'd be too dangerous. Here, come back!' she yelled, as her friend picked up the skirts of her best grey uniform dress and set off at a run. 'Kate, come back!'

But Kate didn't pause except to half turn, wave and call out: 'Just walk him up and down for a bit by the church, I'll be back in a jiffy. So help me, I'll flay the bugger alive if he's hurt our Dermot.'

Ned Swainson, not unexpectedly, met her accusations with bland indifference. He knew nothing about any assault, he assured her. Why should he trouble himself about some ruffian of an Irishman? Hadn't he worries enough with all the work he had on his plate on Mr Tyson's behalf?

'I swear if you've hurt him, I'll . . .'

'What will ye do, Kate O'Connor? I'd heard you were nicely placed up at the big house, so I'd think before you speak, if I were you, lass. I don't take kindly to threats, not even idle ones.'

'Oh, it wouldn't be idle, so help me.' She was spitting mad, hating the way he avoided looking at her, even with his good eye, and wanting to throw something at him or wring his scraggy neck. But where would that get her?

'Have you searched the river?' he enquired blithely. 'Happen thoo should fetch t'police and have them drag it. If the lad got drunk he could easily have fallen in and his body be lost. A man can drown in seconds in that cold, deep water, as you well know.'

Kate stared at him, the only sound in her head being the hammering of her heart in loud, frantic beats. She surely couldn't lose a brother as well as a husband to that flaming river? That would be too cruel. And then she realised that if this had been the case, Dermot's body would have been discovered long since. 'He's alive some place, I know it. No thanks to you. I'd not find a nastier piece of work than you, Ned Swainson, in all the muck at the bottom of a dozen rivers, so help me. If you think you can frighten me then I'll have to disappoint you for I'm not so easily scared. But I will just nip into the finishing room and ask around among the girls, if ye don't mind. Somebody has mebbe seen him around.'

Swainson looked affronted. 'You can't go in there without my permission. Them lasses are working and mustn't be disturbed.'

Kate gave a snort of exasperation and went in anyway, running in quickly before he had time to stop her. The huge, brightly lit room was packed with girls and women, all busily stitching the separate pieces together that comprised the uppers of a shoe or boot. They fashioned these with considerable care and skill, and with enviable speed. Kate moved up and down the lines of workers, stopping to ask anyone she recognised and whom she knew to be acquainted with her brother if they'd seen him lately. Heads were shaken, eyes taking on a sad and sorrowful expression, as if they knew something she didn't. But Kate couldn't bear to acknowledge what this might be and obstinately pressed on with her questions. She couldn't even find Dolly, the girl Dermot had been hoping to marry. Within minutes she saw the foreman bearing down upon her with a couple of his trusties in tow.

'I'm not going, so don't you dare put a finger on me. I need to ask these girls if . . .'

She got no further as one of the men grasped her arm, while the second snatched her other wrist and twisted it up her back. As she squealed, a gasp of horror went up from the girls all around, though not one made a move to help her, too afraid of losing their jobs to risk doing so. Swainson was smirking, which provoked Kate's temper all the more and she lashed out at him with her foot, catching him on the shin with the toe of her boot.

'You little bitch! I'll have you for that.'

'If you've done anything to our Dermot, I'll see you hang fer it, so I will!'

Now it was Kate's turn to be frog-marched away, in this case not only out of the building but out of the factory yard altogether, the sound of the foreman's threats ringing in her ears as the big gates clanged shut after her. But instead of this having the desired effect of scaring her into submission, it only served to inflame her all the more, for it convinced Kate beyond any doubt that he did indeed have something to hide. Whatever had happened to her brother, Swainson was involved, she was sure of it.

'You're late, Kate. Where on earth have you been? And why is your hair messed up? And there's mud all over the hem of your uniform . . . This is too bad. What have you been up to? You should have been back nearly an hour since.' Amelia swooped

Callum up into her arms, hugging him close as if to reassure herself he was unharmed.

She'd been sitting at the parlour window waiting for her nursemaid's return. Kate had seen the lace curtains twitch and knew, with a swift sinking of her heart, that she would have to lie. She could hardly tell her mistress the truth: that she'd left Callum with Millie, who'd then taken him back to her hovel in Poor House Lane and fed him on watery gruel with the rest of her brood while she, Kate, had gone off to accuse Tyson's foreman of assaulting her brother, ended up attacking him in the finishing room of the factory, and then been thrown off the premises. Indeed, if she told such a tale she really would be out on her ear, and then all Callum's chances of a good future would go up in a puff of smoke.

Kate made some excuse about playing a game of ball on Gooseholme and quite forgetting the time. 'I'll take him up for his tea and a wash now, shall I, ma'am? And then bring him down to you in the parlour, as usual.'

'Yes, please, Kate. I'm sorry to fuss but he is so dear to me, I got into quite a panic when I saw he wasn't here. The shop has delivered our purchases and I rather expected you would have unpacked them by now.'

'I'll get to them right away. Would you like him to wear his kilt, ma'am, or the yellow silk knickerbocker set?' Another creation she'd bought that morning.

'The blue cotton smock and shorts, I think. It is only tea with his dear mama, after all. What a fright you gave me! Parenthood is so – so taxing. Dear me, my nerves are quite in ribbons.'

Kate could see that Amelia wanted to say a great deal more but was too relieved to have Callum back so was allowing the incident to pass. She was still jiggling him up and down, smothering the wriggling child with a flurry of kisses, and Kate suffered an overwhelming urge to rip him from the other woman's arms and scream at her to leave him alone; to say that he was *her* son and not Amelia's at all. Wasn't it enough to lose the rest of her family?

Instead, she smiled and offered to bring her mistress's tea through for her, once she'd got him properly dressed and presentable for visiting his dear mama.

Three days later, the fever began.

It began as a sniffle and a little shivering, but within hours had developed into a raging headache and by then the fever was all too apparent. Callum lay in his crib, fretting and crying and burning up. Fear struck at Kate's heart. It was *her* fault entirely. She should never have left him with Millie. It hadn't seemed so remiss at the time because Millie had often minded him for her, but things were different now. She should have realised that her friend might ignore her instruction just to jiggle the pram or walk him around, taking him home to Poor House Lane instead. And he wasn't simply her own lovely Callum any longer but belonged to another woman now, to Amelia. Kate had never seen her so angry in all the months she had known her.

Amelia demanded to know how her precious boy could possibly have caught a fever when they took such good care of him, and Kate confessed the whole sorry story. 'I just chanced to meet Millie and she told me what had happened to me brother. I was bothered about our Dermot. He's all the family I have left, after all.'

'Kate, how could you? I've even given up my own charity work for the moment, to keep my boy safe. I trusted you, and you have let me down badly. Because of your rapscallion brother, you've risked the health of my child.'

Kate's instinct was to protest that Callum was *her* child, but she didn't dare. They'd made an agreement, after all. Papers had been signed, a day that would live forever in her memory. She had sat in the solicitor's office and later before a judge in a big room he called his chambers, had agreed to forfeit all rights to her child, for the sake of his future. Everyone was very brisk and businesslike, quite unaware of the fear and misery in her heart. The judge had glowered at her over his spectacles and told her what a sensible girl she was, how fortunate her son to be taken in by such a fine couple as Mr and Mrs Tyson. He'd pushed a piece of paper in front of her and instructed Kate to make her mark, expressing surprise when she'd signed her name instead.

And so she had no say over her son now, no rights at all, and no matter how beneficial it might be to her child in the long-term, for Kate this was a hard enough fact to live with. Losing her position would make it a thousand times worse, as then she might never see him again.

Now she faced a further danger. There was no denying that Callum had an infection of some sort and the doctor was called immediately. He seemed quite unconcerned and, ignoring Kate completely, addressed himself directly to Amelia.

'No rash, no swellings, no sign of anything sinister. But the boy should be carefully watched. He could simply be teething or it may be the start of influenza. There have been a few cases about, quite a nasty strain in fact. As I say, it might be nothing at all. Give him plenty of fluids, try to bring down his temperature with a cold compress, and keep him free from draughts. Children are like this, dear lady, sick one minute and bouncing around the next. There is nothing for you to fear.'

Amelia was unconvinced but his instructions were carried out to the letter, and more. Blankets soaked in vinegar were hung at the doors to the bedroom; gallons of home-made barley water laced with lemon juice were brought up from the kitchen, Mrs Petty doing her bit for the little master despite her disapproval of this scandalous adoption.

'Did he see a gypsy woman or a mad dog perhaps when you took him around town?' she enquired of her mistress, her voice fearful. 'They do say as that can bring on a fever.'

'I don't think so, Mrs Petty. And you'd be much better off not listening to such superstitious nonsense.'

'Nay, 'tis true, you mark my words. No matter what you do in life, thoo has to take special care of the all-seeing eye of God. If he notices summat is not quite right, he takes his revenge.' Glaring hard across at Kate.

Amelia gave a snort of impatience. 'That will be all, thank you, Mrs Petty.'

And then the vomiting and the diarrhoea began.

Now, even old Doctor Mitchell frowned and looked troubled. 'I'm afraid the poor child has colic or gastro-enteritis of some sort. It's a common enough complaint with young children, though more usually found in poorer families, and can become pernicious if we can't stop the purging, or keep sufficient fluids inside him.' He left careful instructions for the little boy to be given an infusion of strawberry-leaf tea to stop the dysentery, feverfew for his headache and colic, and goldenrod to stop the violent sickness. 'He must have nothing at all to eat but give him plenty of boiled water, and let nature take its course.'

It seemed far too inadequate a remedy for such a precious child.

Amelia absolutely refused to leave Callum's bedside, despite Kate's protests and the concern of her husband that she mustn't tire herself. All day and night she bathed his hot little head with a cold compress, struggling to persuade him to sip the boiled water and getting upset when he absolutely refused to take it unless Kate held the feeding cup. No amount of signed papers would change Callum's mind as to who his mammy was, and Kate couldn't help but nurse a secret delight in this.

But then after a while he became so ill that he neither knew nor cared who was at his bedside and from then on Amelia insisted on taking the lion's share of the nursing. Much of the time she permitted no one else to come near him and Kate found herself demoted to emptying the chamber pot and changing sheets, when all the time she longed to hold her sick child to her breast.

IO

The stench of sickness seemed to permeate the entire house. Early on the third morning, Kate was carrying an armful of soiled linen down the stairs, hurrying so that she could quickly return to the sickroom, when she almost ran into Eliot. He grasped hold of her, steadying her when she might have lost her footing and fallen.

'Kate, is he no better?' The concern on his face was unmistakable and she felt a constriction block her throat. So far she'd refused to believe that Callum was in any real danger, hoping that so long as they did exactly as the doctor instructed then in no time at all he would be well, beaming his toothy grin and up to his usual mischief. Now, for the first time, she faced the reality that he might not get better at all. Quite unable to voice these fears out loud, she could do nothing more than shake her head.

'Oh, don't cry. I'm sure he will recover. He's a strong child, a fine boy.'

Kate hadn't realised, until he said those words, that she was indeed crying. Now she became aware of tears running down her cheeks unchecked. The next instant, Eliot Tyson, her employer, master of this household and a substantial business empire, was rocking her gently in his arms while Kate sobbed out her anguish on to his shoulder. It felt so good, so safe, such a wonderful comfort, that she wanted to stay there for ever, feeling the strength of his arms about her, the power of his broad shoulder beneath her cheek.

He took out a clean linen handkerchief and began to dab at her tears. 'There, there, that's right, let it all come out. It's been far too much for you to bear. I've tried to do a couple of hours' work each morning but can't seem to settle at the factory. Despite there being matters crying out for my attention, I have to keep coming back to see how things are here, find out if the doctor has called again.'

This morning Eliot had spotted a set of accounts which had troubled him greatly, but he couldn't seem to concentrate on them through worrying over the child. He hoped that when he went back later in the day, he'd find that he'd mistaken the figures in his anxiety, and there was really no problem at all.

Kate was thinking that she could tell he'd been out by the scent of leather on his skin, mixed with the cold, clean damp of a Lakeland wind. It was utterly intoxicating.

'You must be quite worn out, probably haven't had a wink of sleep for days on end.'

Kate tried to protest that lack of sleep really didn't trouble her in the slightest but then met his gentle gaze, and the words vanished from her mind. She could see a reflection of her own image mirrored in the pupils of his brown eyes. It seemed right, somehow, that it should be there, almost as if it belonged. She also saw concern and sympathy, although really she was seeking something more, something far more personal.

Finally he spoke, a rough, croaking sound, barely above a whisper. 'And what of my wife? How is she coping?'

It was the mention of Amelia which brought her to her senses. The power of this moment was over and Kate took a step back, releasing herself from his grip. She put a hand to her face to wipe away the tears, tucked a strand of hair behind one ear as thoughts cascaded through her brain with neither clarity nor sense. What was she thinking? She was behaving like a fool. He was her master, and a married man. Quickly, Kate bent down and gathered up the discarded laundry.

'I must get this down to the laundry room right away, and grab a bite to eat so that I can hurry back and take over for a while. The mistress needs rest more than any of us. You should tell her to take a nap. She might listen to you, sir. She won't take it from me.'

As Kate ran down the stairs she didn't look back, aware that his eyes followed her, every step of the way.

As if Eliot didn't have enough anxiety to endure about Callum, and the health of his dear wife as a result, he was growing increasingly alarmed about the state of the business. Something was most definitely wrong. He'd been planning to buy new machinery for the finishing room, some fancy sewing machines from America, and now his accountant was telling him the company didn't have the reserves to carry out these plans. This had come as a nasty shock. He may not enjoy the travelling and touting for orders which had been the mainstay of his father's approach to business, but Eliot prided himself on having a good head for figures and on keeping a finger on the financial button.

He considered postponing the purchase of the new equipment. What did it matter anyway? Callum, whom he now thought of as his son, was seriously ill, and there was even a possibility he might not recover. All he really wanted to do was to stay at home and be with the child, and to support Amelia. She was looking so tired and wan, so frightened of losing the child.

Yet now the boy was so sick, it somehow seemed even more important that the business be kept safe and secure, otherwise it would be tantamount to admitting that Callum might not survive. Not that there was anything Eliot could do at home in any case, Amelia having banned everyone but herself from the child's room. So he buried his fears deep and set about ensuring that the company would at least still be there for Callum, whenever he needed it in the future.

Eliot had always taken great care that costings for the manufacture of their shoes were correctly done, and all accounts properly audited; unlike his father who had never troubled himself on that score, working purely on instinct rather than mathematics, being far more obsessed with fussing over every detail of procedure in the factory. And Charles's first rule of economy appeared to be that if he had a penny in his pocket, it was there to be spent. Would he go so far as to cheat his own brother in order to get his hands on more money? Surely not! Yet capital was leaking away and Eliot intended to discover why.

Could Kate perhaps be right about Swainson? Was he feathering his own nest? Or was it one of Eliot's other employees? He had to find out.

Eliot closeted himself in his office with the books and spent hours poring over lines of figures, balancing outgoings against income, searching for any unusual discrepancies or a mistake in the arithmetic. He was still there when everyone else had gone home, and barely noticed Dennis who crept in late in the evening with a plate of sandwiches, courtesy of Mrs Petty. It was some time in the early hours of the morning before his fears were conclusively proved to be justified. Eliot sat staring at his findings, unwilling to believe his own eyes, even as alarm was changing slowly to a deep, burning anger.

Someone was carrying out a meticulously perpetrated fraud. And he rather thought he knew who that someone was.

He went home to bathe and change quickly, though sleep

was impossible; checked on Callum, soothed and comforted his wife. Kate was optimistic that the little boy was over the worst. His temperature had apparently dropped and the loss of fluids had reduced somewhat over the last twenty-four hours.

'He's on the mend, sir, so he is. Look at that bright, cheeky face. By this afternoon he'll be shouting for his boiled egg and toast soldiers.'

Eliot clung to her optimism like a lifeline, feeling it incumbent upon himself to keep faith in the child's ultimate recovery, otherwise where was the point in anything?

The moment the bank opened, he set about his enquiries. Eliot asked pertinent questions about the financial affairs of various members of his staff, including his own brother, but the manager was completely unco-operative, pleading client confidentiality.

Later that day, as he was studying the order books, Eliot noticed that the firm who supplied them with dressed leather had recently changed hands, bought out by an unknown buyer. This was just the breakthrough he had been looking for and he spread his net wider, asking a number of judicious questions among his business colleagues until finally the facts emerged and a picture began to form.

At this point he called an Extraordinary General Meeting of Tyson's board for the very next day.

They all came, the entire family: not surprisingly since most of them were dependent upon the business for their income. Charles, of course, came, looking thoroughly peeved and disgruntled; one or two cousins and elderly uncles; and the two aunts, his father's unmarried sisters – Cissie, who hated to miss out on any fun, and Vera, a stickler for everything being just so, pin-neat and absolutely correct. Heavily involved in church affairs and the local community, she took her responsibilities very seriously indeed.

So did Eliot. Nothing was more offensive to his trusting nature than fraud, particularly when it appeared to spring from within the company itself, possibly within the family.

He'd requested a private interview with Charles before the start of the meeting proper, and while the rest of the Tyson family enjoyed coffee and a little chit-chat, the two brothers stood facing each other in the office. Eliot came straight to the point, which he noticed startled Charles somewhat.

'I'd like to know why, exactly, you have chosen to undermine my business?'

Taken aback by the unexpectedness of this assault on his integrity, Charles coloured up, his bewhiskered cheeks turning a fiery red. 'I don't know what you're talking about.'

'I think you do, Charles, so you can stop the act of outraged innocence. Come on, tell me. I'm waiting to hear.' Eliot's attitude towards his brother had always been one of resigned tolerance. He knew Charles wasn't driven by ambition, as their father had been, but by greed. He was selfish and profligate, a spoiled child who'd been brought up to expect everything in his idle life to be handed over without any effort on his part.

Eliot had no intention of making excuses for him, but nevertheless conceded that much of this attitude was their father's fault. Having endured a long, tough climb from the gutter, George had been insistent that his own sons would never need to struggle so hard or sacrifice so much. The will to succeed had been all-consuming for him; sadly he'd allowed his ambitions to run out of control, and a genuine desire to create a better life for the family had finally split it apart. This had affected George badly, made him even more determined to keep his sons out of trade. By the end of his life he'd done a complete about face and turned into the kind of snob he'd once ridiculed and loathed.

There was a warning there, certainly, but perhaps, Eliot thought, he'd protected Charles from reality too well. He should be more honest with his brother, making him see things as they really were, the true legacy that George had left his sons.

'Haven't I always been fair with you, seen that you were provided with well-paid employment as junior partner here, plus a handsome share in the profits?'

'I should have got my cut of the profits without needing to work, as the aunts do.'

'Don't be childish, Charles. Everyone needs to work, even you. How else could you afford to finance your extravagant lifestyle? Despite your laziness I did my best for you, and yet you've cheated on me like any common-or-garden thief. What is the reasoning behind this attempt to defraud my company?'

'There you have it!' Charles burst out. 'Listen to yourself. *My* business! *My* company! If I were guilty as charged, and I do not admit – not for one moment – that I am, wouldn't that be the reason? Your constant reference to Tysons as belonging exclusively to you.'

Eliot frowned. 'It does belong exclusively to me. Like it or not, that is the situation. The company *is* run by me, and I bear sole responsibility for it. Perhaps I didn't do the job particularly well in the past while I was learning the ropes, but then Father gave me little enough training. Nevertheless, it has provided you with employment, and profit from the few shares you own in it, as it does for several other members of the family. Now, I ask you again, Charles, and I recommend you measure your words carefully before you reply – why are you attempting to steal my profits? Do not lie or prevaricate. It's too late for that, since I'm in full possession of the facts.'

'Then why ask?' his brother said, sounding at his most disgruntled while still endeavouring to give every impression he wasn't in the least concerned. He sensed a prickle of sweat between his shoulder blades as he began to worry where all this might be leading.

'I am aware of your need to borrow, Charles, in order to finance your overblown lifestyle. But I'd hoped to see an improvement in that direction, thinking you might become more sensible with a growing family to consider. That is, until I examined the company accounts more closely. I must say your bank has been most discreet, although the manager did hint that he'd advanced you funds recently. What is it for this time? Racehorses, or that damned steam yacht your wife is obsessed with?'

Charles spluttered with fury. 'Don't speak of Lucy in those disparaging tones! What exactly are you accusing me of, because if you think I've come here to be insulted, then . . .'

'Shut up, Charles, and listen, for once without interrupting.' Eliot leaned back comfortably in his leather chair and waved his brother to a seat with a gesture of barely disguised impatience. Charles ignored the offer, preferring to pace back and forth on the rug, fighting for control, putting his hands in his pockets rather than wringing them as he itched to do.

Eliot was saying, 'The facts are that not all of the profits have been put through the books. Someone has been siphoning them off. My suspicions were aroused to such an extent that I set in motion numerous enquiries, and didn't much care for what I discovered. In short, some person or persons unknown, or at least as yet unproven, have set up their own currying business, using my profits as capital to fund the enterprise. This anonymous individual has taken over the old firm we used to use, Marshall and Stone, and are rapidly expanding and modernising.' A slight pause as he met his brother's troubled gaze. 'Now who do you think that might be, Charles? Any ideas?'

'Damn you to hell, Eliot.' Charles was running a hand through his hair in a most agitated fashion and sweat was pouring down his face.

'Do I take that as a confession?'

'Take it for what you damned well please. I owe you nothing, not a damn' thing. I've worked my guts out for you, and you've paid me a pittance in return.'

'I don't recall you ever sweating quite so much toiling over your desk, Charles, as you are doing now. Why is that?'

Animosity crackled dangerously between the two men. Enraged by the calm in his brother's tone, Charles slammed down a fist on the desk between them. 'That's because you shut me out, drat you! You tell me nothing of what's going on. I'm never consulted on matters of policy, changes of style, new designs or anything.'

'Good heavens, it never occurred to me that you might have the necessary flair, Charles. Perhaps it is somewhat remiss of me, but I don't see you as an expert on fashion, however much of a dandy you might consider yourself.'

'Don't use your blasted sarcasm on me.' Charles was shouting now, and Eliot flapped a hand at him, warning him to lower his voice if he didn't want the whole works to be made aware of their quarrel.

'I don't care who hears, the more the better so far as I'm concerned. I did what I had to do and . . .' Charles stopped, having the wit to see that he was cornered. He'd damned himself from his own lips. He was furious with himself, for the fact that in trying to protect his family's future from what he perceived as a very real and dangerous threat, he'd left himself open to this accusation of fraud. He should have denied it all, kept quiet. It was doubtful Eliot would have been able to prove a thing. Hadn't Swainson assured him of that when they'd conceived the whole scheme together? He shuddered to think what Lucy's reaction would be when he explained that the purchase of the yacht, let alone the motor car they hoped to buy to drive them back and forth to the Lake Windermere house, was well and truly off. 'Dammit, I'll not see my family impoverished.'

Eliot got briskly to his feet, beginning to lose patience with this grasping, obstinate brother of his, and deciding to take a firmer line. 'The point is, Charles, I cannot allow you to bleed the company dry. If you were short of money for good reason, you should have asked me for help. If it is simply to maintain the house by the lake that you neither need nor can afford, then you are nothing less than selfish and avaricious. Wouldn't we all enjoy such a treat? But we have to be sensible. The business is not as strong or as healthy as you might imagine. Father lost his touch at the end, took on too many orders which couldn't be properly filled because of too few staff and inadequate administrative control. The result was damaging to the company. He made a mess of things at the end because he simply wasn't well enough to cope. I inherited a mass of problems.'

'So you say.'

'Oh, for goodness' sake! There's no talking to you. I still don't understand *why* you would choose to steal from me in such an underhand way. Why not discuss your problems openly? Despite our different temperaments I thought we rubbed along well enough and I do believe you've been paid a proper rate. There are certainly plenty who would be glad of such an excellent income. The fact that you can't control your expensive wife is your problem, and not mine.'

'How *dare* you insult Lucy? At least she has given me a son who is legitimately mine, and not a by-blow from some cheap little tart!'

Eliot jerked as if he'd been struck and it was a mark of his supreme self-control that he managed not to plant one furiously clenched fist on his brother's arrogant nose. He drew in a long, steadying breath though his tone was glacial. 'I shall choose to ignore that most offensive remark on the grounds that you are angry and upset, and not thinking clearly. Had anyone but my own brother said those words, the outcome might have been very different. As it is, I suggest it would be for the best if you tendered your resignation forthwith and we'll say no more on the matter. No doubt you would prefer to devote your time to this new project of yours in any case, and I'm sure neither of us has any wish to call in the police. Will you explain all of this to the board, or shall I?'

'The police?'

'You have committed fraud, Charles, that is an offence.'

He was plainly flabbergasted. This was all getting quite out of hand, the last thing he'd expected. To be so peremptorily dismissed, threatened with the *police*, for God's sake? It was unthinkable. 'If I'm not given what I rightly deserve, why shouldn't I help myself?'

Eliot sighed heavily. 'Because it was never yours in the first place.'

'But it should have been. Tyson's Shoe Manufactory should have been ours equally, or else it should have been sold to provide enough money for us to live on for the rest of our lives, as Father promised. Instead, you stole the lot. Robbed me of my rightful inheritance.'

Eliot had heard enough. 'For Christ's sake, Charles, our father didn't *leave* the company to me either. You know damn' well that he didn't want either of us to have it. Nor, if it had been sold, would it have brought in sufficient funds for us to live in idleness for the rest of our lives. Wanting us to be *gentlemen* was his foolish fantasy. Father was living in a dream world. There was never enough money for that. Funds would soon have dried up.'

'I don't believe you.'

'It's true! I wasn't left the company at all. In effect I bought it off him. He said if I wanted it, I would have to pay for it. I had it valued, worked for nothing for all the three years he was ill, and the money I should have earned, plus the sum of money I was meant to inherit on his death, every last penny of it, was used as part-payment for the company. The rest I borrowed from the bank. You had the Windermere mansion and a sizeable chunk of Father's capital. I got Tyson Lodge. Everything else – the company, the machines and good-will, the very land the factory stands on – I've had to pay for, am still paying for, with regular payments to the bank. So, in effect, your inheritance was far greater than mine. Yes, Father did finally agree to let me have the business, but not till he'd bled me, and it, nearly dry. That's the kind of man he was. Obsessive, utterly selfish, and vindictive. You had to do things his way or pay the price.'

Charles's mouth twisted into a vicious sneer, 'I don't believe a word of it! More likely you bullied and bribed him into leaving you the business, not actually paying him a penny for it. You just wanted it all for yourself.'

'Oh, for God's sake, what is the use of talking to you?'

'I'm damned if I'll make things easy for you, Eliot. The board needs to be told that you mean to hand over Tyson's to some pauper child you've adopted on a whim. The child of your mistress, dammit!'

Eliot's voice took on a hard, cutting edge. 'I've already warned you, Charles, to think before you open your mouth. Take care, or you might live to regret those words seriously.'

'No, I bloody won't!' he roared. 'You've deliberately set out to ruin me *and* my family by adopting this workhouse child.

Father would turn in his grave. And as for Mother ... I shudder to think what she would say. Lucy believes that it is sheer desperation which has driven you and Amelia to such lengths, but we'll not let you get away with it. We'll not have some snotty-nosed bastard deprive our children of their rightful inheritance. I'll fight you through every court in the land, if I have to.'

'You don't seem to have understood a word I've said. The company is *not your children's rightful inheritance.*'

But Charles wasn't listening, roaring at the top of his voice: 'I'm damned if I'll apologise for awarding myself a greater share of what should have been mine in the first place.' At which point he stormed out of the office, leaving the door swinging open.

Aunt Vera, Aunt Cissie and all the uncles and cousins stood in the hall watching open-mouthed as he stormed out of the building. After a telling silence Vera said, in her calmest tones, 'He always was an impetuous boy with a penchant for tantrums. Now, Eliot, I do hope you are ready to begin this meeting? I have two more before the day is out, one for the church fête and the other for the repairs to the vicarage roof. Can we get along now, please?'

11

The day Callum was up and dressed, happily playing with his bricks on the nursery rug, was the day Amelia made it clear to Kate that if she was to keep her position, then in future she must obey orders to the letter.

'We've had a close shave, we might easily have lost him, and all because you took a foolish risk. You must have known that your friend would take him into her home, and you, Kate, above all, know well enough what that home must be like. It was a very dangerous, thoughtless thing to do.'

'Yes, ma'am.' There was no point in arguing or defending herself since Kate agreed wholeheartedly. She was bitterly ashamed, stricken to the heart by her own folly. It had been a stupid thing to do, and all for nothing.

Her fears that Dermot had been drowned proved to be entirely unfounded. Someone must have been alerted by her enquiries because before the week was out a note had been handed in at the kitchen door. It was written by Clem in his fine, sloping hand, stating that Dolly had turned up to explain that Dermot was working in Liverpool. He was sorry for not having written to tell Kate where he was, but had been working all summer as a deckhand on board one of the Mersey ships. The note went on, 'Dolly says that he's now settled back in Ireland where he hopes to start his own business, once he has a bit put by. She intends to join him there by the New Year.'

'And good riddance to bad rubbish!' was Kate's furious

reaction to the news. 'Making me worry me head off all this time. Dolly's welcome to you. She'll have her work cut out trying to make something of you, if'n ye ever manage to save more than a penny piece.' No doubt he was at this very moment swilling back the whiskeys in Donegal, so there was fat chance in Kate's unblinkered view. Oh, but she'd miss the daft eejit, so she would. Who knows when she'd ever see him again? Her own brother, the only family she had left. Wouldn't it be grand to live in Ireland with him? But how could she? Not without Callum. She felt so alone, so dependent upon the Tysons, that at times it filled her with fear. If they ever tired of her, or she did something foolish which offended them, they'd turn her out. Oh, but that didn't bear thinking about! She must never make such a mistake again, for the prospect of losing her position, of being sent away and banished from this house, never to see her lovely Callum again, was more terrible than she dared contemplate.

And if that put her in daily contact with temptation in the shape of Amelia's husband, then she'd just have to go more regularly to mass and say a few extra Hail Marys for the sake of her soul.

It took Charles almost two whole weeks before he finally plucked up the courage to tell Lucy what had occurred, continuing to go out every morning and returning at odd hours to throw her off the scent, but one day she confronted him about a rumour she'd heard at Mrs Hetherington's tea table, and that had been it. He'd been forced to own up to the truth. She went white to the gills, picked up a vase and threw it at his head. Admittedly, it was not one of her favourites but even so she burst into noisy tears and blamed him for the loss of it, screaming that he shouldn't have ducked but caught it, and now look what he'd made her do.

'How *dare* you come home and tell me you have been *sacked*, like some common factory hand!' Reaching behind her, her hands closed around a rather nice French ormolu clock and she threw that too, followed by a Royal Worcester figurine and a cut-glass decanter. All he could do was duck and dive to avoid being decapitated. If he didn't stop her soon it was going to cost him a small fortune to replace all the broken items.

'Lucy . . . Lucy darling . . . don't shout at me, beloved. *It's not my fault!*'

Something in the plaintive tone of his voice broke through her fury and touched her heart. 'Oh, my darling, of course it isn't. How dreadful of me to take it out on you. How could I be so cruel?'

And then she was on him like a bitch on heat, fastening her mouth to his, ripping the buttons off his trousers with frantic fingers in her urgency to get them undone, tugging at her own clothes as she did so. The nice silk waistcoat she'd recently bought for him gave an ominous tearing sound as she yanked him on top of her, sending the rest of the china smashing to the ground. 'Don't worry about it, darling. It can be replaced,' Lucy gasped. 'Put your fingers here. Ooh, that's lovely. No harder. Push, push, *push*!' The next instant he was panting like a dog and taking her there and then on the dining room table, amongst the scattered remains of their dinner.

Later, as they lay in bed, sated after repeating the procedure a time or two more, Charles realised that engaging as the evening had been and a great relief to divert Lucy with sex rather than have her berate him over the loss of the Sèvres tureen, now he'd only added to his worries. As sure as eggs make fat little chickens, this evening's work would cost him another mouth to feed, not to mention a fortune replacing broken china. He cleared his throat and tried again to explain their situation.

'A little belt tightening is all that is required, my love, but not for long, I do assure you. Just until we are on our feet again, out on the straight, as you might say.'

'I'm afraid I don't understand what you mean by "belt tightening", or "out on the straight". I never use such common expressions.'

'Something will have to go, dearest. Cuts must be made. Perhaps you could let your French maid go for a start?'

'I couldn't possibly. Celeste is essential. Who would do my hair?'

'I'm afraid I must insist, dear heart. And at least two of the housemaids must go too, and the renovations on the Lake House will have to wait a while longer.' All too aware that her face was growing purple with the effort of self-restraint, he wagged a playful finger at her and rushed on, before she had time to draw breath. 'Once this difficult patch is over, you shall not only have a French maid but a butler as well. How about that, my precious? Only the very best for my little duck, eh?'

'A butler?' Now this was something even the Cowpers didn't have. 'Oh, Charles, you are so good to me.'

'Don't I always do what is best for you, my sweetheart? I only want to make you happy. You aren't going to punish little Charlie Boy for being naughty and dipping his fingers in the family coffers and mucking things up for us, are you, dearest? You aren't going to smack him too hard, are you, my love?'

And since he looked so very contrite, his soft eyes so full of pleading, plump jowls quivering with fear, Lucy sternly informed him that she most certainly was. Slipping from between the sheets, she went to the blanket box which stood at the foot of the bed, aware of him watching the soft bounce of her breasts, the sway of her hips, every movement of her naked body as she pulled out the cane which lay buried beneath the soft blankets. 'Charlie has been a *very* naughty boy, and now he must be a brave little soldier and bend over for the teacher.'

The following morning Lucy sat and glared at herself in her dressing mirror, hating the tired, bedraggled woman she saw framed in it. Although she adored the rascal, he was still not entirely forgiven. How could he be so stupid as to get himself dismissed from the company? At least he should have made absolutely certain that whatever he'd done, couldn't be traced back to him. Let Swainson be dismissed, not her darling Charles. She had come closer to meaning the smacks she'd given him last night than ever before. Only her very real love for this pompous, over-ambitious, opinionated, fascinating man, and her belief that it was Eliot who was really to blame, had checked her.

Lathering her face with cream, she began to smooth the fine lines of disappointment from the corners of her eyes, privately mourning the way her once pretty mouth seemed to be forever turned down in a perpetual sulk these days, already showing signs of bitterness.

And no wonder. This was not how it was meant to be.

When she'd first married Charles Tyson, she'd been promised wealth and comfort, fine gowns and servants to wait upon her every need; a town house, naturally, and one in the country in which to entertain their many friends in style. Now, not only had he cut down on the servants so that nothing was ever quite as clean or as warm as it should be, but he'd absolutely refused to allow her to refurbish their homes or even to have any new curtains, let alone Chinese silk ones.

Once having taken possession of their drab Lakeland mansion, Lucy had dreamed of furnishing it in the French style, with elegant little couches, low tables and desks, a central chandelier perhaps in the drawing room, shaded in a soft pink, and a huge French window opening out on to a regal terrace which would overlook the lake. She'd planned to build a conservatory with marble busts, huge ferns and jardinières; plus establishing a library with bookshelves lining every wall and padded window seats for quiet contemplation. Now, instead, the rooms must remain dull and dark and dreary.

And then there was her humiliation over the motor. Hadn't she told all her friends and new neighbours Charles was about to purchase a Renault or perhaps even a Daimler which would have put her in the very glass of fashion along with some of the best-known hostesses, such as Lady Warwick and the Duchess of Sunderland? Lucy had ordered an entire new wardrobe to accompany it, with all the essential dust protectors, furs, hats and veils in spotted net and fine silk. She would have looked quite splendid, a delightful *chauffeuse*.

And now look at them: up to their ears in debt, the bank pressing for repayment of its loan, and instead of the hoped for equal partnership, Charles had been turned out – *dismissed* – from his own family's company. The shame of it was appalling, degrading, utterly humiliating. Lucy fully intended, of course, to put it about that he'd left of his own free will, otherwise she might never be able to hold up her head again. But deep down she wasn't certain that everybody would believe this fiction.

How she would ever manage to endure Christmas with his dreadful family, she shuddered to think. The whole thing would be a nightmare from start to finish. She would certainly have a few words to say to that impossible brother of his.

Her first Tyson family Christmas was a delight so far as Kate was concerned. Everyone was so happy over Callum's full recovery that even the servants began to speak to her again. Mrs Petty herself invited Kate into her private quarters for a mince pie, piping hot, and accompanied by a generous serving of cream and a large pot of tea. A fire blazed in the cast-iron fireplace and on a polished desk close by stood the household account books, a pen holder, and a photograph of a stern-looking gentleman with one hand resting on his wife's shoulder as she sat before him, a baby on her lap. Kate wondered if these could be Mrs Petty's parents, finding it hard to imagine the stout housekeeper as that baby in the white broderie-anglaise gown.

As the housekeeper poured their tea she cleared her throat, then the words came out in a rush. 'That were a fine thing you did fer Mrs Tyson, sticking by her in her hour of need. In the past you and me didn't see eye to eye over this issue of the bairn, but I'd like to say that happen I were a bit hasty in me judgement.'

'Thank you, Mrs Petty. You don't know how it warms me heart to hear you say so. I'd never have given me babby away if I hadn't thought it was for his own good. It's hard here, with food so plentiful, the Christmas goose and all those puddings ye've been making, to remember a time when I would gladly have eaten the shoes off me own feet, I was that hungry.'

The housekeeper had the grace to pause in the act of lifting a mince pie to her open mouth and look suitably shame-faced. 'Aye, well I've come to realise that like. It's easy to forget need when yer not suffering from it theeself.' She took a large bite of pie and paused for thought. 'Truth to tell, I should under-stand more than most,' she said finally, setting down the pie and brushing away a few crumbs. She glanced back over her plump shoulder as if to check they were not overheard, although since the door of the housekeeper's room was firmly closed it was unlikely. 'I'll trust thee not to let this go any further but I had a bairn of me own once – that were wrong side of t'blanket an' all. Cut me parents up summat shocking, that did.' And she gazed sadly upon the photograph of the solemn-looking pair, and heaved a sigh. 'He were adopted too, my boy, by a fishmonger and his wife. Not so fancy or as well placed as the Tysons, but better off than me, a young lass. I were nobbut fifteen at the time and taken advantage of, if ye get me meaning. Anyroad, I weren't so fortunate as you. I never saw my lad again.'

Kate was deeply moved by the older woman's willingness to share this secret with her, so decided not to correct the repetition of her misconception that Callum was illegitimate. 'Oh, Mrs Petty, I'm so sorry to hear that. 'Tis a terrible thing to lose a child. At least I still get to care for Callum, to be with him every day. God alone knows how I'd manage if I ever lost that.'

Having reached this amicable state of agreement between the two of them, Mrs Petty refilled their cups and offered Kate a second mince pie. 'I don't reckon thoo'll have any more difficulties with the other servants in future. They're all pleased as punch that the little chap is himself again. You'll be joining us for Christmas dinner in the evening?'

'If I'm invited?'

'Aye, 'course you are. Thoo's one of us now, so put yer glad rags on. Happy Christmas, lass.'

'Happy Christmas, Mrs Petty.'

Christmas Day dawned clear and blue and bitterly cold, with a hoar frost sparkling on the grassy banks that sloped down to the River Kent. Breakfast was a jolly affair with bacon and kidneys, and was followed by church for the family which gave Mrs Petty and her band of helpers in the kitchen an hour or two to rush around roasting, baking, stuffing the goose, making gravy and chestnut stuffing, and completing all manner of other festive tasks with a mixture of tears and hysterical giggling over unexpected disasters, such as when the trifle upturned in the larder and the brandy sauce curdled. Fortunately, Mrs Petty always kept reserves of everything, and didn't turn a hair, but it wasn't surprising that the servants were beginning to flag with exhaustion. It had been all hands to the pump for weeks with all the shopping, cooking, baking and preparations to be made.

With several family members staying for the entire holiday period, Christmas Eve had been spent in a whirl of bed-making, airing of rooms, dusting, sweeping and polishing, not forgetting the laying of half a dozen bedroom fires. Fanny had at last allowed Kate to help her, and Callum toddled around with them, putting soap in dishes and hanging lavender bags in wardrobes.

The two aunts had arrived on Christmas Eve at four o'clock sharp, with their Gladstone bags and leather trunk, giving the impression they might be staying for a month rather than two weeks. Dressed in a black bombazine frock, adorned only by a cream fichu of lace at the throat, Aunt Vera looked even more stern than expected: short and square, with her straight dark hair clipped as neatly as the pruned privet hedge in her garden at home. Not that you could see much of it until after she had finished afternoon tea, which was the moment she removed her best black felt hat. She had at least agreed to take off the equally funereal overcoat which very nearly reached the toes of her button boots, handing it over to Fanny with lengthy instructions on where it should be placed and how it should be brushed. She had worn black ever since her father had died some thirty years before, and not even the festive season would make her change the habit.

Cissie, younger by three years, was altogether more brightly attired in a ginger brown tweed skirt and a rather baggy green sweater, somewhat moth-eaten, with cuffs which looked as if someone or something had chewed on them, as perhaps they had, the culprit undoubtedly being one of her dogs, upon whom she doted as if they were children. She kept several pointers and wherever they went they caused pandemonium, always wanting to chase and catch something, and preferably eat it afterwards. Fortunately, on this occasion, they'd all been left at their somewhat untidy home in Heversham, with 'the girl', who had also been left strict instructions to give the place 'a good clean through'.

'Are you quite sure this is wise?' Vera said to Amelia as Callum was brought in for inspection.

'Yes, Aunt Vera, I've never been more certain of anything in my life.'

Cissie held out her arms in an ecstasy of longing. 'Oh, may I hold him?' But then seeing Vera's frozen expression, dropped them again. 'He looks such a dear.'

Amelia chuckled. 'He is indeed. An absolute darling who steals hearts wherever he goes, so do take him, Cissie, and I'm quite sure he'll capture your heart too.'

She sat entranced with the child on her knee while wreaths of holly and ivy were brought in from the garden and Amelia swathed them along the tops of pictures and wound them about the banister rail. A large sprig of mistletoe was hung from the chandelier in the hail, ready to catch unwary visitors.

And so, on Christmas morning, as they all trooped back in from church, kicking snow from their boots, putting off gloves and blowing on cold fingers, Callum, who'd been thought too young to attend, ran to greet Amelia and she swung him up in her arms to give him a resounding kiss under the mistletoe. 'Happy Christmas, darling boy.'

'Kiss for Nursey,' Callum said, and, laughing, Amelia gave Kate a peck on her cheek too. The next instant Eliot was looming over her too, smiling into her eyes.

Kate thought her heart might stop if he actually touched her.

She'd never felt quite the same about him since that moment when he'd held her close on the stairs and tenderly mopped her tears. He'd comforted her then with such sensitivity that he'd captured her heart utterly. Today she could smell his cologne, all tangy and clean, and felt suddenly plain and dull in her crisp uniform dress, forgetting how proud she'd been to put it on not so many months ago. Grasping her gently by the shoulders, he kissed her firmly on each cheek.

Kate carried the imprint of those kisses with her for the rest of the day.

Just before lunch, everyone was ushered into the small parlour where the Christmas tree, adorned with tinsel and tiny candles, and with a fairy perched high on the topmost branch, kept stately vigil over a pile of presents. Everyone laughed as the little boy excitedly set about opening each gift with increasing wonderment and delight. Aunt Vera didn't even bother to preach about the greater good being found in giving rather than receiving. Cissie, who clearly adored him, got down on her hands and knees in her best tweed skirt so she could help him to rip off the paper. Callum's gifts included a farmyard complete with animals, a wooden ship and toy soldiers, a whistle, glossy pictures for his scrapbook, several books and puzzles, plus a money box from Mrs Petty and the servants. A very lucky boy indeed, as Aunt Vera kept reminding him. She'd bought him a copy of the New Testament in white leather, beautifully illustrated and inscribed. Amelia accepted the gift on his behalf with grave reverence. Cissie gave him a woolly toy dog she'd crocheted herself, and promised him a real one as soon as he was old enough.

'One of me best pointers, don't you know? And I'll teach you how to hunt with it, child. We'll have such dashed good fun.'

It seemed that whatever reservations the maiden aunts

might privately hold over this unusual adoption, they were giving no sign of them on this special day.

Charles and Lucy arrived in time for Christmas lunch with their own two children in tow: four-year-old Jack, and three-year-old Bunty, a precocious, blond-haired pair who had clearly never been taught the importance of the maxim of being seen and not heard. And George, of course, the new addition to the family, who was placed in his pram in the hall, although later, Kate would take him upstairs to the nursery for his feed.

As a special treat, the children were to be allowed to eat with the family and as Kate placed Callum in his chair, tied him in with ribbons and fastened on his bib, she thought the atmosphere around the table almost as frosty as the weather. Even though she was kept busy helping Fanny with the serving, she couldn't help noticing that whatever joy and laughter had been present earlier had drained away, to be replaced by a definite air of awkwardness and tension in the room.

Charles Tyson seemed particularly morose. It was the first time Kate had viewed him at close quarters and she didn't much like the look of him. His face was florid, and she noted bloated cheeks and a slack jaw beneath his whiskers. He piled his plate with food in a most ill-mannered way, and then complained that the goose was cold which was absolute nonsense. Mrs Petty would never allow such a thing. Eliot bluntly told him that if he spent less time grizzling and complaining, and more on eating the excellent food set before him, it wouldn't be given the chance to go cold. 'You're running to fat, Charles, take care. You've piled enough on your plate to feed an army.'

Lucy Tyson remarked coldly, 'But then, who knows when we might eat another meal,' which Kate thought a very odd thing to say.

After that Charles kept on casting sidelong glances at his wife, who never spoke another word throughout the entire meal although, like her husband, she certainly ate plenty.

Amelia as always looked lovely in a crimson gown trimmed with silver lace, if a little wan and tired, revealing how much Callum's illness had taken out of her. Her husband was as attentive as ever, showing his concern over her lack of appetite.

'You're losing weight, my darling. You must eat more.'

'Don't fret, my love, my appetite is small. Not like our fine boy here. See how he is eating. Doesn't he look well?'

As Eliot turned to give more attention to his adopted son, he failed to notice the way his wife laid a hand to her side and winced slightly. Kate saw, and hurried over to her, only to be shushed and sent away with a whispered assurance that it was nothing more than the result of too little sleep and too much worry. Amelia was determined that her slight feeling of being off-colour would not in any way mar their first Christmas together as a family. Her eyes shone, her smile never faltered and she devoted all her time and attention to feeding Callum, merely picking at her own food, despite all Eliot's efforts to persuade her to eat more.

12

While the gentlemen were enjoying their port, the ladies and children withdrew to the drawing room. Jack had already broken his Noah's Ark within an hour of starting to play with it, thrown a tremendous tantrum and been in a sulk ever since, constantly pinching his sister's toys. This created friction between them and so Kate was invited to accompany them and supervise their play. Lucy looked not only quite worn out but thoroughly ill-tempered to boot. She'd barely been presented with her cup of coffee before she began to unleash her bad mood upon her hostess.

'Have you any idea, Amelia, what has possessed Eliot to behave in this outrageous fashion towards Charles? It really is quite appalling to dismiss his own brother in such a peremptory fashion. And at Christmas-time, too. What are we supposed to do? *Starve?*'

Amelia flushed bright pink. She hadn't the first idea what her sister-in-law was talking about, but realised instantly that Eliot had obviously attempted to shield her from some unpleasant business or other at the factory. He'd probably thought she had enough on her plate with their lovely son being so ill. She glanced helplessly across at Aunt Vera, who instantly came to her aid.

'It may have something to do with the fact that he no longer trusts him. Brothers aren't always on the same side, don't you know? In fact, my own used to drive me potty, I seem to remember. A martyr to work was our Georgie, never content unless he was out on the road selling his precious shoes – if he wasn't criticising everything his workers did, that is. He was known to take the last out of their hands and do the job himself if he wasn't satisfied with the standard of their workmanship. But then, he was devoted to making the company profitable. Trouble is, unlike Charles, he rarely thought of anything else. Obsessed with business, you might say, and certainly succeeded in what he set out to do, otherwise we wouldn't all be here, would we now?'

'Indeed we wouldn't,' Aunt Cissie agreed, nodding eagerly as she always did at her sister's words.

'Hard work is good for the soul, after all. Charles should follow his father's example and go out on the road too, or serve his time as a shoemaker,' Vera continued in her most hectoring tone. 'Make Tyson's more of a priority instead of simply trying to line his own pockets.'

Lucy gasped, all the colour draining from her face and then rushing back again so that twin spots of scarlet flagged each quivering cheek. 'I will not have him so maligned! Of course Tyson's has always been a priority for Charles, but really, he is not prepared to stand by and see everything destroyed and taken away from him. Why should he be deprived of what is rightfully his? That is too much to ask.'

Amelia stared at her blankly. 'In what way is everything being destroyed or taken away from him? Has something dreadful happened to the company?'

There was a small embarrassed silence while everyone contemplated the open innocence in her face. It was clear that she had given no thought to how the adoption of Callum might be viewed by the rest of the family. Cissie and Vera certainly entertained grave reservations on the subject themselves, though were too fond of dear Eliot and Amelia to own up to them, and it was certainly no fault of the child's. Even so, they exchanged a speaking glance while Lucy drew breath ready for the next attack.

'You know perfectly well to what I am referring.' And she looked furiously over in the direction of Callum, who was happily struggling to make his top spin.

Kate took the full impact of the glare instead, and felt her blood run cold. There was pure hatred in it, an indescribable venom, and she felt a prickle of fear pierce her breast. Like Amelia, Kate had never for a moment considered the impact of the adoption upon the rest of this family. Now she saw the implications and felt a paralysing chill.

Lucy's voice was rising as she grew ever more furious, and nobody seemed able to stop her. 'Some things are beyond endurance. To be ousted by a workhouse brat – one of Eliot's by-blows, no doubt. Let's not mince words: a *whore's bastard* who has robbed my precious darlings of their rightful inheritance. It's too much to bear. No wonder dear Charles was forced to take steps to protect himself. I dread to think what your late lamented brother would have had to say on the matter, Vera, since, as you quite rightly say, he was so passionate about building up the business for the benefit of his *own family*, not snivelling interlopers. Grasping little offcomers. It's utterly disgraceful!'

Vera, for once in her life, was struck speechless and sat opening and closing her mouth like a stranded fish, while Cissie fluttered her hands and kept murmuring, 'Oh dear – oh dear, dear, dear!'

Amelia had gone desperately pale. She felt as if someone had plunged a knife into her heart, robbing her of breath and leaving her throbbing with pain. She couldn't begin to take in the full import of these words yet it was as if she were trapped in a web of unspeakable horror. Was Lucy referring to Callum?

How could she be, since he was not – not what she had accused him of being. Eliot had never looked at another woman. Indeed never would. Didn't they have a perfect marriage? Mistress and maid's eyes met and a message was exchanged. Perhaps it was this silent communication of understanding which gave her the courage to respond.

'I think you've said enough, Lucy. I – I'm not quite sure what exactly it is you are implying but I won't stand for it. It simply isn't true to say . . .'

Bunty, who'd been given a Pollock's Toy Theatre for Christmas, chose precisely that moment to let out a piercing scream as her brother snatched one of the paper actors out of her hand. Having witnessed all of this dreadful scene with growing horror, Kate grasped at the opportunity of a diversion with heartfelt relief. Leaping to her feet, she announced in her briskest, most nanny-like tones: 'Now, Master Jack, I think we are getting a trifle out of sorts. Come along, children. Time for our nap, is it not? Let us tidy away our toys like good little boys and girls, and then we'll all go up to the nursery for a little rest before teatime. Say good afternoon to the ladies nicely, and if you are very, very good, I shall read you a story from Callum's new book.'

She was only too delighted to escape from this dreadful scene, longing to have her child to herself for a while and give him the present she had bought him. It was a lovely book called *Little Stories for Little Folks,* and she looked forward to cuddling him on her lap while she read to him; to kissing the soft, pink curve of his plump cheek and breathing in the dear, sweet baby scent of him.

Gathering her charges, she led them quietly from the room. As she softly closed the door, Kate paused and waited for a moment, fearful that mayhem might again break out but after a long, painful silence she heard Cissie's voice pipe up.

'Got a new bitch the other day, I think she'll be a cracker. Good show dog potential. Bound to be a winner at the County Show in a year or two, mark my words.'

Kate heaved a sigh of relief and left them to it, hoping against hope that Lucy's vindictive outburst would not be repeated. She also prayed that these slurs against her character would not affect the way Amelia felt about Callum, or result in her being dismissed. She paused again at the foot of the stairs. Glancing back at the closed door, she gathered the children safely about her ready for the ascent, anxiously wondering if Amelia had believed all that nonsense about Callum being Eliot's by-blow. Then the door opened and there stood her mistress. Calm and unruffled as ever, she looked the very picture of the perfect hostess dealing with a minor indiscretion on the part of a guest who had unnecessarily upset one of the servants.

'Ah, Kate, I'm glad you haven't quite gone.' She hurried over, grasped the knob at the foot of the banister and peered earnestly up into her face. 'Don't let Lucy's words upset you. I shall make perfectly clear to her your married status and how Callum's father was tragically killed. As for my dear sister-in-law's other comments, I shall treat those with the contempt they deserve. I want you to understand that no matter what she might say, I don't believe a word of it. Eliot is true to me, and always has been.'

'I'm obliged, ma'am.' Kate wondered if she should curtsey or something, but Jack and Bunty had grown bored with waiting, and were starting to climb the stairs on their bottoms.

'As for the adoption . . . well, Callum is our son in every way that matters.' Amelia dropped her voice to a confidential whisper. 'And just between ourselves, Kate, whoever eventually inherits the business is really none of her concern. That is for Eliot to decide. As if I would dream of interfering, or think to intervene on her children's behalf! Tush, the very idea! Not women's business at all.' Kate inwardly smiled at this complete and utter trust and dependence upon the male of the species. But then Amelia had never been compelled to earn her own living, or fend for herself in any way.

'I'm sure you know best how to deal with the matter, ma'am. I'd hate it if you and Mr Tyson were wounded by malicious gossip.'

'It won't happen. We won't allow it to happen. We – I – believe in you utterly.'

'Thank you, ma'am,' Kate felt a surge of gratitude and such a rush of loyalty and love for her mistress she very nearly put her arms about Amelia and hugged her, but stopped herself just in time. Jack and Bunty had reached the first landing. 'I'd best take the children up now, hadn't I, ma'am?'

'Yes, do, Kate. I just wanted you to know that you are not to worry. It has been such a lovely Christmas, with our little boy fit and well again, I refuse to allow one of Lucy's tantrums to spoil it for us.' Then she leaned over and kissed Callum on his soft, flushed cheek. 'He isn't too hot, is he?'

Kate smiled. 'No, ma'am, just falling asleep in me arms, and what a weight he is to hold these days! Yer looking after him too well, I'm thinking.' And both women laughed, united in their love for the child and agreeing that Kate would bring all three children and the new baby down again later, after their rest.

As Kate reached the landing and captured Jack just as he was attempting to slide down the banister, she saw Amelia pause at the drawing-room door before stiffening her spine and walking inside with a bright, 'Now where were we? Vera dear, do you think you could manage a small sherry, it being Christmas?'

★

Kate read the story, enjoying a precious half-hour with her son. The little boy was as good as gold, as he always was for her, rubbing his sleepy head against her breast as if he instinctively knew that here was where he truly belonged. The new baby had been fed and changed and had gone off to sleep again without a murmur. Jack and Bunty were another matter entirely, as naughty as they could possibly be, refusing to get into the beds prepared for them, pulling each other's hair and squabbling the whole time. Bunty kept screaming and stamping her little foot in a fury of temper and Jack peevishly pinched his sister's bottom. A fight ensued and poor Kate had to drag the pair apart and scold them firmly, leaving Bunty in tears and Jack in a scowling sulk.

It took an age but she'd just got all the children settled down, and quiet had descended, allowing her to enjoy a few moments' peace at last, when there came a tap at the door. Oh, no, not more trouble, she thought, putting down the magazine she'd been nodding over. Getting wearily to her feet she opened the door to find Eliot standing there with a parcel in his hands.

'I'm playing Santa Claus and delivering your present.'

Kate gasped, 'I wasn't expecting one.'

'The servants will be getting theirs later, of course, after supper, and there'll be a small one for you then, nuts or a handkerchief or some such. But you are different, Kate, and deserve a little something extra. I know things haven't been easy for you below stairs, so thought it best you should open this in private. We've said nothing about the problems you've been having with the other servants because we weren't sure how we could help, but we want you to know that you are particularly special to us, Kate, for giving us Callum.'

She swallowed down the lump which had sprung into her throat. How she wished they wouldn't keep reminding her of that fact. How she wished she hadn't felt compelled to hand him over to them in the first place, just as if he were indeed a stray dog or cat. Couldn't they understand how very difficult it was for her? There were times, like now when she'd been reading him a story and putting him to bed, when she wondered why on earth she'd agreed to his crazy scheme. But then, would Callum even have lived to see this Christmas if they'd stayed in Poor House Lane? She very much doubted it. 'Mrs Petty and I had a lovely chat only this morning, sir. I'm sure things are going to improve in that department.'

'I'm glad to hear it.' He handed over the parcel, wrapped in plain brown paper and tied with a red ribbon. 'Open it.'

'Thank you, there was really no need.'

'There is every need.'

Kate took it from him, feeling the slightest touch of his cool fingers as she did so, then hurriedly set the parcel to one side. She could tell at once that it was a book, and felt her cheeks growing hot and flushed with the embarrassment of this oddly personal moment. 'I'd like to open it later, when I'm alone, if you don't mind?'

'No, no, I insist you open it now. I need to know if you approve.' He came in and made himself comfortable on the rocking chair she'd just vacated, briefly stroking Callum's sleeping head before looking up at her with a smile. The gesture, and the fact that he looked so very much the excited schoolboy, meant she couldn't possibly disappoint him. Kate found that her hands were shaking as she removed the wrappings. The book was a compendium of flowers and trees, almost as if he were willing her to understand his own passion, and to share it. Her first reaction was to smile, but then Kate experienced a terrible longing to sit down and cry her eyes out.

'You like it?'

'I do indeed, sir. Thank you kindly.'

'I'm a dreadful garden bore, I'm afraid.' He was smiling too but made no move to go. After a moment the smile faded but still he kept on looking at her and, as before, she found herself mesmerised by that gaze. There it was again, that frisson between them, that yearning which seemed to paralyse her brain, leaving her utterly breathless and quite unable to move or drag her eyes from his.

'You won't ever leave, will you, Kate?'

'As if I would leave Callum.' Or you, she thought. 'Never. Anyway, how could you all manage without me?'

He chuckled. Once again he was struck by her apparent fragility, and yet her invincibility. Still too thin, but bright of eye and steady as a rock in her resolve not to complain but to deal with whatever life flung at her. He admired that in her, enjoyed their little chats together, the fact that she felt able to speak her mind freely. She'd certainly given him short shrift that time over his neglect of the business, and she'd been absolutely right. 'That's good. So long as I know you are here, I am content.'

'And why would you not be content, I'm thinking, with all of this?' Her hand gestured to encompass the house, the lovely view of the river, Callum. But inside her heart was fluttering like a wild bird caught in a cage. Did he mean that he couldn't bear to be without her? That he loved to have her near him? Kate could still recall the magic of those kisses under the mistletoe, one on each cheek, and her knees almost buckled as she imagined him doing it again, with no one else around this time.

'Perhaps one must suffer a little before learning to appreciate properly what one has, or else take it all for granted.'

'I'm sure that is so.'

'But then, I often fail in my duty, Kate. Perhaps because I don't have your strength of character.'

'Tch! I don't believe that for a moment. Too soft-hearted for your own good, that's all that's wrong with you. But aren't you the boss of yer own empire, with the power almost of life and death over the poor souls who work for you?'

He was openly laughing now, leaning back in the rocking chair with one leg propped comfortably upon the other, revealing his contentment at being here with her, just talking. 'I reckon the unions would have a say in the matter if that were true, which fortunately it isn't. But I love to hear your frank views. Don't ever be afraid to express them.' They both turned their heads as they heard the sound of raised voices from below. Reluctantly, Eliot got to his feet, a rueful expression on his face. 'You know that I shouldn't even be here?' He sounded sad but not regretful, as if he'd have been quite glad to stay instead of returning to the domestic disharmony downstairs.

'Indeed, I dare say you shouldn't.'

'The gift was simply an excuse. I just wanted to see you.'

Kate's heartbeat hammered in her chest. What did he mean by that? An excuse for what? Why would he want to see her?

He went on to explain that Amelia had meant to give her the book later that evening, when Kate brought the children back down. 'But I wanted to see you, just for a moment, to say how grateful I am that you agreed to the adoption, and stayed to look after Callum so well. His presence has made a world of a difference to Amelia. She is quite her old self again: relaxed and happy. I also wanted to say how very pretty you looked earlier, so pink cheeked and shining that I simply couldn't resist leaving my guests and sneaking upstairs. I hope you don't think me very wicked?'

'I think you very foolish.' Kate chuckled. 'I also think you've drunk too much port and you had best go down now before you wake the children.'

He made as if to obey her but at the door turned back, his eyes were shadowed, unfathomable, unreadable. 'It's very important to me that you are happy, Kate. I hope you understand that? We love having you here. Callum is now my son and I love him, but you are still his mother, in a manner of speaking, and I'm very fond of you too. We both are. How could we not be when you've given us such a fine boy? You are very much a part of this family. I hope you feel the same?'

She wasn't used to people being kind to her. They never had been before, not since Daddy had passed away. Dermot was, well – Dermot, and had gone off to Ireland to seek his fortune, forgetting all about her. Daddy had loved her uncritically, of course, and she him, but that had been different. Only right and natural. The love she felt for this man was of a kind which wasn't right at all. Finding a better life for her son had cost her dear, yet she couldn't help but love him, couldn't even find it in her heart to hate his wife. She should resent Amelia for having so much: wealth and comfort in this lovely home, a radiant beauty, and this wonderful man. Eliot Tyson had turned out to be much kinder than she'd been led to believe, good natured and so handsome, with skin tanned from the long hours he spent in his garden. Dark brown hair falling in shining waves almost to his collar so that the urge to run her fingers through it was almost unbearable. His gentle brown eyes had lines fanning out from the corners, and they would narrow slightly when he was puzzling over something or shrewdly summing up his competitors. Even the fact that he was clean shaven, which was quite against the fashion, set him apart as his own man.

He was looking at her keenly, perhaps attempting to read these thoughts while he waited for her to speak. But Kate could say nothing, merely stand drinking in the sight of him, loving him with a pain that almost cleaved her heart in two. She found that she was trembling, and bit down hard on her lower lip in an effort to control her emotions, desperate to stop herself from doing what she most longed to do: melt into his arms. She could recall the feel of them around her only too clearly.

It was Eliot who broke the silence between them, 'I would never wish to cause Amelia the slightest concern. You understand that, don't you, Kate? No matter what the circumstances.'

'Of course.' Now what would he be meaning by that exactly? She wished she understood the enigmatic expression in those deeply mysterious eyes of his. Was he referring to Callum, saying that Kate mustn't be too proprietorial over him? Or something else entirely? Why was it that every word he uttered left her in two minds over its meaning?

'Nor would I ever risk hurting you, or driving you away. I want you to know, Kate, that you are quite safe here, living under my roof, and will ever remain so.'

He hesitated a moment longer, as if needing a response to this puzzling statement at least – expressions of gratitude perhaps. And still Kate could say nothing, feeling utterly bereft of words, could scarcely breathe, let alone think. Safe from what? Not from her own heart, certainly. Were it not for Callum, wouldn't she pack her bags and leave like a shot? Whatever she'd felt for her husband, and she'd loved him for sure, the sensations of longing running through her now were so tangible she felt certain Eliot must see them radiating from her like heat waves, not to mention the emotion which must be plain in her face.

Fond as she was of Amelia, if he'd made one move towards her then, Kate would not have been unwilling.

13

Over the weeks following, despite Kate's exemplary behaviour the servants were given plenty to gossip about. In due course stories found their way into neighbouring kitchens all along Kent Terrace, Thorny Hills and as far as Stramongate: from maids below stairs to their mistresses above, from workers at the factory to their wives at home, until the whole south end of the town was buzzing with rumours.

There was the quarrel between the two brothers for a start, which had resulted in Charles quitting the company and devoting his time exclusively to running Marshall and Stone, the leather-currying firm. Word had it that this new business was already in difficulties as the days of vegetable-tanned leather were numbered and a new process, called chrome tanning, had appeared.

Old Askew the gardener was heard constantly to bemoan the fact that the master had lost interest in his garden and was now spending most of his days incarcerated in his office at the factory with his accountants and foreman, else closeted in meetings with his bank. This left far more digging, weeding and hedge-trimming for the old man than he could rightly cope with, so he'd taken to hiding away in the shed to smoke his pipe which meant that the gardens were running to rack and ruin.

More entertaining still was the tale of the two sisters-in-law who were said not to be speaking since their little contretemps at Christmas.

Ida, who'd been refilling the coal scuttle and was thus able to slip in and out unnoticed, had heard at first hand how Lucy Tyson had demanded her husband be promptly reinstated, declaring that she didn't in the least mind swallowing her pride in order to make the request as she had her babies to think of – a state of affairs which Amelia couldn't possibly understand since she'd been driven to adopting a poor house brat to fill her cradle.

Apparently, tempers had become more and more frayed as the afternoon had worn on, with Aunt Cissie wailing about not disturbing the children, and Aunt Vera pontificating upon Christmas good-will. By the time Eliot had arrived upon the scene, it had been too late to save the situation and Ida was also able to describe how furious he'd been to discover that his wife had been insulted in her own drawing room. Goggle-eyed, the maid had crept out to tell Fanny, who in turn had told Dennis, who'd mentioned it in passing to Old Askew. Mrs Petty elicited juicy morsels from each of them and filled in the gaps after a little gentle interrogation of Kate herself, who'd witnessed the start of the quarrel.

Embarrassed by his wife's uncalled for defence of him, Charles had taken his family home forthwith, not even staying for the substantial tea of raised pork pie, cucumber sandwiches, Christmas cake and the delicious hot mince pies which Mrs Petty had so painstakingly prepared. Dennis had driven them home in the carriage, earning extra rations in the kitchen afterwards with his tale of how the couple had not spoken a word to each other throughout the entire journey. 'Even those noisy nippers kept their traps shut. You could've cut the atmosphere with a knife, so help me.'

As a result, Lucy Tyson had been banned from the house

save for family occasions when she was accompanied by her husband. 'Almost as if she were a naughty child being kept on a leading rein,' murmured the matrons of Thorny Hills, lapping up the gossip with glee. 'How very shocking!'

Fanny found it remarkable that the master was prepared to allow his brother to continue to visit at all, having caught him in the act of defrauding the company and given him the sack for it.

'The toffs think different from us, girl,' Mrs Petty assured her. 'Family is everything. Blood being thicker than water, and all that. Though how would you know, when you haven't a drop of decent blood in your veins?'

'No, it's pure milk stout,' Dennis agreed with a grin, and was given a slap for his trouble.

And all of this brought about by the fact that Amelia Tyson was unable to produce a son and heir, so that her husband had foisted one of his by-blows upon her, said the matrons as they sat in their church pews whispering behind their hymn books. And as if that wasn't bad enough, he'd forced her to take in the natural mother as well, a no-good piece of rubbish from the Kirkland Workhouse on Poor House Lane.

It was a Sunday in early March, a gloriously bright spring day with the morning sun slanting rays of white-gold over Gummer's How, lighting Rusland Heights and Furness Fells, burnishing the lake to a silvered blue. There was beauty enough in the scene to take anyone's breath away – anyone save Lucy, who was in a rage. She neither noticed nor cared about the majesty of mountains, nor the crisp, sparkling air. She paid no heed to the shy crocuses and snowdrops peeping through the spears of new grass, nor the tightly furled buds bursting open in a pink flush on the horse chestnut trees. The snow-capped peaks of the Langdales did not captivate her, nor the lush green fringe of woodland that stretched down to the lakeside fascinate.

Lucy knew only that she was alone. Charles had swiftly devoured a substantial breakfast of scrambled eggs and bacon but instead of going off for a sail, as he used to do in the good old carefree days, or helping her to devise some picnic or trip out in their newly purchased steam yacht which bobbed in the lapping water beside their very own jetty, he'd dropped a hasty kiss on her brow and said that he must return to the office at once, as he had business to attend to.

Lucy had been outraged. 'Not on a Sunday, Charles, surely?'

'I'm sorry, sweetheart, but that's how it is. We're being dreadfully undercut by the chrome-tanning people, and I have to find a solution. To make matters worse, Eliot has decided to dress his own leather in future. He's bought the patent rights of a process used by a company in Doncaster, and I was depending on Tyson's to really get us launched. He said that if he couldn't trust me to work for him within the company, why should he risk sending any Tyson business my way?'

Charles's face looked grave, lined with worry which she hated to see, but for once Lucy had little sympathy for him. She felt irritated at being left to endure yet another entire day alone, stuck here with the children and the servants right at the bottom of the lake in the middle of nowhere, without even any house party arranged to divert her. Utterly unbearable.

'What nonsense! You must insist. Remind him you are still family and deserve his support.' Details of the business bored her. Why didn't Charles simply insist on his rights forthwith?

'Yes, dearest, though I doubt he'll listen.'

'You give in far too easily, that is your trouble. You must insist that he sees sense and allows you back into the company.'

'He won't have me back. He's made that perfectly clear.

Besides, I don't need him. I prefer to be in control of my own destiny.' Charles spoke with firmness but there was a desperate look in his eye which said the exact opposite. As he made a dash out of the door, he was still wearing his napkin tucked into his waistcoat front.

He'd even forgotten to kiss her goodbye but Lucy didn't run after him to remind him of that fact. Instead she snapped at the maid who came to clear the table, then flounced off to the drawing room in a furious sulk and pretended to read the paper.

All of a sudden she hated this draughty house, hated the mud, the acres of woodland garden that had to be constantly supervised, the packing and unpacking which transporting three children and a host of servants every weekend demanded. And she'd forgotten how very messy it was to live in the country. As a girl, her one dream had been to escape the bleak emptiness of woods and fields, so why had she allowed herself to be persuaded back? Because she had believed it would be different here. She'd thought that this time it wouldn't mean living in an insignificant farmhouse but in a substantial country mansion with huge fireplaces and stately rooms as well as sufficient servants to keep the place clean and the fires blazing. That they would be courted by the country set. But it wasn't like that at all. Throughout the dark days of winter she'd felt trapped behind the glass of rain-streaked windows, and cold, always so cold. It had felt as if she were living in an ice box. Now that spring was here at last, she'd insisted they buy the steam yacht, even though Charles had moaned and groaned that he didn't quite have the money for it, not yet.

'Poppycock! How am I ever to go anywhere without transport, or get to know any of our neighbours without the proper means to entertain them?' And Lucy had kicked her heels and thrown a tantrum until the deal had been struck. Days later the yacht had been delivered, a handsome vessel done out in crimson and gold, its brass and copper gleaming to perfection. Since when she'd spent a small fortune fitting it out, and had been desperately looking forward to their first Sunday afternoon picnic of the season; a practice run as it were before sending out invitations to their socially elite neighbours to join them on an outing. And now, despite the sunshine and all of her effort, Charles had decided he must work instead.

'Will somebody come and see to this dratted fire?' Lucy screamed, although the coal scuttle stood yards from where she sat.

When nobody came in answer to her shout, she jumped up and furiously rang the bell which hung by the mantelshelf. It echoed somewhere for several long moments in the depths of the house. Above her head were the children, no doubt playing and jumping about with their nurse, or whatever they did when not at lessons. Occasionally she went up to see how they were getting along but whatever went on in the bowels of the kitchens and servant quarters, Lucy did not know and did not wish to know, except that if someone didn't come soon, she'd dismiss the entire staff and start afresh.

Fortunately, at that moment the door opened and a maid hurried in, pink-cheeked and out of breath from rushing up many flights of stairs. 'Were you wanting summat, ma'am?'

Really, these common little people. '*Something* . . . were you wanting *something*. And tidy your hair, for goodness' sake. Where is your cap?'

The maid's round face became transfixed with horror. 'Ooh, heck, it must have blown off when I were fetching in the kindling.'

'*Bringing* in the kindling. Oh, never mind, go and find it this instant. No, not *quite* this instant,' as the girl turned on her heel to rush off at once. 'What do you think I wanted? Why do you think I rang?' Lucy then looked pointedly at the dimly burning coals in the grate and managed to indicate her displeasure without saying another word. The maid ran for the coal scuttle and set about her duties.

'When you've found your cap and refilled the scuttle, you can bring my coffee and also a selection of biscuits, if you please.'

'Cook hasn't had time to make any this morning, it being Sunday like and having to make the dinner, and it being her afternoon off.'

'Then we'd best cancel her afternoon off, hadn't we? If she's slacking in her duties, she doesn't deserve one, nor anyone else for that matter.'

The little maid looked stunned. 'Cancelled? Nay, she'll not like that. She were going to see her sister over in Grange-over-Sands, said how nice and convenient it were, us being so close.'

'Well, it isn't convenient for me.'

'Begging yer pardon, ma'am, but does that mean I can't go and see me mam in Arnside? We were going over in the governess cart after t'dinner were cleared away.'

'It certainly does. No one is going anywhere.' If Lucy couldn't go out, why should they? 'And it's *lunch*, not dinner.'

'Oh, ma'am, she'll be that cut up.' The girl gave a great hiccuping sob and then continued, greatly daring, 'Cook won't be happy to lose her afternoon off. She'll be handing in her notice, if yer not careful.'

'Go away, you silly girl, and do as you are told. You could all be without a job before the winter is out if you don't buck up your ideas.' And having reduced her most biddable servant to tears, Lucy watched with some satisfaction as the girl fled, coal scuttle clattering as she attempted to do a proper curtsey and close the door as quickly as possible so as not to let in any draughts.

After she'd gone Lucy screamed with boredom and stamped her foot, then flopped down on a sofa and picked up a magazine only to fling it down again. How she loathed the loneliness without Charles, the emptiness and endlessness of her days. And their games above stairs seemed to have come to a halt. Whenever she suggested one, he would complain that he was too tired, but Lucy knew he was nervous of having another child before they could quite afford one. Money was his overriding obsession these days and he never seemed to have any time for her at all, always making excuses about some business matter or other which required his immediate attention. It had been this way ever since that dreadful weekend when he'd confessed to being dismissed by the company.

Oh, someone must be made to suffer the full weight of her wrath, it wasn't poor Charles's fault at all. Was he supposed to sit by and do nothing while that bastard child took everything, stole the bread from the mouths of his own children?

Lucy got through the rest of the day as best she could, toying with her luncheon which was worse than usual, probably due to Cook's annoyance at having her afternoon off stopped. Serve the woman right, whatever her name was, she'd be dismissed next week and a new one found. Cooks were two a penny.

After lunch the afternoon stretched before her like an empty desert, or rather a freezing landscape. To add insult to injury, the fickle sun had gone in and it had started to rain so there wasn't even the possibility of a walk in the gardens. Oh, how she hated winter here. It seemed to go on forever. Why couldn't they go to Italy or the South of France for a while, as they used to do? What was the point of Charles having his own business and being his own boss if he couldn't take time off whenever he wished? She longed to go straight back to town but no one of any significance returned until Monday.

Finally, bored and disgruntled, Lucy went to bed alone, rather the worse the wear from the several glasses of Madeira she had consumed with her lonely dinner. She would absolutely insist on having a house party next weekend, economy drive or no, and whether Charles had to work or not. There was absolutely no reason why she should endure such unnatural enforced poverty and utter misery. It was too much.

Her plans did not quite work out as the following weekend Charles insisted upon a display of family unity by inviting Eliot, Amelia and that dratted bastard child over for the day. It proved to be a complete failure as the rain poured down yet again, and Eliot refused absolutely to take his brother back into the business or to discuss the matter further. Amelia had not brought the nursemaid with her because she believed the silly girl needed a day off, and so the pair of them were forced to mind their own children for once.

Raging inwardly, Lucy found an opportunity over luncheon to stick a pin into the dreadful little bastard, making him scream out loud, though not a soul guessed why, despite Amelia flustering and fussing over him. The episode, small as it was, brought Lucy enormous satisfaction. She'd do it again, without question. She'd do worse than stick pins into the little monster, if she got half a chance. Oh, yes indeed, she'd get her revenge one day. She just had to bide her time. Nobody treated her precious Charles in this cavalier fashion, least of all his own brother.

Much to everyone's disappointment, conditions and pay for Tyson's outworkers had not improved in the slightest with the departure of Charles from the firm, and Kendal folk began to worry that perhaps the firm itself was in difficulties. None of the workers at the factory was particularly sorry to see the back of Charles, but they did regret the fact that Swainson had stayed on as foreman. Many were convinced he too was involved in the fraud though no proof could be found, perhaps because Mr Eliot was too trusting to look for it. As a result, the man still held sway over the handing out of work. Millie, for one, wished with all her heart he would vanish in a puff of smoke.

Soon after Kate had left, Millie decided she might as well use her friend's departure to her own advantage and went along to see if Swainson would take her on instead. If Kate could stitch uppers, so could she.

Millie hadn't much cared for the way he'd leered at her even then, or how he'd let his hands linger on her shoulder as he'd given her a kindly pat, but he'd agreed to give her some work and for that she was grateful, Clem still having no luck in finding employment. In no time at all, though, she regretted this decision with all her heart, realising that she was to pay a high price to keep her babies from starving. She'd already known the pay wasn't good, that being an outworker brought yet more dirt and disease into the home, and that Swainson had his own set of rules which must be kept if you were to see any money at all.

One of these rules was that two hours' work must be completed before breakfast. Most shoe manufacturers had stopped this practice, on the insistence and advice of the National Union of Boot and Shoe Operatives. When Clem tackled Swainson on this very point, accusing him of exploitation, he'd callously laughed and shrugged his shoulders with contempt. 'Let NUBSO catch me at it first! Your wife isn't going to tell, is she? Not if she wants work from me in future.' By way of punishment, he'd left her without work for two whole weeks during which time one of their youngest fell sick and very nearly died. Millie urged Clem not to complain again.

Another rule was that an outworker was only allowed to call at the workshop to deliver the finished work and collect new materials once a week, but the foreman was permitted to call upon an outworker at any time, to check she was doing the job right. The first time he'd appeared at her door, Millie had been surprised and flustered, worried that he might find fault with her work and not give her any more. She'd thought nothing of it when he'd brusquely told Ma Parkin to go for a little stroll while they discussed their 'bit of business'.

'And wait outside on the steps till I say you can come in,' he'd instructed the old woman.

Only after she'd gone did Millie learn exactly what the bit of business amounted to, what working for Swainson actually entailed. Almost before the door had closed, he'd curtly ordered her to, 'Take off that filthy frock, don't complain and do as yer told, if you don't want your children to go hungry. And look sharp about it, I haven't all day.'

When she'd resisted, loudly protesting that he'd no right to touch her, her being a married woman, he'd given a nasty snort of amusement and pushed her down on to the ramshackle bed where two of her youngest children happened to be sleeping. He'd ripped the dress off her, followed by the equally grubby shift. Millie had whimpered and begged, desperately trying to cover herself with her hands, pleading for mercy, but he'd paid no attention.

'What yer going to do, set that one-armed husband o' thine on to me? Nay, I'm shivering in me shoes. Just remember what happened to young Dermot. Folk who cross me live to regret it – if they live at all. Young Dermot were lucky, getting off with a few broken ribs and a black eye, but it could have been different. Remember that, girl.'

He held down Millie's stick-like limbs and scrawny,

malnourished body with easy indifference while he pawed her breasts, licking and sucking till he was panting with excitement. Then with no further ado opened up his trousers, pulled out his cock and plunged into her, jerking and pushing with all his might. Millie bit down hard on her lip so that she didn't cry out and startle her babies. So fiercely, blood trickled down her chin. Despite being bruised and ruthlessly used, she made not a sound.

'That wasn't so bad, was it?' he sneered as he buttoned his flies and buckled the belt at his waist. 'All you have to do, girl, is keep me happy and the wages will keep on coming. I'd not mention it to that crippled husband of yours, if I were you, not if you want to keep him safe. Mind you . . .' and here he leaned down close to where she lay curled up in pain, desperately trying to stifle her whimpering. Millie could smell the stink of his genitals, see the hairs in his broad nostrils as he breathed heavily upon her '. . . if'n you don't come up to scratch, then you're out. You have to please me with the standard of your work in every respect, do you see?'

She saw very well the trap that had opened up before her and could manage nothing more than a nod of agreement. A great weight of fear had lodged in her chest as she realised with terrifying clarity that Kate had been right all along. This man was evil and pitiless in his demands, and there was no possible escape. Her children were better fed, but at what cost?

Over the following weeks and months, Ma Parkin would quietly withdraw, without being told, whenever the foreman appeared on the doorstep. She said nothing, kept her own counsel, but fussed quietly over Millie on her return. Millie accepted the old woman's ministrations without comment, just as she learned to endure and obey Swainson's commands with silent contempt. He never showed a scrap of kindness to her, or any degree of gratitude. He took what he wanted, making more and more demands as time went by, devising all manner of titillating tricks to amuse himself at Millie's expense. 'Suck it, love. Go on, get on with it! Don't be shy.' And all she could do was obey. He held the power of life and death over her and her children in his vicious hands.

14

With the coming of summer, Amelia and Kate began to go out and about around town once more, perhaps calling in at Robert's bookshop for something to entertain the children, or to John Brunskill's woollen and linen draper in the Moot Hall. Unfortunately, these were not always such happy outings as evil tongues still wagged. The gossip had reached that state of fantasy and make-believe which all malicious talk achieves in the end. Now, not only was Eliot an unfaithful husband who had foisted his mistress and bastard on to his poor wife, but she was actually complicit in the outrage.

'Who knows what goes on behind closed doors?' said the gossipmongers with great glee.

Old friends and acquaintances appeared embarrassed to see her, and would cross the road rather than speak to her, or walk past with their noses in the air. Never once did Amelia remark upon this, though it must have hurt her greatly. Perhaps she realised how utterly pointless it would be; like trying to hold back the tide. The busybodies of Kendal knew a scandal when they saw one, and this one was of enormous proportions.

Worst of all, her friends had stopped calling. Day after day Amelia would sit in the window of her parlour and stare out at what seemed suddenly to be a bleak and empty landscape. The room in which she sat, with its fine display of glass-fronted cabinets, pretty porcelain and pictures, became like a prison to her. She wanted to show off her lovely boy, to boast proudly to her friends about how he had learned to recite 'Mary Had a Little Lamb', how he could manage his own fork and pusher with very little assistance, and looked such a fine young man in his new tartan jacket. But nobody came. Nobody saw. Nobody listened.

Amelia would sometimes sit in the summer house, staring gloomily at the slow passage of the River Kent, not showing any interest in helping Eliot plant dahlia tubers for the autumn. Or she'd saunter down to Nether Bridge, so that Callum could watch the cows wading in the water and the workmen clearing the heap of rubble where the Malt Kiln Cottages used to stand. But depression was taking a firm grip and even her shopping expeditions were gradually curtailed.

Kate became deeply concerned and, unable to bear the sight of her poor mistress so sunk in gloom, made a suggestion. 'Forget the shopping trips, why don't you start your calls again? I expect that's what all your friends are waiting for. Why wait for them to call on you?'

Amelia's eyes lit up. 'Oh, do you think I should?'

'Yes. What harm can it do? You lost the habit from staying home to look after Callum, and somehow never got back into it when the wee boy got better. Time you did. At least you can leave your card.'

'Oh, you're right! Sitting here moping does no good at all. We won't let Lucy's ill manners spoil everything for us, will we, my little man? We'll beard them in their dens. What should he wear?' And in great excitement, she began to get ready. Not for one moment could Kate imagine Amelia being turned away from anyone's door. She was too lovely, too kind, had too much breeding and had always received complete respect from everyone, neighbours and servants alike; surely her mistress was far too nice a person ever to be treated with public contempt? Kate was disastrously wrong.

She had to go too, of course, to wheel the big pram, and so that she could mind Callum while the ladies took tea and chatted. Unfortunately, the afternoon did not go according to plan. Neither Mrs Gilpin nor Mrs Hetherington were at home apparently, although it was quite obvious that the latter certainly was as chattering voices could be heard quite plainly coming from the drawing room. The Greaves' maid accepted the card but made no offer to relay it to her mistress, simply setting it on the tray in the hall. This happened at the next two houses they called upon as well. At the Whiteheads', the moment Amelia and Kate began to walk up the path they saw a curtain twitch in the parlour, but no one came to the door despite their rattling the brass knocker for some moments.

'At least we have given Callum a nice walk,' Amelia said, determined not to be downcast by their failure. 'And I've left my card in several households. Perhaps that will help. But I think we'll take tea at home after all, Kate, don't you?'

By the end of the year, the Gilpins, Hetheringtons, Whiteheads, Greaves et al were further regaled with yet more fascinating news from the Tyson household. Poor dear Amelia Tyson, who had so foolishly allowed her husband to use her in that appalling way and suffered so much as a result, was said to have faded away to practically nothing. She was, apparently, most dreadfully unhappy, which they did not wonder at. Moreover, the girl was still living there, resident in the house together with *that child*. Quite shocking! And poor Lucy Tyson, Amelia's own dear sister-in-law, was still not allowed so much as to set foot in the place.

The matrons blamed Eliot entirely for Amelia's sorry state, not recognising the impact of their own malicious tittle-tattle or thinking to offer any degree of support to their erstwhile friend. And then, just as they thought they had heard everything and could never be shocked again in their morbid fascination with the Tyson marriage, they were startled to learn that poor dear Amelia had discovered she was not ill at all, but *enceinte*.

Eliot and Amelia were naturally both delighted and if their Christmas that year was quiet with no family at all present, not even the aunts, at least it was a happy one. Only Kate worried that perhaps with a child of their own they might reject Callum, and how would that make him feel? She ventured to mention this fear one afternoon to Amelia, as they sat with their knitting.

'As if we would, Kate! What do you think we are? Callum is our son now, and always will be. Another child would be a bonus, not a replacement.'

Eliot showed little of his concern for his wife in front of her, yet he was troubled, and fearful for her well-being. She did not have a good history where childbearing was concerned and he was anxious she should be properly looked after. He urged her to call in the doctor at an early stage, but Amelia only laughed at his fears.

'See how well I am! Now that I have Callum to love, and Kate to look after me, I'm perfectly fine, Eliot, don't fuss. This is women's business, leave it all to us.'

And so he did just that. He had his hands full in any case, now that he had to carry out Charles's duties as well as his own. The business had suffered a serious blow as a result of his brother's fraud and was less healthy than before. The accountants and bankers were concerned by Tyson's heavy losses, and anxious for these to be replaced. Eliot still took no pleasure in acting as a travelling salesman and this was not the moment to start, not with Amelia pregnant. He hated to leave her for any length of time but he was impatient to set matters back on a proper footing.

Perhaps, he thought, the problem lay in the vast number of workers they employed, not only at the factory but as outworkers as well. Although outworkers were still used for some tasks, some time ago Eliot had decided that hand-stitching each individual shoe was too expensive and had brought in machines to do the task at a fraction of the cost, employing girls to operate them as they were much cheaper to pay than men. This move had very nearly caused a strike at the time but the latest sewing machines were even better, and he'd met with no opposition at all to installing them. So the lesson surely was to stick to his guns, to do what he thought best for the company and to hell with anyone else.

Looking at the figures, he decided that their manufacturing costs were still far too high. They needed to expand and bring in more profit. The solution, he decided, was probably to buy in shoes ready-made. What's more, he would employ a salesman dedicated to the task of selling them. If this worked and earned him a fair profit, then costs could be further reduced by trimming down the workforce somewhat. Not that he would allow this fact to be widely known, naturally. Not at this stage anyway.

In April 1907, five months after Amelia's excited announcement of her 'delicate condition', Kate finally persuaded her to call in the doctor. He came with some reluctance since he found pregnant ladies something of a trial, being full of fears and questions over what was, after all, a perfectly natural process in his opinion. Generally, he thought it best to leave them in the very capable hands of Mother Nature until it became necessary to call in the midwife. On this occasion, however, he had stretched a point since this particular patient had suffered more than her fair share of loss in the past. It had come as a great surprise to learn she'd fallen with child again, which didn't bode well for the poor woman.

Now he put his stethoscope to Amelia's swollen abdomen and gave one of his non-committal grunts. He gave her a full examination, embarrassingly thorough so far as Amelia was concerned, and Kate was of course obliged to remain present throughout, watching with anxious eyes.

When the doctor had washed his hands and asked a few questions about whether Amelia was sleeping well, if she was eating properly and so on, he begged leave to withdraw and have a word with Mr Tyson.

'There's nothing wrong with the baby, is there?' Amelia begged the doctor as Kate plumped pillows and smoothed down sheets. She'd done nothing but worry ever since her monthly courses had stopped, despite her excitement over this unexpected development.

'Of course not, dear lady. Do not fret yourself. We don't want one of your attack of nerves, now do we? It is vitally important that you remain calm.'

'For the baby's sake?'

'Of course.' Again the doctor glowered reproachfully. 'For the baby's sake.'

'I do get most dreadfully tired, but it's all so exciting. It would be so wonderful to give Callum a little brother or sister.'

'Indeed, indeed.' Dr Mitchell glanced at the young child leaning against his nurse's knee and sniffed loudly, not quite masking his disapproval of this unconventional situation. So this must be the child from the poor house. 'You must stay in bed and rest, dear lady. Keep up your strength. Perhaps with some beef tea,' he suggested, glaring at Kate from beneath bushy eyebrows.

'Oh, don't say that. Kate is always nagging me to eat,' Amelia laughed. 'Now she'll be offering me beef tea every single day.'

'Then see that you drink it.'

The doctor left Kate to her ministrations and went straight to Eliot whom he found in his study. The doctor felt a twinge of pity as the young man rose to meet him with a smile of welcome on his good-natured face. Dr Mitchell was sorry that he must be the one to cause that smile to fade.

'I don't think I quite understand? What exactly are you implying, Doctor?'

'I am implying nothing. Rather, I am *stating* a fact, Mr Tyson. There is no baby, no child, nor will there ever be one. Your wife is not pregnant, she has a growth which should have been removed months ago. It's a pity I was not called in sooner since now, I fear, it is too late.'

'Too late? No child?' Eliot was staring at him in disbelief. He'd been equally stunned when his wife had told him of her suspicion that she was pregnant in the first place, but as her stomach had swelled, giving every impression of a baby growing within, he had naturally come to believe her. Now he was being told not only that Amelia had been mistaken, but that something was terribly wrong with her.

'You're saying that my wife is ill?'

'I'm saying that your wife is dying.'

'She will get better, Kate, won't she? I truly cannot imagine a world without my darling Amelia.'

Kate couldn't think what to say. Despite all the care the poor lady had taken to keep Callum safe, she couldn't hold back the inevitable so far as her own health was concerned. It had been all too clear for some time that Amelia was fading fast, but she and Eliot had been so wrapped up in their hopes and dreams of a child of their own they'd refused to see it. As her abdomen had swelled, so the weight had fallen away from the rest of her body.

'I'm sure she will, sir. Don't we just have to keep our faith in the Good Lord's mercy?'

Their conversation was being carried out in whispers as they stood together in the dimly lit bedroom, looking down upon the sleeping patient, each loving and grieving for her in their different way, both devastated by the terrible news.

'Are we being punished, Kate, for wanting a family? Is that the reason Amelia is ill, because we weren't satisfied with Callum?'

'Don't talk like an eejit,' was her immediate response, as brusque as ever. 'Of course she was satisfied with Callum. Who wouldn't be? The poor lady tragically mistook nature's signals, that's all. 'Tis a terrible shame, but no fault of hers or yours.' Kate blamed this abiding obsession of her mistress to have a child of her own almost entirely on the gossipmongers. Amelia had been perfectly content over the adoption until they had started brewing their malicious rumours and spreading spiteful lies, making the poor woman feel inadequate.

To be fair, she'd never for a moment believed a word of the evil which Lucy had concocted about Eliot and Kate, and which had spread with the speed of a forest fire. Amelia had maintained a firm conviction throughout that her beloved husband had been completely faithful to her, and that Callum was indeed who Kate said he was, the child of her own legal marriage. But the hurtful comments had cut deep and the battle had taken its toll.

'Oh, Kate, what would I do without you?' Eliot murmured.

'I'm sure you'd manage well enough, though thankfully ye don't have to try.' Kate's love for this man was such that she could even wish his wife would stay well, for his sake, just to keep him happy.

Yet gazing upon the desperately sick woman, breathing so shallowly in the bed before them, they each knew only too well they would soon be obliged to manage without Amelia. Dear Lord but she would be missed, Kate thought. Her kindness, her sweet smile, the joy she'd found in playing with Callum and reading him stirring tales of adventure which he loved, for all he didn't understand the half of them. Her unobtrusive skills at ordering her household, and the thoughtfulness which so endeared her to the servants. The way she would be adamant that Sunday lunch be served promptly at twelve so they could enjoy as much of their afternoon off as possible. How she would insist that the horses not be kept waiting should the family be going out in the carriage, when really it was Dennis she was concerned about, fearful he might catch cold. And never once did she complain to Askew about the piles of leaves he never quite got around to sweeping up. Without exception, they all adored her.

So how would they ever get by without her? Callum was three and a half now and all of Kate's fears and regrets at letting him be adopted had long since evaporated in the face of her mistress's goodwill. This was where he belonged, where they both belonged. Amelia had given them both a new life, made them welcome, a part of the family and been so anxious to share this lovely wee boy that it had been quite impossible to bear any resentment towards her.

Kate and Eliot exchanged a speaking glance, and, looking into her eyes, he saw that their liquid sheen this morning had nothing at all to do with their lovely misty grey colour, and everything to do with the unshed tears which trembled on the golden lashes. He'd wanted so much to believe all was well that he'd shut his mind to any other possibility. Now, as he looked into Kate's troubled gaze, he was compelled to face the truth.

★

The workers at the factory were growing restless, fearful that new machinery and bought-in footwear were beginning to affect the manufacturing output and would ultimately lose them their jobs. Already there were murmurs of disapproval because during the last months Tyson's hadn't replaced workers who'd left through illness, retirement or death. Eliot attempted to allay these fears but since there was indeed some truth in them, his efforts weren't entirely effective. He was depending upon an increase in sales to justify his actions, which so far hadn't happened, so he urged the young man he'd taken on to be responsible for winning orders to work harder, travel further and stay on the road longer.

One morning he arrived at the factory to find the men standing about in the yard, refusing to work. Afraid of eventually losing their jobs, they were out on strike.

'Where is the point in this?' Eliot demanded, standing on the front steps to address the men as a fine drizzle started, coating his head and shoulders with beads of moisture in seconds. It was a dismal morning with a grey mist enveloping the town, blotting out the famous view of the castle and lending another meaning entirely to the title of Auld Grey Town, which generally referred to the limestone architecture. It seemed, in that moment, as if the whole world, even God, had turned against him. The weather certainly did nothing to lighten Eliot's mood as he gazed upon their set faces. This was the last thing he needed with his beloved wife at death's door.

'You know that trade isn't good, profits are down with the extra competition we're up against, and that I'm trying to pull the company back from the brink after one or two other recent problems.' He wasn't entirely certain how much the men knew about Charles's attempt to purloin funds from the company and transfer it to his own business so glossed over that part and hurried on. 'Orders are slack and I'm doing my best to cut costs to encourage more. What else can I do? What more do you want from me? Why aren't we getting the orders we should? Tell me that.'

'Happen because the quality isn't there any more. Have you checked the leather recently?'

Eliot, who dealt with paperwork and was not a man to understand the finer details of different grades of leather, which of course his father had been, looked confused. 'What are you saying? That the company is going downhill because I don't know my stuff?'

'If the company's going downhill then we'll all be in the mire,' roared one man, and Eliot wished he'd kept quiet.

'Stick with quality,' shouted old Harry Crabtree. 'That's what we allus used to produce here at Tyson's in yer father's day. Quality.'

If there was one thing Eliot hated, it was to be compared with his father who'd spent his entire life criticising him. 'I believe we still do produce quality, Harry, but it is expensive and our shoes are not selling in sufficient quantity so we must do something else as well. Market other lines. We can't risk putting all our eggs into one basket.'

Swainson took a step forward from where he'd been lurking in the doorway of the factory listening to all of this, and confronted the crowd, a mixture of angry men and troubled looking women. He didn't like all these awkward questions about quality. Before you knew it, someone would be asking to see the manifests, chits and dockets; wanting to check the bends of leather ordered and how much was actually paid for them, as opposed to what was written in the book. So far, Eliot had not linked Swainson with his brother's swindles. Lady Fortune continued to smile on him as he was still an innocent man in his boss's eyes. And long may it remain so – long enough for him to finish feathering his nest nice and warm before disappearing over the horizon with his pockets heavy with brass. The Tysons weren't the only ones with gentlemanly aspirations. Now the foreman squared his shoulders and took another step forward into the mêlée. 'Happen you're suggesting *I'm* the one not doing me job properly, Crabtree, is that it?'

'If the cap fits.'

'And you can do better I suppose?'

Another voice piped up, 'What happens if this bought-in stock is all the customers want in future? What are we supposed to manufacture then with all these fancy new sewing machines?'

Eliot answered swiftly. 'Tyson's will always be involved in manufacturing, but it's true there may need to be a slight reduction in the work force. I'll do my best to keep it to an absolute minimum, I promise.'

'And what job could we hope to get here in Kendal if we do get the sack? At the sock factory, happen? Well, I can't bloody knit!'

Eliot lost patience. 'No, Ted, I don't suppose you can, so you'll just have to trust me, won't you? And if it's all a bit slow in coming right, then I'm sorry about that. I can't stand about here all day discussing how this company ought to be run. I'm cold, and wet, and damn' well fed up. I've enough on my plate at the moment, as it happens, not to mention a deal of work waiting to be done. As have you. Why not get back to it and leave me to sort out these matters as I think fit. When have I ever let you down before?'

There were a few shamed faces, boots were shuffled on the cobbles and murmurs of agreement voiced, the discomfort of the crowd palpable. There wasn't a man or woman present who didn't know that the mistress was ailing, and without exception they all liked her. She'd always been kind and cheerful, had a reputation for helping those in need without making them feel beholden or being in any way patronising.

A few women began to rail at the men, reminding them how hard it had been for the poor lady losing her bairns, and weren't they only making matters worse for the master? With set faces they began to drift back towards the factory, and one by one the men followed. The heat had gone out of their argument, the danger passed, but Eliot had felt the draught of their anger, and would not forget it.

15

The doctor was sympathetic but recommended Amelia should not be told the true state of affairs. Eliot at first protested. 'But won't she realise when no baby emerges at the end of nine months? Surely that is most dreadfully cruel? She has lost too many babies already, how can I allow her to go on excitedly believing that all is well?'

Dr Mitchell tweaked his moustache and said nothing, but the expression in his eyes silently informed Eliot that his wife would not survive long enough to feel the loss of another child. 'You have your adopted son. Let her spend as much time with him as possible. It may bring her some joy in her final days.'

And so as spring changed into summer, Callum would be taken to visit his mama each and every morning and afternoon, long enough to entertain and cheer her, but not so long as to tire her.

Eliot kept up his strength by working – form of denial, admittedly, as if by pretending that everything was normal, then by some miracle it would be.

Deep down he knew that he could never have coped during this endless, dreadful summer without Kate, who nursed her mistress uncomplainingly throughout a long and painful illness. She didn't seem like his Amelia now. Her lovely face had grown skeletal, there was a brittleness to her emaciated limbs, a yellow pallor to her skin.

But not once did she suspect there was anything wrong. She

submitted to their fussing, and to the enforced bed rest, for the sake of the child she believed she was carrying. Fortunately, in her confused state, she lost track of time and had no notion that the time for her confinement, had there actually been a child, was long past. The doctor had underestimated her strength. Both Eliot and Kate kept up a front of robust cheerfulness, as if they too were looking forward to the new arrival.

Even the servants, who of course had to be put in the picture, were firmly instructed not to weep but always to smile when in Amelia's presence. Mrs Petty spent hours searching through her receipt books for new delicacies to tempt a failing appetite. Dennis took to helping Askew pick vegetables and soft fruit to keep the kitchen well supplied, and Fanny was being unusually agreeable by helping to mind Callum whenever Kate was otherwise occupied, which seemed to be most of the time as she rarely left Amelia's bedside. She, poor lady, tossed and turned in the August heat. Once or twice Kate helped her outside so that she could sit in the sun for a while, but by September even this small treat was too much for her as she soon tired and asked to be brought back in again.

'You must be so bored, sitting here with me all day, Kate.'

'Not at all. Aren't I practising me knitting? We can't have His or Her Majesty, when the babby deigns to arrive, having nothing fit to wear, now can we?' Amelia herself had instructed her in the skill and insisted that a layette be prepared. Kate had continued with the task ever since, even though it was not needed. Privately, she'd made up her mind to take the garments to her friend Millie at some appropriate juncture. She always had use for baby clothes. In the meantime, it kept her hands occupied and provided Amelia with a giggle as she dropped and hunted for stitches.

'Oh, but it seems so long drawn out. How much longer, dear Kate, before my child is born?'

'Not long, I'm sure,' she said, hoping the stiffness of her lips didn't reveal itself in her smile.

'You do know that a child of my own will make no difference to my feelings for Callum? He will still be my beloved son, I'll love him every bit as much.'

Emotion held Kate silent for a moment before she was able to go on. 'Don't I know that already, ma'am? And doesn't he love you an' all? His dearest mama.'

Amelia's eyelids were fluttering closed again, the short conversation already tiring her, she seemed content. 'And isn't he the luckiest of boys to have two mothers?'

Kate did not pause in her knitting, in the hope that keeping her fingers working would stop the tears from falling. She sat on for another hour while Amelia slept. The afternoon waned, and as dusk began to fall Kate heard the front door open and the familiar sound of Eliot's voice, his footsteps striding across the hall and up the stairs, bringing the usual beat of anticipation to her heart. She glanced again at Amelia, saw her eyelids flutter and heard her whisper, '*Eliot?*' followed by that infinite, unfathomable silence which takes place when the anticipated breath never comes. By the time he breezed into the room, still wearing his overcoat in his anxiety to reach his wife, he was too late. She had gone.

Despite the long drawn-out end, Amelia's death still came as a shock to the entire household. It seemed to Eliot that one minute he had a beautiful, lively wife revelling in her adopted son, the next he was a widower, bereft and alone. He shut himself in his room and conducted his grieving in complete privacy, making it clear he had no wish to be disturbed, not for any reason whatsoever. Fanny would creep up the back stairs, tap on his door, and when there was no response, set the dinner tray down beside it and creep away again. The next time she came, the tray would still be there, untouched.

The servants went about their daily duties in doleful silence, mourning a much-loved mistress. Kate did not have time for such an indulgence, nor even to think. There didn't seem to be a minute of the day when she wasn't busy with something or other, not least looking after Callum, who kept asking when he could go and see Mama. Kate it was who washed her mistress's emaciated body, dressed her in a pretty nightgown and laid her out in the satin-lined coffin provided by the local undertakers, in the front parlour. Old Askew brought flowers in from the garden to set at its foot, and Mrs Petty carefully covered all the mirrors so that the devil couldn't capture Amelia's soul. Young Ida insisted on keeping a small fire in the grate, because Madam was so cold. Not one quite had the heart to stop her.

Kate tapped on Eliot's door and said that the undertakers wished to know if he had any particular instructions regarding the funeral. Should she call in the vicar to say a prayer over Amelia? Had he notified all of Amelia's family and friends, or did he want Dennis to take round a note? 'If so, have ye any black-edged cards in yer study we could use? Shall I fetch them to you, sir, so you can write them, or would you be wanting Dennis to give the message personally, from his own lips as it were?'

His only response was to tell her to go away and not to bother him with such trifles, 'I can't make any decisions right now, Kate. I can't even bear to see her like that. You deal with it.'

And so, grieving for the man she loved as much as for her lost mistress, Kate walked sadly away and found she had no choice but to take complete control. She chose the time and place for the funeral, even to the hymns she thought Amelia would have approved of. She'd no idea who to inform, or where they might live, but Mrs Petty listed the most important members of the family and Kate wrote out the cards, in her best handwriting taught to her by her father, for Dennis to deliver. And she personally delivered the notification for the *Westmorland Gazette*. If it weren't so tragic she would have taken a sort of pleasure in the pain this would cause to all Amelia's old friends who had so callously and cruelly deserted her.

It was shortly after she returned from this errand that the front door burst open and Lucy stormed in without bothering to ring the bell or wait for Fanny to show her card.

She roared through the house like a tornado, scouring the drawing room with an all-encompassing glance then rushing up the stairs to the nursery. When she found nobody there either, she ran back down again, only then thinking to look in the front parlour where she found Kate seated by the coffin in silent vigil. 'My God, it's true then? I couldn't believe it when I read the card.'

Kate genuflected and, getting quietly to her feet, respectfully indicated with a slight frown and finger to the lips that perhaps Lucy should lower her voice somewhat in the presence of her newly departed sister-in-law.

Ignoring her completely, Lucy marched over to the coffin and looked calmly in upon Amelia's lovely face, no longer lined with pain and suffering but almost as sweet and beautiful as it had been in life.

'It does not surprise me in the slightest that she's gone in this way. She was never a strong woman. Eliot shouldn't have allowed her to try for another child. A very dangerous thing to do, and now look where it's got her. Though how he'll react to her death, I cannot imagine. He'll be a lost soul, poor man. No doubt he'll give up the ghost, and the business, after this; hide himself away among his trees and flowers and paintings.

Charles will naturally have to return to the company and take up the reins again. Who else is there?'

Kate felt herself growing hot around the collar, anger mounting inside as she became increasingly enraged by the arrogance of this woman. How dare she march in and start dividing up the spoils while standing over Amelia's coffin? The poor woman had barely gone cold and already Lucy was pensioning off her grieving husband, itching to get her own grasping hands on the family company. Kate smoothed down her starched apron and clenched her jaw tight shut to stop herself from saying what was on her mind, though she tried to indicate with a frown how inappropriate she thought this behaviour. Lucy, however, was oblivious to the expressions and opinions of a mere maid.

'Is Eliot in his study or his bedroom? I'll just go up to him and tell him not to worry. Charles will deal with everything from now on.'

'The master has made it clear he is not to be disturbed.'

'I'm quite sure that does not apply to family.'

'To be sure it does! It's more than me life's worth to allow anyone to go up unannounced.'

'Oh, very well then. Pray tell him that his sister-in-law is below and wishes to speak to him.'

Kate went upstairs reluctantly, tapped on his door and, unsurprisingly, received the usual response. As she withdrew, to make her way quietly back downstairs again, she found Lucy had followed her up.

'I wanted to make sure you'd delivered my message correctly. Is he in?' Whereupon, to Kate's utter horror, the woman began to knock loudly upon the panelled door with one neat, black-gloved hand. 'Eliot! I know you are in there and not quite yourself, but there's no need for you to worry about a thing. Charles will take charge.'

'*No!*' The voice that bellowed from within was so loud and forceful that Lucy actually took a hasty step back from the door, startled by the power of it.

The door burst open and there he stood, hair awry as if he'd been tearing it out with his own hands, shirt collarless and open at the neck where the stud should be. His waistcoat too hung open and his trousers looked as if he'd slept in them, which he probably had. 'Charles will do no such thing. You can tell him to leave me alone. Everything is in hand.'

Lucy was flabbergasted. Kate hid a small smile, gaining both reassurance and a deep sense of pride from his instinctive and violent objection to Lucy and Charles taking control. But then, why should they imagine Eliot to be a weak man simply because he had a heart? Something the rest of his family clearly did not possess.

'Someone in authority should be here to oversee matters. There are things which need to be arranged . . .'

'Go home, Lucy. Mind your own business. Kate will see to everything.'

The look of horror on her face was a picture, and Kate suffered a fit of coughing which served to cover a most disrespectful and inappropriate spurt of laughter.

'I never heard of such a thing. Never in my entire life! A nursemaid dealing with a family funeral? Utterly preposterous! And you have no right to speak to me like that. No right at all. I know you are grieving, Eliot, but I think you have quite lost your mind. If you imagine we will stand by and say nothing while this doxy here . . .'

'Go home *now*, Lucy. This minute, if you please, before I personally dispatch you down those stairs.'

'Well, really!' And turning to Kate, 'Don't think you have won, miss,' Lucy hissed, inches from Kate's face. 'You haven't heard the last of this.' Casting her a final and furiously withering glare, Lucy marched down the stairs in a huff, clearly intent upon summoning reinforcements.

Later that night, as Kate was on her way to bed, she heard the unmistakable sounds of weeping coming from the master bedroom. She hovered undecided for some long moments, wondering whether she should intervene, longing to offer him comfort but fearful of being seen to intrude. Men so hated to be caught out in these private moments, and nothing could be more so than grieving for a much-loved wife. At length she proceeded to her own room but found it impossible to sleep. Kate kept thinking about Eliot enduring his grief alone, but what could she do? She was, as Lucy had quite rightly pointed out, only the nursemaid and shouldn't really be dealing with such matters as organising a funeral for the mistress, let alone offering comfort to the master.

And then she heard his footsteps on the landing, and was out of bed like a shot.

'Were you wanting something, sir?'

He was standing at the top of the stairs as if he'd set off with some purpose in mind and had quite forgotten what it was. Kate had quickly pulled on a robe over her nightgown though the September night was warm. Now she asked if he would perhaps like her to bring him a glass of milk, or a small nightcap of his favourite Irish whiskey if he preferred.

He shook his head in a dazed sort of way, showing no real indication of having understood or even heard the question, and still seemed undecided about where he was going, or why. Kate went to his side and took hold of his arm. 'Sure now, 'tis no time to be wandering around the house. Let me see ye back to yer room, sir, shall I?'

Once back inside the bedroom he slumped into a chair while she quickly tidied the bed, which revealed all too clearly what a restless night he'd suffered. The candle on the nightstand guttered and died, and she had to hunt about for a new one and the matches to light it. When the pillows were plumped, the sheets smoothed and turned back, she went and took him by the arm, giving him a little shake to encourage him back to bed. Eliot made no protest as she led him across the room and sat him down on the feather mattress while she attempted to pull off his boots. He was still fully clothed in his shirt and trousers, although he'd removed the waistcoat. Kate considered it too immodest for her to suggest he should undress properly and get into his night attire, confining her attention to the boots. Kneeling, she struggled with the hooks and buttons in the dark and it was as she got to her feet that he seemed to become aware of her for the first time.

'Kate? Is it you?'

'It is so. Now just you lie down and try not to think of anything. Don't ye need yer sleep, with all you have to face over the next few days?'

'Ah, Kate, thank God you didn't leave me too. What would I do without you?' He pulled her close, drawing her between his knees and laying his head against her flat stomach while his arms encircled her. She was stunned but didn't like to protest, the poor man surely being beside himself with grief. Filled with pity, she stroked his dark curls, gently patted his broad shoulders, and as she felt them shudder, held him tight like a child. She could feel the power of his thighs pressing at either side of her hips, his hands at her back, smoothing gently up and down in a rhythm that was producing a most odd effect upon her, weakening her already tired limbs and making her heartbeat suffer odd little stops and starts.

She was never sure afterwards how it came about but somehow she was sinking on to the bed beside him and he was kissing her: her throat, her eyes, her mouth, with an urgency that was growing more fevered by the second. There was an impatience in both of them, and nothing could possibly have prevented what followed, nor allow them time to consider the rightness or otherwise of their actions. Their agony of need was too great to allow pause for thought, too hectic and flushed with the raw necessity to prove that life would prevail and beat back the shadows of death. The cotton robe and nightgown were discarded in seconds and Kate groaned with pleasure as his hands slid over her bare skin, cupped and fondled her breasts. Hadn't she longed for this? Hadn't she ached for him to love her?

Kate was no virgin and not unused to a man's attentions but this was a coupling the like of which she had never known before. Perhaps because she wanted him so much, he brought her to a pitch of desire she could not have imagined possible. As he entered her, she wrapped her legs about his waist, instinctively rocking with the rhythm of his body, discovering a new intensity of joy so that by the time he slumped upon her, sticky with sweat and passion, she was there before him. But then hadn't she loved him for what seemed like a lifetime already?

It was the first streaks of dawn peeping in through the curtains which woke her. His arm was still around her, cradling and protecting her, or so it seemed, and yet his head was turned away, sunk into the pillow. In that instance Kate felt such a rush of love and warmth for Eliot it almost overwhelmed her. She longed to reach out and wake him, to bring him to her again, but sanity slowly surfaced. What had she done? She shouldn't be here at all, not in the master's bed. But then if she'd helped to ease that pain a little, where was the harm? Kate looked down tenderly upon the sleeping figure beside her. So long as she had the good sense not to read too much into this. Hadn't he only made love to her because he was out of his mind from grief over losing his wife? Not for a minute must she imagine that it meant anything else.

Kate slid hastily, almost guiltily, from his bed, fumbled about the floor till she found her nightclothes and, snatching them up in her arms, fled from the room, not even pausing to put them on. She was across the landing and into her own room in a trice, quite certain no one had seen her.

On her way down from the attic to commence her morning duties, Fanny paused when she heard footsteps on the first landing, not wishing to meet the master if he was going to the bathroom to relieve himself. Leaning over the banister she caught a fleeting glimpse of Kate's fleeing, naked figure, and watched, open-mouthed, as she disappeared from view.

Reinforcements arrived later that same morning in the shape of the two maiden aunts who moved in lock, stock and barrel, ready and willing to take charge, indeed positively relishing the challenge. There was nothing they thrived on more than bad news, and Vera's customary funereal black for once was entirely appropriate. Cissie too looked uncharacteristically tidy in an ankle-length black coat and large feathered hat. Both ladies were also swathed in fox fur wraps, despite the heat of an Indian summer.

'Good thing they're here,' Fanny said to Dennis as they enjoyed a quick cuddle in the glasshouse while she collected a few tomatoes for lunch. She'd told him what she'd seen earlier, and he'd been as startled as she, though had warned her to keep mum and say nothing to anyone else.

'We'll keep this under our hats, girl. 'Oo knows when a bit of useful information like that might come in handy?'

Fanny, itching to spread this titillating tidbit and announce Kate's immorality to the world by putting a notice in the

Westmorland Gazette, did her best to smother her disappointment, 'I wouldn't put it past that little madam to think she can get her feet under the master's table, as well as in his bed. If that's the case, the aunts will soon put her right. Selling her child were bad enough. Worming her way into becoming the next Mrs Tyson before the mistress is even decently buried is even worse, to my mind. Nasty piece of baggage she's turned out to be. And if she thinks she can smarm her way round me, she's another think coming.'

Gossip flared again among Amelia's fickle devotees in the tea rooms and shopping halls of Kendal who wholeheartedly agreed that it was far better Vera and Cissie should supervise the delicate matter of the funeral and poor dear Amelia's affairs rather than that dreadful little guttersnipe from the Kirkland Poor House. 'Vera will soon lick things into shape.'

It was certainly true that as the two maiden ladies swept into the hall, and Dennis staggered after them with their trunks, Gladstone bag, several small brown leather suitcases and innumerable hat boxes, Mrs Petty was heard to remark: 'May the Good Lord save us! The aunts have come to stay.'

16

The funeral took place on a typically dismal, wet Lakeland day, with gloomy black clouds and rain hammering on the black umbrellas of the bereaved gathered in the graveyard, and on the shiny roofs of the many carriages. The service, held in the Parish Church, had been planned by the aunts down to the last detail. They discarded most of the hymns Kate had chosen and selected different ones, half of which Amelia had probably never liked or even known. They permitted only white flowers in tasteful wreaths, and printed a special Order of Service filled with prayers and psalms and lengthy readings. Mrs Petty said that if the service finished before midnight, it would be a miracle.

Afterwards they partook of ham and a cold collation, laid on by the housekeeper and her trusty staff, using Amelia's best Royal Worcester porcelain and her finest lace tablecloth. Nobody, Mrs Petty declared with pride in her voice and a challenging glint in her eye, could say that the mistress hadn't been laid to rest with all due honour.

Dozens of Amelia's friends and family, far more than she'd possessed in life, or at least since that fateful Christmas, turned up to remember her in death. Everyone remarked upon how splendid a funeral it was, how suitable was the hymn, 'O Perfect Love', and such a pity nobody had known the words to the others. What a memorable sermon the vicar had given, and how appropriate of him to recall the dear departed's sweet generosity and many acts of charity, her simple and honest desire to help the weak and unfortunate.

It seemed that Amelia had ceased even to have a name now, and certainly no one wished to recall her most generous act of all: that of taking a poor house child into her home to offer him a new life, and even more generously accepting the mother as well.

There was one person missing from this solemn occasion: Kate herself. She'd never expected to go since Callum was far too young to attend his mama's funeral, and so naturally she must remain behind with him in the nursery. When Eliot had called her to his study shortly after breakfast, Kate assumed that was what he was about to say.

'Ah, Kate. Do come in.' She entered with some degree of embarrassment, unwilling to meet his eye in view of what had taken place between them just a few nights before. He didn't offer her a chair and seemed equally reluctant to meet her gaze, standing with his back to her at the window while he addressed the rain-filled sky. 'I've been thinking about Callum. He's far too young to . . .'

'I know, don't worry. I've arranged with Mrs Petty that he and I will stay and keep an eye on things in the kitchen while you're all at the funeral. We reckon that'll be for the best.' And prevent all those busybodies from gawping at him, she thought, and gossiping behind their hands.

'Ah, good, good.' Eliot seemed to breathe a sigh of relief, followed by a long drawn out silence. So long, in fact, that Kate wondered if he'd forgotten she was still in the room, or if she should quietly go now that this matter had been settled. But then suddenly he turned around and made for the door. With his hand on the knob, he again addressed her with his back to her. 'About the other night. I'm not sure how . . . I mean, I never meant . . . I really cannot think what came over me. I've no wish for you to take all the blame upon yourself. It was quite outrageous behaviour on my part, and after all my promises that you would be safe under my roof. I humbly apologise.'

He was apologising for making love to her! That somehow seemed the most shaming part of it. He'd said he didn't know what had come over him. He half turned towards her and she willed him to look directly at her, but he kept his gaze fixed somewhere above her left ear.

Kate felt as if her heart were sinking to her boots, even as she longed to run to him on a flush of warm sympathy, to ease his private torment, to hold him tight in her arms and tell him that it didn't matter, that she loved him and had wanted him to make love to her. She'd known all along, of course she'd known, that it was all a mistake. How could it have been otherwise? His words cut deep, but what else could he say?

' 'Tisn't anything to be ashamed of. We were both at fault, so we were, there's nothing to apologise for. I understand perfectly. It was the pain of – of everything. Of losing your lovely wife.'

'That's it. That's it exactly. A momentary lapse. And I swear it won't happen again.'

It was Amelia he wanted, Amelia he'd longed to hold in his arms and make love to, but Amelia was dead. And so he'd used Kate instead.

Oh, but she really didn't mind. Loving him as she did, Kate had thought of little else since. She would like him to make love to her every day of her life, and couldn't help but hope that he might come to feel the same way one day. For all the inappropriateness of the timing, and the huge differences in their station, it had been lovely to have him hold her and love her like that. Blissful. She'd do it all again, so she would. Didn't care what anyone thought. Kate just wanted him, in any way he was prepared to accept her.

She gave a bleak little nod, unwilling to trust her own voice. After another achingly long pause Kate became aware that he was at last looking at her properly and wished with all her heart that he wouldn't, not now there were tears threading their way down her face. He pulled open the door, a brisk tone coming into his voice. 'Thank you for being so understanding. Whatever there is between us, Kate . . . *was* between us . . . it can't be allowed to flourish. It wouldn't be right.'

She cleared her throat. 'No, sir.'

'I dare say I should ask you to leave, and, in different circumstances, that probably would be for the best. But since the fault was not entirely yours, and because Callum needs you, I hope you'll stay.'

'Leave?' Such a thing had never crossed her mind. Why would he send her away because of something neither of them had been able to help? She looked into his face, startled, and it was then that their eyes finally met and she saw in his no warmth at all, but rather a coldness that shocked her. His chestnut eyes had turned hard, like a pair of polished pebbles, and there was a cynical twist to his wide mouth.

'The last thing we must do is add fuel to the gossips' fire, eh, Kate?'

She could think of nothing to say to this. 'I'd best go and see to Callum, if you'll excuse me, sir.'

'Yes, Kate, do that.' And she practically ran from his presence, wincing as she heard the study door crash to behind her.

If Eliot was sorry, Kate was even sorrier. She stood at the window with tears in her eyes and watched the carriages draw away, so that the scene before her wobbled and spun giddily, as if washed away by the rain. The tears continued to run unchecked down her face till she was sobbing uncontrollably into her sodden handkerchief. Oh, but she would miss Amelia, she surely would. No one could have asked for a better mistress, nor a kinder lady with a sweeter nature.

And yet the night before Amelia had properly been laid to rest, Kate had made love to her grieving husband. How could she have been so heartless, so cruel? What had she been thinking of? That was the trouble, of course. She hadn't been thinking at all, she'd been acting purely on instinct, as had he. Now they must both live with their guilt.

Kate knew she'd been dazzled and astonished by his sudden need for her, wanting only to please him, to show him how much she cared. She'd felt unworthy of his love, grateful almost that he'd even noticed she existed. But of course it hadn't been her that he was loving at all, only his dead wife.

And if, because of a silly family squabble, the wagging tongues of Kendal could so destroy a lovely, innocent lady who had done no wrong save to take a wee boy to her heart and believe in a good and faithful husband, what would they say if they discovered what had taken place that night? In a way, Kate had justified their malice by making the gossip come true. Their former cruelty, lack of charity, and holier-than-thou attitude towards the sanctity of marriage would be as nothing compared to how they would react if they learned that a servant, a girl from Poor House Lane, had pretensions to become the mistress, or even, in her secret dreams, the wife of Eliot Tyson.

He was right. She should leave. Were it not for Callum belonging here, in this home, with the man who had adopted him, Kate would pack their bags and go before ever the family returned from the funeral. As it was, she was trapped, by her love for him, and by the shamefulness of her behaviour.

It was a relief for them when the day was finally over and all visitors and mourners, save for the two aunts, finally left. Kate kept her mind firmly away from troubling thoughts by working extra hard. In the days following, as well as minding Callum, she helped Fanny clean and tidy and restore order to the house. The housemaid had withdrawn into one of her sulks again, for no reason Kate could think of; barely uttering a word despite their working together changing bed linen and laying bedroom fires, dusting and polishing, not to mention the acres of carpet needing to be beaten and swept after all the food that had been trodden in. Kate assumed she too was grieving for the mistress, and made no comment.

Fortunately, there was little time to be morbid, as operations were directed by Aunt Vera with the precision of a military operation.

'Don't you gels imagine for one minute that you can start slacking, simply because your poor dear mistress has sadly departed this life. Standards must still be maintained.'

'Yes, Miss Vera,' said Fanny, bobbing a curtsey.

'Miss Tyson to you. Though you can address my sister as Miss Cissie, to avoid confusion.'

'Thank you, Miss, er – um, Miss Tyson, ma'am.'

The two maiden ladies swooped upon the task of clearing Amelia's room with relish, urging Fanny and Kate to help sort her gowns, day clothes, footwear, even her nightgowns and underwear into different piles. Those which could be distributed amongst the cousins and other family members; those which might be used by carefully selected, needy individuals. The remainder were gathered into an indiscriminate heap to be taken along to the Union Workhouse. Kate grimaced at the thought but selected a few useful items for Millie and secreted these away in her room. She meant to go and see her friend soon. She hadn't seen her in months, not since Amelia had fallen ill. She would take these few items, and the knitted baby clothes.

Lucy arrived one morning with her three children and

nanny in tow for the express purpose of picking over the prime items in Amelia's wardrobe. She gathered together large hessian sacks full of garments, shoes and pretty stoles and purses, even a selection of Amelia's favourite books and jewellery, calling for Dennis to bring the carriage to take her home.

The greedy madam, thought Kate, but prudently kept these thoughts to herself.

Later, in the kitchen, the servants were agog over the visit. 'I doubt there's anything left worth the pinching,' Mrs Petty muttered. 'You'd have thought they'd've given us first refusal, being part of the household like and after all the years of service I gave the mistress.'

'I always fancied that long blue velvet skirt meself,' said Fanny. 'Ooh, and I would've loved that taupe costume for me going-away outfit,' casting a coy glance in Dennis's direction. No date had yet been fixed for their wedding and Fanny was getting anxious.

Kate said nothing, thinking it all somewhat unsavoury to be sieving through a person's belongings when they were barely cold in their grave, though who was she to talk? Hadn't she helped herself already to Amelia's most valuable possession?

'Dennis says that Madam Lucy looked like the proverbial cat who'd swallowed a pint of cream. Relishing the fact she'd seen off her rival good and proper, and picked over the spoils.'

'They say as how Mr Charles in't doing too well at that new job of his,' said Askew, unexpectedly taking the pipe from his mouth to join in with this conversation. 'No one expects it to last.'

They all looked at him in surprise, as if they'd quite forgotten he could talk, let alone have an opinion worth noting. 'Bless my soul,' said Mrs Petty, 'if that's the way the land lies, I'd say that Master Charles will be back in harness at Tyson's afore the month is out. You mark my words, the master won't stand by and see his own brother go under.'

She was proved to be absolutely correct in her surmise, as was Askew. By the end of October Charles had paid a visit to his brother and a new deal was struck behind the closed doors of his study. Tyson's Shoe Manufactory bought out Charles Tyson's leather-dressing business, complete with its considerable debts.

'We'll just have to hope we don't all live to regret the master's generosity,' Askew said again, excelling himself in his chatter on yet another evening of below-stairs gossip. No one responded, but there were a good many thoughtful expressions.

Millie didn't seem to be at all herself when Kate finally got around to calling, but oddly withdrawn and sullen. She kept Kate standing at the door for so long, barring the entrance with arms folded about herself, that Kate had to ask if she was ever going to be let in. 'I feel a bit of a lemon standing here. Don't I even get a cuppa?'

They sat in the all-too-familiar, overcrowded little room that seemed to smell more strongly than ever of stale urine and mice. There was the usual gaggle of emaciated, lethargic children scattered upon the bed with its odd assortment of ragged covers and old coats, as well as on the clippy rugs on the earth floor. How many more children had Millie produced in the last eighteen months or so? she wondered. There was also a heap of leather pieces by the chair, as if Kate had interrupted her in the middle of her work, which she made a mental note to ask about later. Best not to charge in with questions, she decided, but come to it gently. She felt like an alien being or, worse, like a lady-bountiful come to visit 'the poor'. Millie confirmed this impression with her first words.

'I'm surprised you'd sink so low as to call in here now you've got so high-and-mighty.'

'What a thing to say! 'Course I haven't gone all high-and-mighty, and you're still me friend, I hope.'

'You've not brought Master Callum, I notice.'

'No, he's out with El— his papa, fishing.'

Millie rolled her eyes. 'Papa is it now, not Dad? And fishing, at three?'

'He's four now, actually.'

'Oh, *actually*, is he indeed? My word, isn't he going to be the little toff? Still, what would I know of such goings on?' She gave a half-shrug and, looking at her skinny shoulders, Kate thought she'd shrunk even more.

'I was wondering how things were with you, that's all?' When Millie didn't respond, Kate tried again, keeping her voice resolutely bright and cheerful. 'So, how are things then? I see ye've added to yer family since I was last here.'

'I had the twins last year, aye,' Millie said, with no inflection of joy in her tone.

'And ye've another on the way, I see, so isn't it a blessing that I called? Look what I've fetched for you and the babbies.' Holding out the parcel of clothes she'd so painstakingly knitted for the baby that never was, as well as a few items which Callum had grown out of, which she thought might be suitable for Millie's brood. Neither the Tyrolean jacket nor the tartan kilt was amongst them.

Millie didn't even bother to unwrap the parcel, just sat pleating the hem of her grubby blouse with her stumpy fingers. It was Kate who, with a tut of impatience, pulled back the paper. 'See, some warm little jackets and knitted trousers. Won't they be fine come the winter?'

'It's very generous of you, I'm sure.' Millie's voice remained cold, distant. Abandoning the blouse, she began to chew on her fingernails instead.

' 'Tis not at all generous. This is me, your old friend Kate, remember? When have I ever had anything worth the giving? I didn't when I lived here with you, and I still don't. The only thing I ever gave away that was of value was our Callum, and I wish to God I'd never had to do that. Aren't these from the mistress who recently passed away, much to our sorrow, and in case you didn't notice?' There was a defensive note in her tone now, a brittleness to her response, clearly adding herself to the list of those who mourned Amelia's passing.

'I – I'm sorry. I didn't realise.' Millie went back to pleating the shabby blouse, every now and then combing her fingers through greasy strands of hair and glancing across at the door every five seconds, as if she half expected it to open and reveal yet another unexpected visitor.

'She was a fine woman, so she was. I'll not find a better mistress in a long day's march.' Kate suddenly realised these weren't just words or false sentiment, that she truly meant what she said, and her throat tightened with emotion. Oh, but she would miss Amelia, she surely would.

And suddenly it was as if her mistress were there beside her, a voice whispering in her ear: What are you doing here, Kate? Didn't I warn you to stay away? I don't belong here any more, in this place which I once thought of as home, Kate thought.

It seemed that her life had changed radically since the days spent in this room, not only in physical comforts but in her attitudes too. Once she would have hated the ruling classes, no matter what. She'd never have thought to take their part or defend them, and now here she was, not only speaking up for her late mistress and mourning her, but sleeping with the master. At least, she'd slept with him once and would again, given half a chance. Now there was something she'd never dare tell Millie. Kate found she was blushing simply at the memory of that night, let alone the hopes and dreams she'd foolishly entertained of repeating it. At least until they'd been so firmly dashed by Eliot's apology.

She considered her friend with shrewd speculation, brow furrowed in thought. 'So, are ye going to tell me how y'are, or what's eating into you to make you look so much like a wet fortnight, or shall I go?' Kate suddenly glanced about her, at the familiar muddle, the muck and the mess she used to spend her entire day cleaning up. Something was wrong. Something missing. And then it came to her what it was. 'Where's Ma? Oh, no!'

'Aye, she died last back end. Took away by a racking cough.'

'Oh, Millie, I'm so sorry. You'll miss her sorely.'

'I will, Kate. I do.' And Millie stopped plaiting the hem of her blouse, stopped chewing on her fingernails to look up pleadingly at her old friend as if seeing her for the first time and marvelling at the sight of her, her own eyes filling with tears. 'By, but it's good to see you, love, I – I . . .' She couldn't finish the sentence before emotion choked her, and then the two friends were holding each other tight, both weeping and sobbing on to each other's shoulders, Millie for her lost mother-in-law who had cared for her as if she were her own, and Kate for her own sense of loss and tortured emotions.

The tears had been mopped up, a pot of tea brewed, and Millie had even consented to accept a slice of the cherry cake which Mrs Petty had kindly sent – largely because the children's eyes had nearly popped out of their heads at the sight of it, and it would have been far too cruel to deny them this pleasure despite Millie's objection to charity.

They'd chatted about Clem, about the hopes they still entertained of his getting a decent job and them finding a better place to live. Now, Kate was asking more pertinent questions about the pieces of half-stitched leather she'd seen on the mat. 'You're working for Swainson, right?'

Millie's face seemed to fold in upon itself, eyes becoming dark hollows of fury. 'I do it 'cause I must. Our Clem gets nowt, not with his missing arm, even though he lost it at a decent job, working in a factory. No boss gives a damn about workers' accidents. Why should they? All that matters is their profit, and Swainson is another such.'

'I did warn you, Millie, but I can see you've really no choice, not with all these babbies. But watch he doesn't ask for more. I don't trust the bastard as far as I can throw a ball of cotton wool.'

It was as if she'd unlocked a sluice gate. Millie opened her mouth, still full of cherry cake, and began to howl. The whole sorry tale came pouring forth. How he'd forced himself upon her, used and abused her however he thought fit, and how she was forced to submit again and again or else starve for want of work. And the worst of it was that she didn't have the first idea whether the twins were really Clem's bairns or Swainson's, let alone this one she was carrying now. Millie sobbed as if her heart would break, so upset she started vomiting and it took some time to calm her down. More tea had to be made as Kate sat with her arm cuddled about her friend, holding her tight until the storm of weeping was spent and, exhausted, she finally subsided into hiccuping sobs. Seeing that their mother had stopped crying at last, the watching children crept closer, a couple of them climbing on to her knee, hollow-eyed with fear.

'There, there, love, I'm fine. Don't fret, our Susie, yer mam's just a mite poorly today. It's helped a bit just talking about it all and getting it off me chest like. It'd all built up inside, now Ma isn't here to help any more. She knew what he were up to but never said nowt, not to Clem, nor even to me, never chastised me once. She'd just clean me up, mend whatever he'd ripped or broken, and mek me tea till I'd stopped shivering and got a hold of meself again like. Oh, but it's terrible hard without her. He's got worse now he knows there's no one here at all during t'day. He comes at all times and stays for hours, making me do all sorts o' mucky things to him.'

'Oh, Millie, you must tell him to stay away. There must be other ways you can earn a living.'

'Oh, aye, there are, and you know what they'd be. And happen I will go on t'streets in the end. At least I'd get paid for everything I did then.'

'Don't say such terrible things! I can't bear to hear you talk like that. So help me, I'll see his head on a platter afore he touches you again.'

Millie looked suddenly panic-stricken. 'Nay, don't you get involved, Kate love. You've escaped. I'm that jealous of you, but at t'same time I don't want you back here, suffering same as we do. Tha's got away and Ma were right to tell you to stay away. Say nowt. I'll sort it, one way or another.'

'But there must be something I can do, and Jaysus, I'll find it, so I will. And before you say it, don't ye fret yerself, I'll make sure that whatever it is I decide to do, it won't rebound back on you and yours in any way.'

Promises that were easily made, but Kate hadn't the first idea how she was going to keep them.

17

Aunt Vera and Aunt Cissie made it their task that winter to stay and support Eliot in what they judged to be his 'hour of need'. Their first duty each day was to speak to Mrs Petty and ensure that something suitable would be served to dear Eliot when he returned home from business (they never referred to it as the factory – far too common). The next was to ensure that the maids were made fully aware of their duties for the day, and woe betide them if the linen closet should become untidy or the brass fender tarnished.

Much of the aunts' own day was spent in sewing for the needy. When they were not thus engaged, Vera kept herself busy with her innumerable committees, at the church, the hospital, or the various charitable institutions within the town, and Cissie would often go off fishing or walking her pointers. Fortunately she'd brought only two with her, known as Napoleon and Josephine, although the pair created mayhem enough, digging up Askew's newly planted leeks, and leaving dog hairs all over the drawing-room sofas, not to mention unsightly scratch marks on the kitchen door in their efforts to beg food off an obdurate Mrs Petty.

Following a frugal lunch the aunts would permit themselves a short nap, generally taken in the drawing room, ensconced in matching wing chairs with their heads thrown back or nodding in time to their accompanying snores.

After this short respite, they would wake refreshed and set

about the main business of the day: paying calls. They kept a diary of the ladies they had called upon most recently, those amongst their near neighbours who merited more frequent attention, and invitations which must be issued, counting out the cards they would need for that particular afternoon with punctilious care before ever they set off. They prided themselves on not being in the least judgemental, although anyone who had not attended poor dear Amelia's funeral was likely to find themselves cold-shouldered, even if those who had cut her so cruelly at the end of her life were not.

Nevertheless, they were careful to confine their conversation on these occasions to more general matters, such as their charity work and the church, and avoid any mention of the 'domestic situation' at Tyson Lodge.

Kate found that with the aunts in residence, her own duties multiplied threefold, and the work she did to help Fanny was no longer voluntary but an expected part of her day. Maintaining a proper nursery routine for Callum who, as a lively four-year-old was much more demanding, appeared to be very by the way, given no priority at all. The aunts did not approve of him trailing after her while she carried out her duties of sweeping, bed-making, cleaning windows or brasses, which meant that he must remain in the nursery unattended for short periods alone, which greatly troubled Kate.

'What possible harm can he come to?' Vera would stoutly remark when once Kate expressed her reservations on this practice.

'He gets upset when he's on his own, and what if he should wander about looking for me and fall down the stairs, or have an accident of some sort? I should be there to watch over him.'

The aunts, in particular Vera, were privately of the opinion that delightful as the little boy might be, actually adopting him had been one step too far. Naturally they blamed Amelia and her obsessive need for a child for this decision. Nor did they wish to consider too closely the unpleasant rumours about dear Eliot which were still rife. Who the father of the Kirkland Poor House child might be was certainly none of their business. Men were a law unto themselves, after all, and the aunts didn't consider it their place to act as judge and jury on the subject.

The mother, however, was another matter entirely, and showed every sign of getting above herself. Actually writing and sending out the announcement of death notices, giving orders to the undertaker and attempting to organise poor dear Amelia's funeral without any prior discussion with the family, had been quite beyond the pale. Shocking! And imagining she could plan the entire day exclusively around this child of hers, and at their expense, was sheer impertinence on her part.

'Stuff and nonsense, girl. I can't be doing with molly-coddling infants,' Vera declared in stentorian tones, just as if she were an expert on the subject. 'You have your duties to attend to. We can't have you lolling about all day in the nursery, playing with your child.'

'Will he be going to school when he turns five, do you think?' Kate dared to ask.

'I'm sure I wouldn't know. That is entirely up to Eliot. He may well decide to send Master Callum away to school. Indeed, I would advise it. Certainly something must be done if the child is not to turn into a savage.' And having issued this dreadful indictment of Kate's son, Vera's small, solid figure marched briskly away, not a hair on her neatly clipped head moving an inch as she did so.

Charles was in deep trouble. His currying business had been under-financed from the start, and having been hit by the new process which left vegetable-tanning outdated and expensive, something he hadn't even seen coming, it was a miracle it had lasted as long as it had. The fact that Eliot had agreed to buy him out and take over the failing business should have been the answer to all his problems. Hadn't he wanted to return to the fold, to have his old job back at Tyson's? And he'd got it, admittedly with strict limits curtailing his power. He no longer had access to the accounts, of course, and all orders he made had to be double-checked and any decisions discussed with Eliot first. It made him feel all the more inadequate, unwanted and useless.

'Don't you trust me?' he would demand of his brother.

'No, why should I? The last time I did that, you robbed me. A person has to earn trust, Charles, not assume it by right.'

'I'm your brother, for God's sake.'

'Exactly. That's why I thought I could trust you in the first place. I was wrong. Have you done anything to curb Lucy's spending habits, or your own for that matter?'

Keeping two fine houses going was proving to be a considerable drain on Charles's purse, alarmingly so in fact, and yet it still didn't seem to make Lucy happy. It was certainly true that he'd managed to restrain her spending for a while, but the moment the takeover had gone through, she'd reverted to her old ways.

'Thank goodness for that,' she'd declared. 'Now we can get on with enjoying life again. We shall have the Cowpers over for dinner on Sunday.'

Charles attempted to explain that money was still tight, that in fact none had actually changed hands. Eliot had simply agreed to take the debts of the currying business off his hands, which was a great relief but did nothing to solve the problem of their other substantial debts, which seemed to be growing at an alarming rate, nor pay off the mortgage.

Lucy either didn't listen or wasn't interested. She set about furnishing and equipping the lakeside house to the highest of standards. He had the latest bill in his hand at this moment: two hundred guineas for a fine mahogany dining table, not even counting the set of twelve chairs. He couldn't imagine how one piece of furniture could cost so much, and why on earth they would ever need to seat twelve people in any case.

And that wasn't the only one. He flicked through several more bills that he kept stuffed in a box at the back of his desk which were equally frightening. Fifty pounds for a Persian rug. Seventy-five each for some gilt chairs she'd had specially made in the French style. And then there were any number of pieces of Chinese porcelain, tapestries for the walls, screens, mirrors and pretty little tables which had happened to catch her eye. The house looked more like a French château than a Westmorland country home. She'd even started looking at masterpieces and talked of buying a Gainsborough or Reynolds, a prospect which made his blood run cold.

Charles felt close to despair. He picked up a letter from his bank manager, read it through one more time then tore it to shreds and dropped it in the waste-paper basket. Where was the point in going to see the man simply to receive another lecture, particularly when there was nothing to be done?

Perhaps he should try one more time with Lucy. He began to rehearse what he might say, pouring himself a large whisky to help the process along. It certainly wasn't going to be easy but he must find some way of imparting to her the severity of their situation.

It was almost as if Eliot was avoiding her. Kate hadn't set eyes on him for months, following their painful discussion in his study on the morning of the funeral. A part of her wanted to avoid him too, and yet another part ached to be with him, to have him hold her as he had done that night; to have him need *her* and not confuse her with the memory of a much-loved wife. If only she could catch Eliot alone to speak to him about these fears. But he seemed to have forgotten all about Callum in his grief, and was making no provision at all for the child's welfare.

Fortunately, Callum was a good little boy. Kate would set him small tasks of reading or writing, or some sums to try, hoping that Eliot would find him a school soon, though one in Kendal. She couldn't bear the thought of her boy going away. And what would happen to her then? She would no longer be needed, no longer have access to her son. The thought filled her with fear.

Besides her concern for Callum's education and her own future, in order to keep her promise to help Millie, she must somehow confront Eliot with what was going on behind his back where the outworkers were concerned. He couldn't be allowed to remain in ignorance, and who else would have the courage to tell him but herself? Kate had been twice more to console her friend, reaffirming her promise to help but explaining it might take longer than she'd hoped. Millie seemed oblivious, expecting nothing.

Eliot always seemed to be fully occupied at the factory and Kate didn't like to trouble him too much. She went there once but had been refused entry by a sour-faced woman who told her the master was too busy for visitors and wasn't taking on any more operatives. Kate had objected, saying she wasn't seeking employment, that she was his son's nursemaid. When Eliot had appeared, looking fraught and bad-tempered, waving her away with a dismissive hand, she'd seen at once that it was a waste of time.

'Not now, Kate, not now. Can't you see I'm busy?' And he'd walked away. Swainson had given his supercilious smirk as he'd turned and followed his master back inside.

Kate had tried twice more, to no avail. Now she was

hovering about in the passage, hoping she might catch sight of him on his way home from the factory, when Aunt Vera bustled by.

'And what do you think you are doing here, girl? You should be upstairs in the nursery with Master Callum.'

'I was hoping to have a word with himself, so I was.' Kate winced, knowing her Irish brogue came out all the stronger when she was anxious.

'Haven't I told you a dozen times, there is a correct and an incorrect way of going about such things? Lurking in the passage, hoping to waylay the master and waste his time with a lot of foolish nonsense, is not the proper way at all. If you have any problems, you must address them to me directly, each morning after breakfast. Should I deem it necessary for you to see the master, an interview will then be arranged at his convenience, not yours. Is that clear?' Not waiting for a reply, Vera briskly continued, 'Now be off with you about your business. You are not paid to stand around doing nothing.'

Aunt Vera and Aunt Cissie firmly believed that domestic routine must be shaped to suit masculine needs and requirements. The fact that during Amelia's lifetime Eliot would always defer to her on most things not directly connected with business was quite by the way. His wishes were now paramount, or whatever the aunts imagined his wishes should be.

The aunts themselves had never done paid work, spinsters or no, as this would have reflected badly upon their father for not having properly provided for them, and latterly upon Eliot, their favourite nephew, who ran the family business in which they held shares. If this meant at times that they must deprive themselves of small treats and excursions, they looked upon this as a way of instilling fresh fortitude against life's adversities. They had never expected nor called for equality, and yet they were formidable adversaries whom few men would have had the temerity to cross. Kate certainly didn't attempt it now. She hastily apologised, bobbed a curtsey and beat a hasty retreat, aware of Miss Tyson's stern glance watching her every step of the way. When she returned to the nursery it was a relief to find that Callum was still sleeping soundly. She should have asked Fanny to sit with him while she went downstairs but the maid was being particularly contrary these days, never quite agreeing to anything Kate suggested.

Yet somehow, despite the two old aunts' interference, she must find a way to speak to Eliot alone. How to achieve it, that was the question.

Lake Windermere was at its most magnificent, the woodlands thick and lush and green, the summer days endless and golden. Charles sat watching the public steamers chug back and forth the length of the lake with the last of the season's cargo of trippers and felt deeply depressed, almost as if he were spinning downwards into a dark pit from which there could be no return. There was an actual pain in his chest, as if he were about to succumb to a heart attack. And was it any wonder? In his hand he held the bill for the completed conservatory, yet another expensive monstrosity Lucy had insisted on having built at vast cost, and for which the builders were harassing him for payment, threatening court action if there were any further delay. But how could he pay if he had no money?

In his heart, Charles knew that the evil day could be put off not longer. He must speak to his wife.

He found her among the ferns and lilies. She looked enchanting, of course, as always. Soft red lips that he so loved to kiss; shining ebony hair curled and teased about her brow, rising into a delightful coiffure that could only have been achieved by the new French maid. And her breasts . . . so full and round and comely. He almost reached out and fondled one there and then before he thought better of it, reminding himself that he had come to play the role of scolding husband and must stand by his decision not to give in to her charms.

'Sweetheart, there you are.'

Just looking at her lovely face should make it all worthwhile but somehow, even though she'd turned to him with the smile she used to give him in the early days of their marriage, when he was in funds, her radiance didn't excite him the way it had then. Perhaps he was too concerned by what lay behind the smile, that she might be about to ask for some other treat which would then assume the proportions of an essential require-ment to complete her happiness.

Before he had the chance to speak, to say a word of his carefully rehearsed speech or broach the subject which had become a nightmare for him, she flung her arms about his neck and, squealing with delight, said, 'What do you think I've found?'

His spirits plummeted. Dear Lord, let it not be another picture. He'd been thinking of sneaking the Constable back to the gallery to get a refund until he'd realised he hadn't yet paid for that either. How she charmed these people into giving her so much credit was quite beyond him, yet she never failed to do so. Presumably brandishing the name Tyson as if it meant he was some sort of walking bank vault. 'Not another work of art, sweetheart, I trust? We don't have the wall space.'

Lucy giggled girlishly. 'What a darling you are! No, no, this is much more fun. Come and see.'

She pointed through the arched, conservatory windows, and there it was, standing on the drive. A motor car. Not any old motor, but a brand new Daimler. 'Didn't you say you liked those best, darling? Well, I've bought you one, for your birthday. Isn't it wonderful? Aren't you excited?'

Charles thought he might very well pass out on the spot. Lights were spinning in his head, rose-coloured, green, purple, yellow and blue, all the colours of the rainbow pounding and beating behind his eyes, the only benefit being that they blotted out all sign of the expensive motor which was completely hogging his drive.

Lucy was still talking. 'I've engaged a chauffeur, of course, to go with it. Can't have my sweet darling tiring himself out by driving. Didn't Eliot always say that a gentleman never drives his own carriage? I'm sure it is even more true of the internal combustion engine. There, aren't I clever to have learned such words? And I picked all of it up from my *Woman At Home* magazine, would you believe? Well, what do you think? Are you thrilled?'

Charles managed to discover his voice at last. 'You really shouldn't have, beloved,' he said weakly, as if she'd bought him a new puppy and not this – this most expensive, unasked for, unexpected, *disastrous* piece of merchandise. 'But, dear heart, when you say you bought it for me, how did you do that exactly? I mean, how much did it cost?' He could hear his own voice rising hysterically and valiantly attempted to curb it, finishing more quietly, 'Where on earth did you get the funds?'

She kissed him lightly on the cheek. 'Now you aren't going to start getting all grumpy about money again, are you, pudding? Well, of course I didn't actually have the money on me. I never carry cash, silly boy. I gave them your name at the garage, and instructed them to deliver it today, for your birthday. You don't mind paying for your own pressie, Charlie Boy, do you? I mean, it's the thought that counts.'

Later, when Lucy went into the study to check why Charlie Boy hadn't come down in answer to the dinner gong for his birthday repast with at least twenty invited guests, she found him sitting looking out of the window, a great smile on his face.

Except that when she got closer, she found that he was holding his hunting rifle between his knees, and it wasn't a smile at all.

Charles's funeral was nothing like so grand as Amelia's. Besides, following on so swiftly after that previous sad event, no one quite had the stomach for it. Nor could it take place at the Parish Church since he had sadly taken his own life. A few stalwart members of the family stood around while he was disposed of as quickly and discreetly as possible, and then returned to their respective homes without another word. Charles would probably never be spoken of again, certainly not in polite circles.

Lucy was too numb to react. She showed no sign of hysterics, shed not a single tear. Whether she grieved for her husband in private, nobody quite liked to enquire. She didn't seem to hear if anyone offered their condolences, mumbling odd remarks about a motor car having to be sent back and how it was such a pity that Charles would never get to drive it now. The only spark of animation came when she was brusquely informed by Eliot that the house by the lake must be sold and she would have to make do with the one in Stramongate; she could very well lose that one too, if Charles's debts proved too heavy.

She did not take this threat lightly. Embarrassed members of the household tiptoed past the door of Eliot's study, pretending not to hear the shrillness of her voice within, only thankful that they were not the one suffering the blast of her temper. 'You wouldn't *dare* to deprive my children of their only home as well as their heritage? You do realise, Eliot, that he wouldn't be dead at all, if it weren't for *you*! And she'd stormed away, giving him no further opportunity to defend himself, managing to look both brave and forlorn all at the same time.

In the weeks following, life itself seemed to be taken on

tiptoe with everyone, servants and family alike, speaking in low, hushed tones, not quite knowing whether it would be proper to smile. It was the aunts who put a stop to this nonsense and came to the fore yet again, privately remarking how wise had been their decision to stay on. They certainly had no intention of leaving now.

'Dear Eliot will need us more than ever,' Vera declared stoutly.

'Oh, indeed, yes. To lose a wife *and* a brother. Dear, dear, dear. Poor man,' Cissie most heartily agreed.

'Charles was always a loose cannon, a wild boy who grew into an unstable man,' Vera stated in a tone which would brook no contradiction. 'It does not surprise me in the slightest that he chose the coward's way out.'

'Nor I,' agreed Aunt Cissie.

'All we can do is pray for his soul. Meanwhile there is work to be done, and life to be lived.'

'Of course there is. So true, so true.'

And having made their point most firmly, they got on with the task of living, expecting the rest of the household to do the same.

The death of Charles, the trauma of disposing of his Lakeland home and effects, settling his debts and so forth, had deprived Kate of any opportunity to carry out her promise to Millie, for surely Eliot had far more important matters on his mind. But she had not forgotten her pledge and visited her old friend regularly, growing increasingly concerned by her condition. One morning Kate managed to snatch a moment with Eliot before he set off for the factory. He looked surprised to find her patiently waiting for him on the landing, and not particularly pleased.

'What is this, an ambush?'

'I need to talk to you about Swainson. Didn't I say what a dreadful man he was? Well, now he's . . .'

'Kate, enough! I'm well aware of your dislike for this man but he is my foreman. So far as I am concerned, he does his job well and I'm not prepared to stand here and listen to tittle-tattle.' He made to walk on past her down the stairs but Kate grabbed at his sleeve.

' 'Tis not tittle-tattle, 'tis the gospel truth. He's after the women, so he is.'

Eliot drew in a long weary breath but the expression on his face was one of disbelief. 'And who told you that, I wonder, one of your women friends from Poor House Lane?'

Kate's cheeks flushed a guilty crimson and she saw by the way his eyes narrowed to ice-cold slits that she'd made a bad mistake mentioning her old yard.

'You've been there again, haven't you? I understood my late wife had put that dreadful place out of bounds to you. Are you saying you've risked Callum's health yet again by venturing down there? Have you?'

All Kate could do was hang her head in shame.

'I'm of a mind to dismiss you on the spot.'

'Oh, please don't, sir! I'm that sorry, so I am. It's just that my . . .'

'Have done, Kate, and get back to your duties. And leave my blasted foreman in peace.'

18

September arrived and with it that mellow softness so often found in a Lakeland autumn before the bite of winter takes hold, with the smell of leaf mould, sunshine and garden bonfires in the air. Life at Tyson Lodge slipped back into its familiar routine: the servants going about their daily chores, Kate minding Callum, still worrying about what would happen when he turned five, as he soon would do. Would he then have no need of a nursemaid? Would she be dismissed and a governess engaged, as Eliot had once implied might happen? She daren't risk pushing the subject of Swainson too hard, in case it backfired on her. The result of her last effort and Eliot's threat to dismiss her on the spot had chilled Kate to her very soul.

And still the two spinster aunts showed no sign of leaving.

Their favourite occupation was to call upon 'unfortunates', wearing a suitably gracious expression and carrying their parcel of charitable offerings before them like a flag of honour. The recipients were generally carefully selected women who had fallen upon hard times, and deemed to be in need of their time and attention. The aunts would offer a modicum of sympathy, larded with a great deal of worthy advice, largely of the 'converting them to come to church' variety, as the sisters firmly believed that poverty was somehow only inflicted upon the un-Christian. Occasionally they might agree to provide a small amount of cash to buy coal, a much-needed overcoat or

pair of boots, but mostly they preferred to make their offerings in kind as they didn't quite trust 'these people' to spend
the money wisely. And souls, they declared, were in any case
of far greater importance than bodies.

All of this put Kate in mind of her own time in Poor House
Lane, and when once they directed her to accompany them in
order to carry the parcels, she absolutely, and steadfastly,
refused.

'Wouldn't they all think I was lording it over them?' she
explained.

'Utter tosh!' Vera retorted, quite unable to see the problem.
'Are you questioning my judgement, gel?'

'Indeed no, Miss Tyson, but I wouldn't feel comfortable. It
wouldn't be right.'

Cissie saw her point at once. 'You'd be embarrassed, dear,
is that it, as if you were making yourself out to be better then
these poor people?'

'I would so. Sure and they'd think I was playing the Lady
Bountiful.'

Vera took off her spectacles and polished them furiously,
seeing that she had lost that particular battle, though she
wasn't prepared to let it go without a fight. 'It is my firm
opinion that the poor are an unavoidable part of the system,
one we are no more likely to be able to eradicate than we can
change the laws of gravity.'

'A decent job or mebbe a bit more book learning might
help,' Kate said, unable to keep quiet in the face of such pigheadedness. 'Isn't that what I want – a decent education and
upbringing for me own son?'

Both maiden ladies looked taken aback by this effrontery on
her part. They took their own more privileged position for
granted, as if believing they were immune from such disasters
as poverty. And didn't they do all they could to help the less

fortunate? Indeed, on a regular basis they attended lectures which fully explained the rules of philanthropy versus economics; how it was laudable to nurture and champion the inadequate and the weak, so long as this didn't interfere with the capacity of business to make a profit. Surely everyone knew this simple fact, otherwise how would Tyson's Shoe Manufactory, for instance, ever survive? Clearly, this girl understood nothing.

'My dear girl, education is for those who are worthy of it, not for every Tom, Dick and Harry.'

But there was no stopping Kate now. 'I don't see why not. And a clean, healthy home where a woman can bring up her babbies safe and well, and people don't piss in the yard, wouldn't come amiss either.'

Vera looked as if she might very well faint, this information being far too much for her, as if she never needed to relieve herself at all, let alone in a place where insufficient lavatories were provided.

'I fully intend,' she explained later to her sister, 'to make it my business to see Miss Kate O'Connor learns her place and stays below stairs, where she belongs.'

'Whatever you think best, Vera dear.'

'Unless, of course, we can think of some foolproof plan to rid ourselves of her entirely.'

Some time later, Aunt Vera confronted Eliot at breakfast with what could only be described as her implacable look. 'Cissie and I have found an excellent school for the boy.' Excellent in that it didn't cost a fortune, and its main advantage was that it was many miles from Kendal. 'It was recommended to us by the vicar,' as if that settled the matter, 'and the boy can start after Christmas which will mean that he'll no longer be in need of a nursemaid.'

Eliot sensed the onset of panic. He felt confused, as if he were being swept along by some tide over which he had no control. A tide of his own making, of desire and need, a lust which filled him with bitter shame. But it was the thought of Callum that troubled him the most. He was the most important factor in all of this. Whatever Eliot decided to do about the undeniable and soul-weakening physical attraction he felt for the boy's mother, he'd really no wish to lose his son to a school, however excellent, quite so soon.

'He's too young to leave home at just turned five. Eight is surely early enough to send him away. Perhaps we're rushing matters somewhat.'

'Nonsense! This particular school has a kindergarten department, making it part of their policy to begin educating children as soon as possible. He will come to no harm at all. Far better he is in professional hands than the uncertain care of a naïve young girl. Remember, we no longer have the benefit of poor dear Amelia to be a mother to the child.'

Eliot stared at the congealed bacon on his plate and considered saying that the child did still have a mother, but thought better of it. How could Kate be so described when she'd given up all rights to Callum once he'd adopted the boy? It was no longer proper to think that way. He'd been evading the issue long enough, unable to give the child the attention he deserved because of his grief, not to mention the problems resulting from Charles's suicide. Eliot sighed and set his knife and fork to one side. He really couldn't go on vacillating. It would be much better if Kate did leave, thereby removing temptation from his sight.

'Perhaps you are right.' He stood up. 'I promise that I'll give the matter serious consideration. We'll discuss it at some point during the next few days. We still have a week or two's grace, I am sure, before we must decide.'

The two aunts exchanged a speaking glance which Eliot did not intercept as he was already striding from the breakfast room. Aunt Vera hurried after him out into the hall, Cissie, her permanent shadow, not far behind.

'You mustn't delay making a decision for too long.'

'No, no, not too long. Dear me, no,' said Cissie.

'Places are at a premium.'

'Yes, indeed, at a premium,' agreed her echo.

Eliot snatched up his hat, bade them both good morning and fled from the house.

Kate was sitting on the nursery sofa one evening in October when the tap came upon the door. She set down her work with a sigh, fully expecting it to be one of the aunts come to complain about some unfulfilled task or other. They were rarely satisfied with her work and took every opportunity to point out her inadequacies which generally resulted in Kate having to do every job twice over.

'Yes,' she said with weary resignation as she swung open the door. But it was not Vera standing there, it was Eliot.

'May I come in, or is it too late?'

She glanced back over her shoulder at the child sleeping in the adjoining bedroom and, putting a finger to her lips, answered carefully, with proper respect, 'Come into the day nursery. He's asleep.' She closed the door between the two rooms and returned to the sofa, picked up her mending again. Keeping her hands busy might stop them from shaking, she thought, as Eliot drew near. To her alarm and discomfort, he chose not to sit on the rocking chair opposite but on the sofa beside her. She could hear her own heart hammering and was certain he must hear it too.

Kate cast him a sideways glance, watching as he sank back against the sofa cushions, intensely aware of his nearness. Oh, but he was a handsome man! Just the sight of him turned her insides to water, the way his dark curls tumbled over his brow, the mere scent of his cologne setting her senses jangling. He chanced to look up as she was surreptitiously studying him and their glances held. Try as she might, she could not tear her gaze away. Something flared between them, an undeniable spark of attraction that brought a crimson flag of colour to Kate's cheeks. Only when he smiled, breaking the power of the moment, did she manage to drop her gaze and turn her attention back to the sock she was darning, except that her hand was shaking after all and she was forced to set down the needle.

'Are you content?' he asked. 'Do you find your quarters comfortable? Are you managing all right – on your own?' He meant without Amelia, but couldn't bring himself to say her name.

Kate swallowed her nervousness and managed a weak smile. 'Yes, thank you. I'm very well.'

'That's good. More than anything, I want you to be happy, Kate.'

Oh, how she wanted him. How she needed him. It would be so easy simply to turn towards him, to let his hands caress her bare skin, let him have her and be done with it.

Which, of course, he knew.

She again addressed herself to the sock, compelling her fingers to work properly. She was puzzled and alarmed by this late visit, wondering what exactly was on his mind. Their conversation felt stilted and studiously polite. But then, was it any wonder? This man had turned her life upside down on two separate occasions: when he'd taken her son as his own, and on the night following Amelia's death when he'd taken her to his bed. What could he want of her now?

Kate might secretly adore him, find him the most exciting man alive, yet she remained wary of him. He kept her here, at

Tyson Lodge, because it suited him to do so. Was he now about to tell her that her services were no longer required, that Aunt Vera had persuaded him to send the boy away?

Of all things, Kate hated insincerity and hypocrisy the most. He didn't love her, so why pretend? Why act as if he cared whether she was content or not? Why make comments about wanting her to be happy? How could she be, loving him as she did and knowing that love was not returned?

His first words confirmed her worst fears. 'Aunt Vera tells me she's found Callum a good school.'

'You aren't going to send him away?' Kate looked at him in dismay, her gaze silently adding, And me too?

Eliot's response was a sad smile. 'You know this is all quite impossible. Having you here – after what happened between us. Don't you think that it would be the wisest thing, for us both?'

He saw the small shake of her head, the light from the fire catch a blaze of colour in her hair, how the translucent skin suddenly drained of its normally rosy, apple-fresh colour. Yet Kate's clear grey eyes were as defiant as ever, challenging him even now to brook her defences, if he dare. She didn't want to go, nor would she beg to stay. And then on the tips of her lower lashes he saw a tear. It hovered for a second before it spilled over and ran slowly down her cheek. Without giving it a second's thought, Eliot leaned closer and licked it away with his tongue. Her eyelids flickered closed. He heard her soft moan, felt her body tremble, yielding instinctively to his touch. And as he reached for her, he quite forgot that he'd come to ask her to leave.

The next morning when Kate woke they were still on the sofa, their limbs entwined, the weight of his body heavy and warm against her, the smell of the sun on his skin intoxicating,

making her want him all over again. Kate lay beside him not
daring to move, keeping her breathing slow and even, in an
effort to pretend she was still asleep. She feared that when he
woke he'd be ashamed, and that his sense of guilt would cause
him to turn from her again.

But what else could she expect?

Wouldn't the aunts be appalled if they knew how their
darling nephew had spent last night? No, they'd turn a blind
eye, of course they would. It was all too common for a master
to take his pleasure of a maid. Not for a moment would they
consider it a sign of love. Why should they? There was no question of Kate stepping into Amelia's shoes and becoming the
next Mrs Tyson. Quite unthinkable. Such a scandal would be
the ruin of him. If Amelia's so-called friends could cut her off
so brutally at the end of her life purely on the basis of a false
rumour, when the poor woman had done nothing wrong and
was entirely innocent, what hope could Kate have of them
accepting her? She would forever be looked down upon as a
servant, a pauper, the girl from Poor House Lane. Because that
was exactly what she was.

And wouldn't they take out their spite on Eliot, too? They'd
destroy him, and the business, just as they had Amelia. And
she could never allow that to happen.

Kate smiled softly as he slept on beside her, his face as innocent as a boy's in repose. She stroked back a dark curl, dropped
a gentle kiss on his brow. Oh, but she'd never meant it to
happen, not again. As he'd kissed her that first time last night,
she'd kept her spine rigid with the resolve not to crumble. But
it had proved every bit as difficult to deny him then as it had
that first time. He'd cupped her face with a gentle hand, lifted
up her loose-flowing curls and placed his mouth against the
beat of a pulse deep in the tiny hollows of her throat, threatening to shatter the last of her self-control. She'd tried. Oh, but

hadn't she fought against her desire, pressed her hands against his chest to push him away, despite an ache inside her belly almost too painful to bear.

'You should go. I – I'm tired,' she'd told him, in the way recalcitrant wives had done for generations. But she wasn't his wife, nor even his mistress. She was only a nursemaid.

He'd remained silent for so long, looking into her face as if the very sight of her troubled him, that she'd thought for a moment he was about to do as she asked and leave. But then he'd closed his eyes, very briefly, almost in a gesture of despair, and pulled her close, warm and safe in his arms. And then he'd kissed her again, very softly, on the lips. 'What is destroying me, what is tearing the heart out of me, is wanting you so much. I've been meaning to ask you to leave for weeks now, but I only have to come near you, to pass you on the stair, and all my resolve weakens, my resistance melts.'

'And haven't men wanted women since the beginning of time? What makes you think you are any different?' she'd quipped, determined to challenge him and to keep her wits about her.

'Don't you think I'm different, Kate? Don't you see any sense of decency in me at all? Any honour?'

She'd tried to sit up, to restore some sort of order to the hair that was falling down about her face and shoulders, aware of him watching every move she made. 'And why would I? You're a man so you're used to having your own way, are ye not? Isn't a woman powerless when a man has that need on him, and can only do as she's bid?'

He'd given a soft chuckle at that, his eyes merry with unexpressed laughter. 'You've never struck me as the obedient type, Kate O'Connor.'

'Have I not?'

'No. Never.' He kissed her then till her mouth was rosy from his kisses, exploring it more fully with his persuasive tongue. And in that moment she had known that she was lost.

Nursing these sweet memories in her heart, Kate must have drifted off to sleep again because when she woke a second time she was alone on the sofa. He had gone.

'Top of the morning to ye.' But no, there he was, standing in the bedroom doorway with Callum in his arms. 'Isn't that what you Irish say?'

Kate laughed. 'If we're feeling skittish, we do to be sure. Give him to me, I'll get him washed and dressed.' She suddenly felt shy to be here, half-naked, with the master and her son. She reached for her robe, pulling it on quickly.

'He was bored, all on his own. Let him play. Do you want your train, son?'

'Yes, please, Papa. Want my train.'

Eliot settled the child on the rug with his toys then went back over to the sofa to sit beside Kate, hands hanging loosely on his knees, his gaze never leaving Callum, 'I want it to be right for him. For Tyson's to be a good, strong business. For his future to be secure.'

'Sure and it will be.' Kate curled her feet under her and listened enraptured as Eliot began to talk, to speak of his plans for the business, explaining how he hoped to save it from the current depression it seemed to be in by buying a new warehouse.

'We'll keep certain classic lines always in stock, so that our customers won't have to wait so long. We need to keep their loyalty, and if they feel we have stock ready and waiting, we're more likely to get it.'

Kate was touched by his willingness to share these thoughts and dreams with her. Could he possibly be taking her seriously at last? 'You should consider designing footwear yourself. Aren't you the clever one with your pencil and eye for colour?'

He gave a disbelieving chuckle. 'Maybe I will one day. Who knows? For now I shall stick to the tried and true lines, for safety.' The smile faded, to be replaced by a frown. 'You know there are murmurs of war in the Balkans, that Europe is in crisis? We've had the assassination of the King and Crown Prince of Portugal, and the arms race continues to gather momentum on all sides – one can only assume for good reason. Do you understand something of this, Kate?'

She looked at him with blank incomprehension. 'Not much, but I hear talk in the kitchen.'

'As if that isn't bad enough, Tyson's has been badly hit by Charles's overspending, by my having to bail him out of the near bankruptcy of his own firm, and now by his untimely death. Somehow we have to claw our way back from all of that and strengthen our position before whatever is about to happen in Europe eventually erupts. It isn't going to be easy.'

Kate was silent for a long time, striving to understand what he'd said, to appreciate his confiding in her and to comprehend the implications. 'It won't help the business having that evil monster as foreman.'

Eliot gave a low groan. 'Don't spoil this moment with that old chestnut. Not again, Kate.'

'Old chestnut, is it? I can see why it pays you to turn a blind eye, making a fat profit out of the outworkers in order to rescue the company, but what about my friend Millie? She's trapped by that nasty little toad.'

She was on her feet now, needing to get this worry off her chest once and for all; to give vent to her anger instead of having it fester inside her as it had done for so long. She wanted to see that nasty, no-good Swainson who'd robbed and pawed her, beaten up Dermot and was now practising his wickedness on Millie, get his comeuppance at last. 'You think not? You think he isn't an evil little shite, do you? Then listen to this. I'll tell you about Ned Swainson, so I will, and you can decide for yourself if he is or not.

'The fact of the matter is that Millie, that's her name, me friend, is in dead trouble. I doubt ye've ever met her but she took over my outwork after I came here, and Swainson is up to his old bullying tricks again. Worse, he's making her pay for the privilege of working for Tyson's in ways he shouldn't – ways I wouldn't care to describe to a gentleman such as yeself. But 'tisn't right, and the man should be punished for abusing a woman in that terrible way.'

For once he'd let her speak without interruption. She'd told him all about Millie, what she'd been forced to do in order to earn a crust to feed her babies, and still he'd said nothing. 'So what the bleedin' hell are ye going to do about it, eh?' Kate challenged him.

19

Swainson had believed himself to be safe. With Charles gone, there was no one now to point the finger or cast any blame in his direction. He'd got clean away with his part in their fraud, which made him chuckle with pleasure. Admittedly the factory was struggling, going through some hard times, and Charlie Boy topping himself hadn't helped one bit. Swainson had been ready to fight if he'd been asked to take a cut in wages, although he wouldn't have protested too much had men been laid off, so long as his own job was safe. So Eliot Tyson telling him, with polite but cool detachment in his tone, that perhaps it would be best if he were to find alternative employment elsewhere, was like a bolt from the blue.

'I shall give you an excellent reference, do my utmost to assist you to find something which suits. And you can have more than the usual week's notice, a month if you need it, but I think it best you go.'

Swainson could sense that his employer was not relishing this unpleasant task, was clearly anxious to get it over and done with as speedily as possible. Yet what were the grounds for his dismissal? What could Tyson have on him? It riled Swainson to think somebody might have been telling tales about him; whether they were true or not, he'd like to know who it was. He made up his mind to be as difficult as possible. He'd certainly no intention of going quietly.

'And might I ask what offence I've caused, to be so summarily dismissed?'

Eliot had no wish to discuss so delicate a matter. He knew the man would simply deny it. There was no proof, after all, just Millie's word against his. 'Let's say I'm making a few changes. If Tyson's is to move forward in this new century, then we must dispose of old-fashioned systems from the past. Allowing dust and dirt and disease, which naturally come from working with leather, to be taken into outworkers' homes is counter-productive. We must modernise.'

Swainson could feel heat rising beneath his collar, spreading up his neck and jaw; the stink of sweat starting from under his armpits. Admittedly, he had no wife to go home to with excuses and explanations, no children who would suffer from his fall from grace, but *he* would suffer. He would lose face, and he couldn't tolerate the thought of that. The men would laugh at him, saying he'd had it coming, and he wouldn't be able to enjoy his little perks any more. Beaten by a mere girl from Poor House Lane! Oh, aye, he could guess who had split on him. That little Irish whore with the big mouth. He'd seen her round the factory enough times lately, seeking the opportunity to spread her dirty gossip.

'So what have I done exactly? You've never had no complaints before. If this is about that lass from Poor House Lane, she's had it in fer me ever since I chucked her. Had a fancy fer me once over, she did, but she's not my sort. Don't reckon she cared fer being cast off though, silly cow.'

'I really have no wish to hear details of your past love life.' It appalled Eliot to think of Kate and this man together. What was he thinking of, letting himself be captivated by her? Yet he had to believe in her. He must. He thrust the unsavoury picture from his mind as he got up from his desk to move to the window and look out over the factory buildings.

Swainson hated him for that proprietorial air alone. Most men of Eliot's class didn't show the least interest in business, being content to take the profit and leave the dirty work to the employees. Why couldn't Eliot Tyson be like that? Why couldn't he keep his interfering nose out of what didn't concern him?

Eliot cleared his throat before continuing, 'You'll be aware that I've endured more than my fair share of tragedy but I still have my son to consider and, as I say, there are to be radical changes made. I intend to build a warehouse for stockholding which is the most modern way of thinking, I believe. Extend the factory and then, in the fullness of time, outwork will be stopped and all manufacturing done within our premises.'

'Which you do not think me capable of organising. Why is that, exactly?'

A short pause and then Eliot turned to him with a bland and distant smile, 'I think perhaps we need new blood. Yes, that's it exactly. New blood. New ideas. A new beginning. Trade has not been good, as you know, what with the increase in the price of leather, competition from America, and rumblings of war adding to the scarcity of raw materials, not forgetting our personal difficulties. Losing my brother leaves me responsible for his family too, you understand. Money is tight. We must do something fairly radical if Tyson's is to survive.'

The man was lecturing him as if he, the foreman of this dratted factory, didn't understand the first thing about the industry. 'I already know all of this. You do realise I could go to one of your competitors, or start my own enterprise?'

'You must do as you think fit, whatever suits you best. Any future employer can come to me for the necessary character references. And, of course, you'll be provided with a handsome bonus for your long years of service.' There was a note of dismissal now in his tone, of wanting to draw this interview to a close, and nothing he had said had given Swainson one iota

of reassurance. What kind of character reference would that
be? he wondered.

'I feel I must object, most strongly.'

'I'm afraid there is no more to be said on the subject.'

'I could speak to my union. They'd have something to say.'

Tyson's frown deepened and his jaw set into a hard line. 'Not
an action I would recommend. Matters could get even more –
unpleasant were you to make a fuss. Go quietly, Swainson, if
you've any sense.'

And that was it, the end of the line with Tyson's, cast off and
dismissed like a pair of worn-out shoes, to be replaced by *new
blood*! Swainson was almost choking with rage for he knew well
enough who to blame for this decision, who to hold responsible. She'd had her revenge after all, the scheming little minx!
Oh, but they'd find they couldn't cast him off quite so easily.

Fanny tied a sacking apron over her skirt, picking up the first
candlestick and the bottle of silver cleaner with a weary sigh.
The aunts were constantly finding her things to clean and her
fingers were sore with all the scrubbing and polishing she had
to do these days. The work seemed endless. She'd leave this
Godawful place tomorrow if only she could persuade Dennis
to go with her.

Mrs Petty sat opposite, comfortably ensconced in her
housekeeper's chair with her skirt tucked up above her knees
and her feet soaking like fat white fish in an enamel bowl of
salt water. There was just the pair of them in the kitchen, Ida
having gone off to see Askew and bring in the vegetables for
the evening meal. In theory this was supposed to be Fanny's
rest hour after lunch, but Aunt Vera had insisted the silver be
done now, without delay.

'And clean enough to see my face in it, Fanny,' she'd
instructed.

'Silly old besom! Who'd want to see her vinegar face in owt? Sour as an old pickle.'

'What was that, Fanny?' Mrs Petty opened her eyes, dragging her mind away from the blissful warmth of the water soothing her bunions.

Realising she'd spoken her thoughts out loud, Fanny quickly improvised, remembering a tidbit of information she'd heard from Dennis only that morning. 'I were thinking of what a pickle we'd all be in if the factory closed. We might all lose us jobs then, eh?'

'Don't be foolish, girl. The factory isn't going to close, and no one's going to lose their jobs.'

'Dennis told me only this morning how there'd been a threat of another strike. That Jack Milburn and his cronies, Bill Grigson and Tom Perry, weren't they the ringleaders responsible for the last one? Well, they've threatened to call another if Swainson isn't reinstated.'

Mrs Petty leaned forward, all ears. The last thing she wanted was to risk losing her position, not when she was so close to achieving that little house she'd set her heart on, on the Fylde coast. Trouble at the factory had a nasty habit of rebounding on them all. 'What's this about a strike? Don't garble it, girl, draw breath and tell the story proper.'

Fanny set down the candlestick, glad of the distraction, and began to relate her tale. 'Dennis says that Jack Milburn were waiting fer t'master t'other morning, that pock-marked face of his hard as iron, demanding to know why the foreman had been dismissed. The master looked a bit flabbergasted like, Dennis said, but he didn't deny it and Milburn said he didn't recall the subject being mentioned or the union being consulted on the matter.'

'And why should he care?' said Mrs Petty tartly.

'Milburn says Swainson might be the foreman but he's also

one of them, one of the workers. "He might have his faults but the men are used to him. Gives us a fair hearing when we need one." That's what Jack Milburn said.'

Fanny had adopted a masculine tone of voice, rather fancying herself as an actress. Mrs Petty put a stop to it. 'Get on with it, girl. Fair hearing indeed! Did Mr Tyson not tell him there are some would disagree?'

Fanny nodded eagerly, enjoying her performance. 'That's exactly what the master said. But Milburn puts on that snarl of his and says the men can't be held responsible for folk what don't like him.'

'Nasty piece of merchandise, that Milburn. Stoke up trouble in a barrel of herrings, he would.'

Fanny lowered her voice to a whisper. 'Dennis said that at this point, there were a snort of laughter from someone at the back of the crowd. Then one chap, happen Billy Branthwaite, says, "And some women are mighty grateful for his care and attention." Can you believe it? What a thing to say?' Her eyes grew round with excitement. ''Course, Dennis says Jack and his mate Bill Grigson are probably in cahoots with Swainson over nice little sidelines they've got going for 'em, and other little jobs they do for him – like seeing to that Irish lad that time. You know, Kate O'Connor's brother. Gave him a right pasting, apparently.'

Mrs Petty had forgotten all about her feet as she listened with avid attention to Fanny's tale. 'Is this some yarn yer spinning me, girl?'

'Nay, it's gospel truth. Jack Milburn doesn't bat an eyelid over these ribald comments about Swainson. Says how the men were quite happy with him, that no one's bloody perfect.'

'Language, Fanny!'

'Sorry, Mrs Petty, but that were Jack Milburn what said it, not me. Then he reminds the master how it wouldn't do the factory no good at all if there were to be another strike.

"Happen you underestimate the strength of feeling among the men," he says. Then asks if he's had any complaints from the women outworkers, and t'boss says he hasn't. 'Course, who would listen if they did complain, Mrs P? Men never do listen, do they? My Dennis might as well be deaf, blind and dumb for all the notice he takes when I talk to him.'

'Get on with your story, girl. What happened next?'

'Well, then Milburn smiles, if you can call it a smile. With them nasty yellow teeth he looks more like a ferret. Says he's heard of no complaints. Not one. "What about you, lads?" he asks, turning to his mates, who of course all back him up.'

Fanny put on a sneer in imitation of Milburn's expression. ' "We'd advise you to let him keep his job then, Mr Tyson, for the sake of the company. All right? Best all round, wouldn't you say?" '

'And is he going to?' Mrs Petty breathlessly enquired as she attempted to lift her feet, now gone quite cold, from the bowl and dry them off.

'Well, he must, don't yer reckon, since he don't want the firm to go under, and seeing as how he's knocking off the nursemaid. So how can he blame Swainson for doing the self-same thing?'

Mrs Petty knocked the bowl flying as her feet crashed to the floor in shock, sending water splashing everywhere. 'He's *what*?' She really should put a stop to this impertinence forthwith, but hardly able to catch her breath or contain her curiosity, could only warn, 'Mind what you say, lass. You'd best have proof for such an accusation.'

'Oh, I've proof all right. Saw her wi' me own eyes, didn't I? Coming from his room one morning, naked as the day she were born.'

It took no time at all for this delicious morsel to fly all around town and once more Eliot felt the cold shoulder of hostility.

Whatever he had suffered previously was nothing by comparison. On that occasion the rumours had been entirely untrue, a complete fiction devised by Lucy's malicious tongue. This time he knew he had no defence. He was guilty. He had indeed taken the girl to his bed. He could not deny it. Friends he had known for years crossed the road rather than speak to him. Customers cancelled orders. Whineray asked if he might wish to consider resigning from the Town Council, which Eliot bluntly refused to do. Even his own servants either froze him with the ferocity of their disapproval or sniggered behind their hands.

Never having been the kind of man who took advantage of those in his employ, Eliot still couldn't believe how very stupidly he'd behaved, and deeply regretted his actions. The girl seemed to have bewitched him and he couldn't get her out of his head. Perhaps it was time that he at least got her out of his house.

It was a day or two later, a crisp autumn afternoon, and the aunts were out, either 'going visiting' or 'paying calls'. Kate was playing hide and seek with Callum on the lawn. There weren't many places to hide and she didn't allow him to go anywhere near the outhouses but he was still of that age when, if he had his eyes covered and couldn't see you, he believed he couldn't be seen either. Kate would count to ten, pretend to hunt for him and then catch him, swing him up in her arms and kiss his plump, flushed cheeks. His floppy woollen beret, which she had knitted herself and was meant to keep his head warm in the winter sunshine, would slide off and roll away, and then they'd both chase it, pop it back on and start all over again.

'Catch me again, Mammy! Catch me again!'

Ever since Amelia had died, she'd allowed him to start calling her by that name again, so long as they were alone. It was their secret.

The game came to an abrupt halt when she saw Eliot striding across the garden and, grabbing Callum up in her arms, set off quickly in pursuit. There were matters she still needed to discuss with him: not only whether or not Callum was to be sent away to school as the aunts had threatened, but also Millie's situation and whether he had done anything about that yet. This seemed as good a moment as any.

Kate caught up with him beneath the rose arbour. He used often to cut roses to bring into the house for Amelia during her long illness. Now he stood there uncertainly, clippers in his hand, seemingly trying to decide whether to cut a few late blooms or not.

'They're beautiful, so they are. Wasn't the Dorothy Perkins one of the mistress's favourites? Such a heavenly scent. I'm glad to see ye home early from the factory for once, I was hoping ye might have a minute to spare. But then, aren't I always pleased to see ye?' Kate couldn't prevent a smile from twitching at the corners of her lips, and a stain of colour coming into her cheeks as she recalled the night they'd so recently spent together.

He gave not a flicker of a smile, merely frowned and spoke in brusque, clipped tones, and Kate felt herself shrink inside at the coolness in his tone. How was it he blew so hot and cold with her?

'I'm afraid it is but a brief escape. I felt the need for a breath of fresh air but I must return shortly.' As if to prove this fact, he began to walk away, clippers still in hand. She ran after him.

'Please don't go! I'd like to know what's happened about Swainson? It's important that I speak to you.'

Still he didn't pause but rather lengthened his stride, putting yet more distance between them. Once again Kate was forced to trot, the weight of Callum balanced on her hip slowing her down considerably.

'Mammy, let me walk! Put me down, Mammy!'

'Stop wriggling and keep still. It's quicker if I carry ye.' Kate began to feel hot and flustered, angry that Eliot could so mulishly ignore her and quite out of breath with the effort of trying to keep up with him. 'Will you hold on a minute, ye daft eejit?' She must have lost her head to address him like that, calling him names, and without even a 'sir' or an 'if you please', but still he ignored her. He pushed open the garden gate and set off towards the river as if he hadn't even heard her. Kate really saw red then.

'*Eliot*, fer God's sake, will you stop fer a minute afore I drop him?'

He did stop then, but only to march back to her and snatch Callum from her arms. 'If you are not even capable of holding a child safely, then perhaps you're the wrong person to be taking care of him at all and I should dismiss you after all.' The small boy, alarmed by their angry voices, opened his mouth wide and began to wail.

Kate told him to hush and turned her attention back to Eliot. 'And what's that supposed to mean? What's got into you all of a sudden?' She could feel her heart banging like a drum, since she believed she knew very well. She'd become an embarrassment to him. He was out to find fault so that he could be rid of the problem of having her around, rid of the temptation. Couldn't she tell by the way he was glaring at her with such cold indifference, quite at odds from the looks she'd enjoyed from him the other night? She forced herself to be calm. 'Eliot, will ye speak to me properly, fer God's sake, and stop blowing so hot and cold? I don't know where the hell I am.'

'I think you've lost your manners, Kate O'Connor. It's *Mr Tyson* to you. Or sir.'

'Is it indeed?'

'Yes.'

'I didn't notice the need for such formality the other night.'

'It's needed now.'

'I see. And why is that, might I ask?'

'Because I am the master, dammit, that's why. And I'll not have you telling me what to do.'

Kate stood fuming in silent defiance but he was right, of course. Despite what they had shared beneath the sheets, he was still the master and she the maid. How could she deny it? He was as far removed from her as ever. Further, it seemed. She'd been wrong to succumb to her emotions so foolishly, although some would say he was more in the wrong for taking advantage of her. Yet, deep down, Kate knew it hadn't been like that at all. Neither of them had been able to help what had happened, and she didn't blame him, not in the least. She just wanted it to mean as much to him as it did to her. Tears pricked the backs of her eyes which she blinked rapidly away, gritting her teeth in an effort to regain control. She must remember that her main concern was for Millie, surely far more important than any tender sensibilities on her own account. She must concentrate on her friend's problems and stop daydreaming of what could never be, even if she had overstepped that fine line by instinctively using his Christian name; by asking, nay *telling*, him to sack Swainson. But had he done so? Wasn't she itching to know what had happened to the old bastard?

Bored with their lack of attention, Callum was working himself up into a fine tantrum, yelling and tugging at her skirts, urging his mammy to play catch with him again.

'Will ye just wait awhile, me cushla? Mammy's busy. We'll play in a minute. Why don't ye sit on the grass and make Mammy a nice daisy chain? There ye are now. See how long ye can make it.' She gave him a kiss and plucked a few daisies to get him started, and as if by magic the tears abruptly dried. 'I'm sorry, *sir*. Don't I forget meself at times?'

'I think you forget yourself in more ways than one, Kate O'Connor. You are not this child's mammy. Not any more. Amelia was his mother, and will remain so in his memory for ever. See that you remember that simple fact in future, if you please.'

Kate felt her cheeks start to burn and the struggle for control grew harder; tears clogged her throat and her eyes began to smart in raw agony. She lifted a bleak face up to him. 'You're right. 'Course y'are. It won't happen again, only . . .' He started to walk away from her along the path, and Kate saw that through her own folly she was losing him. She ran after him. 'It's just that I'm that upset over me friend Millie, d'you see?'

He didn't pause, not for a second, not seeming to hear her or want to listen, and Kate struggled to keep pace. 'Have ye done anything about poor Millie . . . have you? Answer me, ye miserable git, or have you let that nasty piece of shite off yet again?'

He stopped at last, rounding on her with cold fury in his eyes. 'You really should watch your language, Kate O'Connor. Particularly in front of my son. As a matter of fact, no one else seems to agree with your assessment of Swainson. There have been no other complaints about him. Not one. I've heard some vindictive nonsense from girls at the factory in my time, spreading malicious gossip over this, that and the other, but never any tale as fanciful as yours. And bearing in mind the grudge you already bear against the man, I've decided that your tale cannot be trusted.'

Kate gaped in shock. ' 'Tis the truth, I swear it! You need to sack him, get yourself a new foreman, so help me, before it's too late.'

'Oh, come on, Kate, you've been out to get your own back on Swainson from the very first moment I set eyes on you, all because he refused to pay what you considered to be your dues.'

'And he attacked our Dermot,' she burst out, biting her lip when she realised she'd only made matters worse by this interruption. 'And me.'

He gave her a wintry smile that froze her heart. 'As you once told me, not very convincingly, I seem to recall. And so, as the vendetta continues, you've decided to involve your friend, have you? Very clever. Except that it won't work. I'm not quite the fool you take me for. You're sadly mistaken if you think you can tell me how to run my own factory as well as ruling every corner of my personal life, not to mention insinuating yourself into my bed.'

Kate jerked as if she'd been struck. 'El— Mr Tyson . . . sir . . . Sure and ye can't mean that? I don't believe ye do. Are you accusing me of forcing meself upon you?'

He had the grace to look a mite shamefaced and turn his gaze away. 'More than that. You understand my meaning well enough.'

'You think I lied, just to get me own back on that no-good piece of sh— dirt?'

He pushed his face close to hers but there was no kindness in it, not a hint that he might change his mind and kiss her instead. It was almost as if those precious moments of intimacy had never taken place. 'I'm saying you can push a man so far and no further. That I've reached the limits of my patience with you. The aunts are right, you are a very clever little manipulator and know how to take advantage of a man, how to use your charm, your feminine wiles. But not quite clever enough. Now, I suggest that you pack your bags and go.'

She taking advantage of *him*? Now there was a laugh! Wasn't she the victim here? Kate didn't understand exactly what being a clever little manipulator meant, though she could guess.

Wasn't he just trying to run away from what he'd done, as all men did, particularly bosses, and had done so throughout generations of abuse upon women? And she'd been stupid enough to believe this one might be different. Hadn't he himself claimed to be? Oh, but she'd never felt such rage in all her born days.

Kate stood her ground, arms akimbo, and shouted after him as he strode away. 'Ye've no right to speak to me like that. No right at all. Jaysus, Mary and Joseph, I'll make you take back every blethering word, so help me! Damn you to hell, Eliot Tyson. And will you stand still when I'm shouting after you, or do ye want all the neighbours to hear what ye've been up to, cause I've a mind to tell 'em?'

Not even this threat gave him pause. He strode away without glancing back, let alone returning to plead for her silence or to continue an argument he considered closed.

She was furious that she had failed on all counts: failed Millie, failed to keep control of her emotions, failed utterly to win his love, even failed Amelia who had become her friend. Blinded by tears, Kate stormed back across the lawn towards the house. Only when she reached the nursery did she realise that she'd left Callum behind. Drat the man! He'd got her into such a rage she couldn't even think straight. Dashing back out again, she saw the boy wasn't on the lawn either. Wouldn't she just strangle Eliot for this! He'd taken Callum with him. He'd rob her of her only son when she was at her most vulnerable. Well, he'd see that she wasn't so easily disposed of.

20

Kate made no attempt to leave. She didn't pack her bags. She made no mention to the aunts, when they returned, that she'd been given the sack. She politely took their coats and hung them up, carefully sticking a hat pin into each discarded hat, then handed them the silver salver where a collection of cards waited for them from afternoon callers.

'Oh, dear,' said Cissie. 'We missed Lucy again. She has called every day this week and found us out. We must pay her a return call tomorrow, sister dear.'

Vera did not respond but addressed Kate directly. 'Did you clean out that closet, as I asked you to?'

'No. I mean, I've not quite finished it yet.' And, seeing Vera's frozen stare, she hurried back upstairs to get on with the job forthwith. Sure and wouldn't Eliot regret his words the minute he calmed down? He'd not want her to leave then, not at all. Hadn't they made a pact for her to allow him to adopt her lovely boy so long as she could stay on as Callum's nursemaid? Even if Callum was sent to a fine school, or Eliot employed a governess, surely to goodness he'd need her in the holidays, so how could he sack her? It would be breaking their agreement. It could never happen.

Deep inside, Kate was filled with uncertainty, but still she made no move to pack. She cleaned out the closet, as directed, and filled the rest of the time cleaning and tidying the nursery, carefully following all of Amelia's rules, using all the skills she'd learned from her lovely mistress.

Kate heard the front door bang around seven o'clock and rubbing her hands clean on the back of her uniform dress, tidied her hair as she set off down the stairs to face her employer. That afternoon while she'd worked she'd given herself a thorough talking to, sternly reminding herself that Eliot Tyson was the master of this house, and of the factory, and she really should remember that. What had happened between them, on two separate occasions, had been a mistake: the result of grief after the loss of his lovely wife, or pure physical need, and not some deep-rooted attraction on his part. But that didn't make it a sin, no matter what the gossips might say. She loved him even if he didn't love her. Though what she wouldn't give to see that smirk wiped off Fanny's face!

He was standing in the hall, taking off his coat, handing his scarf and hat to the maid when Kate hurtled down the stairs, almost tripping over the last few steps in her eagerness.

She bobbed a curtsey and gave an awkward little laugh, wanting to show she bore him no ill will. After all, didn't they both know that he couldn't manage without her? And she, for one, was more than ready to apologise for her impudence, fully anticipating that he'd do the same, then wouldn't they be right as ninepence again? All well between them. After that, she'd collect Callum and enjoy a quiet half-hour bathing him before putting him to bed. She had the water all ready and waiting, and his favourite currant biscuit to go with his cocoa.

'I'd like to say again how very sorry I am for me impudence this afternoon. It surely is none of my business who ye employ at the factory.' Kate desperately attempted to put proper sincerity in her voice. She certainly hadn't given up hope of getting rid of Swainson, but she'd obviously have to bide her time. She really couldn't risk losing her place here, the chance to be with Callum.

Eliot frowned down at her. 'You are absolutely correct in the assumption that it is none of your business, as I believe I've told you before.' He gave her a sideways glance and saw that her smile, as always, was entrancing. He could feel his anger draining away, his resolve weakening. Yet he was determined not to show it, not wishing to be seen as easy meat. He'd lost his temper this afternoon, perhaps said things he shouldn't, but a part of him did wonder if what the aunts said was correct: that Kate was indeed a clever and manipulative liar who had planned the whole thing from the start. The adoption, her being taken on here as nursemaid, even their lovemaking. She was still talking and he hadn't heard a word.

'So, where is the little monster? Hasn't he been the lucky one, going to the factory and being allowed to stay up so late? I'll never hear the last of this.'

'What are you talking about? What do you mean – staying up late? Hear the last of what?'

'Of Callum – of Master Callum, I should say, being allowed to visit the factory with you. What else?'

'Callum? But he's not with me. He's with you, isn't he? I certainly left him with you this afternoon in the garden. Why in heaven's name did you imagine he was with me?'

Kate became very still. 'Dear God, then if he's not with you, where the hell is he?'

Lucy had never felt more pleased with herself. What marvellous luck that she had chosen that very moment to call. What an opportunity. She hadn't quite been able to believe her good fortune.

She'd tried for weeks to catch Eliot in, to demand to know why her allowance had been reduced to an almost penurious level. The man simply didn't seem to understand how very expensive children were to feed and clothe and educate. But then how could he, with only a workhouse bastard to care for who'd be grateful for any scraps off his table? And then, as if by magic, the child himself had appeared before her, grinning in that inane way of his and holding out some daisy chain or other. It had been the easiest thing in the world to pick him up and simply walk away.

She'd walked quickly, rapidly turning over possibilities in her mind. What could she do with him? The river was the obvious solution. Children were constantly wandering off. What could be more natural than that he should get too near the water and fall in? Yet there were too many people about, nannies walking their charges, maids cleaning the steps of the fine Georgian houses along Kent Terrace and Thorny Hills. Schoolgirls coming out of the High School building. People strolling on the wide sward of grass by the river on this pleasant autumn afternoon. Someone might easily spot one small boy struggling in the water. And how could she make good her own escape?

But she must do something. It was essential that she take full advantage of this piece of good fortune. There would be no question then but that her own darlings would inherit the company, as they should, as they deserved to do after what Eliot had done to Charles.

If it hadn't been for Charles being sacked by his own brother, for God's sake, her beloved husband would be alive today, and she wouldn't be reduced to begging for the little comforts in life she surely deserved. No tears welled in her eyes at this thought, no sense of bereavement. Lucy felt only a searing, burning anger, one which culminated in a powerful need for revenge.

And then it came to her, the perfect solution. She would take the child back where he belonged: to the workhouse. This time to the big Union Workhouse up on Kendal Green where the guardians would keep a better watch over him, or perhaps pack him off to some other, more distant, charitable establishment. She didn't have the time to search for such a place herself, but she was quite certain that once he was incarcerated in the workhouse, no one would think to look for him there.

And then her own children's future would be assured.

She would insist on positions in the firm for both Jack and Georgie, at the appropriate juncture. Hopefully, Eliot would not live to a ripe old age, or else would retire and ultimately hand the firm over to his two nephews. In the meantime, she would make certain that she at least squeezed a decent allowance out of him. The thought suddenly came to her that he might marry again, arresting her galloping progress across Gooseholme and making her hide behind St George's Church to catch her breath while she considered this possibility.

The child was starting to whimper. 'Where's Mammy? I want Mammy.'

Paying no attention to his distress, Lucy's thoughts remained fixed on the problem of Eliot. What if he did marry again? Another, younger, more fertile bride would ruin everything. She dismissed the idea at once. By the time he'd got over grieving for Amelia, she would have thought of some way to put a stop on that too.

'I want Mammy.'

'Hush, child. Stop your noise.' She gave him a little shake, which made him cry even louder. 'Oh, for goodness' sake, shut up!' she shouted.

Callum was so startled he jumped as if he'd been physically struck, then opened his mouth wide and began to howl. Lucy was furious, but felt obliged to pick him up in order to stop the terrible din he was making. She couldn't bring herself actually to cuddle the child but did jiggle him up and down for a bit, which, after a few minutes, seemed to do the trick. The sobs faded somewhat but he had a disgusting mess all over his face now, dripping from his nose. She put him down again quickly and set off at a cracking pace with a firm grip on his hand, dragging him behind her so that the small boy had to run to keep pace, his little plump legs going like pistons. Once or twice he almost tumbled over his own feet, and she had to jerk him upright, but the crying continued unabated.

Lucy took the precaution of finding a quiet corner of a back street, where she took off his smart little smock and shorts and removed his nice clean underwear. She then set about rubbing dirt and mud all over the sobbing infant, including his carefully washed hair till it stuck out in spikes all about his little head and his tears made tracks of dirt down his round cheeks. She couldn't do anything about the fact that he looked well-nourished but she ruthlessly ripped and muddied his clothes before putting them back on him, minus the underwear, of course. That was much better. Now he looked as he should: a pauper in need of care.

'*Want Mammy!*' the small boy screamed, stamping his feet. '*Where's Mammy?*'

'Mammy has gone. You must come with me now.'

He resisted, dragging his feet as she tried to pull him along, then threw himself to the ground, screaming and kicking his heels in a frenzy of temper. For a moment Lucy panicked, looking frantically about to see if they'd been observed. Fortunately, there was no one around. And then she smacked him, very hard, on the backs of his legs, and that quietened him beautifully. He was staring at her now with shocked and fearful eyes, mouth agape in deep distress as he gave great hiccuping sobs.

'Now be a good boy and do as you're told or you'll get

another smack,' she warned, and was gratified to see that he understood perfectly. Probably the only language bastards like him did understand.

At the back of her mind, Lucy had been planning what tale she would tell the guardians, turning over possible circumstances. Perhaps she should say that she'd found the boy wandering in the middle of the road, in dire danger of being run down by a carriage or motor. She felt wary of exposing herself too openly by crossing over the river and walking through the busy part of town.

Also, it occurred to her that the Poor Law Guardians might ask his name and Callum was perfectly capable, at five years old, of remembering it. They might even ask her own name, or insist she fill in a form or something, which would never do. Not that they knew her at the workhouse since, fortunately enough, she'd never been one to go in for charitable works as Amelia had done. Even so, she must take care to get it right. This operation was proving to be far more problematic than she'd first thought.

Undaunted, she readjusted her plans. She wrote 'My name is Allan' on a luggage label she bought in a shop and tied it to his wrist. No one would have any reason to doubt that, and the name was near enough to the sound of his own to cause the child confusion in his present, distressed state. No doubt he was young enough to forget his real name, if they called him by the new one often enough. And looking so messy and dirty, they'd simply assume that his mother was dead, or couldn't care for him any more.

Lucy was perfectly certain that despite the workhouse being only a short walk from Thorny Hills, it might as well be a million miles away for all the good it would do one small boy. Once incarcerated within those solid stone walls, he'd never see his mother or his adoptive father ever again.

She went the long way, taking a detour behind Sandes Avenue and up through the woods and back streets to Kendal Green. It was with great thankfulness that she finally spotted the limestone walls and high windows of the workhouse. She sat him on the step, the child's head now nodding with exhaustion, and ordered him sternly not to move. Lucy clanged the bell using the attached rope and rushed back across the street to hide round a corner, where she could safely watch proceedings. She saw the door open, light spill out and a woman appear. She noticed the child at once and didn't seem in the least surprised, merely took his hand, spoke a few quiet words to him then brought him to her side. Pausing only to glance up and down the length of the street, she led him inside and closed the door.

Lucy smiled to herself. Good heavens, if she'd known it was as easy as this, she'd have done it long since.

At first they weren't too concerned, thinking he might have become locked in one of the many garden sheds or outhouses as Askew had gone about his work during the course of the afternoon. But when there was no sign of the boy there, nor anywhere in the house or conservatory, Kate gradually began to lose control. Where could he have gone? She found his soft wool beret lying discarded on the lawn, not far from where they'd been playing. Kate snatched it up and sank her face into it, breathing in the scent of him.

She felt numb with fear, convinced that he must have wandered off while she and Eliot were quarrelling, that he'd fallen into the river. Eliot's reaction too was to turn and run down to the slow-moving water but it wasn't too deep in this part and, after a desperate search, it seemed that this had not been Callum's fate.

'How far could he have got though, in the time? As far as the weir?'

They both looked up river to where the water slid over a shallow ridge below which it became fast-moving, dark and deep. Standing on the bank, soaking wet, they considered this dreadful possibility in silence for some minutes. 'I hope to God not that far,' Eliot murmured at last.

Kate was haunted by visions of Callum running away, frightened by their raised voices. Perhaps he'd even got as far as the town, and who knew what might have befallen him there? Been knocked under the hooves of a runaway horse, run over by a motor. Or maybe he was still playing hide and seek and it had gone wrong and now he was trapped somewhere: in an outhouse, or stuck under one of the bridges. She was frantic to decide where to start searching, which might be the most likely spot, there being far too many places hereabouts for a small boy to hide. And while she shivered and wept and dithered, Eliot took charge.

'Askew, go round the neighbours. Look in their carriage houses, their garden sheds and outhouses. They all know you, so you'll meet with no objections.'

Dennis was dispatched to alert the local constabulary, and Fanny and Ida ordered to search every corner of the house, though they'd done it twice already. 'He might be hiding in the attic, playing some silly game. Search every cupboard, every chest, every corner.'

It was Mrs Petty who put forward the possibility of abduction. 'He could have been taken by gypsies. They're often about at this time of year, heading north with their horses. Maybe one of them has pinched the li'l lad. He'd fetch a good price, being so bonny and red-haired, if'n they sold him on to some childless family.' And then seeing the master's stricken face, she flushed bright crimson as she realised what she'd said. Her warning was dismissed as another of her silly superstitions, something she was prone to.

Everyone searched for the rest of that day and all night, and for days afterwards: the servants, Eliot and Kate, the local police, friends and neighbours, even the two aunts grudgingly did their bit to help, but they found no sign of him. Kate refused to rest, couldn't eat, could no nothing but walk about in a daze of exhaustion, calling his name. Endlessly and restlessly searching the same places over and over again.

'We'll find him in the end, I know we will. I feel it in my heart. He isn't dead. I would know it if he were dead.'

In the days following, the entire district was alerted to keep a look out for the missing child. Sadly, it was over a week before a description of him appeared in the *Westmorland Gazette*, and then it was to describe him as wearing a smart blue smock and shorts, and polished patent shoes. A small, fuzzy picture was reproduced, taken the year before, which didn't look like Callum at all.

'He's grown so big since then,' Kate groaned, still clutching his floppy beret to her breast, carrying it round with her like a talisman, as if to prove that he would soon be found, alive and well, and would be in need of it again. 'Oh, why didn't we have his picture taken again?'

'We'd need to take one every single month to keep a check on his progress,' Eliot responded sharply, not a jot of kindness in his tone.

Had anyone up at the Union Workhouse read the paper with more than their usual cursory glance, they would not necessarily have made any connection between that pretty little toddler seated on his mama's lap with any of the half-dozen or so pauper children who'd turned up on their doorstep in the last few weeks.

*

Another week went by, and then another, and still there was no sight of Callum. Deep down, everyone was beginning to lose hope, yet couldn't quite bring themselves to admit it, or to stop looking. Eliot was sorely neglecting his business, and Kate could think of nothing but her son, filled with a conviction that it must all be her fault. If only she'd not let him loose to play on the lawn. Why hadn't she kept a proper eye on him? How could he simply disappear in a matter of moments?

It was late in the evening and she and Eliot sitting in the parlour sipping a hot toddy, exhausted after several more fruitless hours of searching, when for the first time the two of them talked as they never had before. Mostly they shared their feelings about losing Callum, their fears over what might have happened to him. Eliot even took her in his arms and Kate clung to him as she wept, united in their grief. His kindness brought a sort of comfort, and at the same time an increase in her pain for Kate could tell by the way he sorrowfully patted her shoulder that he still saw her as nothing more than a young, naïve maid towards whom he felt a considerable sense of guilt. She so longed to tell him that she didn't care about what had happened between them, didn't blame him in the least, not deep down in her heart. Didn't she love the bones of him, so wasn't it the most natural thing in the world that she would give herself to him?

Instead, thinking of the loss of her lovely boy, the words came out all wrong. 'If only you'd listened to me about Swainson, instead of arguing and shouting, Callum would never have run away.'

Eliot looked at her and sighed. 'Oh, Kate, is that all you can think of? Swainson? He is the least of our worries right now. If you hadn't been so obsessed with your petty vengeance against him, I agree, we might well have paid more attention to Callum.'

'And if you hadn't started shouting and frightened him,' she grumbled.

His brown eyes narrowed, taking on their familiar cool, distant expression, all too clearly reminding her that he was the clever, arrogant male and she a mere woman. 'I quite understand that as hope has begun to fade, fear has turned to despair, but we mustn't let it turn into anger and blame. Where is the point in that?'

'Where is the point? I'll tell you where the point is. Because he's my child. *My* son. That's the bloody point!'

'*My* son, Kate,' he softly reminded her.

She bit back the denial which sprang to her lips, swallowed the bitter taste of it. 'So what if we don't get him back? Ever?'

Eliot had lost a beloved wife, and now the child he'd come to think of as his own. He too could taste the bitter aloes of defeat and was irritated and annoyed by her obstinate determination to place all the blame on him. 'Why can't you accept that not everyone has the same way of going about things as you? Swainson may well be a harsh taskmaster, a foolish man perhaps but not necessarily an evil one. Otherwise why would the men at the factory support him?'

'No doubt because it's in their interests to,' Kate shrewdly surmised.

'Oh, Kate, you are growing paranoid.'

'Don't use your fancy long words on me.' And she burst into tears.

She rather hoped he would draw her into his arms once more but instead he leaped to his feet and his chestnut eyes blazed with fury. His jaw tightened, mouth twisting with shock and disgust. 'How can you stand there arguing about Swainson when your child is missing? Have you no heart, woman? How can I believe in your innocence when you are so utterly callous?'

Kate gasped, realising with disbelief and horror that it was not the foreman he was angry with but her. He didn't see himself as being responsible for Callum's loss at all. He laid the blame for that entirely upon her. 'You d-don't understand. It all springs from that – from our argument about him and your stubborn refusal to listen. You're an obstinate, arrogant bastard, that's what you are, Eliot Tyson!'

'Am I indeed? And had you not been so set against Swainson from the beginning, I might have taken more seriously what you had to say. As it is, I don't believe a word of it. You're making it all up so that you can throw the blame for Callum's disappearance on to someone else. Well, it won't work, Kate O'Connor. Don't think you can wriggle out of your responsibility so easily. Had you been a decent mother to your child in the first place, none of this would have happened. You were utterly feckless and irresponsible from the start.'

'I was not!' She wanted to leap at him, to claw that damning expression from his face, or else fall into his arms and have him tell her he didn't mean any of it, that all would be well and her darling Callum would be found at any moment.

But Eliot wasn't even looking at her. He was pacing the parlour in a lather of temper, pausing only to brandish a fist or wag an accusing finger in her face as he raged at her, their moment of rare intimacy quite gone. 'First you almost get the child run over by wandering in front of my carriage, then you take him back to Poor House Lane where he picked up a sickness that was almost the death of him, and *now* you've lost him altogether. *What kind of mother are you?*'

Kate felt as if she'd been slapped. She stared at him in stunned disbelief, the snarl of contempt on his face, in his voice, seeming to vibrate through every jangled nerve in her body. She couldn't quite believe that his kindness had evaporated so swiftly, and so completely. She took a steadying breath, desperately striving to calm herself. 'Is that what you really think?'

He snorted his contempt. 'Don't tell me you're going to pretend that you didn't benefit from the adoption? You were far more concerned with getting yourself a fine job, not to mention eagerly climbing into my bed at every conceivable opportunity, to pay proper attention to your own child. But then, what else would one expect from a girl from Poor House Lane?'

It was as if he'd stuck a knife into her heart, and then twisted it. Only when he saw the shock in her eyes did Eliot see that perhaps he'd gone too far. But it was too late. The words couldn't be taken back so he continued to glare at her in cold fury, stubbornly refusing to retract a word, or to allow a shred of pity into his heart.

Kate turned on her heel and walked calmly away. Up in the nursery, she slipped out of the uniform dress and pulled on the only other frock she possessed, a plain brown fustian which had been provided in place of the one burnt on the garden bonfire. Then she wrapped her shawl about her head and left the house, all too aware of Fanny trailing after her, standing at the door and silently watching as she walked away.

Within a short half-hour, Kate was back in Poor House Lane, back where she had started, back where she belonged; only this time with no hope of escape, and knowing her child was lost for good.

21

It was worse than before. This time she not only had no work
but also no hope of getting any. Bad enough to be without
references, and live in the hovels of Poor House Lane, but she
couldn't even go to Swainson and ask for outwork, not now,
after all that had happened. And somehow she'd lost the
stomach for living here; for the stench of sharing her bed with
a gaggle of urine-soaked children while Clem and Millie made
low grunting noises of love in some shadowy corner; for the
overflowing privy and the groaning pain in her empty belly.
She found herself thinking with longing of clean sheets, of her
lovely nursery and lost privacy, of Mrs Petty's roast lamb
dinners, and crisp clean uniforms.

And all the time, Kate was haunted by the loss of her child.

She got through each day in a daze, spending much of it
endlessly searching the back streets and yards of Kendal, just
in case Callum had got himself lost and someone had taken
him in, like a stray dog or cat. She would see his small, beaming
face everywhere, recognise the bright copper of his hair and
run to grab some child who proved to be a perfect stranger to
her. There were no tears now, just a terrible choking pain
clamped like an iron band about her chest. But then she didn't
have time for tears. She was too busy searching. He must be
somewhere. How far could one small boy travel on his own?
And if he was in Kendal, she would find him, she was sure of
it. If only she looked hard enough.

Every evening she would wend her weary way back to Poor House Lane and Millie would fold her arms about her friend, and the pair would weep silently together, grieving for this golden child they had both loved.

And then there were the nightmares: an awareness of some dark presence lurking in the shadows waiting for him, of a great weight pressing down upon her, stopping her from breathing, from running to save him from this unseen evil. She would hear the sound of tiny feet running away from her, she knew not where, nor with whom. Sometimes these images were so powerful that she could smell Callum's fear, see the river, the dark woods or the fellside, sense a terror greater than she had ever experienced and know that some dreadful disaster was about to befall him. She would wake in a sweat, jerking upright, calling out his name at the top of her voice. Then she would get up from the bed in the middle of the night, pull on her shawl and search for the place of which she had dreamed.

Every night as she lay down to sleep, Callum was the last thought in her mind. Every morning when she woke, he was the first thought to come into her head, and her heart would be filled afresh with grief. But then, unexpectedly, she woke one day with an idea in her head, filling her with new hope. She pulled on her clothes and ran to Millie who was already working on the leather by the dim light of dawn that streaked in through the single filthy window. Without fail she got in her two hours before stopping long enough to make breakfast for her family. Not that Clem would be bothering much with that this morning. He was still fast asleep in the drunken stupor which was becoming all too common for him, snoring like a pig under the heap of tatty bedclothes.

Kate grabbed Millie's arm, stopping her in mid-stitch, to get her attention. 'I've thought where Callum might be! If he got lost, he could have been taken to the Union Workhouse. Someone might have found him wandering about and taken him up there. Whyever didn't I think of that before? I'm going now, this minute. I'm going to find out.'

'Be careful,' Millie warned. 'If they take one look at you in your present state, they'll lock you up too.'

'Don't talk daft, it isn't a prison.'

'Could've fooled me.'

Secretly alarmed by this warning, Kate hesitated for two more precious days but, in the end, couldn't get the idea out of her head and so decided to take the risk and go. She spruced herself up as best she could, aware that Millie's concern was valid. She didn't look anything like as smart as she had in her nursemaid's uniform, particularly after a few weeks back in Poor House Lane. But she was prepared to lie if necessary, should anyone ask any awkward questions, by pretending she was still employed by the Tysons. In the event the officers there weren't in the least bit interested in her. They had more than sufficient inmates to cope with already, and nobody at the workhouse recognised the picture of a curly-haired two-year old sitting on Amelia's knee in any case.

So although Kate was allowed to scrutinise every child, to her bitter disappointment he was not there. Callum was not among them.

What she didn't know was that Lucy had grown nervous. She'd never seen Eliot in such a rage as he was in now, and all because that stupid girl had left him. You would have thought he'd be pleased to be rid of her. Worst of all, he was still searching for that dratted child. She'd begun to fear that perhaps he might suddenly take it into his head to visit the Union Workhouse on Kendal Green, and would discover the boy among the other pauper brats. Lucy decided that drastic action was called for.

She was not normally one to indulge in charitable works but this was different. Fortunately, she had always been a regular church-goer as this was the expected thing for someone in her position and quite the best place to be noticed by the aristocracy, and she knew the vicar to be a promoter of good causes. It took no more than a few words after Sunday service, suggesting that perhaps something should be done to find new homes for the poor workhouse children, coupled with the promise of a generous personal donation, and her plan was swiftly put into effect.

'What a wonderful idea,' the vicar enthused. 'A truly kind thought. How very perceptive of you, Mrs Tyson, that you should understand how important it is for these children to find real homes, with proper families. And most generous of you to aid our efforts in this respect.'

Lucy didn't have any money, nor did she allow that to stop her. She would find it from somewhere: the bank, the sale of one of her last remaining pictures, even from Eliot himself, which made her laugh out loud at the irony of such a thought. How wonderful if her brother-in-law actually financed the removal of his adored adopted son from the neighbourhood.

'Of course I understand, Vicar. Haven't I lost my own beloved husband and am left to bring up my deprived children alone? My heart bleeds for these poor innocents, it truly does.' She even managed to shed a tear, which quite touched his heart.

The vicar helped draw up a list of suitable foster parents, travelling far and wide to visit colleagues in neighbouring parishes to see if they knew of other good people willing to offer a home to an orphaned pauper. And while he did that, Lucy found several farmers who were willing to offer bed and board, at least, in return for an extra hand with the labour. She made no effort to check out whether they were suitable people to provide a home for such a child.

When they had their lists, Lucy visited the Union Workhouse, wearing her smartest costume and her sweetest smile, and found herself received with heartfelt gratitude. The place was apparently overrun with inmates: men, women and far too many children. Not that this surprised Lucy who had always known that the poor bred like rabbits, which was why they were such a drain upon the country's resources and needed to be kept very much in their place.

It took no time at all to choose the lucky recipients of her largesse and nobody noticed that among them was a copper-haired boy named Allan; nor that Lucy selected for him a remote farm high in the Langdales. Not even his own mother would think to look for him there.

The Union Workhouse had been Kate's last hope but she'd missed finding her son by a mere twenty-four hours.

There seemed to be nothing left for Kate to live for now. She no longer showed any benefit from her time spent with the Tysons nor from Mrs Petty's plain but wholesome fare. Her face was pale as parchment, her hair lank and lifeless, and the bonny plumpness gone from her body as weight fell from her. Millie would anxiously spoon porridge or watery soup into her, save her the choicest bits of meat or bruised fruit whenever Clem was fortunate enough to acquire any from the market, tempt her with home-made oatcakes, but her efforts were wasted. Whatever food Kate did manage to get down her, was as quickly vomited back up again.

One morning, just as she had finished heaving up her breakfast and was trying to settle her stomach with a mug of hot, milkless tea, there came a loud rap on the door.

Millie opened it and Kate saw her glance quickly back over her shoulder as if by way of warning, not needing to hear his voice to understand the silent message her friend shot her and know that Eliot was here.

'May I come in?'

Millie wavered in confusion, uncertain what to do. It seemed unthinkable that Eliot Tyson should want to come into their hovel, and yet he was already stepping over the threshold, ducking his head as he came into the gloomy, filthy room they optimistically called home. She saw the way he reeled slightly at the smell but quickly recovered, and after a swift assessment of the room's occupants – the huddle of children, Clem seated by the smoky fire, Millie with her arms full of babies – fixed his eyes on Kate.

'I thought you would be here.'

'Where else?'

'There was really no need for you to leave.'

'There was every need.'

He fell silent, perhaps confused by the fact that she had not moved, not even got up from the table let alone come to him, and again allowed his gaze to rove about the room. Kate became acutely aware that he was staring at a mouse, quietly grooming itself in a corner after having evidently breakfasted on the contents of a nearby cupboard, watching as it scuttled beneath the floorboards to join its mates. She saw him take in the skein of cobwebs she hadn't bothered to remove, the cockroaches crawling over the dirty dishes in the brown stone sink. He cleared his throat and spoke in a hushed whisper. 'Could we – perhaps – speak outside?'

'Why? Does this place offend you?' For God's sake, said a voice in her head, it would offend anyone with a nose to smell, and eyes to see.

Millie moved over to her, gave her shoulder a little shake.

'Go outside with him so's you can speak in private. Go on! The morning air, fresh or not, will do you good.'

They stood in the yard, on the slime of the cobbles with rain drizzling down their necks and the smell of pigs strong in their nostrils, not quite looking at each other. A boy trundled past, pulling a small handcart in which were a few pieces of coal, several broken boxes, and a collection of indeterminate items he'd obviously picked up on the midden, the better pieces to be spruced up and sold, many no doubt destined for the fire so that his family could keep warm and cook.

'Morning, Kate.' The boy nodded at her, then suddenly spotting a rat scurrying up the side of his cart, shouted, 'Gerroff, yer bugger,' and kicked it away. 'Bloody things!'

'Morning, Jonty. Quite a collection you've got today.'

'It'll do.'

Kate noted how Eliot's horrified gaze followed the boy as he went on his way. He looked as if he'd been found in a midden himself, dressed in rags, with a tousle of filthy hair and sores on his face and hands. She heard the low exclamation of disgust in Eliot's throat when, on reaching the end of the yard, the lad paused, opened his trousers and peed in the gutter that ran down the length of it. Nodding again to her, he happily took off his cap before going indoors.

The look that Eliot turned upon Kate said everything.

Shame enveloped her. Kate felt degraded by her very presence in this place, as if it robbed her of all pride in herself. She felt defiled by it, and bitterly ashamed. She had hoped for so much, and yet so little. A decent, clean home for herself and her child. What was wrong with that? She'd so wanted Callum to be safe that, against her better judgement, she'd agreed to give up her rights as his mother. Yet look where her efforts had got her. He had no mother at all now, no mama, no mammy, no home nor father even. He was lost, probably imagining she'd abandoned him altogether.

'I know I made mistakes,' she suddenly blurted out. 'I never meant to fall under your carriage, or for him to get sick. And I never meant him to get lost. I swear I thought he was with you.'

'I know. Things were said that shouldn't have been said. You must come back, Kate. You can't stay here.'

She shook her head. 'Where would be the use of that? You blame me, I know you do. You made that very clear. I just wanted Swainson to stop hurting Millie.'

She heard the small sigh of impatience. 'Oh, Kate.'

'All right, don't believe me then. Just promise me you'll not give up – that you won't stop looking for our Callum?'

'Of course I won't stop looking, not ever. And I'm sure we'll find him, I swear I won't rest till we do. Aren't you going to come and help me?'

'I'll do it me own way, so I will. I can look in places you'd never think of, or set foot in.'

'I've set foot here, haven't I? Come home, Kate.'

She looked him straight in the eye now. 'This is my home. Always was, and always will be.' Then she walked back up the steps, back into the awful, stinking room, closing the door softly behind her.

The very next day a note was delivered. It told her that he'd opened a bank account in her name, deposited a tidy sum of money in it: 'To help you build a new future. Let me do that at least for you, Kate. Get out of that place, for God's sake.'

'I'm not touching his dratted money,' Kate said, grey eyes clouding with misery at the thought he could so easily dispose of her with a few paltry pounds. Naïvely perhaps, she'd half-hoped he'd try again, that he wouldn't take no for an answer and come marching back up Poor House Lane, sling her over his shoulder and carry her off like some prince in a fairytale. Girlish fancy. Stupid, romantic nonsense! And he didn't even see her in that light at all. Whenever he looked at her, she could see in his eyes the guilt he felt over betraying a much-loved wife, and losing the son he'd bought off her. 'Does he think he can buy me off an' all? Mebbe this is all some plot and really he has Callum tucked away safely, and this is just a way to rid himself of me for good.'

'Oh, hush,' Millie said. 'Yer seeing plots everywhere.' Another rap came on the door and the two girls glanced at each other in sudden panic. 'It's him! It's Swainson.'

'Right, leave him to me.' And before Millie could stop her, Kate flung open the door and, lifting her chin high, met the foreman's startled gaze with a small smile. 'The work is going fine and will be delivered on time, but ye can't come in right now so be off with you.'

'Well, well, well, I see you're back where you belong, among the pig swill. Step aside, girl, I've business to do.'

'Not here you haven't.'

'Who are you to deny me entrance?'

He made to brush past her but Kate stood her ground, hands firmly folded across her chest. 'Take one more step and I'll punch ye on the nose, so I will. In future, ye can only come in by invitation. And yer not invited today, so bugger off.'

'You can't do that.'

'I just did.'

'I'm the foreman. I have rights.' She could see his face turning purple with rage and Kate almost laughed out loud at the pleasure it gave her to see him so discomfited.

'So have we got rights, and one of them is that we don't have to suffer you bringing yer mucky ways in here, so push off.'

'You'll be sorry for this, Kate O'Connor.'

'Not as sorry as you,' she shouted after him as he stalked off. Kate ran down the steps, picked up a clod of muck and flung it after him, and now she did let her laughter erupt as she watched him slipping and sliding in the filth in his rush to escape.

Back inside she slammed shut the door, wiping the tears of laughter from her eyes. 'Oh, that was the funniest thing I ever saw. That'll show him, the nasty little shite,' dusting her hands as if wanting to rid herself of something unclean.

But when she looked up at her friend, Millie's eyes were filled with fear. 'What did ye do that for? Why do you always let yer Irish temper get the better of you? Now we're really done for. He'll give us no work at all.'

'So we'll find it some place else, or make us own, to be sure,' Kate said on a note of defiance. But as she watched Millie snatch up the leather pieces and begin to stitch with frantic anxiety, she experienced a stirring of doubt. What had she done? In trying to protect her friend, had she merely made matters worse, risked the family's well-being simply for a moment of personal glory? Kate looked around her at the skinny, snotty-nosed children with not even the energy to play properly, and instantly sobered. She laid a hand gently on Millie's shoulder.

'I'm sorry, love. I didn't mean to make matters worse but we can't have him doing – what he does do with you. You can't let him bully you like that. Does he do it to all the women?'

Millie didn't once raise her eyes from her work, fingers flying as she stitched with frenetic speed. 'How would I know? Some, I think . . . all right, quite a few. Not that anyone admits to it but it's easy enough to tell by the look in their eyes after he's come calling. But don't think you can stop it, because you can't.'

'Why not? If all the women stood together, he'd not be able

to take advantage the way he does. Will I ask around, get some evidence?'

'No, keep yer nose out of it. You've done enough for one day. Anyroad, you'd niver get 'em to agree. They'd be too feared of starving to death while they made their protest. We leave all of the argufying to the men – them as is brave enough.' She did stop now, to fix Kate with a fierce glance. 'We women have childer to feed and can't afford to take the risk. So don't you interfere. Don't poke yer snout into our midden, nor into matters thoo can do nowt to change.'

Kate was stunned by her friend's vehemence. It was the first time they'd ever quarrelled and she felt humbled by the stark fear in Millie's eyes.

'But there must be something I can do . . .'

'There's nowt. So leave well alone.'

At the end of the week when Millie took in the finished work, she apologised to Swainson for Kate's rudeness, saying she hoped that it wouldn't make any difference, that he'd not with-hold work from her as a result. 'Me husband can't seem to get any, d'you see? I depend upon this outwork, to feed me childer.'

In truth, fond as she was of him, Clem was proving to be a worry to Millie, a big disappointment in fact. It was as if he'd given up on himself, lost all faith and hope of ever being able to provide for his family, and yet he didn't seem to understand the price she paid in order to earn a few pennies. He'd help himself to the coins in her purse and go off to the Cock and Dolphin to drink with his mates, saying there was nothing else for him to do.

Swainson gave a sneering laugh, his good eye roving over Millie appreciatively. 'I'm sure we can think of some way to avoid that prissy little miss sticking her nose in where it's not wanted. If'n we use our imagination.'

Then he went to the door, pulled it open and glanced up and down the street before sliding the bolt across. With a jerk of his head, he ordered Millie to follow him into the back room where he stored the bends of leather waiting to be cut into soles. 'Look sharp about it. It'll have to be a quick one afore someone comes.' Oh, but he'd make her sorry for defying him. He would indeed. She'd certainly think twice in future.

Millie swallowed carefully, gave a nervous smile, and followed him inside.

It was a week or two later that Kate finally confessed to Millie that she was pregnant. 'I've fallen again, and this time I've no husband and I don't even want another child. I want Callum.'

Millie didn't scold or judge her for what she'd done with Eliot. She didn't ask why she'd done it, or what she'd been thinking of to sleep with the master before even his beloved wife had been laid to rest, nor why she had repeated the same error months later. She understood only too well how easy it was to make mistakes, and how much in control men were. Didn't Swainson give her a fresh reminder of that fact each and every week? Not being able to come into her home and use her bed had made matters worse, not better. Now he took her wherever he fancied; in his workshop, down by the river, or up against a back-yard wall like a common whore. She wondered sometimes if Clem guessed what was going on, but if so, he turned a blind eye, pocketing the money she earned and drowning his sorrows at the pub.

So if Eliot Tyson had shown Kate kindness, of course she'd be ready and willing to comfort him in his grief and loneliness. Now she would simply have to live with the consequences. And if secretly Millie hoped that this new baby, unwanted as it now might be, would help Kate to ease the grief she felt for her lost child, she did not say as much. Millie herself had buried two bairns and knew that however many other children you had, you never stopped loving or grieving for the lost one. Callum couldn't be replaced, but the new little one might help to heal the wound and give her friend a reason for living.

As Kate broke the news, these thoughts flashed through her head, but Millie simply gave a rueful smile and said, 'We'll manage, love. What's one more, with all this lot?'

22

Lucy sat in the small parlour, looking as if the sky had fallen in on her head. She couldn't believe her own ears. This was the most appalling news. Not at all what she'd expected. 'Would you mind repeating that, Eliot? You say you have given a large sum of money to the *nursemaid*? *Our* money, which we need to save the company.'

Aunt Cissie made a clucking sound with her tongue which sent the two dogs at her feet into a frenzy of excitement. Aunt Vera seemed to have lost the power of speech altogether, sitting bolt upright with her copy of *John Halifax, Gentleman*, which she'd been reading when called to this interview, clutched tightly on her lap.

'I believe that it is actually *my* money, but yes, that is what I have done. I thought you'd be pleased to hear that she is to be properly provided for. I believed it appropriate, considering she has lost her son.'

Lucy balled her fists, sat forward in her seat and spat her next words at him. 'You can't do that. You simply cannot do it. We need every penny for ourselves. What *has* she lost? Some pauper brat of no account. No doubt she'll have another baby to fill his place before the year is out. Those sort of people breed like rabbits.'

The muscles in Eliot's face tightened dangerously as he regarded his sister-in-law with frost-filled eyes. 'Might I remind you this is my son you are speaking of so dismissively, even if he isn't the child of my loins.'

'Oh, dear! Deary, deary me,' Aunt Cissie said, sounding flustered, and both maiden ladies shuddered, not wishing to express matters quite so openly as these two seemed able to do.

Eliot felt a stirring of pity for them: for their inflexibility, their mulish snobbery, and their very obvious greed in wanting everything he owned to go to them. Perhaps that wasn't quite so true in the case of the aunts, but he was perfectly aware that it was so with Lucy. She'd made no secret from the start that she resented the adoption, believed Tyson's Shoe Manufactory should go to her own children. Well, she must simply accustom herself to bitter disappointment. He'd no intention of ever allowing them to have it.

He forced a patient smile. 'As well as the money, I also intend to set her up in decent accommodation, a house somewhere other than Poor House Lane which is an appalling place to live. Have you ever set foot in there, Lucy? Aunts? I have, and I do assure you that you would not like to. It's a festering sore which should be a source of shame to this town. Those cottages need to be razed to the ground, and will be if I have any say in the matter.'

Completely ignoring the philanthropic aspect of his statement, Lucy stared at him as if he'd run mad. 'A house of her own? A vast over-indulgence, surely? She gave up the child willingly, used him as a means to gain herself employment. And can you afford to be so generous? Can *we*? Haven't we done enough for the girl already? How much will all of this charity cost, for absolutely no return or benefit?' She paused as if a thought had struck her, and then cast him a sideways glance, pressing her lips into a knowing smile. 'Ah, is it perhaps because you intend to set her up as your mistress, is that the way of it? I've heard the rumours. Dear me, I'm surprised at you, Eliot. And so soon.'

Aunt Vera gave a low hiss deep in her throat and, having found her voice, it came out deep and gruff and condemning, 'I hope not indeed. Poor dear Amelia would turn in her grave.'

Aunt Cissie simply sank into yet another litany of 'oh, dears', varying them only with, 'What a muddle, what a muddle!' The two pointers whimpered in sympathy and licked her hand.

Eliot turned away, not wishing anyone to see the flicker of guilt that he assumed would be present in his eyes, addressing his remarks to the view of the river through the parlour window. 'Now you are talking nonsense. She is a servant girl in need of help, nothing more. And if Amelia were still here, she would entirely agree with my decision. She would consider it entirely proper since she was ever practical and with a generous heart.' He sincerely hoped his much-lamented wife could not see from the afterlife how quickly he had replaced her. The shame of his actions was killing him, making him quite unable to concentrate on his work or do anything properly. He prayed that once he'd set up the girl in safe and decent accommodation, he would finally be able to put her from his mind.

Having got himself back under control, Eliot turned to confront the censorious faces of the women of his family, aware that the more they attempted to boss and organise him, the more he wanted rid of them from his home. 'Kate O'Connor might be a thorn in the side of some people, with her prickly defensiveness and naïve way of viewing the world, but her heart is in the right place and she deserves better than we have given her. And you are wrong, Lucy, about her reason for giving up Callum. It was done with great reluctance on her part, and for the best of motives.'

'Huh!'

'I rewarded her generosity and trust by neglecting him to such an extent that he was stolen before my very eyes.'

'Oh, he was a lovely little chap, it's true.' Aunt Cissie gave a little moaning cry and dabbed at her eyes so that both dogs attempted to climb on to her lap at once, in order to offer her comfort

'Do stop it, Cissie,' Vera scolded, 'and put those dratted animals down. What's done is done and can't be undone. And there really is no need, Eliot, for you to carry this burden of guilt on your shoulders. The girl should have been paying proper attention to her duties. Perhaps it was God's way of telling you that the whole situation was wrong from the start, that you were never intended to father children of any sort.'

Eliot looked momentarily startled by this bleak assessment of his situation. 'I trust you are wrong in that supposition, dear aunt. I had hoped that perhaps one day I may marry again. Who can say? I may yet have a nursery full of children, God willing.'

Lucy regarded him with fresh horror. What was he implying? Surely he wasn't suggesting that Kate O'Connor might fit that role? Not for a moment had she imagined such a possibility. A new bride of any sort would be bad enough, before she'd had the opportunity to put the rest of her plan into effect. Lucy held fond hopes of finding Eliot a comfortable, mature wife, one unlikely to give him children. The very idea of the nursemaid, the girl from Poor House Lane, becoming mistress of this house, inheriting what her own sweet darlings should have, was utterly insupportable. It must not be allowed to happen. In addition to all other considerations, she was far too young, too *fertile*.

'I am sure that when you have had the opportunity to think about my plan a little more, then you will agree it's the right thing to do. We cannot be seen to take advantage of those less fortunate than ourselves. You do understand, dear aunts? Lucy?' He lifted one brow by way of cool enquiry. None of them answered.

Eliot strode to the door, glanced back at the three women still bristling with censure and let out a small sigh of resignation. Why did no one ever appreciate that he wanted to do only what was right? Why did people always perceive some ulterior motive, some personal benefit to himself in what he did? His mistress indeed! The very idea. He inwardly shuddered at what they would say if they knew how close he had come to falling into that particular trap. What sort of employer would that make him? Oh, the folly a man will commit in grief and despair. It was a relief, in a way, that the girl was no longer under his roof. She was far too attractive, too enchanting for words. Dangerously so. But Lucy was right in one respect – he couldn't really afford to be so generous, yet felt he had to do something. How could he ignore Kate's plight after all that had happened?

'Oh, and I intend to continue searching for Callum so pray keep your eyes and ears alert for news, if you please.'

'You won't find him,' Lucy burst out and then flushed crimson as he frowned down upon her.

'I trust you are wrong in that supposition, Lucy. Callum is my son after all, and I love him. Good day to you all.' As Eliot quietly closed the parlour door there was a moment of intense silence and then all three ladies began to talk at once. He walked away with a small, troubled smile on his face.

Thank God, Lucy thought, as Dennis drove her home later in the carriage, that she'd moved the dratted child far from Kendal. She shuddered to think what might happen if Eliot ever discovered the truth. Lucy was adamant that her brother-in-law wasn't going to be allowed to give away Tyson money to a girl of the lowest class imaginable, who had no right to it at all. It was an outrage which mustn't be allowed to happen. Yet she felt utterly helpless, trapped in some sort of nightmare. She certainly hadn't gone through all of that trauma to be robbed in the end of what was rightfully hers. She had to do some hard thinking, and fast!

The bills were still mounting, seeming to come in as thick and fast as ever, with no end to them. How she was going to settle half of them, she really didn't know. And she must still find decent schools for the children. What a coward Charles was, to have left her in this mess. Drat men! Drat everyone! Livid with rage, she knocked everything off her husband's desk with one furious sweep of her hand.

Only when her storm of temper had subsided did she begin to see things more clearly. The answer was obvious. She should take a leaf out of the aunts' book and move into Tyson Lodge, taking her children and maid with her. It seemed to suit them well enough, as they showed not a sign of returning to their own, humbler quarters. In fact, she'd heard Aunt Vera saying just the other day that she was thinking of letting out the house they owned in Heversham, since Eliot had so many empty rooms here in Kendal, and the poor man was so dreadfully alone now that dear Amelia had passed away.

If he has so much money to throw around, he might as well throw some in my direction too, Lucy decided. She was family after all.

She flung open the door and shouted for her maid. The girl came running, as she'd learned to do whenever her mistress called. 'Start packing. We're moving to Tyson Lodge first thing in the morning.'

What with her foolish brother-in-law going soft in the head, not to mention this nasty and persistent rumour of war in Europe, the world, in Lucy's opinion, was clearly running mad. It was indeed fortunate that she, at least, was holding on to her sanity. She would move into Tyson Lodge forthwith, and who knew where that might lead?

It proved to be a wearisome pregnancy, the baby lying heavy, causing Kate to need to use the stinking privy more often than she cared to. She felt listless and tired much of the time, with none of the anticipatory joy which she'd felt when she'd been expecting Callum. Worst of all, she was a burden on Clem and Millie; as if they didn't have enough mouths to feed without her imposing an extra one. She didn't trouble to think about what she would do when the baby came, and a part of her didn't care. If it weren't a sin, she'd almost wish that God wouldn't allow it to survive.

Yet she mustn't give in. She must get this baby born then she could resume her search for Callum.

Her time came, still with no sign of the birth being imminent, and somehow it reminded her bleakly of Amelia and her long pregnancy, which hadn't been a pregnancy at all. The poor lady had suffered so much with, in the end, nothing to show for her labours but her own tragic death. Only Kate's bruised ribs as the baby kicked and turned within her served to remind her that her own situation was entirely different. There would indeed be a baby for her. Unfortunately he, or she, was simply taking a long time making an appearance.

Millie became increasingly concerned by the delay. 'You're a good two weeks overdue, it's long past time this bairn made an appearance. Here, take a sip of this, it'll happen do the trick.'

'What is it?'

'Only a nip of gin.'

'I don't want it.'

'Aye, you do. Get it down you. We've got to get this baby out somehow, and it'll make for an easier labour.'

Miraculously, the very next day Kate did indeed go into labour but it soon became clear that this wasn't going to be the easy birth she'd experienced with Callum, and that Millie had hoped for. Perhaps she didn't quite have the energy she'd had then, Kate thought, as she sweated and laboured, pushed and heaved when Millie told her to, breathed and coughed and panted at her instruction for hour upon hour with still no baby to show for her efforts.

And the pain was dreadful. She could feel it washing over her, blotting out all thought, all will to survive. One minute Millie would shout: 'I can see the head. It's crowning. Push! Push!' But then it would slip back, and Kate would feel too exhausted to go through all of that again.

'Let me sleep for a little first.'

'No, no, you can't sleep. Come on, sit up. Try again. Childbirth is hard work. Wake up, Kate. Push, drat you!' Millie knotted a sheet to the bed posts for Kate to hold on to, and Clem took the children outside so they wouldn't get in the way. Kate pushed and shouted, cursed and swore, and even at one point screamed out loud as the pain became unbearable, all to no avail. She couldn't endure another moment, wanting desperately to sleep, to die.

In her mind's eye she could see Callum grinning at her, his cherubic face bathed in a golden glow, surrounded by a brilliant light, and she wanted to reach out to him, to let some unseen hand pluck her from this bed to which she seemed to be stuck fast, and draw her up into that glorious light.

'Callum,' she called, 'I'm coming. Wait for Mammy.'

White-lipped, Millie ran to the door and shouted to Clem: 'Run and fetch Eliot Tyson. We've struggled on us own long enough. It's his child, drat it! Let him do something useful for a change. And make sure he fetches a doctor back with you, an' all.'

*

It was a girl, finally slithering into the world at two the
following morning, yelling the place down as if demanding to
know why they'd taken so long about it. The labour had
certainly been longer and more painful than Kate could ever
have imagined possible and yet survive, requiring the inter-
vention of Dr Mitchell at his most skilled to pull the baby from
her and stitch up Kate afterwards. She thought she might
never walk, or move, again, watching with bleak indifference
as the doctor washed and put away his instruments of torture.
Then she looked across at the baby, lying serenely in the basket
which had held all of Millie's children and felt nothing for that
either. There were bruises on her head which the doctor said
would fade in time and really shouldn't worry her. Kate wasn't
in the least bit worried. Why had he told her that? Had she
asked? If so, then she couldn't imagine why. The baby somehow had no connection with her at all. But then nothing did.
She felt in a daze, numb with pain, with no clear idea of where
she was, or how long she had lain on this bed, fighting this
endless, pain-filled, battle.

There were voices in the room, raised in argument, though
she didn't trouble to determine whose, letting the sound drift
in and out of her consciousness. And then a face swam into
view, one she knew well, and a voice – firm and demanding –
a persistent hand shaking her shoulder. 'Kate, Kate, wake up!
See, you have a beautiful baby daughter.'

She struggled to focus on the face, on the voice, casting a
sideways glance up at him. He was smiling, his brown eyes
warm on her face, all anger spent.

'I still want Callum,' Kate repeated stubbornly, tears flooding
her eyes and making his beloved image swim in a blur of colour.

'Of course you do. We all do, and we will find him, I swear it.'
He stroked her hair from the heat of her brow, rubbed away

a tear with the back of his hand and she looked up at him in wonder. Did this mean that he cared for her a little, after all? He must have brought Dr Mitchell, come to her aid again when she most needed it. Would he carry her off to Tyson Lodge and love her as she so longed to be loved? His next words seemed to confirm this dream. 'We must stop fighting each other over this loss we've both suffered, and over what happened between us. It's no good going over and over it. It's done now, but I swear I won't rest till I've found our little man.'

Our little man. How she loved to hear him say that, linking all three of them together. 'It's been months. I tried so hard to find him but . . .'

'I know, so did I. But perhaps you've been given another chance, to get it right this time. Just tell me, Kate, I need to know, whose child is she? Is she mine?'

Kate was stunned, not quite believing that she'd heard right. What was he implying? That she lay with just anyone?

Eliot was still talking, a feverish glow in his eyes. 'The doctor says she's fine, astonishingly so considering the circumstances, but if she truly is mine, I refuse to allow her to be brought up here. I can't let you stay here either. We've been through too much together, Kate. Amelia would never forgive me if I didn't see that you were both well looked after.'

Been through too much! Was this evidence of yet more guilt? She gazed up into his face, willing him not to have said what she thought he'd said, for him to offer to look after her himself, aching for him to take her in his arms.

'I've found you a pretty little cottage in a yard off Highgate. A clean and decent one, just as you've always dreamed of. A place where you'll be safe and your baby can grow up healthy and strong. But you must tell me. I need to know. Lucy said you would have replaced Callum within the year, and it seems that she is right. So is the baby mine, or not?'

Kate felt a flood of hot anger course through her veins. How dare he even entertain the possibility of her lying with someone else? Could he not understand that she loved only him? Did he see her as some sort of tart who wouldn't know the father of her own child, because she'd shared her bed with too many men? If she could only get off this damned bed, she'd scratch his eyes out for insinuating such a terrible thing, so she would. Pushing herself up on her pillows, eyes blazing, Kate told him exactly what she thought of his suggestions.

'Seems to me your mind is filthier than Poor House Lane. Why would you want to know, so that you can pinch her too? While I've strength in me body, won't I fight you every step of the way? I gave you me last one, my lovely Callum, and look what happened to him. I'm damned if you're having this one an' all. Get out, damn you. Get out!'

'Now don't lose your temper, Kate. Stay calm. That's not what I meant, and you know it. For once in your life will you stop fighting me? I've no wish to steal her from you. It's just that I don't see how it could have happened so quickly. I mean, Amelia and I – we tried for years, and you and I only twice.'

'I'm not Amelia. Get out, damn you.'

'Kate, listen to me.'

'Get out! *Get out!*'

And this time her screams were such that he took a step backward, startled by her fervour, his face ashen. Millie was at her side in seconds, telling him he'd best go if he didn't want to scare all Kate's milk away. 'Very well. If that's how you want it. So be it.' And turning on his heel, Eliot strode out of the room, tight-lipped.

23

'Oh, Kate, what have you done now? Will you never learn to guard that temper of yours? I think he liked this new little treasure of yours, wanted you to say yes, that she was his. Why didn't you? He'd have helped you look after the wee bairn.'

Clem said, 'He'd've given you more money, lass. He's made of brass, and should be expected to support her. You an' all.'

'I don't want his damn' money. He can't buy another child off me. She's mine.'

Millie and Clem exchanged a glance of exasperation. 'All right, love, don't get upset. It's not good fer yer milk. Would you like to hold her?'

Kate shook her head and turned away, not wanting to look at, or even smell this alien child. Couldn't they see how exhausted she was, that she just wanted to sleep?

But Millie didn't seem to have heard because a warm bundle was pushed into her arms. It felt so tiny, so fragile, just as Callum had once felt, except that this baby was as pretty and delicate as a flower, her small, rose-pink mouth already arrogantly pursing with feminine conceit. A pair of brown eyes looked steadily up into Kate's proudly proclaiming that she'd arrived at last, and hadn't she done well? 'Just look at the little lamb. Isn't she bonny? And she's all yours. Callum's little half-sister. What are you going to call her?'

Kate found her own lips twitching into a smile and a flood

of emotion rushed through her. It was like falling in love at first sight. She drew her baby close, laid her cheek against the dark fuzz of hair and breathed in the sweet, baby scent of her. 'Flora . . . she is to be Flora. My little flower.'

Millie beamed her delight, pleased that mother and baby were bonding so well after what had been a tricky start. 'Right then, now you put her to the breast and get her suckling nicely while I put t'kettle on.'

Kate did as she was bid, feeling the strength of the child's pull, easing the pain in her that still yearned for Callum. This child was a part of her, and a part of Eliot whom she had loved more than life itself, though not for the world would she let him know it. She would have done anything for him once but now everything had changed. Instead of supporting each other in their grief, neither could appreciate the other's loss. If there'd ever been the possibility of something growing between them, all hope of that had been lost on the day Callum vanished.

Now, blinded by unshed tears, she held her new baby to her breast while her heart ached with joy and despair. 'We'll manage, my precious one, will we not? No one is taking you away from me. We'll make sure of that.'

Some miles away, high in the Langdales where the sun was striking the pikes over Dungeon Ghyll, slanting silvered rays right across to Hardknott Pass, a young boy, small for one very nearly six years of age, was carrying buckets of water from a nearby beck up to the farmhouse door where he poured it into a large boiler. He kept spilling it and soaking his legs and feet because he was in a hurry, knowing that if it wasn't filled by the time the farmer's wife came downstairs, he'd get a beating from her husband. He might get one anyway, simply for being there, for existing, although there were times when the boy felt he must be invisible, since it was rare for the farmer even to speak to him, and never by name.

'Hey, you,' he would say, 'fetch t'milk in. Look sharp.'

And young Allan would rush to carry out this order to the letter, fearful of what might befall him if he didn't. He'd come not to expect praise or gratitude for the work he did. He knew that however hard he laboured, he was considered to be of no account on this farm, because he was of less use than the sheep and hens who produced meat and eggs, and the family cow who gave them rich, creamy milk. In comparison with the other children, who were the farmer's own, he was seen as a second-class citizen.

Sometimes he dreamed of what it must be like to have a mother. There were even times when he could see her in his mind's eye. She had glorious red-coloured hair, rather like his own only brighter, and it fell in soft tendrils about her neck and shoulders. Her eyes were a clear grey and her skin soft and pale as silk. He loved that face, nursed it in his heart whenever he was weeping with cold and loneliness, when the bruises stung too much.

Later, when the boiler was filled, he would have to turn the handle on the mangle, pitting his scrawny muscles and stick-like limbs against the weight of the rollers. Unlike the farmer's own children Allan didn't go to school but stayed all day on the farm to help with the chores: chopping thistles, picking stones, mending walls, and endlessly filling water troughs and fetching feed for the sheep. He never went anywhere, save occasionally to market with the farmer, and then only to fetch and carry or to be used along with the sheepdogs to guard and shepherd the flock. Sometimes he'd go into Keswick or Ambleside with Mrs Brocklebank, the big fat farmer's wife, to help her carry the butter and eggs she had to sell or else mind the stall. He loved these outings, the only bright moments in what was otherwise a dull and lonely life.

He was certainly never allowed to eat in the big, warm kitchen, but took his meals in the cold, draughty barn which was also where he slept, among the cobwebs, which he really didn't mind as the spiders were his friends. He would talk to them for hours, telling them of things which might have been memories, or then again only dreams. Sometimes, if there were ewes brought in after lambing, he'd creep down very quietly and sleep beside them where it was all warm and cosy. They never seemed to mind, and even a sheep as a mother was better than none at all.

'I've decided what I'm going to do,' Kate announced to Millie one day. It was some weeks later, the soreness was easing, even the bleeding was starting to dry up and she was feeling well enough to think about the future. In her hand was an envelope addressed to her. It had come days ago but she hadn't yet plucked up the courage to open it although she knew it was from Eliot. She could feel the bulk of a key inside and guessed it was to the cottage he'd promised her.

In these last few weeks while she'd been recovering from having Flora she'd made up her mind to accept the offer, for the baby's sake. Much as she now hated him for all he'd done, not least for taking Callum from her in the first place and now accusing her of being some sort of whore who slept around, she knew Eliot was right when he said they couldn't stay here, in Poor House Lane. Without Kirkland Workhouse at the end of the yard to protect them, it was more dangerous and soul-destroying then ever. They'd be better off living on the open fells, which she could always do if it came to that, Kate thought with a show of her old defiance. Except that she'd made other plans. 'I've got it all worked out, so I have.'

Millie looked up from her work with interest, glad to hear a brighter note in her friend's voice. 'You've decided to tell him he's the father then, have you?'

'I have not! If he can so easily think me capable of lying with another man so soon after being with him, he doesn't deserve to be given a second chance.' Kate settled the baby in the Moses basket and came over to sit by Millie, watching the stubby, stained fingers work the needle and thread in and out of the leather sole. 'No, no, I'm going to beat him at his own game. Since he won't listen to a word I have to say against Swainson, that despicable little swine of a man, then I'm going to find another way to fight him. Fight them both, so I will, if it takes me last breath.'

Millie stopped her sewing to listen, jaw slack as she took in the vehemence of Kate's anger, panic rising in her breast. 'Fight in what way? What are you saying, Kate? And what's it got to do with Swainson? Nay, don't you do owt you might regret, summat we might all regret.'

'Indeed no, I wouldn't regret a thing, I do assure you.'

'Just remember that I depend upon this work I get from that swine of a man as you call him, to feed me childer. Don't ever forget that.'

'I don't forget it, and I don't like it any more than you do. So pin back yer lug-holes and listen.' She leaned closer, dropping her voice as if the filthy walls themselves had ears, or the vermin that scratched within them could comprehend her plan. 'I was thinking that Eliot Tyson was right, we should get out of this stinking pit.'

'Oh, aye, and pigs might fly.'

Kate chuckled and held up the key, reading the note which went with it to Millie. It urged her to accept the cottage, if not for her own sake then for the child's. 'If he weren't such an arrogant, opinionated bastard, wouldn't I still be in love with him?'

'You still are in love with him.'

'I am not!' Kate held up a hand as Millie would have pressed the matter further. 'Are you going to listen to me or what? I was thinking of that money he so kindly put in a bank account for me, an' all. Not that I know much about how banks work, but I dare say they'll tell me how I can get me hands on it. I didn't want to touch it at first because I was soft in the head over him, still suffering from that girlish crush I had.'

'Girlish crush, my Aunt Fanny, it were more 'n that. Didn't you love the bones of him?'

'Are ye going to listen to what I have to say, or sit there and keep interrupting?'

'All right, go on. I'm listening.'

'I was thinking that all these women who work for Swainson could just as easily work for me. That there are men too in these yards who'd be glad of a bit extra and have the skills at their fingertips.'

'Help you with what? How can *you* find 'em work? You don't have any orders for shoes. Have you lost yer mind, Kate O'Connor?'

She chuckled. 'Mebbe I have but I never felt better in me life, so help me. If Eliot Tyson can get orders so can I, with a good workforce to back me up, particularly if we undercut him on price. I swear I could do better than Tyson's lot any day of the week.

'And what about Callum?'

Kate took a few moments to answer this, needing to get that undertow of emotion under control, as always, before she could speak normally about her son. 'Oh, I'll find him one day, so I will. He's somewhere around. I just have to find out where. In the meantime, I have another child to feed, and life must go on, for her sake. In case you haven't noticed, Millie, there's a war coming, and what is it folk need on their feet in wartime? What did they need in the Crimea?'

Millie looked blank. 'There won't be no war. That's just talk. Anyroad, folk don't wear shoes in wartime, Kate. They wear boots.'

Kate beamed. 'Exactly! So all I have to do is get an order from the army to make boots, then rent a room in which to make 'em, and we're away, so we are.'

'And what do you know about making boots?'

'Not much, but I can learn. I can find someone who'll teach me what's needed. Mebbe I could get our Dermot to come back from Ireland and help an' all.'

'It won't happen,' Millie insisted, scoffing at the very idea. 'Even if you did succeed in making a load of boots, there won't be no war, and then where would you be? With a load of stuff you couldn't even sell.'

'The important thing is not if war will start, but that we're ready for it when it does. In the meantime, we make boots. Lots of them. I learned that much from Eliot Tyson. Get a warehouse and put stock in it, and once shopkeepers know you have goods ready and waiting, they'll buy it. We won't be going in for fancy shoes, nor them posh Napoleons or whatever they call them hunting, shooting and riding boots Tyson's make for gentlemen. We'll make good, solid, working men's boots. We can make 'em for farmers or factory hands as well as soldiers, for anyone who needs the dratted things. I'll use the money Eliot Tyson gave me to buy whatever machinery we need, get meself some men and women to operate them, and set up in competition. It'd be worth it just to save the women from that nasty piece of shite Swainson.'

Millie's mouth was gaping open in shock. 'You're serious, aren't you? You've thought this all out.'

'To be sure, I'm serious right enough. If that bastard can steal my son, neglect and lose him, take advantage of me and then accuse me of sleeping with another chap when I've just given birth to his daughter, his first and only child, mind, he deserves everything I can throw at him. He deserves for me to steal his business in return.'

'Ooh, Kate, ye've lost yer senses.'

'No, Millie, I've just found them. Eliot Tyson is about to learn that Kate O'Connor is not the sort of woman who takes ill treatment lightly, not on me own account nor for the women in his employ. We'll put him out of business, see if we don't.'

Getting started was the hardest part. Her first problem was to persuade people to trust her. Everyone thought her quite mad. Kate went round the neighbouring yards, seeking workers, but many bluntly told her she'd lost her mind and slammed the door in her face, while others politely declined on the grounds they daren't take the risk. Women such as Sally Sibson, Joan Enderby and Nell Benson told her that anyone would be mad to give up secure employment to come and work for her; untried, unsafe and ignorant as she was. It was made clear that despite their distress and unhappiness over the current situation, the women were fearful of change. Children still had to be fed, and if Kate's new business didn't survive, Swainson might not take them back. Then where would they be?

'What will I do if no one will work for me, Millie?' Kate complained, night after night, 'I never thought of that. Why won't they trust me?'

'Because they're scared. Give 'em time. They'll come round.'

Undeterred, she rented an old abandoned ropeworks which would provide the space she needed, and give ready access to the railway. It took all of her nerve to approach the landlord but, despite the scathing disbelief in his face, he was willing enough to draw up a three-year lease in return for six months' rent in advance.

'Tha'll have gone bump by then,' he said scornfully, clearly thinking he could let his property all over again to some other fool.

'Oh, no, I mean this business to thrive and prosper.'

She wrote to Dermot, hoping he might come back from Ireland to help her, and spoke to one or two of the old chaps who sat about doing nothing all day because they'd been 'turned out to grass' as they put it, by Swainson. When she suggested they might like to put their skills back in use again, they looked doubtful.

'D'you mean work for thee? How can a li'l lass like thoo offer us a job?'

'Why not?' Her heart beat fast at the temerity of her answer, and she wasn't in the least surprised when the old men burst out laughing.

Kate shrugged her thin shoulders. 'It's up to you. You can believe in me or not, as you choose, but what have you got to lose? At worst you get a few months' paid work. At best, you get steady employment for years to come.'

They considered her then with greater attention, knowing she'd had a bairn recently, and yet was a widow for many a long year. They'd heard the gossip, listened to their wives sniffing their disapproval and tearing her to shreds. But there was something about the lass, no one could deny it. A certain audacity in the way she tilted up her chin and met their scepticism with a steady gaze, challenging them to dispute the feasibility of her scheme if they dare. With her arms folded, shoulders back and spine rigid with purpose, no one could doubt Kate's determination to succeed. She'd stand on her own two feet, this one, and not beg for pity. So they agreed to give the plan a try. As she rightly said, what did they have to lose?

These men proved more than able to help her find second-hand Blake sewing machines, wooden and iron lasts, and the right finishing machinery needed for her to get going. And old Gabriel, who'd taught her brother his trade, stood at her elbow when she went to buy the leather, pointing out the flaws, the marks and small holes made by the blow fly, all of which damaged the quality of the finished product. All she needed now was to get the women on her side, the very ones she'd wanted to help in the first place.

The first to come round was Sally Sibson from the next yard. She came late one night, sporting a black eye and bruised ribs. 'That bugger has beaten me once too often. *And* he's refused to pay me wages, all because I told him he couldn't have any how's yer father this week because I weren't feeling so bright. Nasty bugger clocked me one, then punched me in t'stomach, right in front of t'childer.'

'You mean Swainson?'

''Course I mean Swainson. Who else?'

'Have you not thought to complain to Eliot Tyson about what he does to you?'

Sally's face filled with a mixture of fear and scorn. 'When have the toffs ever listened to the likes of us? Swainson is the one wi' the power, because he's the one what hands out the work, week after week. Thoo knows that as well as I do, lass. So think on, when you get up and running, let me know. I, for one will be willing to give you a try. I surely can't be any worse off.'

'Tell him to sling his hook, yer working fer me now,' Kate said, eyes bright with hope. This was the breakthrough she'd dreamed of – for one of the women to give her a chance. 'Here's yer first week's wages,' she said, slipping several shillings into the astonished woman's hand. 'Be at the old rope-works first thing tomorrow. I'll find ye summat to do, even if it's only sweeping the bloody floor.'

'Hey, watch that generosity of yours,' Millie warned her as the other woman scuttled off. 'You will be going bump if you throw yer money around so freely.'

'You have to invest in folk, in order to win them over. And what about you, Millie? Will you be giving me a try, or are you sticking with Swainson?'

There was a long drawn-out pause while Millie cast her eye over her sleeping children. Clem was at the Cock and Dolphin, as usual. Even when he wasn't, he rarely brought home more than a shilling or two. Nothing had improved in all of these long weary years. In fact, quite the opposite. There were more and more children to be fed, eleven the last time she'd bothered to count. And who had stood by her all this time? Who had provided clothes for their backs, food for their empty bellies? She looked at her friend and gave a rueful smile. 'How can I refuse? But I want one o' them top jobs, soon as yer mekking a bit o' brass.'

Kate hugged her tight. 'You and me stick together, right?'

Word got around and Sally proved to be the first of many. Once they realised that there was an alternative to Swainson's bullying, and when they saw how hard Kate was prepared to work herself, how determined she was, they were soon queuing up for jobs.

They flocked to the workshop she'd opened in the old rope-works, knocked on her cottage door at all hours of the day and night till, in the end, she was turning folk away, although promising to keep a note of their name, just in case. She paid better wages than Tyson's, offered shorter working hours and no outwork, no dust and filth going into people's homes. None of this business of two hours' work before breakfast, and therefore no children forced into labour too, no blind eye turned when they 'helped Mum out' a bit too often.

'And best of all,' Millie reminded them, 'no Swainson coming round to leer and poke his filthy fingers, or his cock, where he shouldn't, using and abusing us women whenever it takes his fancy.'

'Thoo can count me in,' they said, one after the other.

'This is going to work,' Kate said, hugging her friend with glee.

'All you have to do now is sell the boots we make, otherwise we'll have the bleeding things coming out of us ears.'

24

Even the sound of the words 'the Great War' brought a chill to Kate's heart. How could there be anything great about a war in which thousands of people would die? She supposed it meant that millions more would be saved, that men would be fighting for 'Honour, Justice, Truth and Right', or so it said every day in the newspapers. But how many mothers' sons would need to die before that was achieved? Not hers. She no longer had a son, although today, 10 October 1914, he would be eleven years old. Too young to fight in any case, thank God. Wherever he might be, he would at least be spared that.

Not for a moment, let alone a day, had the memory of Callum slipped from her mind in all of this time. He was forever there, a part of her soul, living and breathing inside her head. And she had never given up hope of finding him. Without that, she might truly have gone mad. Somewhere, Kate was certain, Callum was alive and well, just waiting for her to bring him home.

'Where are ye, me cushla? Mammy loves you,' she would whisper, a dozen times a day.

There were times when she'd wonder what on earth she was doing working herself into a state of exhaustion when she should be out looking for her son. Days when she would find herself falling into a reverie, confronting the stark reality that she had no family, no one to call her own with her brother off somewhere in Ireland. She'd had only one letter from Dermot in all these long years, and that begging for money. She'd sent it, of course. Rapscallion or not, he was her only kin.

But if she ever decided she was wasting her time, she'd think of Millie and all the other women she'd saved from Swainson's unwelcome attentions, wipe away the tears of self-pity and get back to work. There was nothing more to be done about Callum, but she was at least doing something useful with her life.

And she did have a daughter. Kate counted her blessings every day for that fact, hardly able to bear being separated from Flora. Even now she still sometimes woke with that sinking feeling in her stomach, that familiar sensation of loss rushing in upon her like a great black tide. Her first instinct was always to reach for Flora as the child was never far from her side, not for a moment.

Kate glanced across at her now, where she was playing with her doll on the clippy rug: a pretty little thing with dark brown wavy hair, like her father's, that had a hint of red in it too to mark her Irish background, together with his chestnut brown eyes and Kate's own pale complexion. A beauty in the making with her pert little chin, snub nose and sparkling personality. Very much the little madam, and quite able to twist anyone who came within smiling distance around her smallest finger.

The last five years had not been unkind, had proved surprisingly profitable in fact. Perverse to a fault, Kate had returned the key to Eliot and declined his offer of a cottage, determined to do things her own way. But she'd held on to the money, viewing it as a loan, making the decision that he owed her that much at least, for all the pain and loss she'd suffered.

It had been hard at the beginning, taking much more effort than Kate had anticipated to get going properly. The money Eliot had given her hadn't been anywhere near enough, but the bank had been willing enough to lend her what she needed later, once they were satisfied that money was flowing and some profit being made. In addition to the women and the old men who first came to work for her, Kate had soon found a few younger men ready to make a bit extra on top of the wages they already earned at Tyson's by doing a bit of part-time work in the evenings.

And so, with everything in place and boots being made, she'd gone out on the road two days a week, taking her box of samples with her, and if at first shopkeepers had given her quizzical looks and been reluctant to trust in her because she was a woman, had appeared sceptical when she promised to deliver the very next day should they require it, Kate hadn't allowed their negative attitude to deter her.

'I'm selling these fine strong boots at sixteen shillings and ninepence a pair, twopence less than you'd pay Tysons. It's an opening offer to encourage you to give us a try and if you buy more than twenty-five pairs, I'll give you a five per cent discount. Like I say, assuming we have all the sizes you want, ye can have them delivered tomorrow, first thing.'

'And will you give me ten per cent if I buy fifty?' asked one astute customer.

Kate swallowed, swiftly decided to take a chance and agreed that she could. She'd worry about her costings later. What they needed right now was cash flow, or so the bank manager had carefully explained to her.

In the end her charm and winning smile won through. Few could deny her at least the opportunity to prove herself. Within eighteen months, she was seeking more men willing to work for her, needing them to be full-time. And then she secured an order for two hundred pairs of boots from a customer supplying several large engineering firms in Birmingham, with the promise of more later.

She'd gone back to Kendal in a lather of excitement and worry. 'Do we have two hundred pairs? Can we deliver them?'

They did, and could, sending the goods by rail. It was the first of many such orders and Kate had known, at that moment, that the future of her business was secure.

Today, she had twenty clickers working for her. These were the men who cut the leather, and in the closing room she had near on a hundred women and girls putting it all together to form the uppers. The soles were cut by thirty or so men in another room using machines designed 'specially for the purpose. In the final part of the process, the machinist eased the boot on to the last, bringing welt and boot together. Last of all, the boot was burnished and buffered and polished, paired off and strung together. After that they were sent to the packing room, where they were marked, sized up, and packed ready for dispatch.

She'd acquired the much hoped for order from the army, and her own workshop, small by comparison, was way ahead of Tyson's in providing boots for the forces. She'd succeeded to such an extent that recently she'd been approached by the Russians, to supply them too. Kate fully intended to open a whole new department for them alone soon.

Once having got the business going, Kate and Flora, together with Millie, Clem and the children, had moved into one of the other yards off Highgate, renting a white-washed limestone cottage which had three bedrooms, in addition to a kitchen and a privy all to themselves. Luxury indeed. Here, with her friends she'd found a sort of peace, if not exactly happiness. That was a state she could never entirely achieve, not without Callum. Happiness would have to wait until the day she found him, although she still hoped to attain contentment some day, were she ever able to fill that other void in her life, the lack of a good man's love. There were several around who would have been more than willing to fit the bill, of course.

In this yard alone there was Josh the cabinetmaker who'd begged her to wed him as he was in need of a wife to mind his three children. Then there was William the printer, a shy man who had sent her a very formal letter listing his not inconsiderable assets. There was Mervyn, who worked at the tannery down by the river, not forgetting Thomas Hodgson, who'd taken quite a shine to her and offered to share his large corner property and thriving metal workshop with her.

'Thoo's a bonny lass, and I'd do me best to mek thee happy,' he would say. 'How can you resist my ample charms? Aren't I handsome enough for you?'

' 'Course you're handsome, Tommy. I really don't know how I resist you, but I fear I must try. I'm far too busy even to think of marriage right now. Sorry, love.'

Just as well she did. Tommy was one of the first to join up, attending the Territorial Army training camp in July 1914, and leaving for France only a few weeks later.

'I'm that excited,' he told her. 'I've never been further than Blackpool afore. You will write, won't you, lass?'

She wrote every week, gently ignoring his oft-repeated, and increasingly ardent proposals. But he never did see even one Christmas on foreign soil as he was returned to his elderly mother in a coffin before the year was out.

Kate was sad but didn't regret her decision. She was content to remain single and devote all her energies to her business. She'd wanted only one man and he had let her down, supposedly because he was way above her in station and therefore never properly understood or trusted her. The reality, in Kate's mind at least, was that he had failed her at a much more intimate level. Now, five years on from their last meeting, she saw herself as very much his equal. She'd made something of herself, achieved a great deal, and if initially it had been with the money he gave her, the major part of her success had been down to her own efforts, her stubborn determination not to be beaten by life.

Further contingents of optimistic young men continued to leave from Kendal station, new boots highly polished, and with hope and fervour burning high in their hearts. Many, like Kate's devoted suitor, did not return. Some were drowned when their ships were sunk, others died of festering wounds, or returned home having lost their sight or a limb. Some were more fortunate and came home to Kendal to be treated for their injuries at the VAD hospital that was set up in the Friends' Day School, before being sent back to the front, into the 'jaws of hell', for more punishment. By the spring of 1915 over a thousand young men had joined the Kendal Pals, each being given the guarantee that they would be kept together, through thick and thin. And so they would remain, to the ultimate end.

Eliot saw men from his own factory joining up by the score, clickers and doggers and clerks. He made up his mind to join them. How could he not, when his country needed him? Besides, he had no family, no wife, no children to consider, and it would be one way of escaping the strangulating hold Lucy and the aunts had upon his life.

Eliot realised that he had lost much more than Callum, the adopted son he'd come to love so much. He'd come to terms with the fact that his beloved wife was dead. He would always love and miss Amelia but life went on and he accepted that fact. She would not have wished him to waste it in endless mourning.

Losing Kate was another matter entirely. It had come as a nasty shock how very much he did miss her. Her cheerful presence, the challenging way she would take him to task if she disapproved of something he did or said, that enchanting smile and the teasing gleam in her eye when they had one of their spats. That's what he missed the most, in a way, the little verbal combats they'd had.

He could see now that he might have been a touch hasty in his condemnation of her, made in the heat of the moment when he'd been at his lowest, in the depths of despair. But then he'd never expected her simply to walk out and go back to Poor House Lane. Apparently he'd even said the wrong thing the day he'd taken the doctor to help her through that difficult delivery. Even though he'd swiftly responded to her call for help, she hadn't been in the least little bit grateful. And all because he'd asked her to name the father of her child. Wasn't he entitled to know the truth? Could the child indeed be his? He was haunted by the thought that she might be. Why wouldn't the dratted woman tell him?

Kate O'Connor was as obstinate as they come, refusing to answer his questions or even to accept the cottage he'd offered to buy her, although she'd made use of the money he'd sent, he noticed, and set up in competition against him. It felt very much as if she was hell-bent on destroying him.

Worst of all, life was dull now that she was gone, so boring, with the aunts pandering to his every whim. As if on cue, there was Cissie even now. He heard her irritatingly gentle scratch upon the door, as if she had no real wish to disturb him but would do so anyway, for how could she get in otherwise, if she didn't knock? And if *she* didn't scratch on his door, one or other of her pesky dogs did it for her.

'Come in, Aunt Cissie,' Eliot called, striving to keep the irritation out of his voice.

'How did you know it was me?'

He closed his eyes, uttering a silent prayer for patience as she came fussing into the room. She was carrying a tray on which was set a coffee pot, cup and saucer, and a small plate of chocolate biscuits. Under her arm were tucked his slippers. He gave a resigned sigh as she set down the tray, pretending to be engrossed in *The Times* so as to avoid further conversation as she proceeded to add milk and sugar to the coffee she painstakingly poured into the cup. Aunt Cissie was fond of finding tidbits of information in the local *Westmorland Gazette* which she thought might amuse him. Unfortunately they were generally concerned with such gems as the county show, which dog had won first prize for obedience, or who had caught some huge fish or other in Lake Windermere or Ullswater, and generally did not interest him in the slightest.

'There you are, dear, now see that you drink it while it's hot. Don't let it go cold this time. Shall I put your slippers by the fire to warm, dear?'

Eliot managed to stretch his lips into a smile even as he ground his teeth in frustration. 'As you wish, Aunt. As you wish.' He felt as if he were being suffocated by their good-will, as if he were choking from lack of air. Every move he made was noted and remarked upon.

'Did you have a nice walk, dear?' they would say when he returned. Or, 'Was it an interesting meeting, dear? I'm afraid your comments at last week's council meeting were not particularly approved of by the *Gazette*.' Wagging a chiding finger as if he were a naughty boy.

And they had an uncanny knack of always knowing where he was and what he was doing there, or else somehow knew about it in advance. 'Isn't it today that you have the meeting about the almshouses?' they would ask blithely, clearly knowing full well. Or, 'Don't be late for the office today, dear. Isn't the accountant coming this morning?' Sometimes he wondered why they bothered to ask what he was doing, when they clearly already knew everything about his life down to the last detail.

It was a puzzle to him how they did know so much. Did they listen at keyholes, or read his diary? He found himself becoming increasingly paranoid about his personal affairs.

They even commented upon every morsel of food he ate, or when he chose to eat it. Should they tell Cook that he didn't care for haddock? Would he like something different? Was the time convenient? Were they correct in assuming he would not be in for dinner this evening? It was true that he was growing increasingly fond of eating out but Eliot had reached such a level of desperation in an effort to guard his privacy that he would often pretend to be out when really he was hiding in his study, hoping they wouldn't notice. But of course they did notice, and that's when the fetching of small snacks had started, muffins or ham sandwiches, thinking that he'd missed dinner.

So on this occasion he would do his best to remember to drink the dratted coffee, otherwise he'd have to pour it in the aspidistra yet again which surely did the plant no good at all.

And no doubt tomorrow it would be Vera's turn to wait upon him. The sisters fiercely competed with each other to fetch and carry, to bring his whisky, his cigar, his slippers, as if by doing so they could make certain that he wouldn't send them packing, back to their dull lives and their claustrophobic little cottage in Heversham.

If the aunts were a constant source of irritation to him, Lucy was even worse.

Dear Lord, what was he going to do about Lucy? Why he hadn't told her and her spoilt children to leave years ago, he couldn't imagine. But no, that wasn't strictly correct. He knew well enough why he didn't ask her to go. It was all because of the foolish sense of guilt he still nursed over his treatment of Charles. He'd been compelled to sell both his brother's properties in the end, so how could he tell his brother's wife to go? She wasn't entirely to blame for what had happened. She too was a victim of Charles's greed and stupidity, and of what he had led her to expect, as his wife.

Of course, Charles had been wrong to attempt to perpetrate that fraud but Eliot felt he should have realised how very deeply in debt his brother was, and done more to help him. At the time, he'd believed it was enough to urge him to curb his wife's excesses. Having Lucy live in his house these last five years had taught him how optimistic and unrealistic that hope had been. Money went through her hands like water, yet still he couldn't bring himself to throw her out.

If she was a spendthrift, Eliot felt it incumbent upon himself to attempt to rectify that flaw. He arranged for her to be paid a monthly allowance and set Aunt Vera the task of offering sensible advice on how to manage a budget, thinking that as an upright Christian lady she would make the ideal candidate. Despite the sale of Charles's property, furniture and works of art, and the steam yacht of course, none of which had brought their true value, there were still an astonishing number of outstanding debts. Eliot had settled as many as he could, though he'd been forced to ask for time to pay the outstanding balance due to the financial disasters the company had suffered.

Sadly, none of this succeeded in penetrating Lucy's blithe determination to continue spending regardless. She simply could not comprehend the skills of good housekeeping, of keeping a check on her expenditure or restraining her outgoings in any way. Aunt Vera would scold and lecture, cajole and bribe. A case in point recently had been that of Bunty and the dratted new dance shoes.

'No, Aunt Vera, you don't understand. The display is next week and she simply must wear pink, so her old white shoes will not do at all.'

'But why must she wear pink when she has a perfectly good white pair and ballet frock to match?'

'It's called a tutu, Aunt, and the white one was for when she was a snowflake. Now she is to be a pink rose.'

'Couldn't she be a white rose?' The faint shadow of a moustache along Aunt Vera's upper lip was very nearly bristling.

'Dear me, no. I really think white was a mistake. Darling Bunty's skin is far too fragile and pale, like mine, for her to look good in white. No, no, it must be pink. Shoes and a new tutu to match.'

'But the last outfit cost a small fortune, and she'll have grown out of it before ever she gets her proper wear from it. Buying a second set so soon is profligate, dear girl. Utterly profligate. Let the child be satisfied with one.'

Lucy responded by going into a sulk. 'Really, it would be far more useful if the company made the shoes for her, instead of concentrating entirely upon leather.'

'Don't be foolish! It isn't the job of Tyson's to make ballet pumps for silly little girls. I repeat, let the child be satisfied with white, and have done with the matter.'

'*I want pink! I want pink!*' screamed Bunty, stamping her small feet and going very red in the face.

'Why are we being persecuted in this way? I really don't see what all the fuss is about, that a little girl can't be permitted to have a pair of new shoes,' Lucy sobbed above the din.

'*And* a new dress.'

'*Tutu!*'

Bunty lay down on the floor and started to beat her heels in protest until Aunt Vera was almost tearing out her hair with frustration, and of course in the end she caved in and agreed to the purchase of the pink ballet shoes, matching tutu, or whatever other non-essential item was in dispute.

And so the battles continued. Eliot was in despair. His sister-in-law remained as greedy and extravagant as ever, with not the slightest degree of common sense, and short of cutting her off without a penny and turning her from his door to care for her three children as best she may, which of course was utterly unthinkable, he saw little hope of his succeeding where Aunt Vera had failed. Lucy would do as she pleased, and no one seemed to have the power to prevent her.

25

Always, after one of these battles, Lucy would storm to her room to vent her rage upon her pillows. It was Eliot's fault, and the aunts'. That dratted family didn't want her around, didn't even want her precious children.

Darling Bunty was now twelve years old with hair her mother's shade of ebony screwed into inappropriate ringlets, a pale, insipid complexion and small blue-grey eyes that darted about as if afraid of missing something. Even her mother had to admit that she was not a particularly pretty child, her face and body being too round, almost stocky, with very little grace or beauty. Nor could Lucy deny that her daughter's mouth possessed a decidedly peevish twist to it. Jack, at thirteen, had mouse-brown hair and a weak chin, and was already growing quite chubby – very much his father's son. Last but by no means least came Georgie with his cherubic smile and contradictory behaviour; always full of mischief and naughtiness. At nine years old he had recently started preparatory school, while the two older children had been enrolled into the most expensive academies Lucy could find for them.

'Dear Lord,' Eliot would say whenever she presented him with an account for fees, sports equipment, riding lessons or whatever. '*How much?* I'm not buying the whole dratted school, am I?' He really was the meanest man imaginable. Far worse even than poor Charles.

Lucy regarded herself as a doting mother. She was always

pleased to see her children during the long vacations, wearing though they undoubtedly were, and would beam proudly upon them, pat her son on the head and give her daughter an affectionate peck on the cheek, declaring her delight at seeing them look so well. She would claim to be looking forward to enjoying their company over Christmas, or Easter or whatever, but then would sigh with relief when they returned at the end of a long vacation, leaving her in peace.

But peace to do what? Without a husband she held no status in the household. It really was quite outrageous that in all of this time she had found no other likely suitor, or none rich enough to qualify as one, that is. Nor had Eliot made any effort to find her one by introducing her to some of his more affluent friends. He was entirely dilatory in that respect.

But then nothing ever went smoothly where she was concerned.

Look at that dratted whore of Eliot's for a start. Lucy had very cleverly managed to abduct that stupid child of hers and whisk him away so that they'd never find him again – and what had Kate O'Connor done? Had she gone into a tearful decline? Not a bit of it. She'd resurrected herself, stronger than ever.

Lucy made it her business to keep abreast of everything that went on in that slut's affairs, knowing how Kate still searched for her child, still asked questions of everyone she met.

At least Lucy had had the far-sightedness to move the boy far away from the workhouse. She'd once visited the farm over in the Langdales where she'd sent him, sitting in her pony and trap just out of sight under the shade of an overhanging tree and watching the boy as he laboured on the fells. She would have known his bright copper nob anywhere. The farmer had come out at one point and yelled to him across the yard. When the boy hadn't immediately responded, he'd marched across and slapped him about the head before dragging him back to the house by his collar. Oh, Lucy had enjoyed that so much her mouth had positively watered with pleasure. It was perfectly plain that he was being treated as a farmhand, not a son of the household, which was exactly what she'd hoped. Satisfied, she'd whipped her horse to a trot and hurried away, entirely happy.

Now, as she sat in her room weeping with frustration, gloomily going over her failing hopes for her own future, the solution came to her. She would marry Eliot! Goodness, why hadn't she thought of this before? By far the best solution. There would be no danger then of his finding another, more fertile wife, or of her own three children not inheriting the business. The tears dried instantly and Lucy set about repairing the damage.

She waited until the house was absolutely silent and even the aunts had switched off their light and, so far as she could tell, were fast asleep. Then she went to her brother-in-law's room and quietly slipped inside without even tapping on his door.

She realised at once that she'd made a most dreadful mistake. You'd have thought she was the wild witch from the dark woods judging by his horrified reaction as she slid between the sheets beside him. He leaped from the bed as if it were on fire.

'What the hell are you about now, Lucy?'

'I thought it might make sense if we got together. Isn't that what you want, deep down? After all, it's not as if we're blood-related. I'm only your sister-in-law, your dead brother's widow. It's not against the law.'

'It's against all laws of decency! For God's sake, Lucy, leave my room this minute, and pull yourself together.'

Perhaps rather foolishly, she did not do so. Still believing she could win him over, Lucy slid her nightgown from her naked shoulders sufficiently for him to enjoy the ripe fullness of her breasts, regarding him with the kind of provocative lust in her violet eyes that had once excited and entranced Charles, resulting in three handsome children. This thought suddenly brought her to a startled awareness, giving her exactly the ammunition she needed. She wasn't too old for more children herself, not quite yet.

'Wouldn't you like a child of your own?' she challenged him, crawling across the bed to slide her body against his, put her arms about his neck and press kisses over his bare chest. Evidently he slept only in drawers and very fine he looked in them too. His body was leaner, harder and far more exciting than Charles's had ever been. Her decision to offer herself to him had been for reasons of security only, insurance in a way, but this really might be quite fun. She was surely not without powers of persuasion still, and men usually needed little prompting to take pleasure of this kind. She was willing to please him in any way he liked. Wasn't she used to all manner of nonsense with dear Charles?

'Aren't you absolutely desperate for a child? Unlike poor dear Amelia, I have proved myself fertile. My children are already Tysons and we could have more. Together. What could be more sensible? You might even enjoy the getting of them, once you stop pining for a dead wife.'

It was as if she had put a light to touch paper. Never, in all her life, had Lucy seen a man so angry. Eliot went white to the lips. So angry was he that she half expected him to throw her physically her from his bed, which might have proved rather interesting and erotic, come to think of it. Sadly, he came nowhere near her but instead snatched up his robe and stalked out of the room, presumably to spend the night on the couch in his study. Lucy didn't set eyes on him again, although she stayed in his bed until Fanny brought in breakfast next morning, and dropped the tray all over the bedroom rug when she found Lucy there, instead of the master.

★

'You'll never believe what's happened now,' Fanny told Mrs Petty when she scuttled back to the kitchen to collect a second tray of breakfast. But Mrs Petty did believe it, every word, though the tightening of her lips showed that she didn't like it, not one little bit.

As she sliced more bread, wafer-thin as madam insisted, and added a scraping of butter, Mrs Petty gave a loud sniff of disapproval. 'I never did like that piece of baggage. Allus with an eye to the main chance, and too full of herself by half. The poor master would've been much better off with that other one.'

'Which other one?'

'That Kate person, the girl from Poor House Lane. She had more grace in her little finger than this mucky little madam has in all of her nasty body.'

Dennis paused in his cleaning of the harness and other trappings to think about this for a moment. 'I'd call Miss Lucy's body more tasty than nasty,' he said, and earned a clip round the ear from Fanny for his trouble.

'Well, you would know, I suppose,' she told him tartly. Dennis had proved to be a great disappointment to her, never having produced the expected ring or shown any inclination to make their relationship more permanent. She suspected he had a fancy woman somewhere but didn't like to question him too closely on the subject, in case it were true.

'She's doing well for herself an' all these days,' added Mrs Petty, setting a freshly brewed pot of tea on the tray beside the plate of bread and butter.

'Who is?' Fanny picked up the tray and swung away, deliberately turning her back on Dennis to let him see that she didn't care a jot whether he had another woman or not, and certainly had no intention of allowing him a quick fumble at her breasts, as he was so fond of doing. But in her keenness to avoid him and escape back upstairs before Miss Lucy got in one of her tantrums, she'd quite lost track of the conversation.

'I've just told thee, that other one . . . Kate whatever she were called.'

'O'Connor. Kate O'Connor,' Dennis said.

'Aye, that's her, that's the one he should have taken up with. Couldn't be any worse than Madam Lucy.'

'Aye, yer right,' Dennis agreed. 'Her business is doing well enough to worry the master, I'll tell you that fer nowt. I heard him saying to someone in the carriage the other day that she's stopped using a boy on a bicycle for her deliveries and bought a van, a big 'un, and means to buy another soon, happen a whole fleet. What do you reckon to that?' His eyes were shining, and Fanny could see with a rapid sinking of her heart the thought processes running through his daft head. She wasn't far wrong.

The day the van was delivered, Kate's entire workforce turned out to cheer.

'All I need now is someone to drive it.'

She found the answer in the shape of Dennis, who turned up on her doorstep the very same day to offer his services.

'I heard you'd bought a motor vehicle and were in need of a driver,' he said, coming straight to the point.

She laughed. 'My word, gossip still spreads fast round here. But would you want a job with me?'

'Too right. Even Askew's gone now, pushing up daisies, the poor old soul, and I'd do owt to get out of that house of nagging women. It's driving me mad.'

Kate made no comment to this, except to offer her condolences over the old gardener. 'Where would you live? There's no accommodation comes with this job.'

'I'll find somewhere, then mebbe Fanny and me can happen get wed at last. She's right fed up that I've done nowt about it so far but that madam has done everything in her power to stop us. Doesn't approve of servants marrying.'

Kate pretended not to understand. 'What madam would that be?'

'Mr Charles's widow, Lucy Tyson. Taken over the place she has, even giving the two aunts a run for their money, which they don't care for at all. Do nothing but squabble over who's in charge, them women do.'

'I did hear that she was living at Tyson Lodge.'

'Oh, aye, she's living there right enough. Nicely settled in she is, in every way. Very much so. Not that I don't think the master isn't regretting it. Spends most of the day in the factory, or locked in his study. You couldn't call him entirely happy about the situation but he's got himself lumbered, you might say. Driven by his own loneliness, I reckon.'

'I see.' There was a small silence while Kate digested the unspoken information Dennis was giving her with his winks and nods and insinuations. She understood well enough what he was trying to tell her: that Eliot was sleeping with his sister-in-law. Information she would much rather not have been privy to, since it made her feel sick to her stomach. Kate drew in a quick, steadying breath, and hardened her heart against any possibility of weakness which might lead to pity. If he was so lonely and unhappy he was driven to the arms of the dreaded Lucy, didn't he deserve to be miserable and harassed to death by women? Serve him right. Hadn't he treated her with heartless cruelty, making her out to be some sort of whore, when all the time he was as bad himself? Perhaps he would be equally heartless with dear Lucy in the end.

'The job is yours, Dennis, if you want it.'

★

As well as Dennis, Kate felt confident enough to take on a foreman: someone to keep a better eye on the work in progress. His name was Toby Lynch. Toby was a short, wiry man in his early-thirties with tousled blond hair and a cheery grin.

'Just so's we're clear from the start, I'll stand no nonsense, no messing about wi' the women, if'n ye catch me drift. Or you'll be out of here faster than a fart from a bottle. Understand?' she told him.

He grinned. 'Perfectly. Me mam and two sisters work for you already, so I know how the land lies. I'm grateful you've got 'em out of Swainson's hands.'

Toby soon proved himself capable of the task as he'd had plenty of experience in the shoe trade and, best of all, Kate liked and trusted him, feeling quite safe leaving her precious business in his hands which released her to go out on the road every day to seek yet more orders. And with Dennis to drive her, she was able to cover a much wider territory as well as carry some stock with her, making deliveries along the way.

The farmers' market took place in Kendal every Wednesday. It had been doing so in one form or another since King Richard the Lionheart had first granted the charter back in the twelfth century. The big two-wheeled farmers' carts today, in the spring of 1915, stood in a tidy row the length of the market place, and the housewives who walked by would stop to buy butter and eggs, potatoes and green vegetables, as well as the famous damsons from the Lyth Valley.

With the business running smoothly and it being May Day, Kate had awarded herself a morning off. She walked along swinging her basket, Flora skipping beside her. The little girl was wearing a pale blue pinafore, yellow blouse, and a straw sun-bonnet to shade her head from the sun. They'd already watched the Morris Men, and the dancers around the maypole up on the green, though there'd been no beating of the bounds this year because of the war. This was a tradition where the aldermen and burgesses of the borough walked the boundaries of the town, scrambling over walls and ditches in order to do so. The townsfolk would often follow on behind to enjoy the fun. But at least the sun was shining and Kate felt happy and content, enjoying the rare treat of a day out with her daughter.

'Now isn't this a grand sight? What would you like, my princess? A stick of coltsfoot rock, a glass of lemonade or a twist of candy sugar?'

'Candy sugar, candy sugar, Mammy.'

Laughing, Kate bought the stick of pink candy and gave it to Flora who instantly stuck it into her mouth. 'Don't eat it too fast now. Oh, look, I must buy some of these delicious damsons then we can make some jam later. Won't that be fun?'

While Kate waited for the farmer's wife to weigh out the fruit that she needed, Flora gazed about her with open curiosity, quickly growing bored as her mother seemed to be taking forever, talking and talking to the woman, choosing other items which were not quite such fun, like a turnip, cabbage, some potatoes and onions. Sauntering along the line of carts she came to another which sold only butter and eggs, apparently being minded by a red-haired boy.

Flora had been warned not to speak to strangers so she sucked on her sweet, gazing at him wide-eyed and saying nothing. But she could tell by the way his gaze was fastened on the sticky pink candy twist that he was hungry.

'Give us a lick,' he said at last, his need overcoming good manners.

Flora considered, but she was a kind little girl at heart and had begun to feel sorry for the boy. He looked nice enough if a bit hot and tired, with his round face and bright copper hair. She broke off the bottom part of her sweet and handed it to him. He snatched it greedily from her and stuffed it into his mouth in one gulp, crunching on the candy so that it was gone in seconds.

'Flora . . . Flora, where are you?'

She rolled her eyes. 'That's my mammy.'

The boy stepped forward for a better look. 'Who, the one with red hair? She looks nice.'

Flora let out an exasperated sigh, 'I suppose so. A bit of a fusspot. Won't let me do anything or go anywhere, but you know how mothers are.'

'No, I don't, s'matter of fact. I haven't got a mother.'

Flora's eyes widened. 'No mother? Don't talk soft, everybody has a mother.'

'Well, I don't. I'm an orphan, see. I live on t'farm with Mr and Mrs Brocklebank.'

'Flora, where are you?'

'Got to go.' And spinning on her heels, Flora skipped happily back to where Kate stood waiting for her, her basket heavy with produce.

Grabbing the child's hand, she gave her daughter a little shake. 'What did you think you were doing, wandering off like that? That was very naughty. Haven't I told you to stay by me?'

'I was only talking to that boy.'

'Never mind what you were doing. You do what I say and stick by my side. Is that clear?'

Flora nodded silently, and with her hand clasped firmly in her mother's, meekly fell into step beside her, glancing back only once when they reached the end of the street. The boy was still watching them and Flora lifted a hand to wave goodbye.

'Who are you waving to?' Kate asked, feeling guilty at her over-reaction. The child had only gone to the next-but-one cart, not even out of sight. She really must allow her some freedom and not be so consumed by the fear of losing her. She turned now to see who it was who had caught her daughter's attention, but saw no one of particular importance other than a fat farmer's wife berating her child by clipping him about the head. Poor boy, what had he done to deserve such a cluttering? she wondered. How cruel some mothers were.

She smiled down at Flora, who was looking quite distressed over the little scene, and attempted to distract her. 'Come along, my precious, we shall go home and make damson jam, then a whole batch of scones to eat with it.'

And so Kate didn't notice when the young boy wriggled free to escape the thrashing and ran after her for some distance, at least until she'd turned into Finkle Street, where he stopped and stood by the lamp-post and watched her walk away, still laughing and chattering to her pretty little daughter, until she'd quite vanished from sight.

A few weeks later, Fanny walked into Kate's workshop with a swagger. It amused Kate to see the housemaid flush with embarrassment as she came towards her. 'What a joy it is to see you again, Fanny, and looking so well. What're you doing in my neck of the woods then?'

Fanny glowered, cheeks flushing pinker than ever, for this Kate O'Connor cut a very different figure from the one whose feet had been filthier than her own boots all those years before. She was no longer a nursemaid, after all but an employer, and one who had won increasing respect around the town. And Fanny needed work.

'I'm all right, I suppose, but me and Dennis, we're not gerrin' wed. He's tekken up with some shop assistant or other. Right little floozy, no doubt.'

'Oh, dear, I'm sorry to hear that, I am so.' Since Dennis was her driver, Kate was well aware of his new domestic arrangements, but thought it best not to admit as much at this juncture.

'Don't be, I'll survive. Only I'll ring his flamin' neck and throttle the bugger if the Hun don't do it first!'

Kate nodded sympathetically, waiting patiently for whatever Fanny had come to say. When still she hesitated, showing no sign of coming to the point, Kate was forced to prompt her with, 'So what can I do for ye on this bright morning?'

The housemaid cleared her throat. 'The fact is, Kate – er – Miss – er em . . .'

'Kate will do fine.'

Now that Fanny had finally started it all came out in a rush, on one swift indrawn breath. 'The fact of the matter is, Mr Tyson has decided to take the King's shilling and be an officer and I can't stand being a housemaid no longer, not in that house anyroad. I'm fed up with all the work and being bossed about, and me wages haven't gone up in years. What with Mr Askew dead, and Dennis gone, that only leaves Mrs Petty, me and daft Ida to look after that big place and the two aunts. Not forgetting madam herself, of course, who never lifts a finger. So I'm not stopping on, I've had enough.'

Kate's understanding of what Fanny had told her got stuck somewhere around the part where she'd said Eliot had joined up. Dear God, no, don't let him do that!

'By heck, I don't mind telling you, Kate, 'cause I know you'll understand, she's a right one and no mistake. A nastier piece of work you wouldn't find in a long day's march. Why, just the other day she med me clean and blacklead all the grates twice over because she said I hadn't done 'em proper. Called me a lazy slut an' all. Lazy my eye, when I spend me bleeding life on me knees in that house, and not saying prayers neither. And you know what I caught her up to t'other morning . . .'

But Kate had heard enough servants' gossip. 'You say Mr

Tyson has joined up. When did he do that? When does he leave?'

'Sometime in the next week or two, I imagine. Off to do his training first, though. Anyroad, like I were saying . . .'

Kate set her hands flat on the desk top, since they'd started to tremble, and leaning closer, fixed the girl with a stern glare. 'Fanny, I haven't all day to sit here listening to your tittle-tattle. What is it exactly you are wanting from me? Would it be a job, by any chance?'

The housemaid looked shame-faced but admitted that it was. 'I'm looking for a fresh start, a new beginning. I thought you might help me to get one, since we're old chums like.'

Kate thought this description a somewhat exaggerated view of their relationship but made no comment on Fanny's assessment. 'You know, of course, that Dennis is working for me too. Would that not bother you, in view of your current differences? Because I don't want any trouble, Fanny. I don't want you imagining you can win him back, and then causing mischief when you don't succeed.'

Fanny's cheeks flared bright crimson, for of course winning him back had indeed been on her mind, but her voice was quite steady as she told the lie. 'I wouldn't have him back if he were wrapped up in a parcel and tied with a scarlet ribbon. No, I'm finished wi' men. And I'm done wi' being an housemaid an' all.'

Kate was still doubtful, remembering the way the girl had sent her to Coventry, been so imperious in her manner, as if she were God's gift and Kate something the cat had dragged in. Yet she didn't blame her for wanting something better. Domestic service was a thankless task, particularly working for the likes of Lucy Tyson, and she'd earn much more money in the workshop. 'I'm not really taking anyone on at the moment, but since you and I are – as you say – old chums in a manner of speaking, I'll make an exception in your case. You can start tomorrow in the tongue department.'

'Oh, Kate . . . oh, thank you, miss, thank you. I'm that grateful.' Fanny's eyes shone and for one dreadful moment Kate thought she might actually be about to hug her before Fanny hastily backed away. Yet the girl's obvious joy brought a smile to Kate's lips. There were many kinds of abuse, and perhaps Madam Lucy had bullied this lass once too often. Fanny deserved a chance too, just as much as the women of Poor House Lane.

'That's settled then. You can go now, Fanny. I'll see you in the morning, sharp at seven.'

'Yes, miss.' It was only when she reached the door that Fanny thought to ask, 'What's the tongue department? What do I have to do there?'

'Certainly not use your own tongue, Fanny. We can hear quite enough of that at other times.'

Fanny had the grace to giggle.

'I've girls to make the eyelets in the boots, others to put in the lining if there is one, some to fold the leather in a process called sciving, while others close up and stitch the toe. You, Fanny, will join the girls whose task it is to put in the tongue. But don't worry, you'll be given very clear instructions tomorrow. Don't be late.'

As Fanny dashed off, thoroughly pleased with herself, Kate sank back into her chair before her knees quite gave way. She just hoped she'd done the right thing and that Fanny would suit, and would change her mind about throttling poor Dennis. Yet all she really cared about was that Eliot was leaving. *He would soon be going to war.*

26

Lucy slammed down her knife and fork in a fury. As if things weren't bad enough, Eliot had taken it into his head to play the hero. It had come like a bolt from the blue when he'd made the announcement over dinner, quite ruining her appetite. She hadn't even guessed that he intended to enlist which would obviously mean that he'd escape her clutches.

Lucy was against the war; had joined the Women's Peace League to raise money for the pacifist cause, campaigning for it to be stopped largely because they said so. However genuine the emotions of the other pacifists, Lucy was simply concerned with the disruption to her own life. And she'd had quite enough of that already.

The aunts, fools that they were, entirely supported Eliot's decision. 'Quite right,' Aunt Vera said, pursing her mouth into a prim line of approval. 'The right and proper thing for a gentleman to do is join the call to arms.'

'Oh, indeed,' agreed her sisterly echo, patting and stroking the dog leaning against her with great excitement.

But it was Lucy who gave a small growl of annoyance, which Aunt Vera heard. 'What did you say, dear?'

'I said, how can Eliot be so foolish as to enlist when he is needed here, to run the company? How are we supposed to manage without him? Who on earth will run the business while you're away, playing the hero?' she demanded, fixing him with an icy glare. 'Surely you don't expect me to keep an eye on things for you?'

Eliot gave her a cool, distancing smile. 'I've made all the necessary arrangements. And no, indeed, you will not be troubled. I have my accounts clerk to deal with the day-to-day issues of paying wages and outstanding bills, including, dear sister-in-law, your own allowance, so you will not be inconvenienced in any way. Although I would remind you that there is a war on, and prudence and thrift are the order of the day.'

'Poppycock! I'm not letting some jumped up little Hun ruin my life. Isn't it bad enough that I have no home of my own and am forced to live on handouts and charity?' Lucy felt trapped, stifled, living here with the two dragons, as she privately thought of the aunts. She'd been patient long enough. She wanted, *deserved*, a home of her own, a husband and money in the bank to see her comfortable and secure. She wasn't old like them, but still young with more than half her life still to be lived and enjoyed. She should never have been deprived of the house on Stramongate, she thought, quite forgetting that it had been her own decision to move into Tyson Lodge, not to mention her own reckless spending which had put both her homes in jeopardy.

'Why don't you do something to stop that girl from destroying us? Why don't you fight back and beat her at her own game? Surely, with the power of the Tyson name, it would be an easy matter to put her out of business?'

'By *that girl*, I assume you mean Kate O'Connor?'

'I mean that no-good chit of a whore, the girl who sold you her own child and then lost him through her habitual carelessness.'

Eliot winced at her bluntness, biting back an instinctive urge to defend Kate for hadn't he accused her of the self-same thing in the past? Yet he felt honour bound to speak, for nothing of the sort had been proved and he'd lived to regret his hasty judgement of her. 'I'm not sure that is correct. And, however irritating, her business is nothing more than normal, healthy competition. She has substantial orders from the army and is even now negotiating a contract with the Russian Government.'

'Tch! The woman must sleep with every Tom, Dick and Harry in order to achieve so much, so quickly. She's a self-seeking slut . . .'

Lucy went on talking, going on and on about Kate O'Connor, but Eliot had stopped listening. He felt thoroughly wearied of women. He'd be glad to get away and be in the company of men for a change, war or no war.

'. . . you could at least stop being so damned honourable. She's deliberately set out to ruin you, any fool can see that. And having stolen Dennis, Fanny's gone to work for her now. She's taking us over. Why you allow her to get away with it is quite beyond me. I would've thought you'd have put your own niece and nephews first.'

'If that is another complaint about money, may I simply say in my own defence that I hope I do my duty, what I believe to be right. However, my pockets are not bottomless pits over-flowing with brass, Lucy. Times are hard.'

How tired she was of hearing those words. 'Kate O'Connor is doing well enough, despite the war, stealing business from Tyson's hand over fist. So why aren't you doing something about it, instead of running away?' His lack of response to this barb as he continued to eat his meal, even politely commenting on the tenderness to beef and making Cissie flush with pride at the compliment, infuriated her all the more.

The damned woman was advancing herself at their expense, that of Lucy and her precious children, and Eliot didn't seem to care whether there would be a business left for them to inherit. Why didn't he do something to stop her? Lucy felt rage building up inside her. She could feel the sour taste of it in her throat like bile. She refused to allow this dreadful family to treat her so callously, as if she were of no account. Not for one moment had she imagined her life would turn out this way, stuck at the Lodge as some sort of dependant with no say over what went on. She was the mother of three children who should join this business one day. And it was surely her duty, as their mother, to ensure that there was something worthwhile for them to take over in the fullness of time, especially considering all the trouble she'd taken previously. She needed to make that point clear at least. 'If you weren't so selfish, you would provide me with a home of my own *now*. Don't my children deserve that much, at least?'

'I was under the impression that your children were very well provided for. They certainly cost me enough.' Eliot sighed as he reached for the wine decanter to refill his glass with a rather fine claret, though how much longer he would be able to afford such luxuries was a moot point.

'And *you* resent paying for them.'

'That's not what he said, Lucy,' Aunt Vera chipped in. 'Dear Eliot is merely advocating prudence.'

'And thrift,' echoed Aunt Cissie, slipping a slice of beef to her favourite dog.

'What about my precious darlings? Don't they deserve the very best of care? You destroyed their father, would you destroy them too?'

'My word, Lucy, that's a bit below the belt,' Aunt Vera reprimanded her in vinegar tones. 'We all know that Charles was the author of his own misfortune, as are you, my dear, to a degree.'

'I beg your pardon?'

Eliot patiently flapped a hand to calm heated tempers. Poor

Vera was puffing like an old train; he rather expected steam to issue from her ears at any moment. 'Speaking for myself, I can't help admiring Kate O'Connor's tenacity and entrepreneurial spirit. But fear not. It might be a struggle but Tyson's will survive. One cannot expect to have things all one's own way in business. Matters could change radically after the war. The army won't require so many boots then and she might be the one in difficulties, whereas Tysons will have its classic lines to fall back on.'

'There you are, Lucy dear,' said Aunt Vera with waspish satisfaction, 'you will simply have to be patient.'

She smiled at the older woman with all the sweetness of acid.

Fanny took to her new job without any problems whatsoever, finding it quite a treat to be with girls her own age, and to Kate's enormous relief paid no attention whatsoever to Dennis, walking past him in tight-lipped silence, with her nose in the air in that stuck-up way of hers. Kate wondered how Mrs Petty and Ida would cope without housemaid, gardener or chauffeur, doubting they'd manage to replace any of them just now. Coping with the aunts would not be easy, and who would Lucy find to boss? Not that it had anything to do with her what went on at Tyson Lodge. She had her own problems to think of, after all, but she was finding it difficult to concentrate on practical concerns today. All Kate could think of was that Eliot had enlisted.

She sat plaiting her daughter's hair, listening to her chatter on about what her teacher had thought about a picture she'd drawn, what she was going to do today in school and how many gold stars she'd won lately.

A small hand tugged at her sleeve. 'Mammy, are you listening? I want to go to Maggie's for tea. Will you let me?'

'Of course, darling, if her mother is happy to have you.'

'Oh, she is, she is. We're going to make jam tarts. Maggie's mummy does things like that with her all the time.'

Not like me, Kate thought, with a nudge of motherly guilt. 'Well, perhaps Maggie's mummy doesn't have to go out to work, as I do.'

' 'Course she don't. Maggie's got a daddy to do that.' Flora shook her head, making the streaks of fire in her dark auburn curls dance and bounce with health. The child was vain enough to be constantly demanding that they be allowed to fall loose on her shoulders in soft waves, but Kate insisted that plaits were far more practical. Then, as if asking the question for the first time, which wasn't the case at all, 'Why don't I have a daddy?'

'Oh, my, now look at the time. Aren't we going to be late, if we don't get a move on?' Callum had been too young to understand that his daddy was dead, that he was never coming back from the river. It had been easy to talk of heaven, and Jesus needing him more, since he didn't fully appreciate the finality of death. It seemed to be much more difficult with Flora, who was a child filled with questions and curiosity. But how could Kate tell her the truth, when she couldn't bring herself to admit that Eliot was her daughter's father?

Kate found the image of Flora's pretty little face blurring as her eyes filled with unexpected tears. Flora's daddy was going to France to fight and she didn't even know it. Dear God, how would Kate herself survive, not knowing how or where he was, not being able to write to find out if he was still alive? Kate wanted to hate him, but couldn't. She wanted never to think of him again, never to need him, but that seemed quite impossible. She felt trapped by her own weakness.

Flora said, 'And will we go to the market soon? I want another candy twist, and to see my friend again.'

'And what friend is that?' Kate said with a laugh. 'Now will ye fetch yer coat, or your teacher will give you a black mark, not a gold star.'

'The one I shared my sweet with. You know, I told you, the boy on the farmer's cart with the red hair.'

Kate felt as if she had been drenched in cold water. But if so, then why did she instantly feel all hot and prickly, her fingers going numb so that they became paralysed, unable to fasten the buttons on her daughter's coat?

'Let me do it, Mammy. You're so *slow*,' Flora complained.

'Where did you see him, this boy? How old was he? What did he look like? Which cart was it? Did it have a name on it? What was the farmer called?'

But these were too many questions for Flora. Besides, she'd grown tired of the conversation, was far more engrossed with showing off her newfound skill with buttons. 'Mammy, look, I can nearly do shoelaces too. My teacher says I'm the cleverest girl in the class.'

'Flora, listen to Mammy. I want you to try to remember. How old would you say the boy was?'

It took some time and a great deal of patience before Kate could get anything more out of her. 'Oh, I don't know. He was bigger than me. And he was hungry. That fat lady hit him.'

And then an image of a fat farmer's wife clouting a boy about the head, whom she'd taken to be the woman's own son, came into Kate's mind and a wave of sickness hit her. Had that been Callum? Could it possibly have been him? Oh, dear God, had she been so near, and never realised it was him? Oh, let it not be him. Much as she longed to find him, let him not be so ill-treated.

Kate walked her daughter to school that day, as she did every morning, but this time, instead of hurrying back to the work-shop to get on with the mass of orders and tasks piled up on her desk, she dashed to the Town Hall in a frenzy of agitation, demanding to speak to councillors, to the Town Clerk, to anyone who could tell her the names of the farmers who attended the market. She was told only that it was a free market, that farmers came and went at will.

For the last five years Kate had studiously managed to avoid Eliot Tyson, catching no more than the odd glimpse of him at a distance, for all Kendal was a small town. She hadn't wanted to see him. The mere sight of him had served only to bring back all the pain of loving him, and the agony of losing Callum.

Occasionally, she'd see the two aunts going into the post office on Finkle Street or shopping on Branthwaite Brow. And once or twice she'd spotted Lucy marching into Berry's the draper's on Highgate, her three children trailing after her like a line of ducklings. But Kate always made sure that none of them ever saw her.

She'd also made a point of steering clear of the far side of the river, where she'd be sure to run across him. Yet Kate was ever aware that Eliot was not too far away. On her way back from her fruitless errand at the Town Hall, she looked across the river to the grey-stone, square mansion, to the turrets and windows that she'd once known so well, imagining him closeted in his study, a fire burning in the grate, a book on his lap. But no, he would be taking breakfast with the aunts and Lucy, before hurrying on to his work, as she should be doing. She'd often hoped and prayed that he might be missing her, that he was lonely too, while at the same time telling herself that he deserved to be so for rejecting her so heartlessly. That he might, perhaps, come looking for her one day. But of course he never had, and in the end she'd come to see that it was foolish to go on hoping, telling herself she didn't want him anyway.

Didn't she hate him for choosing Lucy over her? Wasn't she at least *trying* to hate him, and to prove that she could stand on her own two feet? And, damn it, hadn't she succeeded? Until now.

Should she tell him about this possible sighting? Did she need his help? Maybe later, when she had more information.

She went to the market place, empty today, it not being the right day, but she visited all the shops, asking shopkeepers if they had seen a red-haired boy minding a cart for a fat farmer's wife. None had. No one knew his name. None could help her.

Kate stood in helpless misery and wept. If only she had paid more attention at the time to what Flora had been saying. If only she'd gone back to remonstrate with the woman for clouting the boy. But she'd thought it none of her business. Didn't it happen all the time, mothers chastising their sons? It didn't necessarily mean that he was being ill-treated, that he was unhappy. Or even that it was Callum. There must be any number of other red-headed boys in Westmorland. But somehow, in her heart of hearts, she knew that it was him, that this was a clue, and felt a stirring of excitement despite her despair. How many farmers were there in this county? Not so many surely that she couldn't find him. All she had to do was visit all the other markets: Ambleside, Buttermere, Coniston, Keswick, Kirkby Lonsdale, wherever farmers gathered to sell their produce. Somewhere amongst them she would find him.

Wasting no time, she ran to find Dennis. 'Forget the deliveries today. I have a more important job for us to do.'

'Are you sure, Kate? That Mr Rumley don't like to be kept waiting, and Joseph Webster is a stickler for his boots being delivered on time, even to the hour. He'll have his lads on standby, waiting to unpack the boxes the minute we arrive.'

'Well, he'll be disappointed today.' She was flying around, answering queries, giving out hasty instructions, calling for Millie, wanting to tell her friend what she'd discovered. When she succeeded in finding her, gabbling out her tale at breathless speed, Millie's eyes opened wide in wonder. She hugged Kate tight, instantly promised to collect Flora from school and keep an eye on things here, and sent her friend on her way with all her love.

'I shall have every finger crossed. Bring him home, Kate. Bring him home.'

They drove miles that day, through town after town, it seemed as if it might be the length and breadth of the county, though how could it be, pottering along far too slowly for Kate's liking, and with far too many stops. Dennis would frequently need to refill the tank with petroleum, mend a puncture or simply cool down the engine. It was an exhausting trip and utterly fruitless as it turned out. Either there was no market that day, or no sign of a red-haired boy with or without a fat farmer's wife. It was nearly midnight by the time they arrived back home again, tired and discouraged.

'We can try another day,' Dennis consoled her, fully understanding what it was all about by this time. 'But not tomorrow. We have to deliver those boots.'

They tried again of course, only days later, deliveries or no, but with equal lack of success. And as if this wasn't bad enough, on Sunday a train was leaving with the next batch of recruits off for training. No doubt Eliot would be amongst them.

The last thing Kate wanted was for him to go to France and run the risk of being killed. She couldn't begin to contemplate a world without him, a time when she didn't know that, whether or not their differences were ever settled, she could at least see him about town and know that he was safe and well. However much she might deny it, didn't she love him still? Wouldn't she always love him, drat the man.

There was no question in her mind but that she would

have to go on Sunday and see him off. How could she escape it? But not for a moment would she allow him to see that she cared.

Kate could see at once that Eliot was surprised to see her. He stood on the station platform in his smart overcoat, his bag at his feet, and looked at her as if he couldn't believe what his eyes were telling him.

'Is it really you, Kate? You look well.'

'Thank you.' She'd made sure that she did look well. She was dressed in a brand new burgundy coat and ankle-length skirt, a pale blue silk jabot at the throat and a matching hat with a long feather atop her neatly coiffured head. She'd bought the outfit 'specially for the occasion and the open admiration in his warm brown eyes was gratifying, if painful to witness. She came briskly to the point. Without removing her black kid gloves, she handed him an envelope, 'I heard you were going off on training today and wanted to bring you this. It's the money you loaned me.'

'Good lord, Kate, that wasn't a loan.'

'Well, I've treated it as such. I'm a decent, hard-working woman and I don't take money from men, not even gentlemen.' She met his startled gaze, unblinking. Kate had every intention of keeping this meeting strictly formal. Not for a moment must he be allowed to guess the inner turmoil she was suffering.

'I'm sure you don't. I mean – I never thought that you . . .'

'I wanted to make that quite clear, considering our past association. And there was one other thing I thought you should know. A young boy was spotted on the market place the other day, a boy with red hair. I don't know whether it's Callum or not, of course, as I haven't been able to find him yet. But I intend to keep searching, just in case. I've already visited quite a few other markets, to no avail, but I'll keep looking. I wanted you to know – before you went away. I won't give up, and I'll tell the aunts if I get any news. Now, I wish you well, a safe homecoming, and bid you good day.'

She turned on her heel, had walked for some yards before he came out of his stunned paralysis and in two long strides was by her side, looking as if he might snatch hold of her arm but then seeming to think better of it.

'Kate, don't rush away. I can't believe what you're saying. You think it might be Callum?'

She gave a helpless shrug, 'I can't be sure till I find the boy. It might all be a waste of time. I've followed up so many leads already, but there's always a chance, don't you think?'

'The trouble is, he'll have changed so much by now. He's a grown boy, almost a young man, so how can we know what he'll even look like? All these lost years! So much we've missed, been deprived of. He won't have that soft baby voice any more, nor your Irish lilt in it. He won't giggle and chuckle as he used to do. He could look and sound like a Westmorland farmer. He might not even be in the county . . .'

'Oh, don't say that! Don't I drive around in me pony and trap every Sunday, just on the off chance I might spot him? And day after day I've had Dennis drive me over half the county in the van, when really we should be working. If he's here, I'll find him so I will.'

Neither of them mentioned the possibility of his being dead. They never had and never would. Until a body was found to prove it, Callum would remain forever a lost child.

As she turned her eyes up to his, he saw the anguish there, the need for reassurance, and something more.

Impulsively, Eliot took her hand and squeezed it. 'If anyone can find Callum, you can. But please don't go, not like this. At least wait till the train departs. I'd like to see you standing there, on the platform, when it draws out of the station. Will you do that for me?'

She looked sideways at him, at the pleading in his eyes, shielding her own with a sweep of long, golden lashes. She'd meant to be entirely practical and businesslike, simply to return the money, inform him of this new lead which she was desperately trying not to get too hopeful about, and walk away. But soon, when his short training was over, he would be off to the front. Tommy Hodgson had gone to France and never returned. What if the same thing were to happen to Eliot and she never saw him again either? How would she feel about refusing this very simple request? How would she ever be able to live with herself? Kate felt herself weakening. 'Very well.'

'We've time for a cuppa, I think. Would you care for one?'

27

Kate sat almost in a trance, oddly drained of emotion, feeling spent and exhausted, unable to think of a thing to say.

'So, tell me, how you are doing, Kate. How is the baby – er – how is she?'

It was astonishing, though typical of him, that he should start by asking about her child and not the business. They sat on a bench in the teeth of a cold wind, since the tea rooms were heaving with young men and their families, and drank their tea to the strains of 'Tipperary', played by the town band. Kate could see the Mayor in his robes and chain, and what were presumably various members of his Corporation all walking about, trying to look important as they reassured men that they would not lose out by volunteering, that their families would be looked after and well provided for.

She kept her spine stiff, her hands clasped tight on the cup and saucer, as if to a lifeline. 'Flora is grand, ta very much. And she's not a baby now but quite the little schoolgirl. She'd been attending a kindergarten on Aynam Road but last September she started school proper, which she loves.'

'Splendid, splendid.' He looked slightly nonplussed, thrown off-balance by her self-assurance and cool control. Perhaps he half expected her to be scratching his eyes out, or weeping with anguish all over him. Kate heard him clear his throat, as if he didn't know quite what to say next; noticed from the corner of her eye how he glanced up and down the crowded platform, and down at the still unopened envelope in his hand. He slipped it into a pocket of his greatcoat. 'I've maintained an interest in your progress. I heard you were doing well, that you were very busy.'

'Indeed I am, as no doubt ye are yourself?'

He gave a snort of laughter, one which held not a trace of humour in it. 'As you well know, busy is not the word I would choose to describe Tyson's these days. I'm sure you are only too aware of the damage you've inflicted upon my firm, Kate O'Connor, so don't pretend otherwise. But then wasn't that your intention all along? The ship won't go down, but it is badly holed and taking in water. We are a shadow of our former selves.'

She opened her eyes very wide as she stared innocently up at him. 'Indeed, I'm shocked to hear ye say so.'

Had she done it then? She'd beaten him, or at least wounded him badly. So why wasn't she feeling that warm glow of satisfaction she'd expected to feel? Why didn't she experience the pure joy of triumph? 'I'd've thought you'd be doing grand, what with the war and all. Still, I'm sure you'll manage to survive, Tysons allus do.' She turned her head away and sipped her tea, to prove that she really wasn't interested in whether he did or not, or even if he answered her question.

Eliot gave of snort of disbelief, exhaling a breath that clouded to mist in the cool morning air. 'Oh, we'll survive. I'll make damn' sure of it, even if you did snap up all the orders to supply the army with the boots they need a good twelve months before I even thought to ask. Very forward-thinking of you.'

And now her lovely mouth curled into a tiny smile, relishing her victory, and Kate's clear grey eyes gleamed with delight to see how his jaw tightened with annoyance at being bested by a woman. 'I believe it was you yourself, Eliot Tyson, who carefully explained it all to me. I didn't properly understand at the time, me being only a simple servant girl, but later I got to thinking it might make good business sense, so decided to give it a go. And I must say, the officer I spoke to regarding the order was a perfect gentleman, smothered in badges and ribbons so he was, but still he made time to talk to me.'

Eliot sighed. 'I don't doubt it. Bowled over by that enchanting smile, I should think. No doubt you made him an offer he couldn't refuse?'

'I did indeed give him a price that was beneficial to us both, if that's what yer meaning. But then what else would you expect me to offer?' Kate responded tartly.

'I wouldn't know, Kate, would I? Depends what you considered you had of value at the time, or what you thought might be of interest to him. I'm sure whatever deal you cut, it was to your advantage.'

She could feel a surge of anger at the insinuation behind his words, as if he were implying that she would offer herself, or her child if it was politic to do so. Her fingers tightened on the cup in her hand as she struggled to stay calm but they must have been shaking after all because some of the tea spilled over on to her lap. She leaped to her feet, dabbing at it in annoyance with her handkerchief. 'Oh, no, me new skirt!'

'Can I help?' he offered, and she slapped his hand away.

'I can manage perfectly well, thank you.' It certainly wouldn't do to let him see that he had scored a point and rattled her. Ignore him, a voice in her head urged. He was as arrogant as ever, always so damned sure he was right. Best to pretend she hadn't properly understood. She sat down again, trying to disguise the small damp stain on her lap by pulling her coat close about her. 'In any case, I don't believe my business methods are any concern of yours.'

'They are certainly nothing if not individual, and largely seem to involve theft of some sort.'

'Theft?'

'Of *my* customers.'

She opened her mouth to deny it but then closed it again, nipping her lower lip between her teeth, firmly resolved to say nothing more. He was probably right. She had stolen a great many of his customers.

He sipped his tea, which suddenly tasted sour and unpalatable so he set it aside, brow puckering into a troubled frown. Leaning his elbows on his knees, he deliberately kept his gaze turned away from her, though even when staring at the ground, he could see her trim ankles and her small neat feet in their fashionable button boots.

He sat back, unable to bear being so near to her and yet still at odds. 'It's a pity, in a way, that we don't get on, that we spend so much time at loggerheads. It would make more sense if we were on the same side. I'm sure then we could help each other a good deal, if we but tried. Particularly now, with the war on, and my business needing more attention than I can give it.'

'Who's taking care of it then, the business? Holy Mother, yer not leaving that bloody foreman in charge?'

'I must do my duty, Kate. What else can I do?'

'You're mad. Why do you stubbornly insist on trusting him?'

'Who else can I trust?'

'Me. You could trust me.'

He gave a nostalgic smile, the warmth in his eyes cooling to the chill of polished marble. 'That might have been true once, but not now, Kate, not any more. Why would I risk handing over the running of my business to the woman who has deliberately set out to destroy it? The woman who has stolen not only many of my workers, but some of my best customers by ruthlessly and constantly undercutting me on price?'

'I offer a much faster service. And where was *your* support when I needed it? Isn't it every man, or woman, for themself?

And if your workers leave you, you should perhaps ask yourself why.'

He looked thoughtful for a moment, the first shadow of doubt creeping in, then cast another glance in her direction, noting the sweep of those fine lashes, the curve of her flushed cheek, the proud way in which she held herself, and something strange happened deep inside him, a clenching of muscles, a burning sensation, so that he was forced to look away. The fact that she was a beauty didn't mean a thing, he told himself. Of course he wanted her, what man wouldn't? And he couldn't get it out of his head that many others had probably enjoyed her too, just as he had. He'd no proof of her innocence. She'd certainly produced two children with comparative ease, and God knows who their respective fathers were.

She'd climbed into his bed without a moment's hesitation. Young Dennis had been sufficiently besotted to leave secure employment to go and work for her, and wouldn't hear a word said against her. According to rumour, she'd enjoyed any number of suitors in recent years and had now taken on a foreman, Toby somebody-or-other, whom she was probably getting cosy with. For all he knew she might not ever have been married since her husband had been conveniently dead – drowned, apparently – when he'd first met her. He hated himself for being jealous, but was it any wonder?

'You're probably right. It wouldn't be appropriate for us to work together.'

'And I'm doing fine on me own, thanks all the same.' One moment she moved towards him, then he'd lost her again.

'And at least you don't have to see Swainson every day.'

She gave a small smile. That is a bonus, yes.'

'You must have liked him once over, to dally with him as you did?'

She turned wide, disbelieving eyes upon him. 'Dally with Swainson? Sweet Jaysus, I'd cut me own throat first.'

'He has implied that his advances were once willingly accepted, presumably until that little contretemps over pay when you believed he'd rebuffed you. Isn't that why you've had it in for him so fiercely all these years, out of some need for female vengeance?'

'If he told ye all that, then he's a bigger liar than I gave him credit for, and you a bigger fool to believe him.'

'Is that so?'

There it was again. The old arrogance back in place, the cold superiority of his expression telling her they were as far apart as ever. Kate set down her cup and saucer with a sharp click on the bench beside her, a great wedge of tears blocking her throat. 'Sure an' if I drink any more, I'll be drowning in tea. I've had two cups already, waiting for ye to arrive.' Why could he not trust her? Why did he persist in seeing her in the worst possible light?

Eliot frowned, again feeling confused and uncertain of his ground. He told himself that he would have stood by his decision to sack Swainson, had he thought it would do any good, had he believed for one moment that her accusations of his abuse of women could be true, but he only had her word for that. From the moment Swainson had said, no – implied – they'd once been lovers, he'd had no doubts about revoking his decision. The union had not found it difficult to convince him to do so. Oh, but he wanted to believe in her innocence, yet how could he, when she'd been more concerned with her own welfare than the safety of her own child? If she hadn't been fussing over this foolish vendetta with Swainson, Callum might still be living safe and well at Tyson Lodge to this day. He could very easily hate her when he put his mind to it.

But he wanted her, too. God, how he wanted her.

A silence had fallen between them, long and awkward. Desperately wanting to break it, he changed the subject. 'Once I've completed the initial training, I'll be allowed home for a few days, in order to sort out my affairs before being shipped overseas. Will I see you again?'

Kate deliberately kept her heart hard, a piece of granite with sharp edges even if its core might be soft as mallow. 'I very much doubt it. And I'm sure you'll have enough to see to, without bothering about me. Won't you want to spend time with Lucy? I'm surprised she didn't come to see you off today.' There, she'd said it. Now he would know how she too listened to gossip.

He gave a snort of laughter, as if she'd said something amusing. 'I do assure you that Lucy would be the last person I would want to see. I can't wait to escape her greedy talons, and if she did come to see me off, it would only be to give me her latest shopping list, or yet more bills to pay. The woman drives me demented.'

She glanced up at him quickly, stunned. Then you're not – I mean, you and she . . . I heard that you . . .'

He frowned. 'I haven't the first idea what tales you've been listening to, Kate, but I do assure you there is nothing between my sister-in-law and myself but tiresome duty.'

So he wasn't sleeping with her, after all? Kate found herself smiling. 'Looks like we both have a habit of jumping to conclusions.'

He regarded her thoughtfully for a moment. 'It would seem so. I do assure you that if I could find some way to prise her, and the blessed aunts, out of my house, I would do so.'

Suddenly Kate felt so ridiculously light-headed that she actually giggled. 'I could lend you a lever, or mebbe you could change the locks when they're out on their calls.'

'Now why didn't I think of that?'

'Oh, drat, there's the train whistle.' Her whole body jerked, face naked with fear, and his startled gaze took in the horror she clearly felt over his imminent departure into unknown dangers.

'I'll be fine,' he soothed, as if she had spoken these thoughts out loud.

Kate cleared her throat and gave him what she hoped was a cool and distant smile, keeping her tone brisk. ' 'Course ye will. Only the good die young.' And then she gulped, realising what she'd said, and unable to prevent herself, leaned over and kissed him quickly on the cheek.

He seemed startled but then smiled at her, a smile warm enough to soften any woman's heart. Any, that is, but Kate O'Connor's. 'Thank you for coming. And for that kiss. I'm not sure I deserve it.'

She felt flustered now, wishing she'd managed to stay calm, but his reaction to her mention of Lucy had quite unnerved her, set her pulses racing. 'I'm quite sure you don't, but everyone else seems to be getting one so we can't have you feeling left out, now can we?' As she got swiftly to her feet, tugging at her immaculate gloves, there was the sound of muffled weeping coming from all sides as mothers, wives and sweethearts said their goodbyes to loved ones. Even the band had muted their tone. The Mayoress was handing out packets of sandwiches and cigarettes to the new recruits as they climbed aboard. Eliot got to his feet and picked up his bag, ready to join them.

'You'll send word if you hear anything about Callum?' He raised his voice against the din of banging doors and the persistent hiss of steam.

She nodded, quite unable to answer. The whistle blasted again and, glancing about, Kate saw that the platform was rapidly emptying with very few soldiers left on it. Most had already boarded, holding the hands of sweethearts through the windows.

'At least you have another child.'

'I do so, and I take good care of her.'

'Are you ever going to tell me if she's mine?'

She saw the bleakness in his eyes, heard the plea in his voice, and turned away, unable to bear it. Doors were being banged shut, a porter's whistle, the sound of urgent shouts. 'Ye'd best go.' Still he didn't move a muscle. 'Sure and you'll miss the damn' train, if ye don't get a move on.' The last thing she wanted was for him to leave like this. She wanted to hold on to him, to hold back the train, not let it take him away from her.

Almost as if it were happening in slow motion, she saw how he stiffened his spine, pushed back his shoulders and lifted his head in that proud way he had as he glanced back over his shoulder at the waiting train, hissing like a restive animal in its impatience to be off, then he swung back to her in leisurely fashion, as if he had all the time in the world, his face unexpectedly soft. 'Will you write to me at least?'

It stunned her momentarily that he should ask, that he should want a letter from her. She could feel her cheeks growing hot at the thought, was perfectly sure her heart was making more noise than the damn' band and all the sobbing wives and mothers put together. She very nearly refused, but then remembered his ultimate destination, thought how much a letter from home must mean to a soldier. She gave a little shrug, trying to appear indifferent 'Sure and where's the harm in that? I could send the odd postcard, if you like. I might even knit you a balaclava.'

He gave a shout of laughter. 'That's my Kate.' Then before she guessed what he was about, he dropped his bag and swung her up in his arms and the power of his kiss was everything she remembered.

She was still reeling as he snatched up his bag again, managing to leap on to the train just as it began to shunt out of the station. Kate found herself running beside it, waving to him, doing her best to keep sight of his beloved face till the last possible moment, but it wasn't until she reached the end of the platform and had to stop and let it go on without her, that she finally called out, '*Yes*, she is. She's yours.'

One morning three weeks later Kate opened the door of her cottage and found Eliot standing on the doorstep grinning at her. He was in full dress uniform and looked absolutely marvellous.

'I've got forty-eight hours before I leave for France. I've arranged for us to be married at the Parish Church at noon. Can you be ready by then?'

'*What?*'

'Don't argue with me on this, Kate. Don't go into one of your Irish paddies, I don't have time. You know it makes sense. We were meant to be together so stop squabbling with me the whole damned time and do as you're told for once. If nothing else, Flora needs a father.'

'But . . . but . . .' She wanted to say, 'But you're going off to war, you've never spoken to Flora, you've never even told me that you love me.' Except that her mind was in a whirl and she couldn't seem to get her tongue round the words.

Millie's voice came softly from behind. 'She'll be ready, don't you fret, if I have to carry her there meself.'

Eliot grinned, saluted both women, winked broadly and, turning smartly on his heel, strode away, looking every inch the officer.

'I will not!' Kate yelled, the minute the door was slammed

shut. 'How can you even imagine that I'd marry that no-good, arrogant, full-of-himself bastard who thinks I'm naught but an Irish whore? Jaysus, Mary and Joseph, do you think I'm mad? Why would I do such a damned fool thing?'

Millie was busy rifling through a chest of clothes. 'Because thoo loves the bastard, why else? And think what an exciting forty-eight hours you've got to look forward to. Now, how about this? You always look good in powder blue. Your night-gown is a bit old-fashioned, but I doubt you'll need that anyroad, do you?' She was holding up a crêpe-de-Chine gown, a wicked smile on her face, a gaggle of children gathered about her, giggling behind their hands.

'I can't believe you'd do this to us.' Lucy was almost too aston-ished to be angry. Wasn't it enough that she'd been forced to get rid of that dreadful girl's child? Now the little tart had responded by presenting him with another.

Eliot was smiling happily upon his womenfolk whom he'd deliberately gathered together to impart this latest news, and repeated his statement in a clear and steady voice, steadfastly adding more besides. 'I do indeed intend to wed Kate O'Connor. And, yes, it's true that we succumbed to a moment of attraction shortly after Amelia's death, when I was grieving and at a low ebb. You mustn't blame her for that. It was my fault entirely. I was out of my mind with grief. Later, for no real reason that I can truly justify, we were intimate again, which has resulted in a beautiful daughter.'

The two maiden aunts blushed furiously and made little clucking noises, not quite knowing where to put themselves.

'Dear God, that doesn't mean you actually have to *wed* the creature,' Lucy spluttered.

'In my eyes it does. Had I known about the child earlier, I would have wed her before the birth, but it is not too late to put matters right. I'm aware it won't be easy for you, nor for the servants, what's left of them, but I hope that you will do your best to welcome her into the family and give her the support she needs while I'm away fighting in the trenches. Kate has a kind heart and will, I am sure, prove to be a dear sister to you, Lucy.'

'*Sister*? You want the *nursemaid* to be my *dear sister*?'

Eliot rewarded this comment with a flint-hard glare. 'You may recall that she is no longer a servant. Kate has her own business, in which she is doing rather well. I intend to leave Tyson's in her charge, and have no fears that she'll do a good job. So, I hope you weren't going to say something along the lines of "over my dead body", because none of us would wish you to adopt such an outmoded attitude, Lucy. These are difficult times and we must pull together. I do mean to go through with this. No one will prevent it.' And he encompassed them all with a warning glance. 'Aunts, I hope you too will welcome my new wife to the fold?'

'Dear me. Deary, deary me,' said Cissie, stroking the dog on her lap with such agitation that it woke up and jumped down, yapping excitedly, thinking they were about to play some sort of game. She made a grab for it, trying to calm it.

'What would Amelia say?' asked Vera, in shocked tones.

A predictable response but then the aunts had barely tolerated his taking in one innocent child from the stews of Kendal, let alone marrying the mother. 'Amelia would not object.' He raised his voice above the yapping of the dog. 'She was very fond of Kate, as am I. And she knew how much I wanted children. She wouldn't expect me to ignore this one, particularly not after what happened to Callum.'

'But the child is *illegitimate*.' A word spoken in hushed tones. 'You cannot alter that fact by marrying her.'

'I can try.'

Vera drew herself up in rigid disapproval, spine like an iron rod, her square body seeming to pulsate with shock as she gasped for breath, making little puffing sounds in her throat.

Cissie began to look concerned. Giving up on the dog she'd been trying to restrain, she put out a consoling hand to pat her sister instead. 'Now don't get into a state, dear.'

Vera said, 'Oh, do hush for once, Cissie, and put that dog out before it drives us all demented. *Marriage*, dear boy, is a big step to take. Even I, stickler for propriety that I am, question the necessity for it. Think of the implications, the position she will be expected to maintain, the access she will have to Tyson money . . . and this is bound to create one almighty scandal in the town. The gel does not deserve your generosity, she's no better than she should be.'

Eliot laughed. 'A quaint phrase I've never really understood, but entirely inaccurate. I'm quite certain that we have all misjudged Kate badly.'

Lucy, who'd been happy for Vera to do most of the hard work, now chipped in to offer support. 'Utter nonsense. If there was ever a case of being trapped into marriage, this is it. Don't let her make a fool of you again, Eliot.'

He walked away to take up his favourite position at the window, hands clasped behind his back as he gazed out upon the smooth dark ribbon of the river, the town he loved so much with its cluster of limestone houses huddled together in this wide, green valley with the distant fells; hoping that in some way the view might calm him. But his patience was fast disintegrating. He'd not expected the breaking of this news to be easy, but he'd be damned if he'd allow them to be quite so obstructive. He certainly had no wish to discuss his feelings on the matter with the women of his family. These were far too personal, and he fully intended to keep them to himself.

At length he turned to face all three of them, his expression as blank as if it were carved in stone, his tone when he addressed them uncompromising, making it clear he would brook no argument, that all discussion on the subject was now at an end. The wedding is to take place at noon today. I hope and trust you will all be there to wish me well.' And having made his point, he strode from the room.

Lucy thought she might choke with rage. All her clever planning, all her efforts, all those long years of patient waiting, all for *nothing*! Yet she found, to her horror, that she was powerless to prevent it. The wedding did indeed go ahead that very day, in a simple ceremony conducted by the vicar in a fitting and proper manner. The aunts were present, unwillingly making a show of support, but Lucy herself absolutely refused to attend.

She remained in her room in a fury of temper, railing against the injustice of it. When she heard the church bells ring, she snatched up one of her favourite vases and hurled it to the ground. Seeing it smashed into a hundred pieces, she promptly burst into tears.

Oh, but she'd have her revenge, she surely would. She wasn't finished, not by a long chalk. If that slut thought she'd won, then she was sadly mistaken.

28

Kate was not late. In fact, to her shame, she was early. Fortunately, Eliot was there before her, one of his soldier friends who had volunteered to be best man beside him. All the necessary arrangements had been made, a special licence procured, the vicar probably bribed as he smiled his way through the service with brisk efficiency. It surprised her that the aunts were present, looking unnaturally funereal in their customary black, but much to Kate's relief the sour-faced sister-in-law was absent. In fact, no one else attended the simple ceremony except Millie and a for-once sober Clem dressed in his best suit, looking as if he'd been scrubbed and buffed to a brilliant shine. Even so, Kate could not claim to be lacking in attendants, either from bridesmaids or page boys, as the huge church echoed with the chatter and excited giggles of Millie's children and Flora, who all thought it grand fun.

Kate's first emotion had been one of alarm, worrying how she was to explain all of this to her daughter. 'How on earth do I tell a little girl that this is her daddy who I'm marrying at last, after all this time? How do I do that, fer God's sake?'

Millie had considered the point with grave seriousness. 'You say, "This is yer daddy, pet, and we're getting married at last."'

Kate gave an exclamation of annoyance. 'Don't make fun of me, Millie. What if she asks why we didn't get married in the first place, when she was born? *Before* she was born, fer God's sake, as is the proper way of going about things.'

'You'll say you didn't feel like it at the time, that you hadn't quite made up your mind. She knows how cussed you are, so won't be in the least surprised.'

'But . . .'

'No more buts, Kate, just tell her. Haven't I been saying for years that she has the right to know who her father is?'

And so Kate told her. She went upstairs, sat on her bed and told Flora the whole story, or as much of it as seemed appropriate for a five-year-old, desperately striving to ignore the ache in her heart which reminded her she had another child, who would have loved to hear this news. She and Dennis had been round the markets on a number of afternoons during these last few weeks, in whatever spare moments she could snatch away from the workshop, which admittedly were few. As soon as the wedding was over, they'd go again. Kate wasn't for giving up on Callum, not while she'd breath in her body.

In the event, Flora took it all on the chin, asking only, 'Can I tell me friend Maggie that I've got a daddy now?'

'Ye can so, sweetheart, because that's what ye'll have.'

'And you're marrying him today, so I get to miss school?'

'I am, and ye do.'

Flora thought about this for a long moment, 'I can tell her tomorrow then, can't I? Will I be wearing blue too?'

'They'll never accept me. Never. It's not even worth the trying. Far better if I stay with Millie and Clem while you're away.' They were standing on Scout Scar, an open fell overlooking the town, having enjoyed a pleasant, if rather quiet lunch at the Fleece Inn. The aunts would have declined and beat a hasty retreat back to their parlour were it not for the fact that Eliot had insisted they should stay and celebrate his wedding, and so they'd sat stiff-backed throughout, hardly opening their tightly pressed mouths wide enough to take in a morsel of the excellent Westmorland lamb.

Afterwards, Kate and Eliot thanked their guests for coming to share this special occasion with them, and with Flora skipping along in front of them, the three of them had walked up Beast Banks, on through Serpentine Woods and out on to the fell. It was a long, steep climb but it was a soft spring day with a bright sun lighting the first primroses, the wayside clotted with wild daffodils and blue pools of bluebells forming a haze of brilliant colour among the long green grasses in the woods.

'If you're worrying about the aunts, or Lucy, then don't. I've spoken to them and they are quite resigned, if not exactly jubilant, about our decision to marry.'

'*Your* decision. I don't seem to have had much say in the matter.'

Eliot chuckled. 'Flora seems quite happy with the situation.'

Flora was ecstatic. She'd met her father for the first time outside the great doors of the Parish Church and it was apparent to Kate, to everyone present, that they had liked each other on sight. In typical Flora fashion, she came straight to the point.

'Are you my daddy?'

'I am.'

'And are you going to marry me mammy?'

'If she'll have me.'

'Did you have a quarrel before, that time when I was a babby?'

'I think we must have done.'

'Has Mammy said she's sorry?'

'Not yet. Do you think she might?'

Flora had considered this very seriously for a moment, and then shaken her small head, making the dark curls bounce, the fire in them gleam in the sun. 'Will you say you're sorry to her?'

He gave a rueful smile. 'Sorry enough to ask her to be my wife, will that do?'

A tiny puckering of her brow. 'Mammy says we're to come and live with you.'

'If you approve. I hope you'll like my house. You'll have a room all to yourself, but you can of course see your friends whenever you wish.' He indicated Millie's children standing close by her side, holding on to her hands and watching the proceedings in wide-eyed wonder.

'Will I be stopping in Miss Williams's class at school?'

'Oh, yes, I should think so. If you want to. Do you like Miss Williams?'

At this she nodded, and the matter seemed to be settled. Flora released herself from her friends and went to stand before him, gazing up into his face. 'You can kiss me, if you like.'

'Only if you call me Daddy.'

'All right, Daddy. You can kiss me now.'

And he'd swept her up into his arms and smacked a great big raspberry kiss on her cheek, making her squeal with delight.

'So if we've no problems with Flora,' he said now to Kate, watching the little girl in her pretty blue frock hopping and jumping from one tussock of grass to another, 'what else matters? The aunts will come round once they warm to your charm, as I have done,' he said with a teasing smile. 'Even Lucy has had the opportunity to express her disapproval but gave up when she saw that it got her absolutely nowhere. So you see, I've made my feelings on the subject very plain.'

That's more than you have to me, Kate thought, but didn't say as much, her eyes on Flora, happily humming a merry little tune to herself.

What had she done on a mad moment of impulse?

Kate was in no doubt about his reasons for marrying her. He wanted Flora. Having lost Callum, he needed a replacement child, particularly now that he was going to war. Perhaps this time he felt it incumbent upon himself to offer her something more substantial than a mere job. Perhaps he realised she would never agree to another adoption, or perhaps he thought it might work out cheaper for him in the end to make her his wife, since she could keep an eye on his business too, for nothing.

And why had she agreed?

Because of Flora? Perhaps she was part of the reason, but much more than that. Because Kate had found herself quite unable to refuse. Even without Millie bullying her every inch of the way to the altar, the thought of being with Eliot, of waking beside him in the morning, of being allowed to care for him, to love him, had been overwhelming, too tempting to refuse.

She'd thought of him going to France, of possibly losing him for good, and she'd needed some part of him all to herself, in case she did lose him. She'd wanted a glimpse, however momentary, of how it felt to be his wife.

Of course it had all happened so fast, but these thoughts had raced through her mind. Now, with the knot tied and facing reality, things looked rather different. They were indeed man and wife but Kate couldn't quite come to terms with the fact. How could they ever hope to lead a normal life when the image of Callum still lay between them? What if she never found him? Could she ever hope to banish the guilt of losing him and allow herself to be happy again? When would the agony end? When did time start to heal, as everyone had promised her that it would? The thought that Callum had wandered off and got lost while they were quarrelling, thinking they were angry with each other, angry with him perhaps, haunted her as much today as it ever had, and still brought the occasional nightmare.

Best to turn her mind away from it. Where had agonising ever got her? Concentrate on what was happening now, on the subject in hand. How she was to fit into his life, into Tyson Lodge, as Eliot's wife. 'What about Amelia's friends? The ladies of Kendal society. Would they ever accept me as your wife? I doubt it.'

'Do you want them to? Do you care whether they do or not?'

'No, of course I don't care, but you can't deny that these people matter.'

'Why should they matter? Do they to you?'

'No, not to me. I don't give two pins for any of them.' Her worries changed to anger now, as they always did, and she turned on him, spitting mad that he couldn't, or wouldn't, understand. 'Jaysus, Mary and Joseph, can't you see it's you they'll hurt, *you* I'm thinking of? There will be the most God-Almighty scandal, just like before. We must have been mad to do this.'

He gave her a sideways glance, a long, narrow, considering look which seemed to indicate disbelief, as if saying that she should surely be used to scandal, a woman alone with a child. Kate could almost see the thought imprinted in his gaze, almost hear the words on his silent lips.

'Don't look at me like that, I don't care a jot what they say about me, for all I've more morals than you've ever given me credit for, more than them probably. Wasn't I once decently married afore ever I met you?'

He chuckled. 'Are you accusing me of leading you astray?'

'And isn't that the way of it?'

A smile twisted the corners of his mouth, but he said nothing, unnerving her slightly.

'Oh, I don't know what to think. So why did you marry me? Will you tell me that, at least? You could have come to see Flora at any time. I wouldn't have denied you that much, not with the war an' all, and I was even prepared to tell her that you were her daddy.'

'Why do you think I wanted to marry you, Kate?' They'd stopped walking so he could hold her gently in his arms and his voice had grown softer, mesmerisingly so.

She gave a careless shrug. 'And how would I know?'

'You can't guess?'

Kate shook her head, deliberately stubborn, pretending not to notice the teasing gleam in his brown eyes.

'Then I'll just have to show you. Not now, of course,' glancing pointedly at the happy child who'd come to take their hands, begging them to swing her between them. 'Later, perhaps.'

'I'm not sure I'm ready for this.'

Eliot was at the far side of the room and, having removed his jacket and tie, had begun to unbutton his shirt. Kate stood unmoving, filled with a sudden, girlish shyness, knowing she was trembling from head to foot. Between them lay the vast sprawl of a bed and she was perfectly certain that she couldn't go through with sharing it. She simply couldn't. She'd taken one swift, all-encompassing glance, drawn in a deep breath and decided it was best to make her feelings clear right from the start.

At her words, he stopped folding the silk necktie to look across at her in surprise, then as if recognising something vulnerable in her expression, tossed it to one side and came over to take her gently by the shoulders. That is entirely your decision, of course. If you prefer to wait, we can. There'll be time enough for – for all of that – later, when I get back.'

'Oh, God, I forgot, you're going away!'

He smiled and shook his head. 'No, you hadn't forgotten at

all, you just don't care to think about it. Neither do I. I'd like to stay here, with you, for ever. Why did we quarrel, Kate? What was our problem when the attraction between us is so strong?'

'You know well enough, let's not go over all that now. I just want to wait till I'm ready, that's all,' she said crisply, and snatching up her nightdress, fled to the bathroom. At least she was allowed to use that now she was no longer a servant.

Later, keenly aware that she was lying in the master's bed, that the aunts were in a room not too far away, perhaps with their nasty little ears pressed to the wall, she lay unmoving beside him. He reached out and touched her hand. Kate instantly turned her back on him, striving to make her breathing sound even and slow, as if she were falling asleep. It didn't seem to be working as he began to stroke her back, his hand moving slowly up and down, easing the tension in her shoulders, melting the stone in her heart so that she could hear her breathing quicken, betraying her need. He seemed to have edged closer as she could feel the warmth from his body searing through her like fire.

'Are you warm enough? Quite comfortable?'

'Yes, thank you.' They were lying side by side in this great bed, yet talking to each other like strangers.

'Does it feel odd sleeping here, in a strange bed? Would you like another pillow or blanket? Would you, my love?' He was teasing her, she could tell by the lightness in his tone, and it pricked at her conscience that he should be driven to use such tricks on her which, in turn, caused her to flare with fresh annoyance.

'I didn't say I was cold, I said I was tired.' She thumped her pillow and tried to move away from him as far as the bed would allow but he laid an arm about her waist, capturing her again, and Kate felt certain he would feel her heart beating.

He stroked the back of her wrist with his thumb and, sensing the weakening effect his caresses were having on her, she flounced up in the bed, masking her trembling with a show of anger. 'How will I ever get to sleep if you're interfering with me the whole time?'

To her utter amazement he burst out laughing, lay back against the cool sheets and roared till even Kate found herself smiling reluctantly.

'What? What is it? What have I said?'

'I thought a husband was supposed to *interfere* with his wife on their wedding night, particularly if she is as lovely as you.'

She could see the gleam of his eyes reflected in a shaft of moonlight, the whiteness of his teeth in the semi-darkness, and something inside her began to melt. 'Is that what I am? Your lovely wife? You do think I'm lovely, or are you making fun of me again?'

He reached up and stroked her glorious tumble of red hair, smoothing his hand over her soft cheek, along the line of her throat, sliding the thin nightgown from one naked shoulder and making her shudder with longing.

'I swear you are the loveliest creature I ever set eyes on. I always thought so. Why, in God's name, we've spent so much of these last years at odds, I cannot comprehend. I shall carry the image of how you look this night with me forever. Will you write to me every single day, my love? Will you remember me with perhaps just a little affection when I'm out there in the mud of the trenches?'

She was lost. Kate felt a great lump of emotion rise in her throat, could barely breathe, let alone speak. 'Oh, Eliot, 'course I will. Don't you know that I love the bones of ye? I always have. I'll love you till the day I die. Why else would I have agreed to this madness?'

Eliot felt his stomach tighten in that all-too-familiar way, yet still he managed to maintain his control. One wrong move now and he could lose her for ever. He gave a rueful smile, cupping her cheek with a soothing hand.

'Will you stop being angry with me then? At least long enough to kiss me.' And this time when he pulled her gently into his arms, she came willingly.

When they woke the next morning Kate put out a hand and instinctively reached for him. Amazingly, he was still there. It hadn't been a dream but magical reality. She rolled over to straddle him, kissing him awake. 'Wake up, are you tired of me already?'

'Never!'

She nibbled at his ear, licked the erotic curve of it, rubbed her lips enticingly against his, angling her body so that he could enjoy the soft fullness of her breasts, 'I think perhaps ye don't have the stamina to keep up with me.'

'Minx, I'll show you who has stamina.' And grabbing her around the waist, he pulled her beneath him and began to make love to her all over again.

Out on the landing, as the aunts bustled down to the dining room, they heard the squeals and made small clucking noises with their tongues, 'I really can't think what came over him to behave in such a dreadful, devil-may-care fashion. He'll rue the day,' Aunt Vera said, in her sourest tones. 'Rue the day.'

'Oh, indeed, you are absolutely correct, sister. They will both regret this marriage,' Cissie agreed. And, calling to the two pointers to stop snuffling at the bedroom door, the two maiden ladies made their way down to breakfast: spines rigid, heads held high, deliberately deaf to the noises emanating from behind the closed door.

In the nursery, Flora was already regretting her mother's hasty marriage. Yesterday had been so exciting, what with the new blue frock, the thrill of the wedding, and getting a new daddy. Now, Aunt Lucy was standing by her bed, ordering her to get up in a very nasty, bossy voice. 'You're a naughty girl to be still lying in bed. You should have been down to breakfast fifteen minutes ago. Don't you understand that it's rude to be late for meals? You aren't even dressed.'

'Mammy helps me dress.'

'A big girl like you? What nonsense! Anyway, your mammy isn't interested in you any more, not now that she's got a new husband.'

'She is! My mammy loves me.'

'Not any more.' Lucy whipped back the sheets and eiderdown and Flora instinctively curled up into a tiny ball and closed her eyes, hoping the nasty lady wouldn't be able to see her any more, or that when she opened her eyes again, Lucy would have vanished in a puff of smoke.

'Get out of bed this minute and wash and dress yourself before I take my slipper to you. Don't expect any help from your mammy. She's too busy to spend any time with you now so you must do as *I* tell you. This is *my* house. *I'm* in charge here, not your *mammy*! Come along now, stop shivering, get that nightie off.'

Flora struggled out of bed and obediently began to pull off her nightgown, tears forming at the corners of her eyes although she was desperately trying not to let them fall. She quickly pulled on her drawers and her vest with the little sleeves, but then got confused as she tried to tie the ribbons on her petticoat. She could do a knot on her shoelaces, like Miss Williams had shown her, but didn't always get the bow quite right. Her small fingers went round and round with the loop, in and out, but somehow it wouldn't stay in place. It kept coming undone and now she could hardly see what she was doing for the tears in her eyes had grown too big to see through them properly.

'Get on with it, child, we haven't all day.'

'I c-can't . . .'

'There's no such word as can't, and don't answer back. You are a very stupid girl. Put your hands on your head. *Now!*'

Flora jerked as if she'd been struck.

'Do it *now!*'

In an instinctive bid to protect herself, the child instantly obeyed. She clasped her hands on top of her head and her lips started to tremble. Even though she pressed them together very hard, the bottom one still wobbled.

'Don't you dare move an inch,' Lucy warned, grabbing her by the shoulders and giving her a little shake, 'or there will be a worse punishment for you. You shall miss breakfast this morning because you've been so lazy. But if you're a good girl and do as I say from now on, then I won't tell your mammy how naughty you've been. Do you understand?'

Wide-eyed, the frightened little girl pressed down even harder on her wobbling lip and dutifully nodded.

29

The workers at the factory found it hard to accept Kate. Simply being Eliot's wife wasn't enough, since the working man's view of women was pitifully low. Wives, in their opinion, had a limited value, a role which should be confined either to minding the children and keeping house, or to the bedroom. Certainly not the factory floor. Nor were they interested in the fact that Kate had made her mark in the shoe industry with her own workshop, which was smaller and entirely different. It produced only boots for the army. She knew nothing about making classic lines, the quality shoes for which Tyson's was famous.

And of course far too many of them, Swainson included, remembered her as a simple nursemaid. Without exception they thought she'd got above herself.

'Who does she think she is?' they would mutter whenever she issued an order, urged to react in this way by Swainson himself.

Kate had expected trouble from the foreman, and she got it. She was aware of these rumblings of discontent, knew the men were deliberately working to rule and not pulling together. One by one they would come to her and complain that a consignment of shoes, or boots, could not possibly be produced in the time she'd allowed; that some order or other had been 'accidentally' overlooked; that the leather was faulty; a machine had broken down; any and every excuse under the sun. She tried talking to them, man to man as it were, appealing to their better natures, their patriotic spirit, but got absolutely nowhere.

'Come on, lads,' she would say, 'there's a war on. You can do better than this. Jump to it.' But they didn't jump to it. They didn't put themselves out in the slightest. And all the while she was aware of Swainson smirking in the background.

She'd left Toby Lynch, her trusty foreman, in charge of her own workshop at the old ropeworks, and with gritted teeth told herself she'd just have to learn to work with Swainson here at the factory. Eliot had warned her not to expect too much, that the men were behind him for some reason and would have no compunction about walking out and destroying the business completely if she did anything hasty they disagreed with, such as sack him. So she held her patience. For now.

Early in the new year Kate found that she had a serious shortage of men. With the falling off of volunteers, the government was bringing in conscription. It was not a popular move and many men objected, but the decision was irrevocable. The war must be brought to a satisfactory conclusion and with all speed. Even Dennis, along with many of her most skilled operatives, had been called up. Kate thought, for a time, that she might be about to lose Toby, but managed to get him excused on the grounds of his being in charge of the production of boots for soldiers.

Finding herself in dire straits, she put an advertisement in the local *Westmorland Gazette*, offering training to any women willing to take their place. She got a surprisingly good response with more than enough women ready to take on the challenge. Patriotism was running high.

Kate took them on and resolved to make some changes. She made adjustments to the shift patterns to allow those women who wished to, to work nights along with the men, so they could be with their families for at least a part of each day. All hell broke loose. The older men strongly objected, resenting the idea of the factory being invaded by a bunch of women, and a strike was called in protest. Each day the men would gather at the factory gates, waving their placards and shouting offensive remarks to anyone brave enough to breach the picket line. Many women stopped trying, refusing to go in to work because they were too afraid. But there were others who valiantly turned up each and every morning, determined to get in somehow. Sally Sibson was such a one, showing her resourcefulness by climbing in through a lavatory window, until one of the men spotted her and bolted it from the inside.

'The buggers'll not stop me,' she cried, gritting her teeth and rolling up her sleeves in a burst of fighting spirit that would have gone down well on the Somme.

One morning, as Sally and her two best mates, Joan Enderby and Nell Benson, marched boldly up to the gates, things suddenly turned nasty. The three women were jostled by a group of angry-looking men who very swiftly surrounded them. 'Hey up, you lot,' Sally yelled at them. 'Bugger off! We've a right to go to work, same as you lot. We allus have worked, harder then you, you daft lumps.'

'Not in our factory, you haven't. Go back to yer bloody kitchen. We don't want no women here, tekkin work from t'men.'

'Don't talk bloody daft. There's no men round 'ere, they're all off fighting in t'war, where you should be, Bill Grigson.' Suddenly becoming aware of other men drawing close behind her, Sally swung round to face them, fists clenched, ready to punch any who dared touch her. 'Here, what the bleeding 'ell . . .' But she got no further as a stone was thrown. It hit her on the back of her head and knocked her out cold. Nell and Joan ran to help but the men refused to let them through, jeering and yelling, pushing and shoving them back and forth like rubber balls between them, till the women were sobbing with fear.

A voice rang out above the din. 'Holy Maother . . . what the bleedin' hell do you lot think ye're doing with me workers? Get yer hands off them, Jack Milburn, if'n ye know what's good for you.'

A hush fell over the factory yard as all eyes turned towards her. Kate was a fearsome figure to behold as she stood, hands on hips, the blazing aureole of hair around her head matched only by the fire in her smoke-grey eyes. 'Isn't your son at the front, Will Barker? And yours too, Tom Perry, and yours Joe? So you can all take those menacing looks off yer daft faces and get back to work afore I sack the bleeding' lot of yous.'

Jack Milburn, ever the troublemaker, took a step forward, not a sign of his expression softening. 'My son will be back when the war ends, probably by next Christmas, and then where will he be, with no job to come back to? Out on the streets, that's where.'

'There'll be work for him right enough, don't you fret, whenever he does get back. And you know as well as I do that this war won't be over by Christmas, not by a long chalk. In the meantime, we have boots to make; if'n your lad isn't to fight the Hun barefoot, so get back to your machines, the lot of yous.'

Kate thought for a moment that they were going to obey her and go quietly back to work, albeit grumbling under their breath, but then a familiar figure emerged from the shadow of a doorway. Swainson. Dear Lord, she should have guessed he'd be behind all of this.

'I'll thank you to get out of my yard. If you've anything to say to my men, you can address them through me,' he announced, in chilling tones.

'Is that so?'

'It is. They do nowt but what I tell 'em.'

'So what gives you the right of life and death over their souls? Because that's what yer saying. If they don't work, they don't get paid, and if they don't get paid, they starve. In the meantime, their sons die on the field of battle, presumably in their bare feet.'

There was a small, telling silence. All eyes turned to Swainson who, with his wandering eye lurching sideways, lip curled into a snarl, said, 'We working men are used to fighting exploitation by the ruling classes, and from them jumped-up 'uns who are pretending to be what they're not.'

There was a collective intake of breath at that, for no matter what anyone might say about the rights and wrongs of employing women, this was the boss's wife he was insulting here, a woman who'd made quite a name for herself already in the town. Kate simply smiled, as if he'd said something to amuse her. 'Exploitation? Is that what you call it? And there's me thinking we were fighting a war here, not each other. I thought it was the Hun who was our enemy, and we were working nicely together, as a team: all British, all Kendalians, all proud to be doing our bit. But then, what do I know? I'm just a daft woman.

'Seems to me like you're the one always giving orders round here, not me at all. Why is that? I wonder. Pissed off, are you, cause you can't get your grubby little hands on my women any more, eh? Is that it? Do these men know how many of their wives you've been poking while they pay you to be their spokesman? I bet they bloody don't.'

The silence in the yard now was oppressive and Kate wondered if she'd gone too far. She still had no proof to back up these allegations. Not one of the women had ever been brave enough to speak up and complain, either to Eliot or to their husband. It had all been hushed up, swept under the carpet as something unclean and best not investigated too closely. Why should she imagine they'd be any different now? But she'd reckoned without Sally.

'Aye, she's right.' Her voice sounded cracked and raw with pain, a mere echo of its former resonant self, but there wasn't a man present didn't hear every word. 'He certainly did his worst wi' me, filthy bugger.'

There was an achingly long pause, and then a second voice. 'And me,' echoed Joan Enderby, stepping forward.

'Me an' all,' added Nell Benson.

Thus encouraged by this show of bravery, other women stepped forward, coming to stand beside these three, silently offering their support; the blazing defiance in their steady gazes challenging anyone to doubt that they'd been anything but unwilling victims in Swainson's climb to power.

They turned on Swainson as one man then and the fear in his ferrety face was palpable. He was driven from that yard by a shouting, rowdy, dangerous crowd of angry men, Jack Milburn, Bill Grigson and Tom Perry along with him. All Kate did was stand by and silently watch, grinning from ear to ear.

Matters improved considerably after that, at least in the factory. At home it was another matter. Lucy continued to treat Kate as some sort of glorified servant, if not exactly a nursemaid since there was only Flora to see to. It was after all useful to have someone to call upon to do her bidding.

'Kate, will you just bring my wrap from my bedroom?' she would say, without glancing up from her magazine or her crochet work. Or, 'Be a dear and go and ask Mrs Petty if we can have tea early today, and some of her delicious cream buns.' Anxious to fit in and be accepted, Kate would obey, until it came to her one day that she was doing all the running about in the household, all the fetching and carrying, even to lighting fires and filling coal scuttles, particularly since Fanny was no longer there to do any of it, and poor Ida could scarcely cope with all the extra duties. But hadn't she enough to do, running the factory? Surely if she could deal with that nasty piece of shite, Swainson, who'd never once set foot in the works since that stand-off in the yard, she could sort out one foolish sister-in-law.

The next time Lucy asked her to fetch something, a handkerchief this time which she could quite easily fetch herself, Kate politely declined. 'Sorry Lucy, but I'm just working on these balance sheets, and might lose me concentration if I break off.'

Lucy was clearly shocked by this lack of deference. 'I beg your pardon? I've just asked you to do a job for me. Are you refusing?'

'Well, would you believe it, so I am. It may have slipped your notice but I'm no longer employed as a servant in this house, that we don't in fact have a housemaid any more. Fanny has left.'

'Gone to work for you in that dreadful little workshop, I understand.'

Kate beamed cheerfully. 'My "dreadful little workshop" as you call it, is now part and parcel of Tyson Industries, so you'd best get used to the idea. But yes, that is where Fanny is happily ensconced. And although I've tried placing several advertisements in the local press, I've found no replacement housemaid, so we are all going to have to pull our weight a little bit more than usual. At least until hostilities are over and things settle back to normal.'

'Well, really! You surely aren't expecting me to sweep and clean? Isn't it enough that I've sacrificed my lady's maid because of Eliot's parsimony? These Tyson brothers were always mean, dreadfully so, considering their vast wealth.'

Kate sighed and shook her head sorrowfully. 'And isn't that what I thought meself once? They appeared that wealthy, certainly from Poor House Lane, but now I'm not so sure. This is a big house to run, the aunts and you live in it and need to be kept, along with your children and their school fees paid. Eliot does his duty, bless his generous heart, but the money has to be found from somewhere. And there are God knows how many other aunts and uncles and cousins who depend upon Tyson's to furnish them with pensions or dividends on their shares. You, *dear sister-in-law*, are not the only one making demands upon him. Perhaps you should remember that occasionally.'

Lucy bridled at being so reminded of their relationship. Had she been a cat, her fur would have stood on end and her claws been unsheathed. 'Is that meant as some sort of criticism?'

'No,' Kate replied calmly. 'It's meant as a comment on the facts. Eliot carries all the responsibility for this family on his broad shoulders, which mebbe you should appreciate a bit more. I'm surprised ye've made no progress finding yerself a new chap. 'Course, it isn't easy now, not with all these men going off to war, and there'll be even fewer when it's over, I shouldn't wonder. So if you couldn't find a husband before, I doubt you'll have much better luck after.' She gave a sad shake of her head. 'What a waste. I'm sorry for your misfortune, so I am.'

Lucy's cheeks fired to scarlet, and she leaped to her feet in a fury. 'I'm not asking for your pity.'

'No, 'course you aren't,' Kate continued, at her most pleasant. 'Only for me to fetch ye a handkerchief, or whatever it is ye've a fancy for next. But we can't find a maid for you, do ye see, let alone a rich husband. And I'm sorry I can't help like I used to, but since Eliot has left the responsibility for Tyson Industries in my hands, and the workers depend upon the company for their livelihoods, not to mention all the rest of the Tyson family, the factory must have first call upon me time. I hope you understand. We'll all have to do our best to pull together and get along, won't we?'

Words which were echoed in Eliot's own letters home from the front. 'I hope you and Kate are getting along better now,' he would say.

And Lucy would write back, 'We are like dear sisters.'

Kate found that once she'd made it clear she was no longer a servant but Eliot's wife, and should be treated as such, she coped quite well with her new role. Her fears for him increased over the long months of his absence. At the end of last year he'd been involved in the Gallipoli bloodbath, an ill-conceived campaign which Kitchener had finally abandoned when he'd gone out there to inspect the situation at first hand. Kate had spent a tense few weeks before hearing that Eliot had been safely evacuated along with his men.

She'd received several letters after that which attempted to give her an insight into the horrors he was facing, although some words had been scored through by the censor. He spoke of the conditions in the trenches, the slush and mud, the stink and blood of dying men, how there'd been times when they were sick with fear or fed up to the back teeth; his pain over losing one of his men, as well as his fury if one wasn't pulling his weight.

'They are so young, Kate. Little more than boys. Some of them can't even . . .' and again obliteration of his words by the censor, but Kate assumed them to be 'fire a rifle'.

Sometimes he spoke of his need for her. Nothing overly romantic, just a few plain, simple words scribbled on the bottom, 'I miss you, Kate,' or 'Thinking of you, my love.'

She thought of him too, every day. And when the pain and worry became too great, she would bury her fears in work, as she always did.

In July, the British launched their offensive on the Somme although even that grand military campaign was soon bogged down in controversy. Despite its apparently careful planning, losses were huge and soon Rolls of Honour were being posted in the Parish Church and Kate became obsessed with calling in, just to make sure Eliot's name wasn't on them and someone had forgotten to inform her. Shrines to the fallen appeared everywhere: at churches up and down the land, on street corners, outside ordinary houses in the streets of Kendal, all with names and flowers, prayers or crosses, set beside them.

Kate helped her women workers make up parcels of cigarettes and Kendal mint cake, socks and even the balaclavas she'd once flippantly promised Eliot, to send out to the soldiers. When once he wrote to say that nothing was getting through, she contacted several food suppliers in town who all agreed to send out parcels to the soldiers, packed together in a great big van, which did get through and were gratefully received.

But as the summer wore on, Eliot's letters became less frequent, their contents more guarded, which caused Kate to worry all the more.

She did at least get a letter from Dermot saying that as conscription didn't apply to Irishmen, he'd not been forced to go. He was doing well with his own little business, he told her:

> Though not as well as yours, mind. Aren't you the grand one now? Me and Dolly have three babbies, and still happy as Larry after nearly six years of marriage. I'd come and see you, Katy love, only we never have two halfpennies to rub together. One day, eh, me lovely? Keep those Irish eyes smiling.

Kate shed many a tear over that letter, reading and re-reading it over and over till she knew every word by heart.

Wouldn't she just love to see her big brother again? Aw, but you couldn't have everything in this world, and he was fine and dandy, safe enough where he was. There were many who weren't so lucky. Too many. Fear and anxiety for their loved ones ran through everyone these days, though it was true she'd little enough family that she could afford to lose sight of any one of hers. She'd never found the red-haired boy Flora had spoken of, had lost faith that she ever would. It had probably not been Callum anyway. Kate decided that the red-haired boy was simply a figment of Flora's imagination. But that wouldn't stop her search continuing. Only right now she'd little enough time, not with two factories to run.

There were times when she suffered pangs of conscience over leaving Flora more and more in the care of the two aunts, and with Lucy. But then Cissie was quite fond of the child and would happily read her stories for hours, much to Flora's delight. Vera, on the other hand, would read only carefully selected extracts from the Bible. Fortunately, Flora liked these too, which softened even Aunt Vera's stony heart, at least a little. It seemed to Kate at times that her daughter was making more progress with them than *she* was. She even got on well with Cissie's hysterical dogs.

But if they had learned to tolerate the child, the maiden aunts rarely spoke to Kate, except to issue her with an order or instruction of some sort, which she generally ignored. Or else it would be to chide her on some supposed failing: 'Eliot would wish you to leave the letters on the tray in the hall, not take them to the post office yourself.'

'But who else will take them, if not me? Fanny works at the factory now. Dennis has enlisted. Dear Askew is no longer with us, and Mrs Petty and Ida have enough to do. Who else would post the letters, will ye tell me?'

But she never won an argument. They would find some

other fault instead. 'Poor dear Amelia always used to have the brasses polished on a Friday. These are looking very grubby dear. Quite dilapidated.'

'Then here's a rag, clean them yourselves, why don't you? Or ask Lucy. She's not got much on this week.'

'Well, I never!'

'Oh, deary, deary me.'

They still hadn't accepted her for what she was, a vital part of Eliot's life. Winning the men over had been easy by comparison.

30

Lucy wasted no time in taking advantage of Kate's distraction. The fact that running the business was taking all her attention was proving to be a positive bonus. It had the wonderful benefit of allowing Lucy long periods alone with the child and she willingly volunteered to collect Flora from school.

'You see how I have taken your words to heart about us all pulling together? This is my way of doing my bit, *dear* sister. One way, at least, that I can help, and with my own children away at school, it is a pleasure to spend time with a child again.'

And the joy of it was, Kate believed her! She would kiss her sleepy daughter while she was still in her bed and dash off without a second thought, completely trusting.

Lucy was really beginning to enjoy herself, growing more imaginative in her abuse of this child who had been foisted upon the household. Not only did the luckless Flora stand in very well as a makeshift servant to fetch and carry her knitting wool, embroidery threads, books or whatever, but from that very first morning when Lucy had made her situation clear, the child had proved to be a surprisingly quick learner.

Dear Flora had a natural instinct for survival which meant she responded well to the fear Lucy induced in her, and proved to be surprisingly easy to control. Disappointingly easy at times, which meant that Lucy needed to devise new trials to provoke her, if she was to remain entertained and not grow bored by the whole enterprise.

It was such a marvellous way of relieving her own personal frustration and fury. So utterly satisfying to take out her revenge on a child.

She would order Flora to stand in a corner for lengthy periods with her hands on her head whenever she didn't instantly obey one of Lucy's instructions to the letter, or else pinch the flesh on her tummy or the backs of her legs, where any unfortunate marks were less likely to show. By way of variation, Lucy would put a blanket over the child's head while she slapped her quite hard, to and fro, with the flat of her hand. That way there would be no bruises. At first, Flora had cried a great deal during these ordeals, but the little girl soon learned that this only resulted in yet worse punishment and would now suck in her breath, bite her lip and keep silent, which, oddly enough, infuriated Lucy all the more. It seemed to issue a further challenge, and she'd be desperate to find some way to make the child cry.

'I'll break your stubborn spirit, drat you,' she would hiss through gritted teeth. 'You are so *very* naughty, no wonder your mammy neglects you and doesn't love you any more. You are going to have to learn better manners, or nobody will love you ever again.'

'Yes, she does love me,' Flora would stubbornly insist, pouting with trembling lips, and be slapped even harder for this show of defiance.

Sometimes, if Lucy should offer to take her for a walk to feed the ducks or up to Serpentine Woods, Flora would object, becoming tearful over this promised treat.

'No, I want Mammy! Mammy, you take me for a walk.' And she would cling to her mother's skirt, or drag her feet and refuse to go.

Kate would panic, worried that Flora wasn't finding it any easier than herself to settle into this new routine with a strange family in a strange home. She would hold her close and soothe her, trying to reassure her precious child. 'There now, won't ye have a grand time? You must thank Aunt Lucy for offering to look after you so well when Mammy's busy.'

'But I want *you* to look after me. You never do. You don't love me no more.'

'Now where did you get that nonsense from?'

'Aunt Lucy said you don't, not if I'm naughty.' A gulp and a guilty swallow, since this was dangerous territory.

'I'm sure she didn't say anything of the sort. Wouldn't she only be telling you to be a good girl so's yer mammy would be proud of ye? And sure, I am proud of ye. Don't I love the bones of yous? Aren't you my precious treasure?' And Kate hugged her daughter tight, to prove it.

'I know it's hard for you to understand, sweetheart, but there's a war on and our brave soldiers have gone out to fight to protect us all. Daddy has left Mammy in charge of his factory. That's my war job, d'you see? Not only do I have boots to make for all these fine soldiers but I must see that the business is run properly, that all the workers are properly looked after and kept happy, orders taken and dealt with so the factory will still be here for Daddy when he comes home again at the end of it all. Do you understand, me cushla?'

Even as Kate patiently offered this explanation as simply and clearly as she could, half of her mind was worrying over what fresh trouble might be brewing there, whether a promised order had been completed, if she could squeeze a free day to go off round the markets again on yet another fruitless search for Callum. And also worrying over when she'd last had a letter from Eliot – not for two weeks surely? So much to think about, so many worries.

'Mammy wants you to be a brave little soldier too, d'you see?' she said, unconsciously worsening the situation.

For Flora it was all very confusing. She understood about the war, and her mammy working hard, but she still couldn't get rid of that nasty feeling in her tummy. Something wasn't quite right and it must be her fault because hadn't they all had that lovely wedding, hadn't she got a new dress and a new daddy and come to live in this great big house? Even her friend Maggie had been impressed. So she should be happy, shouldn't she? And if nobody liked her, and kept smacking her, it must be her fault, mustn't it? Oh, why was everything so muddled? And why couldn't she make Aunt Lucy pleased with her?

Their battles over meals were, to Lucy, a particular delight. Lucy just loved breakfast times. Flora hated eggs. It didn't matter whether they were boiled, fried, scrambled, any way Mrs Petty chose to make them, she absolutely refused to eat eggs. Kate said that she'd always disliked them.

'You're too soft with that child. Always were with Callum too.'

'Callum isn't here now, so let's not bring him into this,' Kate insisted firmly, and Lucy gave a careless shrug.

Mrs Petty offered various alternatives. 'If the little petal doesn't care for eggs, would she like a nice fat sausage for her breakfast instead? Or a bit of crispy bacon?'

'I'm sure that would be lovely,' Lucy agreed, thrilled to have found a new and imaginative way to plague the child. 'But I'll take the eggs, Mrs Petty. You know how I love them.'

The aunts always ate their own breakfast early at seven, so Lucy made a point of waiting until they'd finished before taking Flora in. Then she'd put the 'specially prepared sausage on to her own plate and give the two poached eggs to the child. Flora turned up her nose in disgust.

'Don't want them. Don't *like* eggs, Aunt Lucy.'

'You'll eat what's good for you, like them or not.' And when it became clear, as anticipated, that she was not going to eat them, Lucy began spooning great lumps of the rapidly congealing mess into her protesting mouth, Flora spitting and crying in most satisfactory distress.

The following morning was even better. Lucy stood behind the child's chair, arms folded, and took immense pleasure in watching how she struggled to eat the hated egg through choking tears, gagging over the yolk which she loathed so much.

'You really need far more discipline. Your mammy has spoilt you, but *I'm* in charge now, so you'll do as *I* say.'

Then Lucy had a brilliant idea. If drilling was good for soldiers, she thought, why not for a small child? She conducted these 'exercises', as she liked to call them, out on Scout Scar, far away from the house and any prying eyes, where she could be in complete control. She insisted Flora march back and forth over a given area, arms either raised above her head, or constantly swinging, for hour upon hour. This became a regular routine, often in the pouring rain, till the child was weeping and giddy with exhaustion. Lucy would then generously allow her a short respite before brutally making her start all over again.

'Fifty times! You must walk this path fifty times without stopping. Your daddy drills because of the war, so why not you? Do it right, and I'll tell him what a good little soldier you are.'

There was the odd awkward moment. Should they return home with the child soaking wet, Lucy would hurry her upstairs through the silent house before anyone could see, handing her a towel with the order to strip off and dry herself.

To Flora's credit, she made less and less fuss, withdrawing into a silent shell which she cast about herself, as if she'd grown indifferent to pain and punishment. As a consequence, she did indeed become more disciplined, a great deal better behaved, both at mealtimes and in company.

Kate would remark upon it, saying what a 'good girl' she was, thus seeming to condone the situation in Flora's eyes. Other days, she would look slightly troubled, observing how quiet her daughter had been at bedtime and asking if she was sickening for something.

Lucy always dismissed such a notion as utter nonsense. 'She's tired out from playing so hard all day, that's all. You really mustn't fuss the child, sister dear.'

And Vera would put on her spectacles and frowningly comment, 'We don't like noise here. Children should be seen and not heard.'

Flora's increasing reserve, so far as Lucy was concerned, only proved that the 'exercises' were working. The purpose, after all, was to 'instil discipline' and if the result caused Kate O'Connor some concern, all well and good. A bit of worry was excellent, exactly what that little whore deserved, so long as it didn't get out of hand and she got wise to what was really going on.

Callum had never entirely forgotten his past but it remained somewhat distant and unreal; a muddle of half-dreams, half-memory. Now he had another puzzle to add to it. The day he'd met that girl at Kendal market stood out in his mind like a beacon. Not simply because she'd generously given him half her sweet, which had been pretty much all he'd had to eat that day, bar one apple and a lump of hard cheese, but because he'd caught a glimpse of her lovely mother. For some strange reason he couldn't explain, she'd looked familiar.

Ever since that day, he'd kept a lookout for her, longed to see her again. He never had, of course. They rarely went to

Kendal, it being a long way from the farm, and Mrs Brocklebank didn't always let him go with her to the local markets at Keswick and Ambleside, more often leaving him with a list of chores to keep him busy on the farm while she was away. Now that he'd grown bigger, his workload had increased considerably.

'Great lad like you needs to pull yer weight, since you eat so much,' Mr Brocklebank would say. ' 'Bout time you were some use round 'ere.' As if he'd never done a hand's turn in all these long years.

'Nay, he's a growing lad, aren't you, Allan?' Mrs Brocklebank might add, if she was feeling kindly towards him.

If she did take him with her, he'd be kept working the whole time so he was never able to wander off and do any exploring on his own account. Mrs Brocklebank didn't allow any show of independence.

But now he was thirteen and a half he was not quite so biddable, and he'd grown big enough not to be so cowed by her bully of a husband. In his bed in the dusty, cold barn, Callum would work on his plan of escape night after night. He was haunted by his vision of that woman: her lovely face, the red hair so like his own, those brilliant, clear grey eyes. She'd stood just yards away from him, calling to the girl, so he'd had several moments in which to study her. It had felt almost as if time were standing still in that instant. And then she'd smiled at the child, hugged her close as if she were precious, gently scolded her for wandering off and hurried her away, not even noticing him standing there watching.

And if, at the back of his mind, he wondered if she was the one, if this lovely woman could possibly be the mother he'd been dreaming of all these years, he didn't dare let the thought grow. Then one of the other stallholders told him once that someone had been asking after him. He'd hoped it was she, but soon put that notion from his mind too. He knew that hope was a dangerous thing.

But the possibility that she just might be looking for him had never gone away. The idea that she might indeed be his mother intrigued and excited him. Somehow he had to find her, and ask.

Today was May Day, 1917, and as luck would have it they were once again off to Kendal to the butter market. Mr Brocklebank hadn't been available to drive the cart, so that task had fallen to Callum. As usual, he helped the farmer's wife set up the stall and arrange their wares. The morning was busy with shoppers, as always, but all the time he was looking for an opportunity to slip away, to put his carefully laid plan into effect. His chance came early in the afternoon when Mrs Brocklebank began gossiping with the woman on the next stall. Normally, he would have taken the opportunity to have a bit of a rest on the edge of the cart, if no one was wanting butter and eggs, but this was the best chance he'd get to look for the red-haired woman, perhaps his only one, and he meant to take it.

With her back turned, Mrs Brocklebank didn't see him slip under the stall and crawl away. When Callum believed himself to be out of sight, he got to his feet and ran hell for leather. Hopefully, she wouldn't spot that he was missing until he was several streets away. What would happen later, when he returned, he didn't care to think about too closely. Best just to run for it, even if he hadn't a clue where exactly he was running to, or where he might find the woman.

He ran helter-skelter down Branthwaite Brow, boots clattering on the cobbles, and instinctively turned left when he reached Finkle Street, not pausing until he'd run the length of Stramongate and reached the bridge where he skittered to a halt and stared in astonishment at the river.

A prickle of recognition made the hair at the back of his neck rise. *He'd been here before! He knew this place!* But how and why? So far as he could recall, he'd only ever been to Kendal market a couple of times before with Mrs Brocklebank, and never once been permitted to wander anywhere on his own. When they drove into town on the farmer's cart, they always came down Windermere Road. He didn't remember them ever crossing the river at this point, over this particular bridge. Or could he be wrong about that? Had he travelled this way as a boy with the Brocklebanks on some occasion or other? Was he simply confused?

He had a sudden vision of a woman in a smart grey coat and a big hat with a feather. She was holding his hand, shaking him quite hard and shouting at him. He was crying, because he was frightened. Who was this woman, and why was she so angry? Callum knew, with absolute conviction, that it wasn't Mrs Brocklebank. Nor was it the woman whose face had haunted his dreams throughout his boyhood. This was a new memory. Someone else entirely.

His feet were taking him on over the bridge, past a church which made him shiver with foreboding for some reason, then out on to a broad sward of grass.

'What's this place called?' he asked a boy passing by on his bicycle.

'Gooseholme. Where you looking for? Have you to deliver summat to Thorny Hills?'

Thorny Hills. The name hummed in his head like a familiar tune. He'd definitely heard the name before. He *had* been here before. He knew it. He *knew* it!

His excitement was growing but he let his feet make the decisions about which way to go. They led him unerringly across the grass, out through a lych-gate, and stopped by the walls of a big, square, grey-stone house. He drew in a deep breath, unlatched the garden gate and walked up the path.

At the door he spat on his hands and rubbed them over his face, did the same again, this time flattening down his unruly copper curls, and tucked his cap tidily away in his pocket. He could do nothing about the none-too-clean working shirt and fustian trousers, the braces and mucky clogs, so he stretched up and tugged on the bell pull. He heard the sound of it echo deep in the belly of the house, and again there was that prickling sensation that he'd done this before, heard that sound before. Nothing happened. There was no response, no answer and he tugged on the bell pull again.

Callum found he was holding his breath so much that it hurt, and let it out on a gasp. He'd almost given up hope, had half turned away, deciding nobody could be in after all, when the door was pulled open. He swung about, his young face bright and eager for this first meeting with the woman he'd dreamed of for so long. Would she be the one? Was this the moment he would at last meet his mother?

31

'Was that the bell?' Mrs Petty held the buttered scone poised in one hand, a knife loaded with jam in the other while she put her head to one side to listen. 'Did you hear anything, Ida?'

She sniffed, rubbing the back of her hand across her nose to wipe the drip from it. Of course she'd heard the bell, but she'd no wish to leave this warm fire, or this lovely tea Mrs Petty had done for them because Fanny was paying one of her customary visits. Nor had she any wish to miss the ending of one of Fanny's stories, which were always titillating. 'No, Mrs P, I didn't hear nuffin.' Let madam answer. She'd nothing else to do all day. Ida was taking an hour off.

'You'd best go and check. Get along with you then. Don't sit there looking gormless.'

With reluctance, Ida set down her plate, casting a lingering glance back at her scone as she scuttled quickly out into the hall. She could see a boy at the door. He had copper coloured hair and a bright smile on his face, though even as Ida watched, the smile quickly faded as he looked up into madam's face. Not that this surprised her. Madam Lucy wasn't known for her warm welcomes, not unless it was someone she wished to impress. Delivery boys didn't come into that category.

Ida couldn't quite hear what was being said, but madam was flapping her hand, then shaking a fist at the boy. Poor beggar.

He'd obviously done summat wrong. Happen he'd brought the wrong stuff from the shop.

'I'll deal with this, Ida,' she called back over her shoulder.

'Rightio, Madam.' Ida turned to go, but spotted a bunch of grapes sitting atop the fruit bowl on the hall sideboard, and was momentarily distracted while she popped one in her mouth, then another. What a treat! Fortunately the aunts were out, so no one would see her. She heard an angry shout and a cry but by the time she'd rearranged the grapes to cover the gap, the boy was gone and the front door had slammed shut. Ida scuttled back to the kitchen like a mouse into its hole.

By this time, Fanny had finished her story and Ida had missed the exciting part, as she so often did. Why was she always the one called upon to jump up and down to fetch things or answer the flaming door, which on this occasion had been a complete waste of time?

' 'Oo was it, Ida?'

She bit into her scone and spoke through a shower of crumbs. 'Only a lad delivering summat for madam.'

'Nobody special then?'

'No.' Ida reached for another scone, anxious that they might all be gone before she'd finished this one, and got her hand slapped for her greed.

'Yer mouth is still full,' Mrs Petty chided her. 'Nay, I'll never manage to teach you manners, girl, not if I live to be a hundred.'

Ida flushed crimson, Mrs Petty being the nearest to a mother she'd ever known so she did her best to please. But it'd been mighty hard since Fanny left, and she missed Dennis teasing her, and even the smell of Askew's pipe. Nothing was quite as it used to be, in the good old days, as Mrs P was wont to call them.

Mrs Petty removed the plate from her reach. 'You can have

another, Fanny love, and tell us how you're getting on with the mistress. Eeh, it's grand to see you. We get none of the gossip in these parts nowadays. What's she like as a boss, Kate O'Connor as was? Is she managing the factory well in the master's absence? We rarely see hide nor hair of her round here. Mind you, it's that poor child I feel sorry for. Left to her own devices more often than is good for her, poor little lamb. If it weren't for Madam Lucy, she'd be no better than an orphan.'

'Is that why the little lass looks so pasty-faced?' Fanny enquired, plastering jam on to a scone as if it might go out of fashion.

'Pasty-faced?' Mrs Petty looked affronted, taking offence at the implication the child wasn't properly fed. 'Nay, she eats everything I put in front of her. You should see the breakfasts that child consumes. Two eggs at a time, no messing.'

Fanny shrugged. 'Pardon me for poking me nose in where it's not wanted, but I saw little Flora setting off to school after lunch and she looked a bit subdued like, to me. A bit hang-dog you might say. No skipping about and running. Solemn little miss, I thought, holding on to her aunt's hand like a good un though. Is she allus so quiet?'

Mrs Petty considered this question with a frown. 'Aye, happen she is a bit too serious. You hardly know she's there at times. Not normal really, for a child her age. I blame that mother of hers. That Kate O'Connor as was neglects her summat shocking, she does. Heartless floozy where her children are concerned, allus was. I've said as much often, have I not, Ida?'

'Yes, Mrs Petty.'

Fanny frowned, 'I thought you fancied her at one time fer the master? And he's got her, hasn't he? Tekken her as his wife, more's the wonder.'

Mrs Petty sniffed her disapproval, making her opinion on

the matter abundantly clear. I did once think she might suit as his bit on the side, as you might say. The toffs go in for mistresses, don't you know. But never for a moment did I expect him to marry the brazen hussy. Well, I mean, it's not done, is it? 'Tain't right.'

'Aye, but he has done it. Done it proper, some might say.'

'It'll not last. Mark my words, it'll all end in tears. I've said so often, have I not, Ida?'

'Yes, Mrs Petty.' Ida had managed to sneak another scone on to her plate, so again sent a scattering of crumbs flying everywhere as she spoke, earning herself no more than a resigned shake of the head this time as Mrs Petty passed her a napkin.

Fanny surprised herself by defending her employer, stoutly pointing out how much of an effort it took to run a factory, particularly in wartime, 'I don't see why he shouldn't marry her, if you want my opinion. This class business is a lot of old-fashioned stuff and nonsense. You'll see, it'll all be different once this war is over.'

'Well, I never! What's got into you?'

'And she can't be everywhere at once, now can she? Some-one has to run that flippin' factory, so why not her? She's making a good job of it, s'matter of fact. I still say there's summat not quite right with that little miss though, and if I were you I'd keep a watchful eye on things. Look a bit closer to home, and see what's going on right under yer nose.'

'Eeh, do you think so, Fanny?' Mrs Petty asked, mouth hanging open in surprise.

'I do.'

The moment Lucy slammed the front door closed, she stormed upstairs to her bedroom and took out her temper on the pillows by ripping them to shreds, sending feathers flying everywhere. Drat and damn it, this was the last thing she'd expected. Dear God, how had he found them? She couldn't believe her bad luck.

She'd stared at the boy open-mouthed with horror for what seemed like a lifetime before she'd been able to pull herself together sufficiently to think. And she'd certainly had to think fast. She'd heard Ida lurking in the passage behind her and swiftly realised that it wouldn't do at all for the boy to be spotted by any of the servants. Mrs Petty in particular would remember him well. So she'd called out to Ida, saying something about a delivery, that she'd deal with the matter. It was a miracle that she'd bothered to answer the door in the first place, but the sound of that bell clanging on and on had quite frayed her nerves, and it had become patently obvious that no one else in the house was going to.

She'd known instantly who he was. For all it had been years since she'd set eyes on him, the likeness to his mother was uncanny.

Heaven help her, but it was fortunate that Kate had not been home. As always at this time of day, she was at the factory. Even more fortunate, little Flora was still at school and the aunts out paying calls.

Lucy began pacing the room, wringing her hands in agitation. What should she do? What should she do?

After Ida had gone, she'd very cleverly scolded the stupid boy for coming to the wrong house, just as if he really were a delivery boy. She'd boxed his ears and sent him packing. Therefore she did not expect to see him again; not after the roasting she'd given him.

Lucy paused in her pacing to consider the situation more rationally and felt a film of perspiration break out on her brow, her hands grow clammy. What if he did come back though? What if he called when she wasn't in? What if Mrs Petty answered the door this time or, worse, Kate herself? Dear God, this was a disaster. All that time and effort, all these years of planning and patient waiting, and she could be right back where she'd started.

Lucy put her hands to her head, thoughts buzzing round and round like angry bees; none of them making any sense. Eliot had married the boy's mother. He'd rejected Lucy's own offer and made that little whore his *wife*, for God's sake! And he'd adopted Callum legally, so if the boy returned from the dead, as it were, they'd be able to play happy families all over again.

And her own children would get nothing!

All three of them would be out in cold with nothing to show for her efforts; all her planning and clever scheming. Lucy almost let out a scream of rage; was forced to bite down hard on her lip to prevent herself from doing so, since the noise would be sure to bring someone running to find out what on earth was wrong with her. She was going mad, that's what was wrong. Half demented with fury. There must be something she could do. But what? *What could she do?*

Lucy regretted sending the boy away now, since it left her with no idea what he might do next. She should have gone after him. Found out why he was here. Taken him some place else, somewhere safer, somewhere from which there could be no return.

Should she go and look for him now? No, that could be dangerous. He might not have recognised her, after all. Might stay away. Then again, he might not. *How could she be sure?* Oh, she was in a fever of indecision. Biting her nails, wringing her hands, scarring furious wheels along her arm with her own sharp nails, Lucy continued to rage helplessly about the room. She'd *kill* the little bastard if she got half a chance. Wring the life out of his scrawny neck.

*

Lucy still hadn't thought of a solution two hours later, despite turning the problem over and over in her head, considering every possibility, each new idea wilder than the last. Then it suddenly occurred to her that she was supposed to be collecting Flora from school, as she always did.

By the time she arrived, the child was nowhere in sight. Dear God, now she'd lost her, and would be in trouble for that too. Perhaps that was the answer, Lucy thought. She should get rid of Flora as well. But how? She couldn't take another child to the workhouse, not with the war on. They'd only ask if her daddy had been killed on the Somme and did her mother need special assistance to cope? Everything had changed now. The world had gone soft, become more caring. No, she would need to be taken somewhere far away, where no one would think to look. Somewhere much further than the Langdales.

'I'm here, I'm here, Aunt Lucy. I thought you'd forgotten me. I've been playing while I waited for you, but I've been a very good girl. Honest.'

Lucy snatched up Flora's hand and began to march her along the street. 'I don't believe you. You were very naughty to go wandering off like that. Didn't I tell you to stay and wait for me at the school gate? What your mother will say I cannot imagine.'

Flora began to cry. 'Don't tell Mammy I've been bad. Please don't. Mammy has to work for the war. You aren't going to smack me, Aunt Lucy, are you? I didn't wander off, honest I didn't. I was just . . .'

'Never mind what you were *just* doing. I've told you to stay by the school gate.' All the fury and frustration that had been building up inside her seemed to explode in that moment. How *dare* the child disobey? How *dare* that stupid boy have the effrontery simply to walk back into their lives? Lucy pushed Flora up a back street and swinging back her hand, slapped her with all her might. Flora screamed and fell over, knocking her head on a wall as she went down. She lay very still, not making a sound.

'Get up, child. Don't just lie there in the dirt. Get up, I say!' Flora didn't move, not even an eyelash fluttered. In that moment, Lucy realised that this time she'd gone too far.

'I really don't know where she is,' Lucy said, trying to appear concerned and anxious, 'I thought at first she was simply playing a game and hiding from me. I'll admit I was a little late getting to the school, but then I'd had so many interruptions this afternoon. Heaven knows what the servants do with their time, they are certainly never around when needed.'

Both the maiden aunts were looking troubled. Vera said, 'Do you think we should call out the police?'

'No, no, I'm quite certain she's playing some prank or other. Making me worry because I was late. I'm sure she'll turn up at any moment, chastened and apologetic, and so she should be. I, for one, shall certainly give that little miss a piece of my mind when she does.' And Lucy picked up her embroidery and proceeded to apply her needle. After a moment, Vera and Cissie did likewise, while the clock ticked on in the small parlour.

The sound of it pounded in Lucy's head like a drum.

But although all three women sat and waited for the better part of an hour, Flora did not arrive home from school, as Lucy had known that she would not. Cissie had grown quite demented with worry, constantly getting up to look out of the parlour window, the dogs anxiously padding back and forth behind her on each occasion. Even Aunt Vera was fussing a great deal, constantly glancing up at the clock, or examining the silver fob watch she had pinned to the bodice of her woollen frock.

'Dear me, I'm beginning to think we should perhaps call the constabulary,' she began, when the door opened and Kate strolled in. She glanced about her, taking in their solemn expressions, and her usual sunny smile instantly faded. 'What is it? What's happened? Oh, God, it's Eliot.'

Cissie ran to her at once. 'No, no my dear. Don't fret yourself. It's not dear Eliot at all. It's Flora. She's not yet home from school, that's all. She's being a naughty girl and is playing pranks on us. But it's true that we are all becoming just a little anxious about her.'

'Didn't you collect her as usual, Lucy?'

'Am I your maid? Good gracious me!'

'But that was our arrangement. We agreed. In fact, you offered.'

'Out of the goodness of my heart, since the child was obviously neglected. And, yes, I did indeed go to collect her, as I always do. She was not there. No sign of her waiting at the school gate, as there should have been. She's obviously run off to play some stupid game or other.'

Kate looked as if she might collapse and Cissie attempted to lead her to a chair, urging her to sit. Kate shook her off. 'She would never do that. Oh, Lord, where can she be? Where the hell is she?'

'Don't you swear at me in that common way. I'll not have your workhouse manners in here.' Lucy had had ample time to think long and hard over the last hour and believed she had the answer to her problem. 'You are the one to blame here, not me. You are the one who neglects your own child and leaves her to the care of others.

'And this isn't the first child you have lost, is it?'

Aunt Vera let out a strangled gasp and reached for her sal volatile.

'Oh, my word! Oh deary, deary me,' murmured Cissie, and then for the first time in her life put forward a question on her own behalf. 'Surely you aren't suggesting, Lucy, that this was all deliberate? That Kate . . .'

'That is exactly what I am saying. Who else had the opportunity? Who else would do such a terrible thing? Didn't this girl from Poor House Lane give away her own son for adoption, sell him in order to gain herself employment? And as if that weren't bad enough, she inveigled herself into Eliot's bed and got herself pregnant by him so that he felt duty bound to wed her. Now, having got her grasping little hands on his business and full control of his financial affairs, that child too has become a nuisance. She's disposed of her as swiftly and mercilessly as she did the first. First Callum, now Flora.'

'Oh, my goodness me,' said Aunt Vera, stunned by this turn of events.

'That is an abominable lie.' Kate could barely manage to get the words out, her throat felt so constricted, her fear so great. 'Tell me what has happened to Flora. Where is she?'

Lucy longed to say – 'lying dead in a gutter', but that would give the game away. Inside, she was glorying in her victory, unexpected perhaps but all the better for that. She felt jubilant, exhilarated. She'd thought she was about to lose everything but now she had won after all. She'd not only rid herself of both of those bastard children, but, if she had her way, would soon be rid of their dratted mother as well. There would be nothing then to stop her from having Eliot all to herself. He'd be putty in her hands, only too willing for her to look after things for him. Lucy saw herself running the factory, with Jack, now fourteen, taking over in just a short year or two. Oh, it was all going to work out splendidly.

Kate said, 'Tell me! I'm waiting for you to tell me what has happened to Flora.'

Lucy straightened her spine, wrinkling her nose with distaste as she regarded her rival, just as if Kate were still that ragamuffin child who'd crawled out from one of Kendal's worst yards. 'Don't try to wriggle out of this. Your guilt is plain for all to see. What did you do with them both? Throw them in the river, as you probably did with that husband of yours, assuming you ever had one in the first place. Was that the way of it? Did you dispose of Callum's father too, once he was of no further use? Is that what you plan to do to Eliot?' She turned to Vera. 'Perhaps we should ask Ida to go for the police constable, after all, Aunt. This is all beginning to look dreadfully serious.'

For once in her life Vera seemed utterly incapable of making a decision of any sort. Cissie appeared as stunned as her sister, Kate frozen to the spot, white with shock. Lucy carelessly shrugged her shoulders and marched towards the door. 'Then I shall deal with the matter myself. See that she doesn't run away, Vera, while I find Ida.'

Long before she reached it, the door swung open, revealing none other than the child in question, face streaked with mud and blood in just about equal quantities, school gym slip torn, knees scraped but with a smile of pure delight on her young face.

'Mammy! Mammy!' cried Flora. 'Look who I've found. You remember that boy I told you about, my friend from the market with the fat lady? I found him sitting on a wall near my school. And what do you think, Mammy? He believes he already knows you. Does he Mammy? Do you know him?'

32

Did she know him? What a question! How could a mother not know her own child, even if she hadn't set eyes on him for more years than she cared to count? But then he wasn't a child any more. No longer the sturdy toddler she'd once cuddled on her lap, sung lullabies or read to from his *Little Stories for Little Folk*. Thirteen years old and on the verge of manhood, he was as tall as Kate now, if more scrawny for his height than was healthy. Why was he so thin? Had he not been properly looked after? Where had he been? Why had he left? Why had he chosen to come home now, and not before? Or had he been held somewhere against his will? As these questions and a dozen others raced through her head while Kate stood rooted to the spot, frozen with shock, only vaguely aware of the other people in the room: of Vera making clucking noises of disbelief, Cissie quietly weeping, Flora hanging on to his arm as if she might never let go, and Lucy as pale and ghostlike as Kate must herself look.

'Mam, is it really you?' He was gazing at her with rapt attention, his bright eyes troubled yet filled with hope.

Kate tried to speak but no sound came out. She put a hand to her mouth, struggling for control, then tried again. 'Indeed it is, son.' She felt an urge to snatch him to her and yet, over-awed by the strangeness of him, was quite unable to move a muscle.

He was frowning at her, the vaguest hint of hostility creeping over his handsome face. 'Why did you send me away? Why didn't you want me no more?'

It was as if a hand had taken her heart and squeezed the life out of it, leaving her momentarily breathless. 'Sure, and of course I wanted you. I never sent you away, m'cushla. Haven't I spent the last eight years searching for ye, hunting high and low in the desperate hope I'd find you again? Why in God's name did you run off in the first place?'

'I didn't run off. I was *taken*!'

A muted gasp from the aunts while Kate felt her knees give way, forcing her to sink on to a nearby chair.

'I allus assumed you didn't love me no more, that you wanted rid of me.'

Kate gave a low moan, eyes filling with unshed tears as she slowly shook her head, lips trembling as she whispered, '*Never!*'

There followed a long drawn-out silence, one filled with the pain of those lost years, in which the emotion in that small parlour was palpable, almost too much to bear.

In a voice raw with agony, quite unlike her own, Kate asked, 'Taken by whom? God in heaven, Callum love, will ye tell us where've you been all this time?'

And then seemingly in slow motion, Callum's eyes swivelled round to Lucy. 'Ask her. She knows everything.'

Not understanding, Kate frowned. 'How can Lucy know? Have ye told yer aunt already, before ye'd tell yer own mam? Aw, Callum sweetheart, don't break me heart again.'

He was vigorously shaking his head, 'I don't need to tell her. She knows already. Mebbe she planned it all from the start.' As he said this, he instinctively put a protective arm about his half-sister's shoulders and Flora hugged him tight. '*She* took me away. I couldn't remember owt till I come to t'market again today and walked over that bridge. Me feet found this house and the minute *that woman* opened the door, it all came flooding back. Like a bad dream, the nightmare what runs in me head over and over. And from the state of Flora here, you can see she weren't satisfied wi' ruining my life, she intended to ruin the bairn's as well.'

Mind in a whirl, only then did Kate think to look upon her daughter and her heart clenched with fresh fear. Hair matted with blood, bruises on her lovely face, Flora looked as if she'd been beaten black and blue. Kate blinked in disbelief. 'What on earth . . . ?'

Thrusting herself forward, Lucy tossed her head in that arrogant way she had. 'He attacked her, of course.'

'*I* attacked her? Nay, that's rich, that is. I were the one what found her up that alley where you left her. I *saved* her. What were you going to do to the wee bairn after you'd thumped her, take her to t'workhouse an' all, or were you hoping she were a goner?'

Kate looked upon Lucy with eyes dazed in bewilderment. 'What is he trying to say? What's all this about an alley, and the workhouse? Do you understand a word of it?'

' 'Course she understands.' Callum pointed an accusing finger. '*She* were the one! It were *her* what took me away that day, give me a good hiding and dumped me in t'Union Workhouse. I thought I'd struck lucky when I were sent up to that farm in the Langdales, but the Brocklebanks weren't kindly folk. Fer all I know, *she* might've had a hand in that an' all.'

'He's lying!' Lucy snapped, spitting the words in the boy's face, fingers curling with fury as if she itched to scratch his eyes out. 'What else would you expect from a workhouse brat?'

'Calm yourself, Lucy,' instructed Aunt Vera in her sternest tones.

'Oh, deary, deary me,' echoed Cissie, wringing her hands.

Callum was growing agitated, his now quite deep voice rising on a note of desperation as he stood before a bemused Kate. 'Ask Flora then, if you don't believe me. Ask yer flamin' daughter.'

It was all too much for Kate to take in. Had she lost him? Was it far too late for them ever to be close again? When she'd dreamed of this moment it hadn't been anything like this. Why weren't they hugging each other? Why wasn't he weeping in her arms, glad to be home? Kate knew it wasn't unusual for a child to blame its mother if it got lost. Was this his way of dealing with it all, by placing the blame on someone else, first on herself, and now on Lucy? She put out a hand, wanting to soothe him, to calm this beloved son of hers with the assurance that she did indeed love him, but he brushed her hand aside. Beside him, Flora was ashen, which made the cuts and bruises on her small, pinched face stand out more livid than ever.

'Is this true Flora? Did someone hurt you? Was it . . . ?' Kate couldn't find the words. She'd trusted Lucy. Despite her initial doubts, largely due to her sister-in-law's innate snobbishness, yet she'd come round to accepting the woman's help, pushing aside the guilt all working mothers feel when leaving the care of their child to another. But Kate had to know the truth. She had to understand what, if anything, Lucy had done. Could this stuck-up sister-in-law who'd looked with contempt upon her from the start, constantly scorning and disparaging her because of her humble origins, truly have set out to steal and damage both her children?

Flora glanced fearfully up at her aunt then burst into tears. Nothing could have been more damning.

Kate got slowly to her feet, an eerie calmness creeping over her. It must be true then. *This woman had indeed hurt her children!* But why would she do such a thing? And then the answer came. She'd done it out of jealousy, from fear of losing what she considered to be her own children's inheritance. And she still blamed Eliot for Charles's suicide.

The gaze Kate turned upon Lucy now was ice cold. 'Mother of God, what an unholy mess.'

'Don't you dare look at me in that condemning way, you Irish whore! Who are *you* to judge *me*? Your children got the treatment they deserved, no worse than they received at your own hand, feckless, selfish mother that you are.'

Kate had never felt more calm, more in control, instinct warning her that this was not the moment for unleashing her fiery Irish temper, though she might well inwardly burn to defend herself. Entirely ignoring Lucy, she quietly addressed the aunts. 'Whatever the facts in all of this, Flora's wounds need attention. Cissie, perhaps you would . . .'

'Of course, my dear. Of course. Come along, Flora love. Come to your Aunty Cissie.' And Flora willingly flung herself into the comfort of the doggy-scented embrace, sobbing her heart out.

'Go with her,' Kate urged Callum, but he stubbornly shook his head.

'I'll stay here, with you.' Their eyes met and a flicker of hope stirred in Kate's heart. Perhaps it wasn't too late after all and she hadn't quite lost him.

With the aunts and Flora gone, Kate drew in a steadying breath, clenching her fists in an effort to hold on to her hard-won restraint as she faced her sister-in-law. 'So it's true then. You abducted Callum and battered Flora. Can you deny it?'

'Why should I? A doxy like you deserves everything you get.'

Callum leapt forward, scarlet in the face with outrage. 'Don't you call my mother names or you'll have me to reckon with. You're the villain here, the nastiest piece of work I ever clapped eyes on, and I've seen some bad 'uns in me time.

Nobody could call the workhouse easy, and the Brocklebanks weren't soft either but then they weren't gentlefolk, not like you. You're supposed to know better.'

Kate rested a calming hand on her son's shoulder. This time he didn't shrug it off, but let it lie. 'The boy has a point. Is this then the hold ye've had over me all these years? Did it give you satisfaction to watch me pine for me lovely boy, knowing all the time where he was? What kind of woman are you? What sort of mother?'

'One who would go to any lengths, *any lengths*, not to see her own children disinherited,' Lucy hissed.

'That is a decision only Eliot can make, which he will do, I am sure, in the fullness of time when this war is won. For now, I'd be obliged if you would pack your bags and leave. I don't want you any longer under his roof, under *our* roof.'

Callum gasped. 'Nay Mam, aren't you going to call the coppers in? She should be prosecuted, locked up.'

Deep down Kate agreed, yet knew herself incapable of bringing about such a thing. She was only a girl from Poor House Lane after all, so it wasn't her place to act as judge and jury on her social superiors, even if she did see Lucy as morally inferior. She felt some small degree of satisfaction as she saw the colour drain from her sister-in-law's cheeks, the tightness of her jawline slacken with fear. 'No laddie, it's not revenge we're seeking, only justice. Besides, I've no intention of seeing any more children damaged by this woman's evil, even her own, who are surely innocents in all of this. They need a mother, same as you did. Best she leave now, without delay, and have done with the matter.'

Lucy let out a mocking laugh of disbelief. 'You aren't casting me out into the streets, surely?'

'I am so. Now isn't that a wonder?'

'But where would I sleep? How will I eat?'

'Well now, the Kirkland Poor House is closed, as ye know, so mebbe you could try the Union Workhouse on Kendal Green, since you're so well acquainted with the guardians there.' She heard Callum's soft chuckle and gently squeezed his shoulder, warning him to hush, before crossing the room and throwing open the parlour door. 'For all I care, you can sleep in the gutter. You're no longer welcome in this house. Your allowance will continue to be paid, for the time being at least, on condition that you stay away; that you never come anywhere near my children ever again. When Eliot returns, once he's been given the full facts, he will no doubt make a decision on whether or not you deserve to receive any more assistance from this business, having attempted to destroy his family.'

The violet eyes flashed, revealing panic for the first time, yet Lucy remained obstinately defiant. 'You think he'd abandon me, that he'd take *your* word against mine, a whore against a Tyson? Never!'

Kate smiled. 'You're only a Tyson by marriage, as I am. But yes, I think he might well take my word, and that of his son, don't you? He'll be only too delighted to have Callum home safe and well, and you know it.'

'You'll poison his mind against me.'

'Oh, I think you've achieved that by your own efforts, without any help from me. And don't see this as weakness on my part, or as any sign of forgiveness. No one abuses my children and gets away with it but nor will I see evil flourish by repeating it. So you can pack yer bags and go.'

As the door swung closed on her furious, departing figure, Kate turned to Callum and held wide her arms. 'Welcome home, son.' And grinning from ear to ear, he walked into them to hug his mother tight.

*

Mrs Petty declared, and Ida and Fanny heartily agreed, that they hadn't enjoyed a more entertaining afternoon in years at Tyson Lodge. The raised voices in the parlour had naturally attracted their attention, bringing them creeping out into the hall so they could all the better hear what was going on. There'd been a slight interruption when the aunts had appeared with a sorry-looking Flora and Ida was duly dispatched to fetch hot water and iodine. Cissie carried the child upstairs while Mrs Petty, Fanny and Miss Vera remained in the hall, ears pricked. Sadly, the exchange in the parlour had become somewhat muted so that they were forced to draw ever nearer in an effort to hear properly. Fanny swore that if blood looked like being drawn, she'd swallow her pride and run for Dennis. Ida, having scooted to the kitchen, drawn the hot water, flown up the stairs and back in record time, quickly returned to join the curious eavesdroppers. Mrs Petty felt quite certain that at any moment Miss Vera would notice their presence, scold them all and send them scurrying back into the kitchen. But she did nothing of the sort, being far too busy cocking an ear herself. And then the door was flung wide and all of them had to dip back into the shadows quickly .

The voices within rang out loud and clear at this point, all about the wickedness done to those poor children by madam Lucy, of her being cast out into the streets and there being no chance of forgiveness, which Mrs Petty later declared was too good for her by half and she should be hung, drawn and quartered at the very least.

Then Lucy herself stormed through the door, a veritable dervish of fury, ordering Ida to pack her bags and Fanny to fetch a cab as she refused to stay a moment longer in this house simply to be insulted. Not a soul among them moved an inch.

'*Do you hear what I say?*' Lucy screamed, stamping her foot and going red, white and all shades of purple by turn.

It was Vera who had the temerity to step forward, 'I believe no one is preventing you from leaving, dear Lucy. And perhaps it would be for the best, in the circumstances. As ye sow, so shall ye reap.'

Lucy had no option but to obey. She stormed upstairs to her room, compelled to pack her own bags and stagger down the stairs with them moments later before the humiliating gaze of the gathered household. No punishment by the judicial system could have been more devastating, no departure more mortifying for her, witnessed as it was by everyone, including the servants, in condemning silence. No one offered to open the door for her and Lucy found herself out in the porch with not even a cab waiting, her instructions on this, too, completely ignored. She would be forced to walk to the station to find one, though where she would go after that, she really hadn't the first idea.

Perhaps she should settle for a night or two at the County Hotel which might give tempers a chance to cool. Lucy felt instinctively it would be a mistake to go too far away at this juncture. Who knew what might happen in the future? War was a risky business and Kate O'Connor might be less sure of her ground if she were left widowed, for instance.

Dear God, but she'd make the Irish whore suffer for the shame of this day. Lucy decided instantly to write to Eliot and make sure she put her case personally, then they'd see what he had to say, if and when he returned.

In the meantime, she'd keep out of the whore's way, watching and waiting for an opportunity to strike back. Her chance would come. She had only to be patient. And what about that foreman who was dismissed with equal callousness? Perhaps it might be worth putting out a few feelers to find him. Oh, she wasn't done yet, not by a long chalk.